THE ARCHITECT KING

WOLVES OF THE TESSERACT BOOK 3

CHRISTOPHER D. SCHMITZ

TREESHAKER BOOKS

CONTENTS

SPECIAL OFFER!

Stay up to date on the world of Wolves of the Tesseract... you'll get access to a bunch of special freebies, bonus content, and the author's newsletter. You can unsubscribe at any time.
To get access to this exclusive group, just follow this link:
https://www.subscribepage.com/wolvesofthetesseract
and add your email to be added immediatley!

PROLOGUE

During The Syzygyc War, The Desolation ...an eon ago.

Disguised as one of them, Krenyr the Hunter walked through the camp of humans. He stood tall and walked with nobility and grace, even if the stench of the invading mammals from the Prime assaulted his nose.

Krenyr was vyrm—one of the Shades and a master infiltrator. Nobody gave him a second glance.

All assumed he belonged exactly where he was, that his presence was guided by some higher purpose and came from higher up the chain of command. Krenyr the Hunter certainly had orders from the top-he was Nitthogr's chief assassin. Today he played the role of Luciannus, the eldest son of the King and the Commander-in-Chief of the military.

As Luciannus, Krenyr strolled directly through the encampment of the enemy. The shade's purpose was to cause pain and chaos, disrupting the enemy wherever possible and sinking their morale as the war against the vyrms' Brothers of the Apocalypse waged on.

He smiled and nodded to a few of the soldiers who passed them by. Krenyr didn't bother to mentally register them any more than one might notice a flea or tick. Spotting the tent where he knew his target would be, the shade ducked through the flap.

"Ah, Lord Luciannus," welcomed General Vangdahl, the leader of the Guardian Corps, as he looked up from the battle plans he'd helped draw up; a hint of surprise shone through his voice. "We were not expecting you until the evening."

Vangdahl pushed a book to the edge of his table. The title, gilded with inlaid silver, read *Meditations of J'v-Ellah*. Krenyr recognized it as a religious text common to the Veritas and the devout who lived in the Prime. He refrained from scowling, though the writings mere presence enraged him deep within.

Luciannus furrowed his brow and put an edge of arrogance into his voice as he addressed the general. Krenyr assumed all royalty spoke with a kind of jaded tone. "I could not wait, Vangdahl. These monsters have captured my sister and their cultists are threatening to use her blood and split open the veil between reality and the nether."

The General nodded his sympathy and understanding. "It was bad enough when they'd gained just a small amount of it—that event is what instigated this whole conflict. Think what they could do with *all of it*."

Vangdahl frowned, realizing the distastefulness of what he'd brought up. But the reptilian vyrm were not beyond spilling all of her blood for their foul magics, and avoiding the topic would not make its probability go away.

Luciannus frowned and leaned over the map of Neggath, memorizing troop movements and placements as indicated by the tokens laid out upon the table. He spotted one in particular. The Architect King's direct whereabouts.

The creator-king of the Tesseract and all reality was the hunter's top priority. If he could get to him, Krenyr knew he could win the war. Krenyr had strong beliefs he wished to prove to the multi-verse: that this god-king was neither invulnerable nor immortal. He already knew firsthand that the King's children could bleed—and so would *He*.

Krenyr smiled as Vangdahl leaned over the table to discuss the impending assault, which would hopefully reclaim Luciannus's sister. He was so close to his prey that he could taste the man's scent upon his sensitive olfactory glands. Luciannus was known as a brilliant strategist, nearly the equal of Basilisk, his lord's brother. He played the role.

"We'll need to send a team of specialists through this channel here where they will have cover. Perhaps the Veritas can assist. A member of the Flame Order could use their magics to camouflage a strike team of your best corpsmen to reclaim the princess and escape with her before these beasts have bled her dry."

Vangdahl pointed to a spot on the map. "We could bring our entire army to this point here and draw all eyes away to make sure they are not watching the gulch?"

Krenyr nodded, feigning excitement.

The General smiled. "My lord, we have already done that—or it appears that way. Our magicians have used an illusion spell that made it appear we camped right outside of that same location, between the cities of Straruck and Sharonash." He traced a finger through the gully that they'd discussed and smiled. "Our team has already been deployed, just as you suggested." He beamed with pride. "My son is among them. I am pleased to tell you that the Princess was already rescued safely."

"I know," said Krenyr as he placed his hand over the top of Vangdahl's wrist and let his scaly skin take its true form. He ripped the wolf embossed band from the general's forearm to prevent him from shape-shifting into his lycan form.

Vangdahl's eyes widened with dread realization, and the hunter brandished his knife.

Both looked up just as a boy, maybe eleven years old, but wearing Guardian Corps armor, walked in. "Shardai, run!" Vangdahl yelled.

"Grandpa!" the boy screamed as he reached for his pistol.

Too late, Krenyr had already dragged his dagger across the general's throat. The hunter ducked behind the body as it collapsed atop the strategy table, splattering the pieces with hot blood.

Shardai's blaster bolts ripped through the canvas of the tent as his enemy rolled to the ground and cut a slit through it to escape.

Krenyr scrambled through and leapt to his feet, taking the face and form of any number of soldiers as he went. A siren blared, announcing the intruder. Krenyr abandoned the faces he wore as quickly as he acquired them while he meandered through the camp, pretending that he, too, was responding to the alarm. Word of the general's assassination spread quickly.

The Hunter smiled and quit the camp, sneaking out the rear side by the latrines. He knew where his next mark would be: the ultimate target. Krenyr had vowed to Nitthogr that he would kill the Architect King, and by tonight, either the King would be dead, or Krenyr would be.

The Desolation: Limbus...
...a short while ago.

Chartarra gasped and jerked awake in a panic. He grabbed at his throat instinctively, reaching for the wound he knew he'd just taken from Basilisk—the Tarkhūn Emperor; Chartarra knew that he'd bleed out within seconds if he didn't get pressure on it—even then, survival was unlikely.

He could barely move, though, and it took everything he had just to move his hands across the wet, sticky tear across his neck and chest. Dread realization washed over him: he'd already died. At least, the tarkhūn guards had mistaken him for dead and thrown him out with the trash.

Pain burned across the slash marks when he touched them. They'd clotted enough that they wouldn't tear if he moved and Chartarra wondered how long he'd been lying in the heaps of refuse in the garbage trench beyond Limbus.

The vyrm tried to roll over, but struggled to do so. The fact that he'd somehow lived was a miracle, but it would not do him much good if he laid in the festering pits for too long.

Finally getting to his hands and knees, he recognized the spongy, squishy things below him. Faces. The bodies of comrades who had also been executed by Basilisk in his attempts to strike at Caivev's power base.

Chartarra served Caivev, Nitthogr's successor. That fact had sealed his fate the moment he'd stepped into Basilisk's stronghold—even though he'd been on diplomatic business. Diplomacy was a treacherous thing for vyrm—and he *had* been sent with orders to kill the Emperor at the first available moment.

A terrible smell of trash and rot wafted across the hole.

Chartarra's guts turned and his stomach threatened to revolt. The vyrm warrior bit back the urge to vomit, but he identified the colors in the odor as decay and disease. He knew if he stayed too long in the gulch with his open wounds, something would infect him, if it hadn't already.

Staggering to his feet, he ambled through the uneven footing. Heaps of trash, corpses, and debris shifted underfoot and threatened to topple him on several occasions. Simply walking was the hardest physical challenge he'd ever endured, and every step nearly caused him to lose consciousness as the pain radiated from his neck.

He took step after agonizing step. The slow, zombie pace felt like an eternity spent slogging through the waste.

Chartarra spotted a figure in the distance. He didn't know if it was friend or foe—he was in Basilisk's capital city, after all. He could not assume the person was anything but a loyal minion of the enemy... but at this point, Chartarra didn't care. His strength was failing, and he thought the wound might have reopened with all the movement. He might've bled more, had he any left to lose.

The figure ahead became his only choice.

He croaked out a call and tried to call for help. It was not words that came out, but something more visceral and primal. The words that were not words got the point across and he gained the silhouette's attention. The fellow vyrm hurried over to him just as Chartarra's legs gave out.

"Easy, there. Be at peace, friend. I have you," the other vyrm comforted him, picking him up and dragging him from the trash, careful not to exacerbate the wound.

Chartarra tried to ask about his allegiance. "Bas... Bas-sil?" He couldn't get the words out and his voice barely worked because of the damage to his throat.

"It's okay. I don't care who you work for," the scavenger said, setting aside a bag of collected items he'd scavenged from the trash piles. "You're in my care. I will see that you are mended and then you may return to whoever or whatever cause you are a part of. I am not one to judge."

Chartarra noticed that the vyrm had a huge scar down his face, discolored and ugly. As a warrior, Chartarra admired it. Surely, his rescuer had a story.

"W-who?" the injured vyrm croaked.

"Your wound is grievous. We will have time to speak later—I must get you to the healers immediately. For now, know that you are in the care of the Seekers of Maetha."

Chartarra's eyes widened. The rover cult had a long history, though he doubted much of it was true. Nonetheless, his pulse spiked despite his veins barely having enough blood to operate. His pupils widened and his lungs constricted. Finally, the vyrm warrior passed out.

Chapter One

The Prime

"He... he killed him! He killed my father, General Za-haben, all over again. Just when I'd gotten him back." Zabe's eyes burned as he shifted from his lycan form back into his human shape.

They'd locked firmly, murderously, on Jenner, the soldier who had just split the General Zahaben vertically with his sword. The man had only been reverted to flesh and bone for moments before the attack.

Mangled, the bloody victim laid twisted and visceral upon the floor. Shocked looks painted the faces of the bystanders as much as Zahaben's blood painted the tile floor of Respan's pod where the murder occurred.

Jenner struggled against the guards who detained him. They'd all but saved his life by arriving in time to arrest him rather than let Zabe, the werewolf captain of the Guard, murder him on the spot.

Zabe had always been a model of self-control and duty, but now? After such a sudden murder, and of his father by his protégé? He'd just gotten his father back when Shjikara Stonehand, the High Priest of the Veritas, discovered a way to reverse the flesh-to-stone curse and restore the famous General who'd been petrified during the last great war.

Zabe had worked so hard to help find a way and gained perhaps a mere fifteen seconds with his father... only to watch aghast as the sudden murder overshadowed all of it.

With him still struggling, the guards knew better than to let their commander gain an angle on the young man. He was clearly in shock and capable of reciprocating the violence.

They kept a tight grip on Jenner, as well. The murderer was a Guardian Corps soldier, trained by Zabe and his cousin Wulftone. If he'd gone rogue, there was no telling the damage he could do in this room.

Wulftone stood near the back; he crossed his arms, crestfallen with disappointment. Several members of the Veritas's council of Elders stood with him, equally shocked.

"He's not your father," Jenner yelled. "Whatever he... whatever that *thing* was, it was a spy and not Zahaben. It was certainly vyrm in origins."

Zabe's face softened. He'd come to trust the kid, but he'd also been keenly aware that a spy had been in their midst these last several months. Zabe might have let Jenner explain his line of thought, except that a spy turned to stone could not have fed information to the enemy during the Akko Soggathoth debacle.

Shjikara sighed. "I'm afraid you've killed the only one who could have confirmed that, boy."

The corpse certainly resembled Zahaben. It lay lifeless and split nearly in two by the sword Jenner had used, which also lay nearby. The young man had grown acutely introspective and brooding since the trickster demi-god's defeat at the Kith and Koth gates; his friends had worried about Jenner's mental health in the weeks since.

"I'm telling you, he's a vyrm shade," Jenner insisted. "That's what I've been spending all this time doing: researching the vyrms' spy tactics. Whoever that statue was, he was not your father and I can prove it."

Zabe put his hands on his hips. "Alright. State your proof." His voice was calm, but his eyes burned dark and severe. No one doubted that Jenner would die in the castle dungeons should his evidence prove insufficient.

"Both Basilisk and his brother Nitthogr used shades to..."

"Nitthogr is dead." Shjikara's emphatic words silenced the room momentarily.

"Yes, yes," Jenner clarified. "Everyone knows that Zabe fed him to Sh'logath, the Devourer God, at the Battle of Nebraska... *a conflict you and your Veritas refused to fight in*," he shot back, silencing the leader of the religious order. "The Guardian Corps remembers."

Jenner continued. "*Basilisk* has vyrm shades, face-shifting soldiers, who are expert infiltrators. Because of the conflicts between Basilisk and his brother, the two vyrm leaders stamped their shade troops with a small tattoo in order to know his or her allegiance."

"Thank you for the lesson," Zabe spoke sardonically. "Everyone here knows what a shade is and who uses them."

Respan stood next to Tay-lore, the last remaining member of the technological *homo diurnus* race, an android-like species that once threatened humanity as much as the vyrm ever did. They nearly overthrew the Prime dimension without any assistance from the arcane arts.

The scientist had searched relentlessly for a science-based answer to restoring Zabe's father. He'd come up empty every time, but he had made several discoveries along the way, including a new scanner tech that helped identify auras. The old researcher wore one now and flipped through the settings. He nudged Tay-lore and shot him a quizzical look as he handed over the scanner.

Tay-lore busied himself with the device. The two had worked closely together for many years now, and knew each other better than anyone else.

"But it implicates Basilisk is behind this," Jenner insisted. "We know he's been trying to spy on us, even though he's tried to broker a political peace."

Zabe kept his mouth tight. Thin lipped. "I've never doubted that fact. But there is a problem with your theory... shades take their true form when they die." He motioned to the body. "That man is certainly a dead human."

The guards began to haul Jenner from the room.

"No, wait!" Jenner screamed. "My research says otherwise—my research showed that *some* vyrm are far more talented than others. Some are so good that they retain their form even at post-death levels because they can transform themselves even at a genetic level."

Zabe looked at Shjikara. The old cleric with a stone fist merely shrugged. Neither of them had heard that before. The two had been political opponents for years—but they aligned in this matter: if Jenner was a traitor, he had to be dealt with.

"Just check!" Jenner howled. "It's behind the left ear!"

Zabe stayed the guards with a hand as Shjikara bent over the corpse, blocking their view.

He had been holding his scepter in his available hand and turned it over to the nearest guard. "Don't drop that, son. It is the most visible token of my authority."

The soldier gulped and looked over the scepter, holding it gingerly. The orb atop it was inlaid with the sigils of the Veritas and its four orders. Wherever the High Priest went, the scepter went, too.

Shjikara turned the pieces of head back and forth, examining each side thoroughly. He finally stood and shook his head. "There's nothing here."

Tay-lore cocked his head and continued cycling through the device on the aura reader. "Interesting," he said in his monotone voice. "There is a strong darque-dimension aura coming from your fist. The stone one," Tay-lore stated.

Zabe scowled at him. *This was not the time for discovery!* "I don't care how he was able to reverse the stone-form," Zabe decried. "What matters is that he found a way… and then Jenner murdered my father!"

"He's not your father!" Jenner argued, looking very serious. "You don't think I know what it's like to lose my father, Zabe? Huh? Do you? My father was taken from me by those psycho cultists—Nitthogr's minions from Earth, *and we still haven't done a damned thing to get him back!*"

Shjikara narrowed his eyes. "I do think that sounds like a motive," he said to Zabe.

Zabe flexed his fists. His blood boiled and feral instinct demanded that he shape-shift, extend his claws, and slay the soldier. He grumbled beneath his voice and thought of Gita, another of his orphan soldiers. She and Jenner had a special kind of bond—one their mutual friends claimed had turned romantic, even if Jenner shot her on their most recent missions, putting her in the hospital.

The equation stopped adding up. It made no sense except when Zabe assumed the outcome was that Jenner was the spy.

Wulftone recognized the look on his cousin's face and shouted for the guards to take Jenner away before Zabe snapped and did something rash.

"Do you think I hadn't considered this?" Jenner yelled as they dragged him off. "I knew the risks! I willingly bet my life that he was a shade and not Zahaben—think about it! Wulftone—you believe me, don't you? You've got to believe me…"

Jenner's voice trailed off in the distance, leaving behind only an empty, blood-stained room.

Wulftone looked at the body. The split face was so familiar, yet so irreparably damaged. His uncle had practically raised him as Zabe's surrogate brother, groomed him to be one of his prized soldiers—one of the three sons of the great General Zahaben.

They'd lost Zurrah years ago, only to recently find and then lose him again beyond the multi-verse, trapped in the Darque dimension. They'd lost Zahaben during Nitthogr's assault of the Prime dimension, only to have him returned... and then murdered.

Wulftone looked at his cousin and tried to rest a comforting hand on his shoulder. Zabe would not meet his gaze. Their family had experienced such pain and loss in service of duty to the throne.

Shjikara broke the silence. "We have... not always gotten along, Zabe... you and I," he admitted. "But this thing... this travesty... I will see to it that justice is done."

Zabe wouldn't meet anyone's eyes. He didn't say a word, but only set his jaw. He turned and stormed out of the room in silence.

Wulftone watched him go, noted the look on his cousin's face and empathized with Zabe's need to be alone at this very moment. Only Wulftone, with his advanced senses, noticed Zabe shift into a massive, half-wolf lycan form as the Captain of the Guard leapt over the castle wall and then stormed off towards the distant wilderness.

Manhattan

Vikrum Wiltshire removed the belt he wore and set it at the table of the security kiosk with a *clunk*. Several different ammo pouches, each containing alternate types of bullets, balanced the weight around his hips when Wiltshire wore it. Next, he unholstered the nine millimeter at his shoulder and turned it over.

The security officer wore a bored look as he filled out the paper slip to check on Wiltshire's belongings. He waved the private detective through with barely a second glance.

Wiltshire had been here before on a number of occasions, both in his days as a police detective and also in his subsequent time as an agent of the Red Order. Knights of the Red Order were part of a secret, underground society: those who understood there was more to the world than Earth's citizens understood. The world was plain, demure, and ordinary if you only looked at the surface. Vikrum Wiltshire knew better; he had peeled back the thin veil of normalcy and seen things that cannot be unlearned. Cursed with knowledge, he joined the Order, which used its connections and resources to remove dangerous, arcane artifacts from the world.

He sniffed as he turned the corner and kept his head down. The arcane detective had many contacts in the New York City Crime Lab, but not all of them remained positive. Wiltshire's past hadn't exactly been spotless, and now that he'd flamed out of the Red Order, he'd burned bridges on both sides of him.

His life had become something of a train wreck as of late.

"Hey Wiltshire," a voice called.

Wiltshire turned. The voice had been warm enough to get his attention without a feeling of dread in his gut, although he felt disappointed that his incognito tactics hadn't gone as well as planned. "Hey Jimmy," he responded.

He liked officer Jimmy Cain well enough. The kid seemed bright and positive, the kind who probably made a friend out of every classmate at the academy.

"How are you doing?" Wiltshire kept his voice low as he walked, nearly hugging the wall of the corridor to keep from crossing any extra person's paths and attracting their attention.

"I'm good," Jimmy took the hint and lowered his volume to a more personal level. "I heard you lost your partner a little while back. I'm sorry... did you ever find any leads?"

Wiltshire shook his head. Gloom clouded his face.

"I'm sorry," Jimmy walked alongside the older P.I., headed in the same direction: the basement labs. "Atticus was a great man. He was always so nice to me when I was first starting out on the force."

Wiltshire bobbed his head. "He really was." He noticed the sample bag in his hand; Wiltshire couldn't tell what was inside except that it was organic. "You going to see Becky, too?"

Jimmy nodded. "I need the four-one-one on this. A fresh case the boys are working on."

"What is it?" Wiltshire didn't hide his disgust.

Jimmy shrugged with a laugh. "Heck if I know. How about you?"

Wiltshire held up his item, a glass vial with a slip of paper the size of a pinky finger. "Nothing super special—definitely not a body part," he lied. He wasn't entirely sure.

The younger cop gave him a sly look. Jimmy knew just enough of Wiltshire's story to be intrigued by him and his work, but not enough to be terrified.

Wiltshire wished deep down that Jimmy *had been* terrified. It was safer not knowing about what went bump in the night, but Wiltshire also knew that he needed every resource and contact he could get—especially now. "Just a piece of ancient paper," the detective said.

They entered the lead forensic investigator's office together and Becky looked at them both with a bright smile. She always lit up a room, even when surrounded by the grotesque and macabre. An observation window behind her revealed two corpses that laid opened up for examination. A couple of physicians conducted autopsies on them in the background.

Jimmy tossed her the pouch, and she caught it with a wet slap. It didn't seem to interest her all that much, but her eyes lit up when she saw Wiltshire. "Hello, honey. You always bring me the most interesting projects," she said with a twinkle in her eye. She pressed an intercom button and sent Jimmy's package off to one of her teammates for analysis.

The young cop, still fresh-faced and inexperienced, stood in the background and watched.

"It's a scrap of paper," Wiltshire said, "from an old book I found."

"Is it though?" she asked skeptically. Becky examined it thoroughly; the mystery had her full attention. She pointed with her blue gloved finger. "See the way it frays differently than paper? Its vellum, right?"

Wiltshire nodded with a grin. *She was good.* "But vellum made of what?"

Becky bit her lower lip as if seductively. She was in the thralls of the mystery, now. She spilled the sample onto an examination table and began readying it for testing.

"What's vellum?" Jimmy asked sheepishly.

Wiltshire kept his voice low and let Becky work. "A kind of paper made from animal skin. Ancient books were often made of it because it outlasted parchment."

The beat cop nodded as Becky subjected the sample to a number of tests.

Becky looked up. Anxiety spread across her face. "Vikrum?" she asked.

He looked at her, but already knew it was bad. People only used his first name when news was bad—everyone except Atticus, that is.

A knowing look passed between them and both swallowed dry throats in silence.

"What? what did I miss?" Jimmy asked.

"It's not animal skin... it's human," Wiltshire said. "I just wanted to confirm my suspicion."

Jimmy blanched, but kept a neutral face. "And you think it's related to Atticus's murder?"

Wiltshire nodded slightly. "It's from an ancient book, but I think there's a connection. I'm also not positive Atticus is dead." He turned to Becky. "Can you run the DNA? Get me whatever information you can? Get creative if you have to."

She nodded.

Jimmy ventured a question. "That can't be light reading. What book is it?"

"You wouldn't believe me if I told you."

The Prime

"I haven't seen Zabe in days," Claire sighed.

Jackie, her best friend in the whole multi-verse, sat across from her at the table in her royal apartment in the citadel. She cocked an eyebrow at the untouched cup of coffee in front of Claire's hands. As happy as Jackie was with her announcement of her recent engagement to Wulftone, Claire seemed equally dour.

"I'm sure he'll be back soon. I've gotten to know him fairly well through the Guardian Corps, and I've only seen him like this once before—that time the Heptobscurantum cultists planned to sacrifice you and summon Sh'logath."

"Yeah, the Battle of Nebraska," Claire remarked. "Losing people you love will drive you to rash actions."

"Zabe is probably just cooling down and putting some distance between himself and Jenner, so he doesn't kill the guy," Jackie remarked. She mumbled, "Poor Gita. She gets out of the hospital soon, too; this is going to wreck her. I don't think anyone has told her."

"I don't know," Claire said. "Something about this feels different from mourning."

Jackie chomped on a donut. A local chef, with Tay-lore's help, had learned to cook them just how the Earth-girl liked. She washed her bite down with coffee and mentioned, "Yeah, something has been wrong with him for weeks now, ever since you three came back from being trapped in the Darque, you two, and Tahnak. He's seemed... off?"

Claire turned the warm mug before her, rotating it in a nervous circle as she contemplated telling her about it. Finally, she settled on agreeing with her friend. "Yes. Very *off*."

Jackie watched the mug spin. "Well, we're friends, right? Friends help each other. Let's go and get him and do our best to fix whatever is bugging him."

With lips and chest tightening, Claire said, "It's not that easy." She knew Zabe's melancholy existed before Zahaben's revival and murder—it was all connected to what she did, what *Bithia* did, in the Darque. "I can't even find him."

Jackie raised her brows. "I suppose he's one of the few with detailed knowledge of planeswalking, but surely Tay-lore or Respan could help find him. We tracked down Akko Soggathoth multiple times—if *he* couldn't hide, surely Zabe can be found? Besides, aren't you two, like, psychically bonded or something? Just ping him, or probe him, or whatever you magic-brain people call it."

Claire bit her lip and shook her head. "He is not in his lycan form, so Respan's scanners cannot locate him, and our connection... well, he knows me as well as I know him. That means he knows how to hide from me if he wants to be left alone."

Jackie said nothing. She didn't want to pry into her friends' cooling relationship, but as she thought about it, things began clicking into place. Everything suddenly made sense. "When did you become Bithia again?"

The princess couldn't hide her surprise. "How did you know?"

"We've been friends since, basically, forever," Jackie said. "I would have guessed, eventually. But it was really the coffee. Claire was a fiend for it... *is a fiend*," she corrected. "I guess you two really *are* different in your own ways, even if you two *are* the same." Jackie frowned, knowing her words wouldn't make any sense except to people who knew of the two personalities and souls living within the single body.

Bithia nodded measuredly. "I shall attempt to maintain appearances." She sipped the black coffee and shuddered as the taste disagreed with her. "We can not let others know—the kingdom is still fragile since the Nitthogr war and Basilisk might not be as benevolent as he is trying to appear. Besides, the vyrm are not our only enemies."

Jackie bobbed her head and made a mouth zipping motion. "Who else knows?"

"Our circle is small. Sam Jones, er, my father, knows. You. Perhaps Wulftone, if Zabe told him. I will speak with him later to ensure he is in the loop."

"And of course Zabe."

Bitha acknowledged her as correct.

"Wow. It really *is* important," Jackie noted. "Zabe is going through with the wedding still, even if you are Bithia and not Claire?"

Bithia's face saddened at the comment, but she agreed. "He did love me once, and he loves Claire as well. We lead a complicated life, not made any easier with our duties to the throne."

A moment of silence passed between them and Jackie broke it. "Is Claire really gone? Will she come back?"

"I—I hope so. I never meant to push Claire out. I just..." Bithia trailed off. Pain and guilt riddled her face. "It's more like she has gone dormant... I think. I hope."

Jackie leaned forward and gave Bithia the opportunity to vent. "What happened?"

Bithia confessed her overwhelming need to help while they were trapped in the alien dimension and how exerting her power paralleled the sudden disappearance of Claire's presence. She spilled her guts about growing insecure while riding shotgun in her doppelganger's body and admitted that it may have been her fault... attempts at helping might have caused more harm than good.

"I feel so guilty..." Bithia finally trailed off, choosing not to mention how burned out she felt without Claire's mind in the driver's seat. Deep down, she felt like an empty shell. "I'm not worthy to be the daughter and heir of the Architect King."

Jackie sat in silence with her fractured friend. She didn't have any words that she thought could help, and so she remained quiet.

Bithia stared into the cup of black and took another sip of the bitter coffee and let it wash over her senses. In the back of her mind she felt a glimmer, faint and fleeting, of Claire's mind. When she reached out for it, though, she found nothing. *This was all my fault... I didn't want this, did I?*

The rogue thought kept niggling at her. Maybe she had done this on purpose. Maybe she had sealed Claire away because of jealousy and spite. Bithia had to admit the truth, that human hearts were jealous and deceitful at their core. Only by constant vigilance and self-examination could they be kept in check.

She pushed her coffee away and committed herself to being better—trying harder.

I may not be a worthy daughter of the Architect King, but I am a princess, nonetheless. I'd better start acting like it.

Chapter Two

Tay-lore cocked his animatronic head quizzically and watched the footage again on the monitor. Respan sat next to him in the lab as they reviewed the murderous video from a few days ago.

The old scientist sniffed. His laboratory still smelled like cleaning solvent where the floors had been scrubbed of blood.

"I don't understand why his fist glowed," Respan noted, reviewing the data again. "On the darquescanner, Shjikara's stone fist is definitely glowing with some kind of reading. Hypothesis?"

Tay-lore speculated. "Perhaps there is an item inside his fist... an item crafted of darquematter—some kind of hierophanticus?"

Respan twisted his mouth. "Shjikara said that was not the case when I asked. He has no cause to lie to us. And if it *was* something like that, how could it undo the stone curse? We haven't even been able to use the stone glaive's magic to reverse the stone form."

The android pulled up the data for reference. "The glaive does not register an aura on the darquescanner. They seem unrelated."

Respan nodded and stared at the columns of data which threatened to make him go cross-eyed. He silently wished he could try a few additional tests with the mystic weapon now that they had some additional data to develop some tests with, but Zabe had taken the blade with him when he'd disappeared. Nobody had heard from him since he left to cool down.

Tay-lore pointed to a cell on the spreadsheet which showed a range of variables on the mystic energy spectrums which Respan's sensors operated. "This range reveals a discrepancy."

Respan looked at him inquisitively. "How so?"

Tay-lore pulled up the readings from Zahaben's murder and pointed. "The sensor readings are outside the resonance range of all known darquematter."

The scientist said nothing, but he squinted and stared at the screen. He rummaged his hands through his hair as a silent indicator of agreement. "But it somehow registered on the scanner... whatever the scanner is picking up, it is emitting a powerful signature that is *similar* to darquematter."

Tay-lore nodded and completed his thoughts, "But it *is not* darquematter. Speculate?"

Respan furrowed his brow. "Maybe the Veritas emit a kind of aura when engaging in arcane arts or in their mystic disciplines? Perhaps Shjikara's fist is just where we first detected it."

"Perhaps."

"I think we need more research... and we also need more input, maybe from outside sources. It would be nice to get some perspective from the Veritas, but they are such a secretive lot," Respan lamented.

"Should we bring in Sam Jones to ask about our theories? He seems like an intelligent and skeptical sort of man. He may have divergent perspectives based on his experience and background."

Respan shrugged. "Perhaps, though, he is quite taken with Shandra of the Veritas. They have been spending a lot of time together lately. He may have lost his impartiality... then again, he may be able to access unknown information through Shandra."

"Excellent," Tay-lore said. "Surely he could get secret information from her, or perhaps he could sneak a data collector onto Shandra so we could gather information from within the Veritas's headquarters? For the sake of data collection, we would not want her to be aware of it."

Respan leaned back and looked at him screwy. "No. No, I don't think we will ask that of him. It could ruin our relationship with him for asking; it would certainly ruin her standing within the Order if a spy device is discovered."

Tay-lore cocked a head, failing to understand. The android found human relationships difficult to understand.

Respan had promised to help his robotic friend unravel the humanity mystery and so he explained, "It would be an overstep to ask such a thing of him and it would feel like a betrayal to Shandra if he asked. She expects that Sam will know and understand her well enough to know her thoughts and feelings without being told…"

"Even if she has not made them known?"

"Right," Respan said.

"I don't understand. Does Sam have psychic rapport with her?"

Respan grinned. "No. He does not know what she is thinking."

"But she expects him to know, anyway?"

Respan nodded.

"Humans are confusing," Tay-lore lamented, worried he'd never figure it out.

"Humans, yes. Love? Even more-so. The more time they spend together, the more interest they have, the greater their bond, the more the two will walk in step. They won't know what the other thinks… but it will seem like it because they want the same things and share the same goals and dreams. Their feelings, mind, and bodies are braided together with purpose and commitment."

Tay-lore said nothing. Analogies and word-pictures often eluded him, but not this one. Despite people's opinions and thoughts regarding the android, Tay-lore knew love. Respan made perfect sense to him; he'd long watched over Zabe and Bithia, ever since they were children, in fact. He'd experienced their sorrow when Zabe and Zahaben had lost Zurrah and also when Bithia merged personas with Claire. Tay-lore had watched the changes in them as they came into their own and pursued each other romantically; he felt their joy. Recently, he'd lamented further changes; something was different between Zabe and Claire. With Zabe's absence, he felt the need to remain as close as possible to the princess. There was no doubt in his robotic mind, *Tay-lore loved the princess.*

"Speaking of the royal couple," Respan changed the subject, "Has there been any word yet of Zabe's whereabouts?"

The Desolation

With the steady cadence of a glass beetle, Trenzlr walked across the broken and baked tiles of the Plains of Neggath. The wasteland spread out across the main continent and down the slopes and away from Limbus: Basilisk's capital city was a three-day journey east under good conditions. Brushing the sand from between his scales, the reptilian wanderer lamented the deplorable condition of his world.

He did not look up. Nobody ever looked up in the Desolation dimension, a broken place and fallen realm which had once been known as the promised land of Edenya. Its green and lush landscape had long since burned black, corrupted by war and rot. Above it all hung the dark pall: the lurker on the veil. The Great Devourer, Sh'logath, hung on the edge of reality; the anti-god was not real, but was nearly called into existence during the Syzygyc War, so many generations ago.

In the distance, Trenzlr spotted the rovers' tents in the foothills near a mountain range of Kortath. "So many," he mumbled aloud. "They must have all gotten the message, too."

Trenzlr put one foot in front of the other and kept walking. He would arrive before nightfall. The vyrm was tempted to look up and gauge the time by the sun's position, but he did not. He trusted his gut.

A memory wafted through as he slogged through a patch of fine sand: an unpleasant memory from childhood. Even for the Seekers of Maetha, the keepers of truth and of the old ways which predated the wickedness of the Sh'logath cult, kids would still be kids.

Trenzlr recalled the group of children that had grown up with him. He and the other whelps had all dared Klyrtan, the tribal chief's son, to stare at the lurking form of Sh'logath for a full ten-count. None of them had been very old, and the game had been around for generations before them. *Nobody ever actually did it*—nobody could look fully upon the face of the madness in the sky and remain sane. *Except Klyrtan had.* After being taunted for cowardice, after merely *pretending* to look, which was what all kids did anyway, Klyrtan stared straight into the eyes of madness.

Nobody ever looked for real—but Klyrtan did, Trenzlr chastised himself for old sins. Klyrtan had collapsed after ten seconds with eyes turned milky white and mouth foaming. The eyes eventually cleared, but he'd had to re-learn to speak.

Trenzlr swallowed the pang of guilt in his gut for his role in the events. Klyrtan, much to the dismay of the tribal chief, had remained a simpleton ever since. Soon after Trenzlr pushed those dark thoughts from his mind, two vyrm waved at him from the distance, giving the tribal signal of welcome—a test to see if the visitor was friend or foe.

Recognizing them as Hirdac and Klyrtan, Trenzlr gave the proper response and hurried to meet them. Hustling, it took only a few minutes to cross the gap.

Hirdac put away his spyglass and embraced Trenzlr. Klyrtan followed suit; Klyrtan always did whatever Hirdac did. The elder vyrm, a graying widower and faithful Maethan, had made it his life's priority to watch after poor Klyrtan.

"Praise Maetha," Hirdac said. "We were unsure you would get our message. That you are alive at all is a miracle."

"Praise Maetha," Klyrtan echoed behind them as he faded lock-step into the background.

They walked together and chatted. Trenzlr explained how he'd been accidentally flung through an activated dimensional gate while he and his family were on an expedition. A party of tarkhūn hunters had attacked their party and only he had survived, as far as he knew.

Hirdac nodded solemnly. He filled in the gaps in Trenzlr's knowledge, realizing that the lost vyrm had been trapped in a foreign realm for years now. "A few of your relation got away and returned to us, but most of your family perished. Of course, your cousin still lives." His breath caught in his throat as he spoke excitedly.

Trenzlr chuckled and shook his head, "Of course Gerjha lives. He has been on that mountaintop forever."

"The circle is broken," Klyrtan said in a detached sort of way that both vyrm ignored.

"Tell what happened," Trelzlr said. His cousin had been in the mountains for nearly all his life, confined to a circle as large as he could draw in the sand while staying in its center. Gerjha had proclaimed himself a prophet of Maetha after receiving a dream when he was twelve. He'd dedicated himself to remaining inside the circle and devoting himself to prayer and meditation for almost two decades now.

"Gerjha says all things are shifting. Something new is coming," Hirdac explained.

"That sounds like Gerjha, speaking as cryptically as usual. He usually sounds like he's giving revelation but actually says nothing, claiming that Maetha has 'nothing new yet to say.' So what is different about it this time?" Trenzlr asked.

Hirdac looked him fully in the face. "Gerjha has left the circle and come down from the mountain."

Trenzlr rocked back on his heels. "He did what?"

Hirdac nodded enthusiastically. "He came down from the mountain and claimed that the end will arrive soon: something new is in motion, he says—I guess he really means it."

As they grew closer to the edge of the village, a sense of hope seemed to ripple through him at the size of it. They had grown exponentially.

Basilisk's tarkhūn would not dare to attack such a gathering and he'd never seen so many Seekers of Maetha gathered like this before. "This... this could really be it?" Trenzlr whispered as he walked through the camp. Optimism and zeal seemed to ripple through the community. At the center of it, Trenzlr spotted his cousin Gerjha standing next to chief Klewdahar and an unknown vyrm with a puckered scar across his neck; he did not recognize the scarred one.

They made quite the scarred pair. Trenzlr recognized the chief's scar that raked from forehead to chin; he could never forget a mark like that and how he'd gotten it. Klewdahar had been captured by enemies as a young adult and been given a permanent reminder of their opponents' hatred of the rovers.

Regardless of the melancholy he felt when he saw the wounds his people had received, something warm swelled in Trenzlr's gut. *Finally. I am home.*

Earth

Jacob Sisyphus walked through the hall of the German high-rise. He and his Heptobscurantum cult owned the building as part of their corporate holdings. The uppermost floors held a secret; it hid Doctor Pietro Walther's laboratory and the cultist's private quarters.

"Good afternoon, Doctor," Sisyphus said in his trademark voice. As a mountain of a man, he towered over the average-built and middle-aged scientist. Sisyphus was more than a wealthy business mogul and avid cultist. He'd become the most powerful sorcerer on earth thanks to his blending of science with the arcane.

Even during his professional wrestling days, he had been a powerful specimen of humanity, but now? He bordered on godly.

Walther's eyes lit up as they always did in Sisyphus's presence. He'd been Sisyphus's biggest fan when he'd been a mere upstart pro-wrestler, ever since the early days. Walther knew most of it was fake, but Walther had always been a fan of the stories, the athleticism, and the pageantry of professional wrestling. "I heard on the fan forums that you purchased your old wrestling association. Is there any chance you will return to the ring?" he asked excitedly.

Sisyphus shook his head slowly. "No. Those days are far behind me, my friend."

Walther was disappointed only momentarily by the revelation. Being called *a friend* by his hero quickly smoothed over any sadness he felt. "That is too bad, but how may I help?"

Sisyphus grinned. "Doc, I know you're a man of science and that you can see science doesn't have all the answers. You've witnessed what I can do with magic and you've broken through into the other dimensions with your equipment. I'm admitting that magic can't provide all the answers, either. I need your help, Doc."

Walther beamed. "Of course; I'll do whatever you need."

The wrestler smiled. "You and me, Doc. We're gonna take reality by force and bend it to our will. There are whole other worlds out there, whole other fights to win. Power to gain," his growl shifted ominous. "After Caivev's departure, it's important that I know who I can trust." He leaned down and pinned a tiny button to the scientist's lapel, identifying him as a member of the Heptobscurantum.

Doctor Walther lit up. "Of course," he said. "Whatever you need."

Sisyphus grinned. "Magic is potent stuff, my friend." He unrolled a sheet of paper with a sketch on it and a second leaflet fell out; it depicted a metallic pendant dangling from a string.

Walther rushed to grab it for his hero. He turned it over in his hands. Strange, foreign words which seemed written in an unearthly tongue had been scrawled near the drawing.

"I do believe I'd like to acquire one of those to make sure I have adequate protection from others like myself," but his primary attention was on the larger scroll.

The scientist looked at him quizzically.

"Wizards tend to possess both great aspirations and resources." He tapped Walther on the shoulder and showed him the larger manuscript. The stained, ivory papyrus contained more of the mystic writing and a full, detailed sketch of a cheval-style mirror, except that it stood on a solid mount which would not swivel.

"You need a mirror?" Walther asked. "I have one you can borrow."

Sisyphus shook his head.

"Not a mirror then... it provides something—a power or an ability? What does it grant you?

Sisyphus looked at it covetously. "Anything I want." A devious grin spread across his face. "Fire up your machine, Doctor. An old pal gave me a lead on where we might find this particular artifact." He channeled his best theatric, wrestler voice, "And you're gonna have a front-row seat to the rumble of the century!"

Cerci Heiderscheidt flashed her partner a pixie-like grin. She turned her Houston Astros baseball cap backwards and pulled her shielded goggles down over her face. "I have solved science!" she cackled and threw a switch.

She was in her mid-twenties and possessed a perky kind of air, though she was prone to wide swings of mood.

"I really think you're over-doing it," Zurrah said, returning a playful grin. Skinny, but still muscular, the boy laughed at Cerci's mad-scientist bit. He knew it could be true, even if he'd only recently learned what a mad-scientist was from Earth movies—she *could* be a mad scientist. He'd been trapped for many years inside the time-tomb of the Hidden Temple, kidnapped and secreted away by Nitthogr only to discover later that his father had died and his brother had grown up to take his place.

Within the mystic stasis room, he'd remained a teen for a decade, and then Cerci, a scientific genius and underling of Doctor Pietro Walther, befriended him through the door. After becoming trapped in the Darque dimension for many more years, which only passed like days for Cerci Heidersheidt, his body had finally aged up to about nineteen after a dimensional chaos wave hit him. In truth, he was older than her by three years and he'd nearly caught up to her, now.

"I would never over do it," she spoke in sarcastic, theatrical tones. "I am the great Cerci Heidersheidt—genius of a new age!"

Zurrah grinned. "Well, I think you're pretty great," he winked at her.

Cerci kissed him. "You'd better. Or I'll leave you hanging over there." She threw the final switch on her contraption built inside a loading dock of the immense, empty space littered with discarded sports paraphernalia. The machine whined and a triangular aperture split the air near the beam emitters and widened.

Zurrah slapped her on the rump as he walked by. "I thought you wanted an adventure?" he asked. "So why are we spending all this time stealing and pulling heists?"

"This *is* an adventure," she laughed from the controls. "Besides, we're only robbing from people who can afford it and I've still got a mountain of debt to repay. Student loans cost practically more than the parts for the Dimension Cracker." She paused, recognizing another cultural norm he had no exposure to. "I'll have to show you Robin Hood right after I teach you about baseball."

He paused in front of the energy gate and fixated on the first part of her speech. "Seriously? We are going with the 'Dimension Cracker?'"

Cerci shrugged with a chuckle. "Hurry through the hole, sweet cheeks. Mama's got a loan to pay off."

"You know I'm actually older than you?" he bantered as he stepped through.

"Shush, now. This is *my* fantasy... don't ruin it for me or I'll ground you."

The room Zurrah entered was well lit and well-provisioned. Cerci shouted to him through the portal between space. "Oh. Grab that, and that!" she pointed to the two heavy sacks of cash and a tray filled with stamped gold bricks.

Zurrah spun a small circle, taking stock of what else might be within this rich man's vault. Only those few items he'd already thrown through were immediately valuable and easy to liquidate. Rows and rows of shelving contained all manner of ancient books, idols, and other kinds of arcane fetishes.

"What in the world is this place?" he wondered aloud. "It looks like the Sacristy Vault in the temple of the Veritas," he mused.

"I don't know what that is," Cerci said. "Time to get back. I think we got everything of value—at least valuable to us and our creditors."

Zurrah nodded, but then paused right before leaping through. A massive page hung on one rack. Three feet tall, it boasted ornate drawings upon the enormous sheets of vellum. Two other pages were present, but his eyes were drawn to the one. It bore an illustration of a wolf-man stepping through a triangle-shaped door and into another world.

"What are you waiting for?" Cerci hissed.

Zurrah cocked his head, still looking at the page. His father had been known as the werewolf protector of the throne, and from what he'd gathered about his brother, Zabe, from Cerci, his brother had gained that ability as well. Zurrah snatched the page from its place and rolled it up into a manageable scroll.

He ignored the other pages left behind and abandoned the other items of immense power. Zurrah knew that Cerci had a mind for science and the arcane held little interest for her... but the ancient graphic called to him. It seemed too relevant to his family to simply abandon it.

Zurrah flashed her a smile and stepped through the triangular portal. "Mission accomplished," he said, and then kissed her while the energy gate winked out of existence.

CHAPTER THREE

T*he Prime*

Gita leaned on the crutch as she walked out of the hospital. Jackie walked alongside her diminutive friend, just in case she faltered. "I'll be okay, you know," she said. "The physicians said I'm basically fine… only a little sore—more than usual, at least, given the way Zabe makes us exercise on drill days. I guess that being shot will do that to you."

Jackie faked a smile at her humor and gave her a little more space.

Gita's eyes searched for someone at every turn they took through the hallways. They looked around expectantly right up until they exited the building. They finally locked on Wulftone with disappointment.

Wulftone hurried closer, carrying a box of the glazed donuts that Gita had come to love as much as his fiance. She shook her head when he offered her a pastry. "No appetite? You can't be the Gita I knew," he joked. Wulftone caught Jackie's eyes, and he realized that Jackie hadn't told her about Jenner's arrest yet.

"I'm sorry," she said as she climbed into the skiff that would ferry her back to the Guardian Corps barracks. "I was hoping you'd be… someone else."

Gita's friends followed her into the vehicle. Wultone sighed, "You were hoping for Jenner?"

Her eyes twinkled slightly at his mention. "Yeah. I know you said that he survived the final battle, Jackie, and I really thought that he'd have come to see me by now—*especially now*." She grew silent for a moment. "Especially since he's the one who put me here," she mumbled. Gita continued, "I dunno. Maybe I was reading too much into things; I could've been wrong about him."

"We *all* could have been wrong," said Jackie. "But it's got nothing to do with you."

Gita looked from Jackie to Wulftone. "What do you mean?"

Wulftone grimaced. "Did you ever feel like Basilisk was always one step ahead of us? The upper-level leadership didn't talk much about it with the Corpsmen." He screwed up his face and then leveled with her, taking on his superior officer voice, "What I'm telling you is confidential. We have been searching for a mole within our ranks for a long time, now... since before Akko Soggathoth. Evidence came to us, indicating that it was Jenner."

"No," Gita said, surprised. "No, that can't be—*I know it for a fact.*"

"He's currently in prison and awaiting a trial," Jackie said.

"I refuse to believe that. Jenner is no spy—you can believe me," Gita exclaimed. "I can guarantee it; you guys have got to look again. I just know he's innocent."

"I wish we could," said Wulftone, "but a tribunal will handle it, now. It's out of our control. He will most likely be executed," his somber tone emphasized finality.

"What? For *spying*? And on what so-called evidence?" Gita practically exploded in the back seat.

Wulftone and Jackie traded reluctant glances. Finally Wulftone took up the duty of explaining the grisly details. He sucked in a sharp breath. "Jenner murdered someone in cold blood. Right in front of Zabe and Shjikara... in front of almost all the leadership team."

Gita stared at him, incredulous. It was simply not the Jenner that she knew. Tears reddened the rims around her eyes. She sat for a few sullen moments as the skiff jostled along towards the barracks. Finally, she asked, "Who was it?" Last-ditch optimism hung at the frayed edges of her voice; maybe it was someone who had it coming? Maybe it's a misunderstanding and was self-defense?

Wulftone exhaled a hot puff through his nose. "Zabe's father. My uncle. General Zahaben."

"I thought he was dead?"

"We all did, but he came back... he's definitely dead now." The words tasted bad in Wulftone's mouth and he frowned.

Gita chewed her cheek for a bit and spoke softly, like a widow. She shed a few tears and stared out the window. "I loved him, you know?"

Jackie reached back and grasped her hand, giving it a gentle squeeze. "I know you did. I think he knew it, too, for what it's worth."

With a pending tribunal and the severity of his crimes, only high-ranking officials would be granted access to the prisoner. Gita would likely never be allowed to tell him in person.

They rode the rest of the way in silence.

Earth

Vikrum Wiltshire felt the weight of his pistol against his left pectoral muscle. It provided some comfort at least as he followed the strange fellow through the spacious mansion to which he'd been summoned. He asked, "What did you say your name was again?"

"Mister Theera," he stated, leading the way through a polished granite corridor and deeper into the heart of the mansion.

Wiltshire chuckled. "What is that, some sort of family name?" He didn't try to mask the disbelief in his voice.

Theera curled a lip in a kind of snarl. His teeth didn't look convincingly human, but Wiltshire had already suspected as much based on the waxy makeup that seemed to terminate at the major-domo's brow-line; Theera's makeup was good, but not perfect.

"Let us not make the mistake of trying to deceive each other, Mister Wiltshire. We both know that I am no mere human, and we both know who I work for."

"Yeah," Wiltshire sniffed, "You're a Heptobscurantum toady. I've dealt with your kind before, or at least the human version of whatever you are. I really only answered your invitation because I was curious as to what Percival Wainsmith's house looked like on the inside. Look at that woodwork and those sconces. Beautiful." His voice dripped with derision.

Theera frowned. "I thought we agreed not to speak falsely? I know of your feud with the Hidden Seven, the Heptobscurantum council. You have foiled many of their individual plans, plans which my master is not typically a part of. Actually, he appreciates the dose of chaos that you have introduced to the system; it has provided him with much entertainment."

"Speaking of Mister Moneybags, where is Wainsmith?"

"He is... away on business at the moment. Legitimate business takes up much of his time. More than he cares to sacrifice. He will be back, though I know not when."

"Alright," Wiltshire said. "I'll bite. Why did you call me all the way out here, then? I've got very important things I am working on right now."

Theera grinned mischievously. "Yes. I am aware. You seek to solve the murder of your partner, and we both know who is responsible. I sought you out because you are the foremost detective and have proved a repeat foil in our world. When my master left, he placed me in charge of his affairs until his return. Only recently, someone stole from me."

"So call the police."

"I am not concerned about the money or lost gold and gems. I want returned what was taken from my vault. One of the missing pages from the Codex Gigas was taken from the collection." He held up a hand to forestall any questions about the missing pages. The Codex was an ancient work said to have been penned by the Devil as an agreement between the Benedictine monk, Herman the Recluse, and Lucifer. It contained many scripts, including an early version of the Christian Bible, several historical works, and a number of magic formulas and rites. "I am aware that you recently went to Sweden and secured a sample from the binding of the Codex... it would seem you buy into the belief that the missing pages might contain otherworldly rites, spells, and prophecy? If so, you would be correct.

Theera paused for a breath and examined Wiltshire's posture. He had him hooked. "We follow some of the same sources online. There has been much discussion about images recently posted that claim to be a missing page from the Codex. It is certainly authentic. I was a part of the conversation."

"Sounds like you know a lot," Wiltshire quipped.

"Of course I do. I was the one who posted the images and blurred out the references to everything save the Scholomance."

Wiltshire set his jaw at the mention of the name. His nostrils flared and his heart pounded. As an enemy of the Heptobscurantum, he hated that they kept talking him into taking jobs from them.

"Do you have that page? That is my fee. I want it." Wiltshire stopped walking, firmly in negotiation mode.

Theera laughed at him and kept walking. "No. I don't think so."

"Hey. Get back here; I'm talking to you!"

He kept moving onward until Wiltshire yanked his pistol from its holster and racked it once for dramatic effect. The distinct sound of a nine millimeter's slide action had a profound way of getting answers, even if direct threats were not normally Wiltshire's style.

Theera turned and grinned at him. "My, my. You really are riled up by this case. I assure you I will give you the information you seek if you return my missing page."

"A page for a page," Wiltshire insisted. "That's the deal."

"Or what? You'll kill me?" Theera said with a chuckle. He walked towards the occult detective. "I thought we agreed to speak honestly? If I am dead, you cannot open the vault and you won't get any of your precious information. You will never find the Scholomance without me." He stepped closer until the gun barrel rested against his head. "You cannot kill me, Mister Wiltshire. I promised to speak the truth, and I have."

"You think I won't pull the trigger?"

Theera interrupted, "I did not say you *would not*. I said you *can not*." He reached inside Wiltshire's jacket and snatched his backup handgun hanging on the right side; in one smooth action, he stepped back and leveled the gun at the detective. After looking him squarely in the eye, he called Wiltshire's bluff. "You neither could nor would fire. But I will show you that I mean what I say when I claim you cannot kill me." Theera pressed the barrel against his own temple and fired.

Wiltshire howled as the man crumpled into a heap. The detective's gun lay under the collapsed body of Wainsmith's assistant, whose blood and brain were sprayed across the walls and floor. He panicked and paced back and forth. The dead man, or whatever he was, had just killed himself with Wiltshire's gun—there's no way that would look good on a police report.

After a few seconds, the gaping hole in the side of his head began to close itself at a snail's pace: slow for movement, but rapid for healing. A couple minutes later, Theera stirred and began crawling to his feet. He turned the gun back to his guest and spoke raggedly, as if he'd just ran a half mile. "Now that we understand each other... I have no need of this weapon."

Wiltshire couldn't speak. He stood dumbfounded and rooted in place. He'd seen a lot of strangeness in his line of work, but this was a first.

"You will be allowed to take a digital photograph of the missing page," he offered. "It describes, in detail, the Scholomance: the school of the thirteen strigoi, the Solomonari and their legendary Zmei. Whatever you might do when you catch up to them... that will be interesting to see." He leveled a long gaze at the detective. "Will that suffice?"

Wiltshire swallowed the dry lump in his throat and nodded. "I agree to your terms. Show me the vault."

Theera led the way further into the mansion.

The Prime

"I'll see you in one hour," said Wulftone as he kissed Jackie at the doorway to Claire's apartment.

She pulled away and winked. "One hour," she confirmed, and then headed inside.

Normally, she would jump at the chance to hang with her bestie, Claire, but real life seemed to intervene at every possible turn, derailing every plan made to simply enjoy each other's company. From what Jackie had gathered from her older friends, those opportunities would not grow easier the further she got from her young twenties. Her upcoming marriage and new life would make it only more difficult, she assumed.

Jackie dropped her jacket in the hall and noticed two suitcases packed and left by the door as she entered.

Bithia and Jackie were supposed to hang out tonight, and Jackie had planned to bail early, but with good reason. She'd felt a little overwhelmed lately and wanted to be more than just a sounding board for emotional friends. With Zabe presumably brooding in some foreign dimension and Jenner sitting incarcerated, Jackie just couldn't take letting her friends cry on her shoulders much longer; she had an escape plan.

"Oh good," Bithia said when she spotted her. Jackie was one of the few who knew that Claire Jones was no more: there was only Bithia, Princess of the Prime. Claire's body had long possessed both personalities, separate persons each, until Bithia's psychic powers drove out her long-time friend from Earth. Bithia confessed, "I'm something of a wreck lately, but especially today."

Jackie smiled, thin-lipped. She'd expected nothing less. "What's with the suitcases?" Muffled sounds came from one of the bedrooms where her father packed and made last-minute preparations.

"Professor Jecima died," Bithia said flatly.

Jackie sat next to her friend and squeezed her hand. "That's too bad. He was such a nice old man, and a wise and good friend."

Bithia bobbed her head. She still had Claire's memories to draw on and remembered him fondly. Jecima had helped Claire and Jackie in the early days when Nitthogr's forces sought to capture her.

"My father is taking Shandra to Earth for the funeral."

"That's expected... hey? Do you remember the time Jecima slapped you?"

Bithia rubbed her cheek. Even though he'd slapped Claire, and to prove a point, Bithia still felt it, as if the cheek had been her own. She smiled. "Yeah. He certainly had a way of making a point."

"He certainly did," she laughed.

Sam Jones left his bedroom with a suit coat on a hanger draped over his shoulder. Shandra argued with him, "I don't care if it's tradition. It's a foolish tradition."

Jackie raised her eyebrows. "I see you folks have very strong opinions on funerals here in the Prime."

"I'm not against funerals," Shandra said. "I think the required clothing is ridiculous."

Sam held up a black suit and matching tie.

"I don't see anything wrong with it," Jackie said.

Shandra was a member of the warrior class of the Veritas, the Order of the Merciful Hammer. She scowled and snatched the necktie. "This? Why would anyone wear a noose? And to a funeral? This thing serves no purpose."

Sam threw the tie across the room. "Fine. I'll go without it, but we need to leave right away or the gates won't align properly and we'll miss our portal window." He picked up a suitcase.

Shandra followed after him, carrying luggage of her own.

The door shut behind them and Jackie said sarcastically, "They're such a cute couple."

Bithia shrugged and loaded nine spoonfuls of sugar into the freshly brewed cup of black coffee. She bit back a grimace after taking a sip and then added one more scoop. "You know, this stuff is starting to agree with me."

Jackie shot her an incredulous look. "Yeah... I'm not sure it does, really." Jackie told Bithia about Gita's reaction to the news about Jenner and Bithia's own emotional floodgates opened. Jackie nodded a lot and repeated, "I understand," so many times she lost count.

Someone knocked on the door and Bithia pulled herself up from her pity party. She wiped her eyes to make sure she was respectable and as regal as expected of royalty.

Jackie glanced up at the clock. "Oh, look at the time. I should probably go."

"But it seems like you only just got here," Bithia said. "And who knows who might be at the door?"

"It's Wulftone," she leveled with her. "He promised to pick me early. We have a special thing planned tonight. Sorry," she said sheepishly.

"Well, what is it? What's so special about tonight... maybe I can tag along?"

"Ummmm... no. Sorry." She lowered her voice. "We decided to avoid all the ceremony and drama of a wedding and elope. No offense—I'm sure you'll need to have the big wedding with all the pomp and circumstance and what not. You're the princess, after all, and the people need it maybe more than you do... but I just want to marry that man."

Bithia looked her friend full in the face with warm eyes and then grabbed her for a big hug. "Of course not. I just want you to be happy." She squeezed tighter. "If you're happy, I'm happier for it."

Jackie thought her friend might even mean it, despite her currently sad state. "I'll be back soon," she said, hurrying towards the door, which knocked again. "Right after a little honeymoon. He's showed me so many interesting things on the Prime, now it's my turn to show him Earth." She flashed a nervous smile, "and introduce him to my parents... they're going to freak out."

The door opened and Wulftone stood there, tall and handsome. He wore a smile and carried two travel bags.

"Before you go, Wulftone," Bithia asked, suddenly aware of her growing isolation, "who will be in charge of security? With both Zabe *and you* gone, I should like to know..." she trailed off. Ever since her teen years, Bithia's life had constantly been in peril; security was a constant need.

Wulftone grinned as if he'd expected the question. "Chira will take the lead," he said. "He's been the head of the Royal Military force for weeks now and he is up to speed on everything you will need and on your itinerary."

Jackie gave her a hug again before departing. "We plan to get to Earth by a roundabout way and visit my parents right after we get hitched, but we'll be back before you know it. Take care. Be strong. Zabe will be back soon—I'm sure of it. But so what if he isn't, right? You're a strong independent princess. You got this."

The princess released her embrace. "Tell your mom and dad I said hi," Bithia said, almost as if she had channeled Claire for a brief moment. She offered a melancholy smile, and her friends slipped away.

The door closed, and Bithia was alone once more. After a few moments of stark silence, the princess called out to the emptiness inside of her. After the princess had sacrificed herself for her friends long ago, she'd always been with company, dwelling alongside Claire's consciousness. She hadn't ever been truly alone... until now.

"Claire? Claire, are you there?"

Her words echoed through the hollowness inside of her. The loneliness threatened to consume her with one final trick played by the Darque and its nefarious trickster demi-god.

She gave up calling after a few minutes and sat to sulk by the window when she thought she heard it: a faint sob in her subconscious.

"Claire? Claire, is that you?" Bithia asked aloud. She was keenly aware that she would sound crazy if anyone saw her talking to herself. She didn't care. She was the princess and heir to the throne. If she wanted to talk to herself, she bloody well could.

The words reverberated in the emptiness inside her soul, but then she heard it again, followed by the tiny, faint words, "I am here."

Earth

Wiltshire crouched as he examined the door to the opened vault. He whistled and rummaged a hand through a mane of hair that had just begun to gather a tinge of salt. His normal hubris had somewhat returned by the time they arrived at the scene of the crime. "Someone robbed *this?* They might deserve to keep whatever they took if they pulled it off."

Theera merely glared.

The vault was perhaps the most impenetrable thing Wiltshire had ever seen. It looked like a freestanding room built with steel plating worthy of armor on a battleship and warded by security cameras and multiple door locks. The door was currently open for the detective's benefit.

"How in the world did they get in? This thing looks impenetrable." He mainly jawed so he could stall and get a peek at all the wildly powerful totems stored away in the cultist's depository. He spotted two of the pages from the Codex Gigas where they hung by clips. The one he wanted was further in the back and so he couldn't get a great read on it, plus his Latin was rusty, but the closer one had an illuminatory drawing of a black-cloaked figure holding a blood-red ruby.

Wiltshire caught a few lines of the text from the closest page. They labeled the monster as a demon named Suranvyn. He shuddered; he'd read about him before. The entity was a nasty creature, but not one Wiltshire would normally associate with cataclysmic activity or with the Scholomance, and so he moved past it and tried to get a better angle to glean information from the page he desired.

"I will show you how they accessed the vault. Follow." Theera commanded as he closed the massive door behind them, much to the dismay of the detective. He brought Wiltshire to a bank of screens. They showed a CCTV recording of the heist.

A triangular portal opened and a teenage boy leapt through; he was maybe college aged at most. The subject stole the cash and gold, throwing them back through the mystic opening before turning to leave. The screens cycled between the same heist but from multiple angles; mounted cameras on all four corners of the strong room had captured the entire act.

"Here. Let me..." Wiltshire took control of the video system and slowed it down, watching the invader pause and grab the page as if it was an afterthought. "He's just a kid," Wiltshire remarked, switching the angle. "How is it that a kid somehow leapt through a dimensional gate to rob the rich and famous?" he mumbled. "It looks like he's talking to someone."

The next feed played, showing the angle from the rear, and he spotted a face through the geometric portal, a female face. Behind her, a partial word could be spotted painted on a wall: *n Astrod.* "I can get your page back," he stated. "But I'll need you to send me copies of this video. I have a couple of hunches already."

"I will send it immediately," Theera said.

"Just be ready with my payment," Wiltshire insisted.

"It is already prepared," he said. "I would not..."

"Yeah, yeah. You wouldn't lie, or whatever. Just make sure it's done." Wiltshire turned to see himself out.

"Oh, and Mister Wiltshire?"

He turned and glared at the undying thing that served Percival Wainsmith. Wiltshire gave him his attention.

"Do take care. I would hate to see you suffer the same grisly fate that befell your partner, Atticus Sexton. Be cautious as you deal with the Scholomance. At least, exercise care until my master's page is returned? Then you may perform your duties as recklessly as normal."

Wiltshire grumbled something unintelligible and turned to leave with a frown on his face. The fact that the Heptobscurantum had bad blood with the Solomonari was this jobs only redeeming grace, and right now he hated the Scholomance more. He exited the mansion, still wearing his grimace and vowing internally to bring them *both* down... someday.

Chapter Four

The Prime

Shjikara's feet echoed in the halls as he meandered alone through the royal castle. He understood the irony of his free passage through the capital grounds and so a smirk tugged at his lips. None stopped him, and guards were stationed at regular posts.

No one had reason to stop him. Shjikara was one of the most respected citizens of the realm, perhaps one rung below the royal family, those descended from the direct lineage of the Architect King. The High Priest of the Veritas had access to incalculable treasure, arcane artifacts, and immense political power.

For a long time, Shjikara had been at odds with General Zahaben and again with his son, Zabe. Their philosophy for how the Guardian Corps operated in tandem with the throne had always irked him. The Corps allowed too much separation between the crown and the religious sect, of which he was chief... Shjikara could not control them.

Shjikara chuckled at the turnabout. He knew that deep down, he had never actually valued the religious structure or tenants of faith. For him, the Veritas had always been a way to gain power and influence. Whenever his motives became evident to a peer, he used his connections and political sway to destroy him or her, just as he had used his position to prevent Shandra from advancing ranks for many years.

Of course, *He was not Shjikara*. Not truly... not anymore. Just like Claire Jones had a duality of mind, Shjikara had become infested with another's soul: a powerful mind and will which easily overpowered that of the high priest after he had been transmuted to stone by a clandestine visit from Basilisk.

The high priest walked through the throne room. Only dim illumination lit the place. He had been here before.

Behind the tall seat of power towered two massive stone doors. They stretched from floor to ceiling and the engraved magic sigils they bore kept them sealed against intruders.

He hissed as he read them. The words were carved in the Olde Primal Tongue and encircled the door-posts of the Chamber of Mysteries where the Tesseract and other ultra powerful artifacts were kept. It read *Only ye who enter may be pure and of blood royale—or sealed beneath the power of the One, allegiant and loyal. Ye be warned.*

An ancient spell was woven into the words themselves and they made Shjikara's skin crawl. The foreign skin already felt corpulent and gross, to Shjikara, who was not Shjikara, but the priest's body was a necessary part of the arrangement, and the only way for his dark presence to return.

He looked down at his stone fist. Shjikara approved of the replacement he'd received. In his previous life, he had lost that hand to the edge of the Stone Glaive at the Battle of Nebraska.

This man was not Shjikara. He had only stolen the man's body and used it as a vessel, a mere vehicle. Spewed out through a crack in the Darque's Bone Gate, the fractured soul lodged itself within the stony form of the high priest, who did not know how to use the Rune of Return he clutched in his hand. Now, that form was home to the spirit of Nitthogr.

And Nitthogr no longer served his own purpose; he'd given himself over to the service of Sh'logath. The Mighty Devourer would rise again, and Nitthogr would laugh as reality disintegrated into the eternal nothingness.

He stared at the binding spell engraved upon the Chamber of Mysteries. It angered Nitthogr to look upon them. As one of the loyal members of the Royal family, Shjikara, the real Shjikara, would have had access to it but would have never seized the Tesseract because of his loyalties—even Shjikara, for all his secret ambition, would have never done such a deed.

But Nitthogr was *not* Shjikara and he could not open the doors, even if he owned the man's body. One could not fool such primal magic, and this magic was crafted by the Architect King.

The sorcerer would make no mistakes this time. He would breach those doors to the Chamber of Mysteries, take hold of the Tesseract, and fling wide the gates to release his mighty agod.

Caivev sat in the uppermost section of the collapsed bell tower and stared through a targeting reticle, placing the dot onto the form of an errant vyrm rover. She'd tracked a small camp of them to this abandoned city of Sharonash, which lay a day's travel from Limbus. Sharonash was a vibrant community before the Syzygyc war; it was another victim of the great conflict between the realms, which nearly pulled Sh'logath into existence.

Beyond the wasted structures and husks of once-lived in dwellings, a veritable field of statues stood like a waiting army. Just beyond the reaches of Sharonash was the location where the Architect King had surrendered on behalf of the multi-verse and sold his life as a ransom to the Brothers of the Apocalypse in order to forestall the summoning of Sh'logath.

She grinned as she watched the shadows of rovers sneak through the city. A newly christened dunnischktet, Caivev had gained veritable immortality and a dual nature. The vyrmic dunnischktet meant *born of two*.

Previously, she led the Black, the lesser vyrm caste; it was the more numerous faction, but lacked the mutational abilities some tarkhūn possessed, aside from the occasional face-shifting shade.

Caivev had become Nitthogr's successor, beating out both Charsk and the late general Regorik for the job, and she had very nearly unleashed Sh'logath of her own accord in the years since. But after allying with Basilisk, Nitthogr's brother, she became the wife and Empress of all vyrm. Together, in only a short time, she and Basilisk had unified the race despite the cries of the tribal leaders within the Black. Only these rovers, the Seekers of Maetha, remained beyond the fold of Limbus's imperial control.

Caivev watched them in silence for a little while longer. Something had mobilized the Maethans. Finally, she steadied her rifle.

Their sudden flurry of rover activity did not bother her; they had little power, and no known, unifying force amongst them except a creed that the Maetha, some kind of savior, would arise. They were not deemed a threat, but she had grown interested in them for sporting reasons.

Maethans were fun to hunt, she thought.

Caivev pulled the trigger and a sharp crack rang out. Her invisible, projectile bullet sent one of her prey sprawling with a shower of hot blood.

She followed another in the scope as he tried to elude the sniper. Caivev pulled the trigger and put him down with a grin.

And to think, both Skrom and Basilisk tried to keep me in Limbus, worried for my safety. This was her hobby; she found matters of vyrm court to be as boring as the Prime's had been before she'd slid into a traitorous role, drawn by Nitthogr's power and the simplicity of the Sh'logath cult's nihilistic beliefs. Skrom had dutifully taken orders from his Empress and Basilisk, the great strategist, had quickly understood that arguing with her when her mind was set would prove one game he could never win.

She zoomed in and watched her next prey. Caivev didn't take the shot, but she took others as they scrambled for safety. She tried to split them up and was toying with them. Caivev put the scope on the forehead of one young vyrm who leaned out from his cover and called to another Maethan: a child who was too scared to flee. He looked up and spotted the glint of the scope in the moonlight and locked eyes on Caivev.

The dunnischktet pressed her finger against the trigger, but before the weapon fired, something rumbled beneath her and the ground erupted in a spray of sand and baked clay tiles. Her perch collapsed in a heap that sent her sprawling across the open courtyard.

Caivev tucked and rolled to cushion her fall, but her weapon had vanished somewhere amongst the scattered bricks and crumbled foundations. She'd barely scrambled to her feet when the carrion worm reared up and locked all eighty-six of its multi-sized, shiny eyes upon her. They burned dark and hungry, even in the black of night.

The worm bellowed, flailing its antennae and flinging caustic enzymes from its mouth as it opened its disjointed jaws so that the swarm of larval crawlers could spew forth and seek its prey.

Caivev whirled and fled. Her right leg gave out beneath her. Her ankle had taken a nasty sprain and simply wouldn't work as intended.

The flood of the insect-like creatures swarmed towards her, tittering like eager cicadas, eager for the taste of flesh. The creatures were no respecter of royalty or breeding and had developed a taste for vyrm flesh ever since being released into the plains of Neggath decades ago by Nitthogr as retribution against his brother for accepting the Architect King's terms of surrender.

Caivev stumbled further ahead, but it became clear that she could not out-pace the predators on her wounded leg. She bit her lip and tried anyway, keenly aware that they would soon sting her with their thousands of electrified feet and she would become food for the carrion queen.

A figure leapt out from the alley, swinging a wooden staff to keep the worms at bay. The same Maethan that she'd nearly killed had come to her rescue.

"This way! Hurry," he insisted.

Caivev flailed as she turned, but managed to keep up. Every few steps, he paused to beat back the horde. It thinned out the further he led her.

"The crawlers do not venture too far beyond their mother's range," he said between heaving breaths.

A few paces later, they ran into a bigger cluster of Seekers of Maetha. They locked eyes on Caivev and narrowed their gaze at her.

Her heart sank momentarily, and she wondered if she would have been better off with the worms. She could hear them murmuring. "What should we do with her? She would make a prize indeed—we could barter her back to Basilisk..."

Caivev's rescuer put his hands up. "Brothers. Sisters," he addressed them directly. "You all know that is not our way. We help those we can. We could not expect her to do anything but harm us—she does not know any other way. But that does not mean our calling is to take her path. We must remain true to the ways of Maetha."

They grumbled somewhat under his chastisement but reluctantly agreed. In the near distance, the sound of the crawlers swelled.

"We must leave," the vyrm insisted. "Do you need further assistance? We can treat your wounds at our family's camp if you require it."

Caivev shook her head. "No." She'd hidden her speeder skiff amongst the statues near Sharonash's outskirts. "I can manage from here."

The Seekers of Maetha turned without a sound and fled into the night. Lastly, the young vyrm she had almost murdered for fun nodded his head and flashed her a knowing look that communicat ed things that words were incapable of. He turned and disappeared into the night, leaving Caivev behind to wonder about what the rovers were really about.

These vyrm are not at all what I have believed them to be. But her acknowledgment did not mean that she would stop hunting them. After all, she was still dunnischktet.

"Where are you, Zabe?" the princess called out, stretching into the ether with her mind. She got no response, not even a whiff of him upon the psionic winds that blew through the multi-verse and she was one of the most talented psychics on record.

Respan and Tay-lore had been searching for him as well, she knew. Bithia trusted him, but still yearned to know where he was, even if just so she could check in and make sure of his well-being. It irked her that Zabe had not contacted her since Zahaben's murder and his rash departure. He'd simply disappeared.

She tried to respect that he needed to cool off and collect his thoughts, but it had been almost two weeks since the event, and Bithia was his betrothed. Even if the nature of their relationship had cooled since the events within the Darque, Zabe still owed her some respect and some kind of courtesy call.

Bithia caught herself and paused. She didn't want to grow bitter towards Zabe and shoved any toxic self-talk out of her mind. She was sure he must have had a reason to abruptly leave—even if just so that he would not commit murder by taking an eye for an eye.

Though the temperature outside had cooled, Bithia stood on the balcony overlooking Capital City, her royal home, as it spread out below her. Safeguarded by the thick walls that surrounded it, they'd once thought them impenetrable. The vyrm had proven them wrong.

The sun had begun setting on the second full day since Jackie's departure. Her father was away on Earth, now. Her royal advisers and consultants were just that: consultants. They weren't true friends.

She'd spent much time with Pollando in these last couple of days. As the head of The Mystic Order of the Veritas, he was their most capable psychic; although Bithia had proved on several previous occasions that her raw talents surpassed his, although *Claire's* had never equaled his. She worked through several exercises and Bithia began to suspect that the mute monk had grown wise to her true identity and she considered letting him in on her true name. He would figure it out in a short time, she felt certain.

Bithia sighed and watched a bird flit above the roof line. The loneliness she felt was crippling. She'd been unable, thus far, to establish firm communion with Claire—something she desperately desired, even if just to absolve herself of guilt. She'd only managed to secure a brief moment of contact, which verified that she had not somehow obliterated Claire's presence as she'd feared.

After a few moments of centering herself, she tried to find that glimmer of Claire again, searching deep down inside her. Bithia didn't really believe that she would locate anything and so she hadn't put much effort into it.

Surprised to get a faint reading, she felt Claire's presence like a shadow. Bithia put her full attention into it, only to have it slip away. Whenever Bithia tried to really find Claire, her presence dissipated like mist in the dawn. It seemed that the harder she tried, the less effective she was.

Bithia's thoughts strayed back to Pollando. Before the incident with Akko Soggathoth, Claire had been training with him every day prior to the emergence of the trickster. She had honed some degree of rough psychic talent. But when Bithia had shoved her personality out of the driver's seat, it had been to exercise psionic control in order to save them. Vying for power in the sudden struggle may have given Claire the psychic equivalent of a pulled muscle. But it may have been much worse, too.

She followed her train of thought and recalled a time when she'd had a severe injury to her hamstring as a teen. Physical rehabilitation had been necessary to get her back in shape. *Could there be some kind of psychic equivalent? Maybe I can't connect because my strength keeps overwhelming hers and drowning her out?*

It made a kind of sense to Bithia. Psychic powers were like singing voices. Sometimes the volume from a strong and confident baritone overwhelmed a timid soprano by mere comparison, and Bithia knew she tended to be a loud psychic. She remembered burning away the minds of the vyrm lichs, the race's psychics, who tried to stop her at the Temple of Koth. Bithia knew she could be intense, and for all her power, she sometimes forgot the need for finesse.

A pang of guilty emotion rang deep within her gut and she watched the birds for several more long minutes. She didn't like these long bouts of self-examination. The last few days were filled with them and they only reminded Bithia of her growing loneliness.

Bird watching was a dreadfully boring distraction.

Bithia paced back and forth in her apartment. Finally, she sat down on her couch with a sigh and spoke aloud. "Okay, Claire. I know you're there, even if I'm having trouble finding you. It hasn't been my intention to squelch you; I'm sorry if that's what has been happening."

She closed her eyes and, using only the slightest touch of her abilities, initiated a meditative trance. "I'll leave it up to you to make contact... much like you did the first time we met."

The princess, still entranced, found herself on the astral plane and discovered a familiar environment. She was in an old memory.

Bithia walked through the hallways of the castle; mist crawled across the floor and the lights were low, filling the hallways with shadow. In the vision, she was not a child, but she remembered this day from when she had been a very young girl.

Thinking about the odd nature of dreams and visions threatened to destabilize this one, and so Bithia pushed any concerns away. She simply let the vision exist and operated within it.

The princess hurried through the corridors, frantically searching for any other people. It had been this way when this memory had occurred. Nitthogr had somehow accessed the castle, not a military breach, but an infiltration. The sorcerer could not overwhelm these walls, and so he must have seduced someone from the royal court. The enemy had not been inside the castle since his fall to the vyrm and his presence shattered the seeming sense of security. The childhood fear created this criterion moment within Bithia's mind.

We were not as safe as we thought. If the enemy can corrupt our members, he could gain access whenever he desires—I shall never be safe!

Bithia reminded herself that this was only a memory. Without a cadre of enemy psychics invading the astral plane, these memories could not harm her unless she believed in their power. "I am in control here," she said.

A laugh boomed in the shadows, low and guttural. It unnerved Bithia to her core, and she felt the dark presence: the spirit of Nitthogr.

Every shred of his spirit felt visceral and real. She was something of an expert in the astral plane, and Bithia could tell when a presence there was real and when it was fake.

She backpedaled through the halls. "No. You're dead," she insisted. "I watched you get sucked into the rift between reality and the nether-void where Sh'logath consumes." Bithia tried to convince herself that this was just a part of the memory; this had been the first time Nitthogr had made an attempt to abduct her.

The dark presence reached back, touching her with a terrifying glimmer of icy darkness, and Bithia knew that the presence was real. *His spirit is still somehow alive!*

She turned and fled down the hall. Her footsteps splashed fog into whirling eddies behind her.

Bithia sprinted up her steps and to the door of her room in the same apartment where she now resided. A pang of terror rippled through her. This was the same place where Nitthogr had finally seized her after the castle walls fell, though no furnishings adorned the dream-place except for a full mirror.

The looking glass was one of the many magical kinds that the castle had contained over the centuries. This one in particular she did not recognize, except that it had a kind of aura that glowed powerful on this plane of existence.

She looked into the mirror, half expecting to find Zabe climbing the vines that ensconced the castle walls and coming to her rescue. But that was a different memory, she knew, and he had *not* rescued her on that occasion.

Instead, Bithia spotted Claire in the mirror. She stood on the other side of the glass, looking impatient and with her arms crossed.

Bithia locked the door behind her and approached the mirror. She hoped the barrier might keep the dark presence from entering, at least for a little while.

"Claire?" Bithia ventured, goose stepping towards her, doing everything she could to keep the vision from dissipating.

Looking upset, Claire nodded sternly.

As Bithia approached, she noted her other self's red, puffy eyes and tear-stained cheeks.

"You put me here," Claire accused.

"I'm sorry," Bithia said, trying to understand and find a way to rectify the situation. She asked, "Where is here? Let me help you escape."

"I've been trapped in here for weeks, re-living every failure and meaningless moment of my life. It's made me dwell on my regrets and given me lots of time to think... too much time."

"Claire, I'm so sorry," Bithia repeated. "I really didn't mean to—"

"I think you did, though," Claire interrupted. "Deep down, you *meant* to push me out. You suspected this would happen when that energy wave hit."

"I was trying to save us," Bithia argued.

"That's what you told yourself, sure. You kept insisting that you were the more powerful version of ourself—but you know what? *I have strength too*, and you were jealous of that!" Claire's voice cracked as she yelled at the princess.

Bithia slumped. She didn't admit as much, but she suspected that Claire could have been right. "Let me get you out of here first. It may not be safe here. I sensed the presence of..."

"Of course it isn't safe. That's what this whole vision means, isn't it? No place is safe! And that's your excuse for everything, for taking control of us and for taking *him*."

Bithia looked wounded. She knew that Claire meant Zabe. "Claire, I would never..."

"Of course you would. You got jealous because Zabe grew to love me—perhaps more deeply than he loved you—and then when I began growing in my role as the princess; a role *you forced on me, by the way*—you couldn't handle it."

Bithia only stared at her, shocked by the accusation, and bewildered at the thought that she might be right. *Did I allow myself to do something terrible in a moment of weakness?*

Claire continued, her rage unabated. "I am stronger than you think. And if you're going to take something that I love, then I'll take something that *you* value above all else."

"Oh, Claire," Bithia began to tear up, and she sensed the dark presence closing in. The shadows had arrived at the door and hit it with a violent shudder. "You've got to believe me—you'll never know how sorry I am. But we've got to start working together. Let's go back to how it used to be."

Claire turned her back on Bithia and stiffened her neck to indicate she was ignoring the princess. "I should just let you stew in your guilt and remorse."

Bithia did not know how to make it right, and she felt the spirit of Nitthogr growing closer. The enemy hit the door again, trying to break it down. "We're better together—we always have been, Claire... ever since I gave you the spirit of the Prime."

Claire kept her back turned, and Bithia sensed that no amount of pleading would get her attention.

Again, something hit the door, different this time, and Bithia turned her head to address it. This noise was not in the vision... someone was knocking on the door.

Bithia pulled herself out of the trance, grateful for an actual distraction, any distraction. *Now that I know where to find her, I can always go back and pick this conversation up again. Perhaps Claire will change her mind soon?*

She sighed and answered the door.

Chapter Five

Bitha opened the door to find Gita standing awkwardly on the threshold. The short female soldier looked nervously over her shoulder. A tall soldier from the Royal Military, one of Chira's appointments, hovered nearby with a hand resting on the butt of his blaster. She was not dressed in her Corpsmen armor and Bithia almost didn't recognize her without it.

The princess waved him off, though she was glad that the castle guard was on top of things. Her recent dream walk had left her with freshly frayed nerves. She shuddered and put the sensation of an evil presence she'd detected within her walls far from her mind.

"Gita. How can I help you?"

The diminutive girl leaned in and embraced her in a hug that belied the tiny girl's strength. Bithia had not had the chance to get to know her well, although she'd known Gita and Jackie were close and that Wulftone and Zabe both spoke highly of her. She also knew that they had to specially fit some of the Guardian Corps' armor to fit her.

Where are you, Zabe? Bithia wondered again, as she did each time her thoughts touched on him. He'd had to find *her* a shrunk-down version of armor in the past, too—and Gita was smaller, yet.

Bithia returned the hug, not realizing until right now just how badly she had also needed one. She discreetly pulled several twigs and branches out of the soldier's hair, letting the sprigs fall to the floor in the hall.

Gita pulled away and looked sheepishly at the bramble. "Sorry. I went hiking earlier." She blushed, "Sorry about the hug, too. I'm just... so lonely right now with Jackie gone and with Jenner..." she trailed off.

"Please come in," Bithia insisted. "I'd been meaning to get to know you, too. I've just been so busy with... you know, royal stuff. The whole Akko Soggathoth thing put a damper on my schedule."

Gita nodded enthusiastically and followed her within. "I know what you mean, Princess Claire..."

"Please, just call me Claire," Bithia said. "Any of Jackie's friends are my friends." She made the decision on the fly that the circle of people who knew her true identity needed to remain small, even among friends. "Do you want something? Can I get you some coffee, maybe?"

Gita wrinkled her nose. "No thank you, unless you know that Krispee Kreme recipe for Earth donuts? Jackie usually has some of those stashed somewhere."

Bithia grinned. "Actually, I do. Tay-lore was the one to come up with the recipe. Ironic, since he doesn't even eat."

Gita smiled, and the princess opened a box on the table where they shared a plate of the foreign pastries.

"I feel like I've known you for a while, uh, Claire," Gita made an effort to leave off the honorific.

"I know what you mean," Bithia agreed. "I'm actually glad you came. I've been feeling the same way—desperately lonely. Zabe is... off being Zabe... and Jackie and Wulftone are honeymooning. My father and Shandra are away, too."

Gita's face clouded at the mention of Sam Jones. "Yeah. At least you've got a father, though," her tone darkened.

Bithia remembered that Gita's family had been recorded as casualties of Nitthogr's invasion, much as Jenner's had been. She changed the subject and made a note that it was a sore topic for her.

"Sorry," Gita said, realizing that she'd snapped at the heir and ruler of the multi-verse. "I'm just very testy lately. Do you ever feel like life has gotten away from you?"

Bitha nodded enthusiastically. "You have no idea. I keep waiting for something good to happen—to pull my life out of this tailspin I seem to be stuck in."

"Well, you've got a royal wedding to look forward to, don't you?"

Bithia feigned a smile.

"And then you'll have children to look forward to. At least... at least you've still got Zabe and a plan for your life—a plan that doesn't include someone else controlling you—telling you what to do."

Bithia masked her surprise at Gita's emotional dump. *Is someone blackmailing her? Maybe she's being taken advantage of in some way?*

Gita continued. "I wonder if it's the same with Jenner? I can't believe he would ever do what they are accusing him of. Zabe and Wulftone trained him better than that." Her eyes pleaded for her boyfriend's life, though she wouldn't come out and ask overtly for her intervention as a matter of protocol. That would make her visit seem insincere.

Bithia hadn't been paying much attention, anyway. Her mind still turned over and over with the questions of what was going on with Gita. *Is it somehow connected to Jenner and Zahaben's murder? I've got to get to the bottom of it.*

The princess asked a few questions to try to glean some more data, but Gita didn't give up anything else and Bithia didn't feel like they were close enough that she could come out and ask directly if someone was extorting or abusing her. At least she could be confident that it wasn't Jenner, if someone *was*.

She decided to use her psychic abilities to glean the information from her new friend's mind. Normally, she wouldn't intrude on someone's mental privacy without permission, but something seemed very off.

Bithia bit her lip and stewed in the guilt of it. She knew she was rationalizing her decision. She also knew that she'd made it a habit and that could be a red flag for someone abusing his or her powers; Claire's chastisement burned in her ears, but Bithia pushed ahead anyway.

Gita had continued talking, opening up wide enough that Bithia didn't think she could have stopped her if she wanted.

Bithia nodded along politely but stretched out to psychically probe the girl. Her face fell as she tried.

"Claire? All you alright, Claire?" Gita asked. "You look like you've seen a ghost."

Bithia had frozen in shock. "I... I'm alright," she lied, trying to calm herself and pretend nothing was wrong, even though panic coiled around her heart. No matter what Bitha tried, she couldn't get a reading on Gita and when she stretched out her astral senses, nothing returned.

The princess had suddenly lost all her psychic abilities.

Claire's words from their astral meeting rang in the princess's ears. *I am stronger than you think. And if you're going to take something that I love, then I'll take something that you value.*

Earth

Vikrum Wiltshire stared at the footage of the theft and watched it again. He studied the blue lettering outlined with white and orange. *n Astrod...* The detective thought it could be part of a logo of some sort, but the world was a large place, and every company logo on the planet encompassing every industry for the last eighty or so years meant the possibilities were almost endless.

He growled his displeasure and clicked back through some data on search engines. So far, his efforts proved futile and his mind strayed back to the Codex Gigas.

Time was imperative. The more time passed since the theft and the greater the likelihood was that he would not be able to locate the thieves and cash in on his reward. The reward was everything to him; with it, he would either locate Atticus, or avenge him.

He'd had a hacker friend execute some custom facial recognition software, and it had led him to a couple of possible matches on the woman, but the younger boy was a ghost. Of the three possibilities for her, one jumped out right away: Cerci Heiderscheidt had been a researcher working for a private R and D firm that Wiltshire traced back to a Heptobscurantum shell corporation.

The occult detective practically ignored the other two: a beauty pageant queen from Illinois and a college party diva from Seattle. Neither of them fit the profile, but Heiderscheidt had gotten her passport a couple of years ago and left for Germany when the Heptobscurantum dismantled her program. Shortly after that, Wiltshire's research revealed a rash of similar unexplained robberies which were still unsolved. They'd stopped for a period and then recently begun again.

Wiltshire's best guess linked them together, but why the robberies had resumed, and why Heiderscheidt was now stealing from her former employer didn't make much sense. It didn't establish a pattern... but if another of the Illuminati was robbed in the same manner, he would know for certain. But motive wouldn't help him locate Heiderscheidt and her mysterious companion.

He also didn't have any leverage on her if he could find her, and Wiltshire wasn't prone to bullying or threatening young women. She had been a foster child, raised mostly by CPS and foster homes, and she'd been something of a scientific savant. She'd attended college early, barely had any friends, and was barely in the system aside from the online college ID that Wiltshire's hacker had used to identify her. The only other blip she had on any network was her student loans, which had just been paid off in full, in fact. One lump sum of nearly a hundred and fifty thousand dollars. He felt pretty sure he'd found his girl.

Wiltshire sighed and combed his hair roughshod with his fingers. He didn't have anywhere else to turn for details and his mind had begun to fray under the stress of long and tedious hours coupled with a lack of sleep.

He knew powering down to refresh himself was a necessity, even if he wouldn't be able to easily get much sleep with so many rogue ideas bouncing around in his head. Wiltshire poured himself a standard of single-malt scotch and threw back a cocktail of valerian, melatonin, and Unisom to help knock him out, washing the pills down with the smoky whiskey.

Before Wiltshire got too groggy, he opened a browser window and punched in details for one of his contacts. He typed up as many details as he could think of, including a few frames of the video, and attached them to the message to a mysterious person he knew who went by the handle Tay-lore. Initially, he and "T" had been strictly working professionals. But eventually, they'd come to know each other well enough that Wiltshire considered him an a reliable source, if not a friend... if Wiltshire had such things. He had acquaintances and he had work contacts. But T felt like more than either of them even if he did seem a bit eccentric at times. There was something off about him.

Wiltshire didn't know much about him; their interactions had been mostly professional, but Tay-lore had never second guessed the detective's assumptions, called him crazy, or failed to pay him for information he sometimes brokered for the mysterious person. However, Tay-lore wasn't always prompt about responses... hence Wiltshire's decision to take a much needed eight hours of rest as soon as the message was away.

He typed clumsily, correcting his fumbling fingers that had begun to feel the effects of the sleep aids. "Any idea about this triangle-shaped magic door? I know *you* usually come to *me*—but

I'm running out of ideas and a huge case hangs on the line. Any thoughts would be appreciated. I'll owe you one! V.W."

Wiltshire clicked send and then crawled into his bed and fumbled with the charger for his mobile. He failed to plug it in and so he turned the plug the other way. It failed to insert again. He turned it back, cursing with made-up words until it finally plugged in.

No sooner did it begin charging than the phone went off. He groaned and cursed the phone some more, but looked at the screen. An incoming call came from Becky in the crime lab.

"Hullo?" he asked groggily.

"Vikrum? Man, you sound like crap," she said.

"Just getting some sleep. Or tryin, anyway."

"It's like, only seven PM."

Wiltshire sighed a raspberry into the phone and remembered that he hadn't slept all the previous night. He'd spent the entire last evening searching for a lead. "Don't tell me how to live my life," he grumbled. "What have you got?"

"I thought you'd want to know right away on that DNA result. It was definitely human skin, Slavic, actually. Probably from about the thirteenth century."

"That's what I suspected," Wiltshire said. "Slavic includes the Bohemians, or Czechs, right?"

"Yeah... what are you onto, Vikrum?"

"A thirteenth century Benedictine monk sold his soul to the devil: Herman the Recluse. He authored, well, co-authored, the Devil's Bible... the Codex Gigas."

"The giant book on display in Sweden?" Becky asked.

"How do you..."

"The History Channel had some special about it."

"Yeah. There are several missing pages. Most of the book's vellum was made from donkey... except the missing pages."

"That's crazy," Becky said. "A human doesn't have that much skin. Those pages were huge."

"Have you seen the book? I have, and huge doesn't do it justice. These pages were later additions. Penned by Tebel-El, the Devil, written on skin ripped from Herman's body after he was walled away for thirty years to die a slow and painful death in the monastery. He probably tore them from Herman's body one page at a time. These pages were added in the back and rebound by Rudolf the Mad Alchemist in the fifteen hundreds. You know what happened to him?"

"No." Becky's voice was rapt and breathless.

"He turned into a recluse and went nuts. Then the book went to Sweden under the ownership of Christina the She-King. Then *she* went nuts, albeit in different ways; Christina abdicated and banished herself to solitude. The Swedish library repaired the binding, but I was able to get that scrap out to verify my thoughts." He trailed off. Sleep had begun to take root already.

"Wow," Becky whispered. "Is this the *normal* kind of stuff you deal with? Now I understand why you normally tell me nothing."

"Yeah, well..." Vikrum said. "I *have* been drinking."

"I'd like to unlearn all of that, please."

"You and me both. But it's what I'm going to do when I find those missing pages that will truly terrify you."

"I'm going to hang up now," Becky said.

"Good. I didn't want to burden you with that knowledge, anyway."

"Thanks. Good night." She hung up the phone.

Wiltshire collapsed into his bed, wondering why he still had his shoes on. He'd forgotten to take them off, but he was too tired, now, to kick them off; he thought he could muster the effort, but some still, small voice at the back of his mind told him not to bother... maybe he'd need them. He knew that was absurd, but it was the path of least resistance, and so he took the irrational voice's advice.

Seconds later, he was fast asleep, shoes and all.

The Prime

Bithia summoned Chira, who met her on the balcony of her apartment. Her internal struggles aside, she was still her government's leader and had duties to perform.

"Who are all these people?" she asked, watching them below.

Gathering in the courtyard, a crowd had assembled. It swelled as people filed into the courtyards in clumps. They pressed up against the tightly arrayed line of royal guards who made a line that the citizens knew better than to cross.

The crowd wore armbands and headbands of purple and gold displaying a strange logo. Some were more strategically printed, others were hand-painted, making Bithia raise an eyebrow. Whatever the crowd's purpose, it was a true grass roots movement that had motivated them, and Bithia did not know why.

She leaned over the rail for a better look and cursed the timing of her secret loss of psychic ability. Bithia cursed Zabe while she was at it—the timing of his absence was terrible. She was usually better than this: it was uncommon for a groundswell of public opinion to shift this far with her in the dark.

With a sigh, she forgave Zabe. It wasn't his fault. None of it was. This all started because of Akko Soggathoth, and not her fiance.

Chira grimaced. "They are protesters," he informed her. "There have been a few smaller gatherings in other communities, and they've never been violent. We didn't expect them to gather so many so soon."

Bithia bobbed her head. "They are upset about the upcoming diplomatic meetings?"

Chira agreed. "Among other things."

Bithia kept her lips thin. She thanked him and then let him get back to his work. He had much to do in advance of upcoming peace talks, and this sudden security strain would only require more of his attention.

As soon as it was not suspicious, Bithia left her apartment and went to Respan's lab. Gita was one of the guards stationed outside of the laboratory and she cocked her head. "Princess—err, Claire," she corrected, and then gave it a second thought. "Or is it Princess when you're in public?"

She flashed Gita a conspiratorial look. "That's the thing. I'm trying to not be seen in public." Bithia nodded her head towards the door and both women went inside.

Past the doors, Respan fiddled on a project with Tay-lore. They both greeted her when she entered. "What brings you down here to my lab?" Respan asked.

"I need some kind of disguise and I remembered that you had worked on some kinds of tech in the past that altered appearances," Bithia said.

Respan was notoriously scatter brained. He scrunched his face to try to remember the item she had referenced.

"The DCD," Tay-lore reminded him.

"Oh yes! My Digital Cloaking Device," Respan turned to a bin of gadgets on a nearby table. "It's a bit finicky," he admitted, "but it's mostly operational."

"I need it," Bithia said. "I want to walk through that crowd outside and find out who they are, why they are protesting. People are... less honest when they know who and what I am."

Gita understood and agreed, even, but hedged aside, "I don't think that's such a good idea."

"They're not violent," Bithia promised, "Chira told me so."

Respan hesitated. Tay-lore remained as expressionless as ever. "It *would* be an opportunity to see the DCD live and in the field." The scientist worked his jaw and rationalized, "It's for science."

He set the wearable tech on the princess's head. It was a kind of circlet that rested upon her brow, and with the push of a button, her face lit with a series of heavily pixel-lated patches. The light swatches smoothed out and then seemed to form a skin.

Gita raised her eyebrows, convinced, and Bithia searched for a patch of shiny metal to check her reflection.

She'd gained perhaps fifteen years, according to the altered image which also overlaid digital makeup. Even Zabe wouldn't have recognized her on the street, Bithia thought. "Thank you," she said and turned to leave.

"Oh, no," Gita said. "I can't let you leave. Chira would lose his kittens."

Bithia cocked her head.

"Isn't that how Jackie would say it? Whatever. You know what I mean. I can't let you go out there."

Bithia gave her a mischievous look, which the DCD translated perfectly. "You could come with me—then you'd know I was safe."

Gita scowled, sure that she could not stop the princess if she wanted to. "Fine, but I've got to shuck my armor first so we can blend in."

Tay-lore put on a hat, as if it were a good disguise. "I shall come too. I wish to observe this field test."

Respan had already slung on a jacket. "Same here."

Bithia sighed. She hadn't intended to take a whole team out, but knew it was the price of their secrecy.

A few minutes later, they sneaked through the service corridors. Gita sometimes used them for duty, but Respan felt lost, and said as much.

Bithia almost smiled. "Don't worry, I've only ever had to sneak *into* the castle and never out... but I'm sure I'll manage."

"You snuck in?" Gita said, comically amused by the thought.

The princess nodded. She trusted those in her company with the story and pulled on Claire's memories. "When I first came here from Earth, Zabe and I had to get into the castle. It was during Nitthogr's occupation. His grandfather, Shardai, helped us find our way through the Vangandran tunnels and attempt our rescue of Bithia. He took us all the way from the Veritas's mountain to the throne room, even if I nearly had a panic attack from the tight quarters. The rescue mission worked... in a way."

Her memory had not been as amusing as she remembered, the more she dwelt on it, but it brought some peace to Respan and calmed his nerves. They finally arrived at the scullery access.

The door opened from a maintenance hallway and into the burgeoning crowd. Some people carried signs. Most of them were young, but a few were old. Suspiciously absent were folks ranging from thirty to fifty years old, and then Bithia remembered that most of those in their mid twenties through middle-age had been wiped out in years past by Nitthogr's invasion.

"What's the AVA?" Bithia asked someone holding a sign with those three simple letters.

"The Anti-Veritas Alliance," the woman holding it responded. She glanced at the newcomers and noticed they weren't wearing the purple and gold logo, and so she explained. "We need to make our voice known: the people are fed up with the direction we're headed."

A few of the woman's companions chimed in, boorish and angry. They shouted some harsh words against the crown and muttered empty threats in case their fellow marcher had engaged in a debate with a different ideology.

"Don't mind him," the stranger said. "Some people were hit really hard by the last round of the vyrm wars."

Her male companion growled, "It's not just that! I'm not upset, only because I'm hurt," he snapped. "I'm angry because the Veritas let it happen! They should have helped repel the invaders, instead they sat in their mountainside villa and hid away, hording their power and magic that could have sent Nitthogr packing. At least the crown and army fought—not that I'm any big fan of either."

"Why do you say that?" Bithia asked. Her companions stood stiff, not wanting to engage and risk drawing additional attention.

"It's like they never listen. It ain't like I can just address the Princess directly," he complained. "She doesn't know me, or who

I am. It's not like she cares or would put a stop to things that bother me—like this upcoming meeting with Basilisk! His brother slaughtered our parents and siblings, and what? We're supposed to enter trade negotiations with that monster? He was a traitor. He and all the vyrm are monsters."

"Maybe there's a different plan at play," Bithia defended. "Flipping an enemy to an ally would certainly end the attacks... and hopefully change sentiments, so we aren't killing each other anymore."

He complained, "That sounds good in theory, but when have you ever known the Veritas to be open minded about anything? They have to change or go—and my money's on go. That's why we wear this symbol." He brandished the logo: a block adjacent a skinny rectangle. "It symbolizes a broken hammer. If they won't go, eventually the people will *make them* go."

Bitha raised an eyebrow. "What's your name?"

Suddenly, the circlet on the princess's brow fritzed out with a sizzle and a puff of smoke. Her face flickered, and the disguise dropped.

The stranger's eyes widened. "Y-you're the princess! Princess Claire..."

A crowd immediately began to thicken around her. Everyone wanted an opportunity to voice the AVA's ideology to her.

Gita grabbed her. "Come on—we have to go!" The soldier escorted her back to safety.

In the hallway, Respan turned the DCD over in his hands. "Back to square one on this thing, I'm afraid."

Earth

[We've got to tell our counterparts in Ukraine,] the agitated man insisted, pointing at dots on a map. [They are the region's intelligence hub. Whatever this threat is that is killing our kind, it's heading west.] He traced a line from the Caspian Sea and across the southern tip of Russia, just north of Georgia. [We must prepare for it to come *here*.]

[Calm yourself, Adrik. Three dead cells are not enough to jump to conclusions.]

Adrik scowled and dropped the Russian language and used their native tongue. "Isn't it, Rurik? It will be enough for me—especially if we are the fourth group!"

Rurik put his hands up and motioned for his friend to calm down. None of the other clerical workers in the office knew their true identities, and Adrik's volume had started to turn some heads. [Follow,] he insisted, leaving the map behind.

Adrik grimaced and clamped his mouth shut, but he did as commanded. The two spies clocked out and left the office for a short break. They grabbed a quick lunch from a food vendor on the street to keep up appearances. Adrik tossed most of his into a trash bin; nerves had ruined his appetite. After a brisk stroll walked in silence, they entered an abandoned warehouse where a handful of others had gathered.

Rows of boxes and shipping crates, long since abandoned, occupied the facility. Eventually, some entrepreneur would do something with it, but for now it was a shelved Heptobscurantum investment and made a perfect meeting place.

One of the others who had gathered gave Rurik a signal to confirm that they had swept the place for security.

"Okay, now," Rurik asked, "what is all the commotion?"

Seeing they were alone, the skin of the assembled Russians reverted to their true, scaly form. They were shades, each of them.

"Tell him, Adrik," they insisted.

Adrik had the support of his peers. "If something is truly killing our kind, we must get to the bottom of it," he insisted. "But first, we should alert the other cells in our radius."

"To what end… to raise a panic?" Rurik fired back. "I've yet to see any evidence of your bogeyman. We are vyrm—we do not know fear."

[We only know foolishness,] one of the vyrm hissed from the back in a sarcastic Russian accent.

Rurik snapped a glare in his direction.

"You didn't see it," Adrik insisted. "Our cell in Kirovskiy has been silent for too long without a report. I checked in yesterday when the company business sent me to Makhachkala. They're all dead, Rurik. Something tore them to pieces!"

"You saw this with your own eyes?"

Adrik nodded. "I saw the bodies and burned them to avoid detection—I followed protocol."

"And you know what did this?"

"No," Adrik confessed.

A low growl rumbled in the shadows nearby. "You are about to find out," a menacing voice said in broken vyrmtongue, and then its owner leapt upon them.

Chapter Six

The dank air of the mountain cavern flickered with the light of crude torches. A tear split the low light with a brilliant hole. Three perfect lines burned with ruby laser fire that opened the dimensional gate.

Behind the altar, two rows of students were seated at lecterns adjacent to their chained armarium cabinets; the ancient furnishings stored endless rows of codices. The figures rose, each dressed in black monastic cloth, and looked up to hiss at the invading light.

The burning crimson lines of energy shone against their pale skin. They shielded black eyes and stood to array themselves as a unified force against the intruder.

The leader of the lightless wizards stood at the center of their number. He parted his flowing locks. Reddish, straight hair draped behind his shoulders as he growled at the intruder in his long, black leather coat. The enemy carried an ancient kophesh hook blade and meandered away from the blazing rip in space.

Unimpressed, the pale-skinned wizard growled, "How dare you violate the inner sanctum of the Scholomance?"

"Heh," the big man scoffed. "Looks like I came to the right place, then." He walked around cockily and afforded a wider view for a second man, who watched from the other side of the triangle-shaped door. "My name is Sisyphus." He looked the leader directly in the face, equally unmoved, and demanded, "Where is it?"

"The strigoi answer to no man," their leader hissed. With a dread screech, the thirteen wizards sprang into action. They threw blazing balls of eldritch flame at the unwelcome guest.

Sisyphus conjured a shield of pure magic and easily blocked them. They splashed harmlessly aside as he whirled to blast his own offensive. Strigoi leapt and hurdled his blasts, deflecting them aside with similar shields as they rushed forward to surround him.

The big man's muscles rippled, and he stretched forward, smashing one in the face with a big kick. Other strigoi ducked beneath his massive limbs and clawed for him.

Sisyphus slashed at them with his kophesh and the pale creatures slunk back towards safety, hurling more ranged blasts at him. The wrestler growled and brought his shields up back in time to block them, but barely, and then he blasted them with elemental energy, alternating between ice and fire, trying to catch the scrambling creatures with an array of magic.

Strigoi evaded his spells. They crawled across the walls and roof as if gravity meant nothing to them.

The wrestler cursed. "Tell me where the mirror is!"

"You will not get it from us," the strigoi leader hissed as he ducked beneath a ray of flame. He screeched something in a tongue more animal than man. The other strigoi surged forward again.

Sisyphus groaned as he slashed at one of them. He recognized the tactic: they were testing him, looking for patterns and weaknesses they could exploit. He beat them back again and prepared for the next wave of arcane energy bolts that they blasted him with.

Raising his shields again, thirteen blasts of pure esoteric energy streaked at him from thirteen different angles in rapid fire succession. With each missile that pummeled his shield, the mystic aegis flickered and the thirteenth one broke through, knocking a surprised Sisyphus backwards. His torso smoked where he had taken the damage.

Grinning, the strigoi's spokesman snarled, "Attack!"

Sisyphus yanked a plastic sack from his jacket pocket and sank his dentally implanted fangs into it, consuming the blood pack he'd drained from his doppelganger, Professor Jarfig. He'd kidnapped him from the Prime dimension after discovering he could amplify his mystic power tenfold or more by siphoning the primal energies. Jarfig's blood ran down his chin and neck as the faux-vampire sucked down the viscous red liquid.

He felt the blood magic swell within him. Every cell in his body brimmed with energy. Sisyphus laughed as his body overflowed with raw power channeled from the Prime dimension. He'd baited the strigoi into overplaying their hand. Without hesitation, he unleashed a massive blast of preternatural fire that incinerated his closest enemy, burning him to ash and cinder as the other strigoi scrambled to evade a similar fate.

The wrestler poured energy into the handle of his mystic kophesh and reached out with his senses. He grabbed the next nearest enemy with a telekinetic grip. Sisyphus cocked his head as if working a kink from his neck and broke the vertebrae below his enemy's skull.

"Where is my mirror?" Sisyphus roared with a voice that boomed like thunder and echoed down the lengths of the long cave. He dropped the crippled solomonari and stomped on his chest, pressing him against the stone floor.

He stretched out again with his telekinetic powers and tried to tear the books from all their shelves, but they caught on the chains that bound them to the armariums inset within the carved walls.

Beneath his foot, the creature groaned. Paralyzed but not dead, he gasped pained heaves as he spoke. "It... it is not here. We've not possessed it for one hundred and fifty years."

"Hmmm," Sisyphus brooded momentarily.

The pause proved just enough of an opening for the Scholomance to snatch their friend and drag him to safety. With a quick invocation, they dissolved into mist and evaporated, fleeing beyond Sisyphus's reach.

He meandered through their private chamber, still sensing their nearby presence like a foul order. After a brief inspection of the sparsely appointed room, he rattled off a string of curses.

"The puny wizard wasn't lyin. It ain't here." He turned an arc with a scowl. He wanted to smash something, but there wasn't much in the place that was not made of stone. He shook his head and spat profanities into the darkness until he calmed down. The surge of raw power coursing through him from Jarfig's blood soon evened off and tapered down to its normal levels.

Sisyphus touched the tender, blistering spot on his chest where the strigoi wizard had blasted him and laughed to himself, "Yeah... I gotta get me one of those darque-matter amulets to take the edge off those attacks." He stared into the darkness. "Cuz this ain't over, Doc. We ain't done until we find that artifact... and whoever's got that mirror is probably meaner and nastier than this nest of strigoi, if that's even possible."

He turned and walked back towards the dimensional gate where Walther waited. "We'll find it, Doc—but if the Scholomance don't have it, we're back to square one... luckily I've got plenty of plans for the meanwhile."

Walther enlarged the gate slightly to make sure that it was easily passable. Touching the seams between worlds would prove dangerous, even fatal, as they'd seen in the past. The scientist asked, "Was attacking the Scholomance directly wise?"

Sisyphus shrugged. "I think I've proved my point to them—chased em right out of their house. We won't see them for a while," he grinned. "I'll track them down one at a time and eliminate them at my pleasure. They're already down one of their number... maybe two."

The wrestler nodded to the scientist, and he closed the gate. As soon as it winked out of existence, the shadows melted and turned back into the Solomonari. All but their leader returned to their lecturns. They reset their desks and resumed writing.

With a hiss, the chief strigoi threatened, "That is what you think, Mister Sisyphus."

He whirled on his heel and headed towards the deeper darkness of the subterranean tunnel. "Continue your work," he rested his taloned hands on the shoulders of their youngest member, a cadaverous, gaunt man with a freshly shaven head, "especially you."

"Yes, Weathermaker." He began dutifully scribing texts.

The Weathermaker stalked into the shadows that descended deeper into the mountain. "I go to awaken the dragon."

The Prime

The doors to the throne room opened and someone announced Chira's arrival. Bithia didn't yet raise her eyes from the file which Tahnak had grudgingly delivered her. It contained everything that Tahnak had uncovered about the AVA.

His files indicated a bunch of things—chiefly that it had been run by an extended family who had tried on more than one occasion to incite violence that had only been shut down by accident or direct military intervention. The envelope contained a spread of photos from the leadership's family tree. One photo stared up at her: Chira's.

She understood why Tahnak had been so loathe to give her the documents. They seemed a damning report against his friend. Tahnak had even written a few notes in margins where he disagreed with the findings or data that seemed to implicate Chira might know more about the AVA than he let on.

Bithia closed the binder as her military commander waited, standing at attention. "Thank you for answering my summons," she said. "I am certain that you are quite busy preparing for the arrival of our guests who will arrive shortly."

Chira nodded curtly, as if he very much wanted to get back to that work.

Bithia studied him. She knew that he took great pride in his work; despite their recent adventures together, she did not know his family, and she'd never heard him mention them. *Then again, a good spy never would.*

She sighed. Bithia rarely had need to worry about subterfuge before. It was notoriously difficult to spy on a psychic, though not impossible. She'd already grown tired of the festering cloak and dagger activity that seemed to loom around the shadows of the throne.

"I will make this quick, then," she said. "I want the military to be on special guard against this group called the AVA. You might use the Guardian Corps as additional resources if necessary, though I'll still need them for personal protection detail when the vyrm arrive."

"Princess?" The look on his face revealed it all. He wasn't sure that she'd considered the AVA much of an issue until now.

"What do you know about them?"

Chira set his jaw. "They are activists. They hate the Veritas, that much is plain just from their title, and they hate the vyrm."

"Are they dangerous?"

Chira frowned and then nodded. "Not yet. But I do think that they have the potential to become homegrown terrorists. There is too much hate in them for anything else."

"I suspected as much," Bithia said. "Make sure you clear out anybody associated with the AVA before our diplomats arrive. Use force if necessary; lock them up if you have to, but I don't want them on the streets when the vyrm diplomats arrive. If the envoy suspects weakness at all on our part, they might view us as having lesser bargaining power... and we need all that we can get."

Chira raised an eyebrow.

Bithia leaned forward conspiratorially. "We are trying to talk our way out of a war that has been raging for generations. I won't let the threats of violence forced on us by someone else to hold us in a conflict which will certainly require more of the same. If the vyrm are truly considering peace with the Prime, I want to give those negotiations every chance to succeed."

The princess looked Chira up and down and wondered again about her family. For the first time since losing her psychic ability, she felt the black gnawing of paranoia in her gut.

"As you order, Princess Claire," Chira stated formally. "We will not allow this so-called Anti-Veritas Alliance to ruin the peace that we all so desperately want."

She saluted Chira and dismissed him. Bithia picked up the file and opened it so that no one else in her presence could see her face. She missed Zabe, but right now—maybe more so, even—she missed her ability to read a mind, sense truth, and do all those other minor feats she'd taken for granted most of her life.

Bithia bit back a frustrated tear that tried to escape. Claire had been right about how much she valued her abilities.

Basilisk and Caivev, the royal couple from the Desolation realm, appeared in a flash and a whiff of ozone. A retinue of scaled body-guards and envoys accompanied them at the main dimensional gate that lay a short distance from the royal palace. A large contingent of the Prime's Royal Army met them there, flanked by soldiers from the Guardian Corps and a cluster of Veritas members from its warrior class.

Yardi and Chira stepped forward to greet Basilisk and Caivev. Yardi bowed, swallowing his pride and trying to overlook the fact that Caivev had once been a chief antagonist and enemy of his people. For many of the residents of the Prime, Yardi knew she would always be considered an enemy... but that is the barrier that these diplomatic meetings were supposed to smooth over.

Chira, representing the Prime's Royal Army, remained thin-lipped and followed suit. Yardi's cybernetic leg, lost as a result of Caivev's most recent campaign against them, whined on its servos as he turned to show them the way.

"Princess Claire," Shjikara announced as they drew near a pavilion that they'd erected in advance of the historic meeting, "may I present Basilisk and his *wife*, Caivev."

The vyrm forces gave a curt, respectful bow to her. Those attendees from the Prime did likewise for the vyrm leaders. Neither Bithia nor Basilisk and Caivev bowed. It was against protocol for royalty to bend a knee to any other.

"Please approach," said Bithia, who sat at a table where the two groups could come to terms and discuss future relations: an avenue that Basilisk had sought out just prior to his engagement to the Prime's enemy, Caivev. Bithia hid her frown. If Basilisk had attached himself to Caivev sooner, she might have denied him an audience—or at least Claire might have done so. The discussions had opened under *Claire's* authority... before Bithia seized control. She pushed away the dark cloud that tried to cast a pall across her emotions; this was no time to dwell on her mistakes or her secret feelings.

Taking seats alongside of her were Shjikara and Tahnak, whose trials in the Darque alongside Claire and Zabe had given him a unique perspective—despite that perspective having caused him to attempt murdering her. Tahnak looked uncomfortable for his place to such a high appointment. His eye twitched with a nervous, unstable energy.

Bithia wished again, and not for the last time, that she knew where Zabe had gone; he should have occupied Tahnak's seat. A hollow feeling deepened in her gut, exasperating her sense of abandonment. Zabe should have been here for this—or maybe even Sam, Claire's father. Even Wulftone would have brought her comfort. Instead, her closest companions at the moment were her previously attempted murderer, a religious leader who felt as sleazy as a snake-oil salesman, and an emotionless automaton. Tay-lore stood just behind her, ready to consult from a perspective devoid of emotion or logical fallacy if objectivity was required.

She actually liked Tay-lore's presence; he'd faithfully watched over her and her family for decades. Bithia smoothed the wrinkles from her royal gown and put on as much of an air of royalty and diplomacy as possible.

Caivev and her husband took seats opposite her. Basilisk looked momentarily puzzled at Shjikara's presence. His eyes flitted to the high priest's stone hand and then away. As directed by Sh'logath, he had placed a rune in the man's fist prior to turning him to stone. How Shjikara had been mostly reverted to flesh was unknown to him, and Basilisk did not like to operate in a knowledge vacuum.

"Today we are gathered to discuss opening a possible trade alliance," Bithia said. "We ought to set forth some boundaries and recommendations if we move forward. Of course, all of this is predicated on the ratification of our formal military truce—something more than a simple cease-fire." She narrowed her eyes at Caivev. This woman had once nearly been a bridesmaid in Claire's wedding. That ceremony had never happened because of her betrayal.

Caivev, for her part, looked bored to be present. Her role as the wife of Basilisk required her presence, but it was plain to see that she would rather be anywhere else.

Basilisk bobbed his head. "That is assumed and agreed upon. We have items that would benefit the Prime and the Prime has vital materials which could help redevelop the wastelands into a thriving agricultural base, just as it was when I and my brother discovered it millennia ago."

Bithia bit her tongue, choosing not to point out that Basilisk and Nitthogr's intervention had been the root of the woes for that realm. The vyrm had once called their home Edenya, prior to its change into the Desolation under the brothers' guidance.

Shjikara leaned forward and interjected a new condition to the terms. His solid fist clunked on the table as he set it down. "As a gesture of good faith, you must return all the statues in your famous Statue Garden. We are aware that it is filled with prisoners you have taken throughout the years: men and women you have turned to stone and locked in eternal stasis. Such a fate is worse than death and we demand they be returned to us, so I may seek their restoration."

Bithia batted her eyelashes in surprise. It seemed like a smart request, one which she had not thought of. She nodded, agreeing to his suddenly added condition. After Zabe's father, she'd learned of the eternal torment the victims of petrification endured.

Basilisk looked coyly at Shjikara and grinned. The master strategist recognized that they'd entered a new phase of the game—one in which he no longer knew the rules—but he was ever willing to play. "All the statues?"

Shjikara nodded enthusiastically, letting his jowls flap. "Of course."

"You know that my garden also includes political enemies of my own: vyrm who have plotted against me, both from the Black and the Tarkhūn factions. There are hundreds of statues and it would be difficult to distinguish which was which. Are you prepared to take them *all?*"

Bithia looked to Shjikara, who agreed. He explained, "After Trenzlr the Maethan spent time with us in our monastery, we have come to know some of the vyrm ways. I am willing to accept them and make those decisions at a later time."

Basilisk bowed his head with measured reluctance. "As you wish. Arrangements for their delivery will be made." His eyes lingered again on the stone fist that encapsulated the rune he'd placed there. He wondered just what the high priest had in mind. *And why did Sh'logath insist I deposit the Rune of Return there?*

"And the statue of the Architect King as well," Bithia tried to tack on to the agreement.

Basilisk paused and then shook his head. "That is impossible. He and I made an agreement upon the field of battle. That pact is personal, and he is in my keeping until an appointed time. I cannot surrender him without breaking my word—my agreement was to keep him safe and in my custody as long as I could ensure his protection and the terms of our arrangement were met. I'm not yet certain that the Prime is any safer than Limbus."

Bithia's demeanor darkened, but the tone he'd spoken with implied that he would not be moved on the topic. Besides, the return of the other statues was already a political victory. "Alright, then. Back to matters of diplomacy and trade relations..."

But her mind drifted back to Basilisk's words and tone. He was renowned for his spy network and access to information. Bithia was sure that the vyrm leader knew of the brewing unrest and the AVA—there was little else she could suspect would make the Prime less safe than the Desolation.

Gita stood in the overgrown glade outside of a dilapidated house. Vines wove through the bramble and knots of wild sumac, where unchecked growth had begun reclaiming the abandoned property in the short amount of time that passed since the owners met their unfortunate end.

She sank to her knees between the statues where they'd been frozen only a short distance from the silent house. Their forms were locked in terrified repose as they tried to flee.

Gita frowned. "I don't know what to do, Mom." Her eyes shifted to her father and then to her older and younger sibling. Gita was as old as her brother, now, and her sister might remain a toddler forever. She knew she'd give anything for a chance to talk with them again—to be a family one more time.

Her mother did not answer, of course. Only a small breeze whistled through the reeds behind her.

"I heard that Basilisk is staying at the castle for the next couple days; he arrived yesterday. Something about 'forming new diplomatic relations.'" She frowned. "I suppose he'll pay me soon for spying on the royal family... informing on my friends?"

She choked back some tears. "But he said that he's only ever had one of these mystic runes that hold the power to restore someone. I'll have to pick one person." Her restraint failed, and the tears flowed.

"But... but there's got to be another way. Maybe I can bring it to Respan, or maybe Shandra knows someone in the Veritas... I trust her after fighting alongside her at the Hoia Baciu." Her mouth twisted sour. "Or maybe I can somehow find another of these Runes of Return. If there's one, there's got to be more."

She stood and hugged each of them in turn. Her lungs choked up. "I... I just don't know where to turn. They say the high priest can help... he somehow brought back General Zahaben... but if I go to him, he might discover I was the mole. It's not hard to backtrack the time-line and discover my lies... that you weren't *killed* in Nitthogr's invasion." Gita stared somberly at the ground and spoke hopefully, "You don't suppose I'd go to the same prison as Jenner, do you? I mean... if he isn't executed."

Only a breeze responded by rustling through the overgrown glen that had once been her family's yard. She rested a hand on her mother's shoulder for a long moment, and then departed, deep in thought with the thorny bracken tugging at her hair and clothes along the trail crowded by invasive species. It would eventually lead her back towards Capital City and the more populous areas.

More branches rustled after her departure. They shook more violently than the wind was capable of and the fronds parted where Shjikara emerged from his hiding spot. He wore a devious grin set above both of his chins.

Shjikara gleefully sauntered over to the family of four. "So, I finally found my brother's mole." He cocked his head towards the father figure. "You should have raised her better," he wheezed.

The High Priest grunted and withdrew the scepter he carried. All Veritas were required to carry a hammer beyond the monastery grounds as a matter of tradition—but the High Priest's tool was different, unique, and nearly unbreakable. Though its jeweled head rested above and atop something more reminiscent of a mace than anything else, it was both weapon and scepter.

He slammed his weapon through the man's form. Shjikara hit him again, reducing the figure to rubble.

"And you... mother dearest..." he gleefully busted her to bits, reducing her to whitish gray hunks of broken stone.

Shjikara loosed the evil within. Nitthogr's vile spirit oozed through his body in thought and deed. He crashed the weapon through the defenseless brother who had been holding the toddler by the wrist, trying to speed her to safety when they were still flesh and blood. The brother disintegrated beneath the hammer blows, and the false priest turned his gaze to the youngest child.

"But you, my dear, sweet child. You will come with me... I have a dreadfully wonderful purpose for you." Shjikara Stonefist wrapped his arms around the smallest member of the family and carried her off, leaving only a trail of rubble and scattered scree in his wake.

Chapter Seven

*E**arth*

Wiltshire leapt out of bed. His skin had slicked with a cold sweat and the window drummed with a late autumn rain; the overcast sky kept it dark late into the morning.

The presence within his room was palpable and inhuman. Wiltshire felt suddenly glad to have left his shoes on, and he snatched his handgun and leveled it at the intruder.

Wearing only scraps of black cloth that were tied with cords, he looked much like a homeless man and his disguise might have fooled most. Wiltshire saw through the front and recognized him by an overbite that concealed his fangs and the falling locks of thin, red hair; pale, pointed ears poked through the light strawberry tresses.

The detective kept his gun trained on the nightmare creature, even though he knew the ammunition in his nine millimeter wasn't up to the task of killing something of this breed. Wiltshire hoped the strigoi wasn't aware of that. He glanced down at his nightstand; the magazine containing his silver-laced rounds was easily within reach, but swapping mags would take him at least a full second, and he knew these creatures were capable of moving at incredible speeds when properly motivated.

"Mister Wiltshire," he said, eerily turning his head and stretching the S sounds between his fangs. "I do believe that you have been looking for us."

"I only see one of you," Wiltshire growled. "And besides, the guy I'm looking for *right now* is not strigoi... not unless strigoi can make magic triangle shaped doors out of thin air. You guys get a reprieve for a few weeks, but I'll be back to you soon enough."

The intruder opened his mouth to speak, but paused momentarily. "You do not see my brothers because you only see what I want you to see," he said, "but I come with only the truth at present, and I come alone. I do not wish to play games with you, Mister Wilshire. I represent the Scholomance."

"Yeah. You're right. You broke into my apartment, so I'm looking for you now too... you guys killed my partner. I guess whatever order I chase you down in doesn't matter so much to me. Good thing that I'm uniquely equipped for killing creatures like strigoi. I'm sure my reputation precedes me."

The strigoi smirked with amusement. His curled lip revealed a fang that glistened in the low morning light. "You won't kill me. Not yet. You need me."

"The hell I do..."

"If you kill us all, you will never know for sure what we did with Atticus Sexton. Your police may have found the bodies of his wife and children... and a significant amount of the man's blood... but you will never know his true fate without some assistance."

Wiltshire tightened his grip on the handgun. "Alright. I'll play along, but just for funsies. Talk. Why are you here?"

"I come to you because of your particular skills. *You are uniquely equipped to killing creatures like me.* The Scholomance are quite confident in our ability to handle you... any individual Solomnar I should think is capable... but there is another enemy we face, a creature that has killed one of our number. Now, we must replace him to replenish our ranks."

"Is that what you did with my partner, you bastard? Did you take Atticus and turn him into one of you?"

The strigoi grinned and continued, undeterred. "You will want to divert your attention from us and kill this madman before he burns all your answers away. If he destroys the Scholomance, and if your Atticus *is* in our number, which I'll neither confirm nor deny, then all hope for him will be lost."

Wiltshire bared his own teeth and set his jaw. *Rock and a hard place, Wiltshire,* he thought. *And what the heck? Why are all my enemies trying to hire me?* "What is this sorcerer looking for? Also, you're wrong; I don't really care if he kills the whole lot of you. If he softens you up, it'll be all that much easier for me to swoop in and finish the job. Heh. Maybe I'll join him."

The Solomonar cocked his head, sure the detective was bluffing. "He seeks an item that we once possessed. We guarded it until it became a burden to do so, especially since we could not properly use the thing. Any artifact that requires a reflection is useless to us, and its power was too seductive to risk any of our mortal kindred using it on our behalf."

Wiltshire nodded, understanding that it was a magic mirror of some sort. He knew as well as anyone that vampires actually *had* reflections… except for when the mirror's reflective material contained silver, and all the magic ones he'd ever learned about did.

"We rid ourselves of the Venus Oculus long ago for a specific reason which I will not disclose," the enemy said, "and we no longer know where it is—but surely, if this warlock gets his hands on it, he could become unstoppable…"

"I thought the Scholomance were supposed to be the keepers of all human knowledge… and you guys can't find one lost grooming tool?"

The strigoi did not rise to Wiltshire's bait. He stared at the occult detective with baleful eyes.

Wiltshire set his face like flint and thought about the bullets on the nightstand… formed a plan in his mind. He knew the first slug would have no effect if he managed to swap magazines, but it would take more time to eject the one in the pipe than it would to simply pull the trigger.

"So this Magic Mike guy thinks one of the Solomonari has it and now he's gonna knock you off one by one to get at it?"

The strigoi nodded.

"Good!" He yanked his magazine free and snatched the other one from next to his bed. Wiltshire slammed it home, firing a trio of rounds at his enemy; the whole action took barely a second.

The creature had already anticipated his move, and although Wiltshire had only looked away for a split second, the strigoi evaporated into a black mist before the silver capped hollow-point could blast through where he'd stood a split second ago.

Stark silence reigned in the aftermath of the gunshots.

Wiltshire recognized the strigoi. He was the Weathermaker, the chief of the Solomonari students and he rode the mighty dragon Zmeu, the dragon who makes rain whenever it sees the sky. The dragon and rider controlled the weather, bringing storms and destruction with it wherever it went. A few moments later, the rain ceased abruptly, and Wiltshire knew that any danger had passed.

The Scholomance must truly be in danger if they sent the Weathermaker to try turning my attention. He cursed again and crawled out of bed. Wiltshire didn't like this turn of events... not one bit.

The Prime

"Give me what you owe me," Gita hissed beneath her breath.

Basilisk stood straight, but did not acknowledge her existence. He walked past with a regal air of authority.

She had isolated him in a hallway. The Desolation's emperor did not have many moments where he was alone and so Gita snatched him by the arm, needing to seize this opportunity. There might not be another.

Basilisk stopped and looked down at her. He stiffened and cocked his head. "I could turn you to stone with a wink of my eye," he threatened softly. "You forget your place."

"I think not," Gita insisted. "I've seen you make deal after deal these last few days. You've got too much on the line to petrify me and lose it all right now."

Basilisk smiled when she called his bluff. "It is nice to play the game and discover your opponent offers more challenge than presumed."

"You promised me the rune," Gita whispered sharply. She knew she battled a ticking clock in addition to the master strategist. "I did what you asked; now I demand my recompense." She jutted out her one free hand.

He merely stared at her open palm.

"I'm afraid I no longer have the rune. It is gone, though it's quite unlike me to fail to deliver on a promise, but a situation grew beyond my control."

Gita growled something unintelligible, and she began to squeeze her grip tighter. Her tiny hands proved surprisingly strong, and she trembled with rage.

"Blood from stone, my dear," Basilisk cautioned. "I cannot give what I do not have."

A massive tarkhūn soldier who followed Caivev approached from around a corner. A companion vyrm frostmancer followed a half step behind them.

"Is there a problem here, boss?" Skrom asked in his husky voice.

"No. No problem," Basilisk said. He brushed Gita's hand from his arm like it was nothing and linked arms with his wife.

"It's time we get back," Caivev said, escorting the emperor. "The recess is nearly over, and I know you would hate to miss the trade negotiations."

Skrom led the imperial couple back the way he'd come. The smaller ice lord lingered behind them for a moment longer and glowered threateningly at the frightened girl in her shiny armor. He leered as if plagued by a chip on his shoulder or had something to prove.

"Come along, Idrakka," Caivev called over her shoulder, and the vyrm minion whirled on his heels and chased after them.

Gita stood alone and watched Basilisk go, giving no thought to the person he'd left behind in the wreckage of such betrayal.

Surrounded by her royal entourage, and feeling lonelier than ever, Bithia stood next to the platform of the planes-walking gate nearest her palace. There, she watched the departure of Basilisk and his troupe. Her former enemies stood upon the gate's mouth and one of the vyrm walked to the activation receiver. He cut his hand and pressed the wound to the arcane machinery.

Before Basilisk and his crew disappeared, Caivev met Bithia's eyes. They were not friendly, but neither did they burn with the malice of old grudges. She nodded tightly, almost imperceptibly. Bithia returned the gesture and the reptilian persons returned to their home, all except for Basilisk.

He beckoned for her, as if he had a secret for her. Bithia approached, to the dismay of her guards. She waved them off.

"I have seen the truth of it," Basilisk told her. "When I am done sending you the statues, I will return the one you desire most."

"The Architect King?"

Basilisk nodded measuredly. "But I doubt that it will do you much good. My people have tired of the burden of guarding it. Perhaps you will fare better with him in your collection. Maybe it will ease the tensions between you and your Anti-Veritas Alliance members."

"Thank you," she said, quite surprised by the turnabout. She was not shocked that Basilisk knew of the AVA and her population's disgruntlement regarding peace talks with the vyrm. *He probably knew about them before I did.*

He bowed and retreated closer to the portal. "Let it be a final demonstration of my sincerity."

"The statue will be safe in my keeping," Bithia promised. She wrote down a cryptic equation upon a scrap of paper and pressed it into Basilisk's hand.

He looked at it quizzically. It looked like coordinates and instructions for an astral gate location, but it did not match any of the known records the vyrm had committed to memory. "What is this... a gate I do not know about?"

Bithia flashed him a knowing look. "You're not the only one with secrets. He will be quite safe here. This is the safest passage for me to receive something so precious."

"Secrecy is safety," He agreed. The vyrm emperor bowed and then disappeared through the gate.

Bithia let out an exhausted sigh. Tensions had run high the entire time of Basilisk's stay these past few days. Even the sudden gift that Basilisk had offered did not revitalize her enough to overcome such stress—and she had no idea when he would make the return of their petrified leader, if he would even make good on his promise... though Basilisk had never lied to her that she knew of, at least not directly.

Along with her advisers, she and the vyrm had finally completed a comprehensive treaty between their peoples, but the emotional toll it took made Bithia want to sleep for a week, and she'd had no sounding board to vent her frustrations to. Even Gita had become suddenly too withdrawn to pull into her confidence, despite their foolish spy mission into the AVA assembly. Bithia still felt certain something deeply bothered Gita, but she couldn't nail down what it was. Gita was as good at hiding her secret struggles as Bithia was with her own inner turmoil. *Of all the times to lose my psychic abilities,* she lamented.

Since Basilisk's arrival, she'd seen Gita skulking around the castle grounds. The presence of the vyrm seemed to have visibly upset her. Bithia sympathized. So many had been victimized by them in the past and she remembered that Gita's family had been casualties of Nitthogr's invasion, just as Jenner's had been; Gita was not alone.

The existence of the AVA proved that many citizens of the Prime were less than enthusiastic about any sort of reconciliation. But the princess did what she knew was necessary for the future of her people. If they continued fighting, Sh'logath's corruption would eventually blight *her kingdom,* too.

She turned and began heading back to the caravan that would ferry her back to the castle. Tay-lore pulled her aside for a moment. "Excuse me, Princess Claire. I have something urgent which requires your attention."

Bithia cocked her head. "Follow me. We can be alone in my hovercab, and it's secure." She led him into the private vehicle.

"Do not depart yet," the android said. "I am actually requesting this on behalf of another who cannot speak openly."

Bithia looked at him funny. This was not the first time he'd played go-between. Whether it was rogue vyrm or human detectives on earth, he'd made it a habit to work on behalf of friends.

"You will understand my meaning momentarily," Tay-lore said. The opposite door opened and Pollando entered the cab. The rumpled old psychic took his seat and nodded to Tay-lore. "He and I have an alternate method of communicating, since I have no presence on the psychic plane for him to speak with."

Bithia nodded. "I understand." She turned to look at Pollando, but she could not hear his familiar voice in her mind. The mute, old monk, who she'd been too busy to meet with since her incident with Claire, only ever spoke through psychic projection—and Claire had cut her off from that entire sense.

Tay-lore bowed and then exited, leaving them to have a private meeting... something that seemed unnecessary given the nature of psychic communication.

"You're leaving?" Bithia asked him.

"Pollando will make the reasons clear," he responded in his monotone voice. "As always, I will watch after your safety." The door shut and Pollando locked it.

A few moments later, an uncomfortable silence broke when Pollando used his raspy voice. Claire stood stiff and straight at her surprise. The voice sounded like squeaky gravel on glass, if such a sound was possible.

"My apologies for coming to you like this, Princess," Pollando said, still working the weak vocal chords into a consistent timbre.

His voice unnerved her. Pollando's psychic voice was booming and strong, but here was a ragged and diffident tenor.

"I... I'm... what? I didn't know you could speak?"

"Everyone thinks that and nobody ever bothers to ask." Pollando gave her a knowing smile from behind his long beard. He explained, "I made a vow of silence many decades ago. The fact that I am breaking it now—even if in secret—should stress to you the gravity of what I have to say."

She nodded. "Please continue. That you would speak for me is a great honor."

"We must keep this conversation private," Pollando said. "I have tried to speak to you before, but my astral voice only echoed in the void. You seemed unwilling or incapable of hearing me. The former did not seem at all likely." His eyes flooded with concern, assuming the latter.

Claire's eyes grew moist and her chest tightened.

Pollando's face grew worried, and he continued. "I cannot find you on the astral plane. I cannot sense you at all. It feels as if you do not even exist on the psychic spectrum." He took her by the face. "Even now, I can't sense you."

She told him most of what she knew, or some form of it, and acknowledged that she'd had some recent problems with her abilities. Bithia hid that she knew the reasons for it and hid that she was Bithia and not Claire from even Pollando; her secret was actually easier to keep without a psychic presence. She asked, "What does it mean?"

He fixed her with a serious gaze. "I can only tell you that I am worried, Princess Claire. First, you proved an adept student, but ever since your battle with Akko Soggathoth you have changed. You quickly grew so incredibly strong, rivaling or surpassing even Bithia... but now?" He shook his head. "Something is very, very wrong with you."

Earth

Shandra reached across and squeezed Sam Jones's hand. The minister at the front of the room spoke in warm tones. Many of Sam's previous business colleagues from both the university and the museum were present.

One of their peers got up to share a few short anecdotes and fond memories. "What can I say about Miles Jecima?" he said. "Miles had a way with words..."

Jecima's wife had passed several years ago, Sam knew. He'd been at that funeral as well. But Miles's son was conspicuously absent at this memorial. Sam didn't know their history other than that the son was about his age and there had been some kind of rift in the past; he knew they barely saw each other and whenever they did, it usually ended in pain and regrettable conversations.

He thought hard after it, but couldn't quite remember the name. It finally clicked after a few moments. *Jared... that was it. His son's name was Jared.*

"...I mean, he *really loved words*. His wife once begged me to come over and take the door off its hinges so she could get into his study. I guess he'd holed up on some mad endeavor to decode an ancient manuscript that had no known literary cipher..."

Attendees chuckled softly at the story.

One of Sam's old acquaintances leaned over his chair and whispered, "Hey Sam. You know we tried to contact you. We wanted you to speak—after all those expeditions together, you probably knew him better than any of us. You know, you're almost impossible to get a hold of?"

Sam nodded apologetically. "Sorry. I've been... away."

The man shrugged but eyed Shandra up and down as if her presence explained Sam's odd absence. "Heh. That figures, though. A woman's always a good reason for a bloke's disappearance." He leaned back and the rest of the service passed uneventfully.

After the minister dismissed the congregation, Sam led Shandra into the foyer along with the small pool of mourners. He shook the minister's hand briefly while another colleague apologized to the preacher. More than a couple "Jecima stories" had gone well over the line of church-appropriateness. They may have mortified the minister, but they entertained the attendees.

The minister cut the man off and took Sam by the arm. "Mister Jones," he said. "I need to make an introduction for you." He led Sam over to a man in a suit. "This is Mister Rath; he has been trying to contact you now for several days."

Rath nodded, and the preacher went back to his rounds with the laity. "I am Donald Rath," he introduced himself. "I don't expect you'd know me, but I'm Miles Jecima's attorney and I represent his estate. Can we chat for a moment?"

Sam nodded and followed Rath into an office, where they all took seats. Rath produced some documents from his briefcase. "I know that you were very close with Miles," he said, "though you haven't been around much lately." His gaze, too, lingered a moment on Shandra, who seemed oblivious to the inference that different men had each made.

Rath turned the papers over for Sam to look at.

Sam scanned the sheet. "This is... what? He left me something in his will?"

The lawyer nodded and handed over a pen and some deeds for a signature. "He left you his house and everything in it."

Sam's eyebrows arched sharply. "What about his son?"

"Apparently, Miles and his son had a conversation prior to death. Jared only wanted the cash and a few odds and ends, which he has already collected. The house is yours." Rath turned over a ring with keys that would open the locks. "Miles said he always considered you his second son. And he was very fond of your daughter, too."

Sam rubbed his face, almost overwhelmed by the gift. "I guess... I mean, I feel like I should have been there more for him, then. I'm kind of a crappy son."

"Trust me," Rath insisted with a melancholy smile, "between you and me, I've met Jared. You're the good son." The lawyer held up a hand as he took the signature pages. "One more thing. He also wanted to make sure that you got this." Rath handed over a wooden box that was locked by some kind of turning dial with a series of characters on the rolling sequencer.

"Thanks." he said, absentmindedly fiddling with the code. Rath exited while Sam continued working on the password.

Once the room was clear, Shandra placed her hand on the box. "Do you feel it—the aura? Can you tell what is inside?"

Sam gave her a screwy look. "No. What do you mean?"

"Darquematter," she said.

A moment later, Sam entered the password, which had been a code they'd shared long ago back when they'd worked out of the same office; the code had been their password for the door and alarm systems. He opened the lid and found a cluster of amulets similar to the pendant that Sam's daughter used to wear, accompanied by a hand written note.

Claire. I started collecting these after your adventures brought you to my door. They reminded me of you. Also, you still owe me for a new door—but you can see your father about that.

—M. Jecima.

Shandra read the note and flashed Sam a confused look.

"When they crossed paths after Claire had grown up," he explained, "she and Jackie were on the run from Nitthogr. I guess Zabe broke the door down trying to reach her."

Shandra smiled. "That sounds like Zabe."

Sam nodded and held out his arm. He twirled the keyring on his finger. "Come on. Let's go check out this famous door."

CHAPTER EIGHT

The Prime

Shjikara stood in the courtyard under the shadow of the palace; he oversaw the operations. The AVA had cleared out well in advance of the diplomatic exchange and now the place had sprung up overnight with a growing collection of statues—people encased in living stone. These men and women, frozen by Basilisk, were doomed to remain conscious and in an immobile stasis; time progressed around them, but they were helpless to do a thing about it.

Movers brought even more of the statues in and deposited them in the menagerie that spanned several cultural shifts. The figures displayed older styles of dress through the ages. Curious onlookers meandered through. Many brought printed photos of long-lost relations and ancestors, curious to see if any of them had ended up in Basilisk's collection.

The high priest spotted Gita in the distance. She was in her armored uniform as she stormed through the castle grounds on what looked to be on an assignment from her Guardian Corps superiors. They'd kept her extremely busy these last few days—too busy for her to get away for any hiking.

Shjikara motioned for her and headed her way. Gita barely met his eyes as they crossed paths. "My dear Gita," he said with snake oil charm, "We'd barely gotten a chance to speak since after that dreadful business at the Gates of Koth. I understand that you were wounded in one of the battles?"

She agreed, but downplayed it and tried to move past him. He detained her longer by stepping in front of her. His posture insisted on a conversation.

"I intended to visit you in the hospital, you know. But I was so busy with that Zahaben business."

Gita stiffened. "I understand."

"No... no. I should have made the time," Shjikara insisted. "You have suffered so much under vyrm oppression." He put a hand on her shoulder and flooded his voice with warmth and empathy. It sounded genuine.

Gita barely held back her emotions. She believed him.

"But look," Shjikara told her, pointing to the statues. "I've been able to get all of these victims from Basilisk's rule returned to us. I am still studying *how to do it*, but I think that, given what I accomplished at Zahaben's turning, I will eventually be able to unfreeze all of these poor souls."

"You... you really think you can do it?" Gita asked. The lilt in her voice bloomed with hope and optimism. "Is that really possible?"

He hefted his stone paw. "Only I have the power to do this thing. And I would willingly do it. It cost me a hand, but it will be worth it in the end." He walked towards the collected figures, strolling amiably. "Come. Come... I want to show you something."

Gita hurried after him.

"I have been cloistered away in our mountain fortress for too long. Those AVA fellows might be right," Shjikara said, "The Veritas have a duty to do more. You will see more of me. I've determined that I can have such a greater impact down here among the people. It is people who matter above all, yes?"

Gita nodded. "That is why I joined the Corps. Too many people are helpless and in need. There are those who need rescuing... and I can help," she said as she looked away.

Shjikara took her by the face with a palm on her cheek. "You are stronger than you look, Gita, daughter of... of... I actually don't think I could name your parents. I apologize. I only know that they passed."

Something inside her broke and her eyes welled up. "If I tell you something as my confessor, will you keep it a secret?"

The High Priest embraced her. "It will stay between you and me. I will help absolve you if I can," he said in a warm tone.

Gita sniffed away a tear, but several more came. She confessed everything, that her family did not actually die in the sorcerer's invasion but had been targeted by Basilisk; he thought he could insert a mole where so many shades had failed. She confessed that she was the spy, and that her guilt weighed upon her every day. "I'm so sorry... but I don't know what to do. You'll help me, won't you?"

Shjikara led her a little way deeper into the collection of statues. "What was the price of your betrayal?"

"Basilisk said that he would release my family and restore them to flesh if I could get close to Claire or Zabe and reported on them, or at least on their military operations," she said, wiping her damp cheek.

"Did he say 'restore them to flesh' or merely that he would release them?"

Gita scowled and looked at the ground. "I got a moment alone with him yesterday. He claimed it was the latter, but I don't see how that matters. He would have given me a rune to restore only one of them anyway, something he showed me when he froze them, but now he says that he's lost it."

"That is important because my brother does not lie," Shjikara said. "Falsehood is not one of his tools."

"What?" Gita looked at him, confused and certain the priest had misspoken. "I don't understand what..."

"I cannot absolve you of this crime," Shjikara led her through a row of statues. "Only *she can do that*." He pointed to a tiny stone form. Gita's sister stood on the end of the row with her brother's hand, broken off at the wrist, still attached to her.

"Shara!" Gita's eyes widened with panic. "What... what do you mean? How did Shara get here?" She floundered for a coherent train of thought, trying to understand what was happening.

Shjikara turned on her. His eyes burned with something evil.

Gita finally recognized the vile gleam in his pupils. She had been only a teen when it had happened, but Gita had been with her family when they were rounded up and forced into a vyrm concentration camp. She recognized that look. *Nitthogr had visited her camp firsthand.*

"I now possess that rune," Shjikara held aloft his stone hand. "It resides firmly within my grip and I alone wield its power. I will release your sister, Shara, in my own time, if you remain loyal. As you worked for my brother Basilisk, you will now work for me," he hissed.

"No! No, I won't. I'm going to Princess Claire—she has to know."

Shjikara blocked her path. "I see it in your eyes. You think I can't do worse to Shara than Basilisk has already done?" He playfully fingered the break at her brother's hand. "Your sister is now the only survivor. I smashed the rest and now she is relying on you to save her." Shjikara's eyes burned as they locked with Gita's. "You are responsible for her fate. She is only a child, Gita... will you really condemn her? From what I know of her condition, she is conscious right now and can hear every word—will you abandon her to reveal a security concern? Would they even listen *after all you've done?*"

Gita's eyes poured out tears, and she sobbed uncontrollably. She shook her head. "I... I..."

"You belong to me. You will no longer report to Basilisk—Shara's life depends on it, and while Basilisk is impotent to restore any statue to life, *I can.*" He scanned her broken posture. The outcome was already certain. "Go and confirm that your parents are beyond hope and dashed to pieces. Know that you now belong to Nitthogr. *You are mine now.*"

Gita turned and fled, trying to wipe away the salty, wet redness from the edges of her face. Shjikara smiled as he watched her go and then composed himself in a regal manner. He stepped back into the open air of the courtyard beyond the cluster of the statues even as the movers delivered the last of them, several thousand in all.

Tay-lore paused in front of the High Priest. The android had been walking through on some unknown purpose when he paused to watch Gita rush past, bawling her eyes out. He turned and found Shjikara watching her run... fleeing the priest, it seemed.

"What is the matter with Gita?" Tay-ore asked him.

Shjikara drew himself together like he was hiding something. "Oh, she's just sad."

"About what?" Tay-lore turned to address Shjikara.

"About many things. About Jenner mostly, her friend is in prison and I told her I could not recommend any punishment except for execution after the trial concludes. The books of military code and conduct are very clear on the matter."

Tay-lore stiffened and then watched Gita exit the courtyard. The android was historically bad at reading body language and the nuances of human communication, but even so, he knew that Shjikara had been untruthful.

His robotic synapses ran subroutines and processed data. The result was suspicion and a high probability of danger. *He has access to Princess Claire.* Tay-lore's concern rating spiked, and he knew he would have to keep an eye on Shjikara.

Earth

Sisyphus stalked through the woods alone, searching for a specific, rare creature. He'd abandoned the portal some distance back and did not want to leave his enemy with any opportunity to either escape his grasp or to use its magic or misdirection on Doctor Walther; the wizard knew as well as any that Fey creatures could be the most devious of them all.

Trees towered high above and the lush moss sqwunched underfoot like a magical, living carpet of the forest. It blanketed the vale and silenced the sounds within the natural cathedral, where branches and verdant canopy cloistered them away from the world of man and all its woes and technological pacing.

The solitary human stalked through, keeping his eyes sharp for his contact's home. *I know it was around here somewhere.* Sisyphus crested a rise and sidestepped a massive tree trunk on the spongy hillock of peat and old growth. In the lowlands beneath him, he found the little beast.

A single broken tree stump towered waist-high above a field littered with thousands of plastic cups, lids torn open and their contents licked clean. The pudding cups' labels identified them as vanilla flavored. Sisyphus shook his head; he'd delivered the tiny monster five pallets of snack cups only a week ago.

"Just like a little junkie," he said incredulously and then kicked the stump. "Bwbych! Bwbych, get out here!"

A tiny door made of bark opened on the side of the hovel and a boggart crouched and then made his way out. He looked like any ordinary house-elf, except his skin tone had greened and his features had pointier ends; he bore an almost porcine likeness and a grouchy face that looked prone to biting. This one had no legs; they terminated in wooden posts where they'd been replaced after some tragic tale of the past.

"Sisyphus! Sisyphus, my friend. What brings you..."

The massive wrestler roared and snatched him in one huge paw and then lifted him off the ground. Bwbych was no larger than a toddler.

"What? What did I do?" Bwbych screeched.

"You gave me bad information, you little twit! Now I'm here to make you pay me back for all this." He motioned to the field of empty containers.

"I didn't..." the boggart flailed and struggled, trying to free himself.

"The Scholomance! They did not have the mirror, you little liar, and now I have made a powerful, unnecessary enemy." He shook Bwbych like a rag doll.

The boggart looked around in a panic. "Well, you can take your payment back then."

"I don't want your empty cups—you already ate the pudding, you rotten little creature." He'd offered untold riches for the information, but Bwbych had a weakness for the sweet stuff, especially vanilla.

Bwbych reached up and sank his teeth into Sisyphus's wrist. The wrestler yelped and dropped him. The boggart scrambled on his wooden peg legs and nearly made it inside his door and to safety when Sisyphus held aloft his weapon and used his mind to seize the creature.

"Not so fast." Sisyphus lifted Bwbych from his feet and hung him in mid-air. The wrestler used his mind and forced Bwbych's limbs outward, splayed wide.

"Okay. Okay, you got me. Now let's talk like civilized beings," Bwbych bartered.

Sisyphus glared at him and then shook out the pain in his hand, which dribbled red rivulets from the gash. He exerted power through his mind and pulled all four appendages away from each other as if his prisoner had been put into an invisible rack device. "If you don't have answers for me, this is going to go badly for you." Sisyphus pulled hard enough on the boggart's arms that both elbows and shoulders popped in their joints and made him squeal. "You'll have two new wooden pegs to complete the set unless you have what I want."

Bwbych yelped but spoke through the pain. "Tell me... tell me what you want, and I'll try to help, but I was chained in a tree stump for several centuries—some of my intel was bound to be outdated!"

Sisyphus relaxed his grip and the pressure he exerted, but he did not release his prey.

"I can't track the locations and happenings of every magic user on this miserable plane—nobody can do that—but I'll help if I can," Bwbych promised.

"I only want what was promised to me. *The Venus Oculus.*"

The boggart grimaced, making him even uglier. "I do not know where the mirror is now, but if my interactions with the Red Order are any indication, and if the Solomonari have released the mirror, then it could have been claimed and might be anywhere by now."

"Has it been used?"

Bwbych shook his head. "The mirror can only be used once every hundred years, but its power is strong and distinct. If it had been used, I would have felt it." He could tell that his answer was insufficient to get him out of the wizard's grip. "Here. Take my amulet as payment for my mistake." It pained him to make such a trade after the deal had been done, but Bwbych did not have any intention of using the item—though he might have tried to trade it for another haul of sweets. The mirror was likely to give him an unlimited supply, but just as likely to change the boggart's taste buds, so its flavor was like vinegar to him. All magic had a price, and the stronger the magic, the greater the risk accompanying it.

Sisyphus stared at the circle of baked clay that bore a single rune inscribed upon it. "What is that?" It resembled a cookie on a string. "It looks like some kid's kindergarten art project," he scoffed.

"Very rare," Bwbych promised. "Very valuable. It can open a portal to the Feylands; my home exists apart from your multi-verse. But a word of caution when you break it. I have not used it because I don't have any guarantee of returning. The Spider Queen, who has long ruled there, is loath to let creatures leave her domain once they've entered." He looked across at the scattered field of empty plastic containers and cautioned the wizard. "There is no vanilla pudding in the Feylands."

Sisyphus grinned and removed the fragile pendant. Slipping it around his neck, he hid it beneath the folds of his jacket. "The token will be a part of my arsenal in case I need a backup plan or a sudden emergency escape... but given how unlikely that is, I will only consider it *part* of the debt you owe."

"Then what do you want?" he yelped as Sisyphus used his powers to start slowly pulling on his limbs again as a reminder. Bwbych was pretty sure it was only because the wizard enjoyed inflicting pain.

"There is a secondary prize I am chasing. There are amulets from the darque dimension. I know the daughter of the Architect King used to wear such a one. You know it?"

"Heh. Yes. I know the one. They grant an assortment of boons and curses, but most do similar minor tricks... prestidigitations, but none are as powerful as the mirror."

"There are more of them on Earth, yes? I want one that will insulate me from the magic of others."

Bwbych tried to nod, but he still couldn't move even his head. "There are several, but another has been collecting them."

"Is the shard I seek among them?" He tugged on Bwbych's limbs to reinforce the gravity of his question.

"Yes." He panted and caught his breath after Sisyphus relaxed the pressure. "Miles Jecima. He is an archaeologist, not well known except by a few—but he is friends with the Architect King's princess, and he has acquired a number of them."

"Then he will not be hard to find," Sisyphus said. He released the boggart, who fell to the ground.

Bwbych edged his way towards the door of his tree stump sanctuary.

Sisyphus turned to leave the oddly littered grove when Bwbych called out to him from the stump. "Hey, wizard! You wouldn't happen to have any of that pudding with you? Maybe I could barter for more? Surely I have *something* else you want, perhaps more information."

Shaking his head, Sisyphus kept walking and left the boggart to rot in his own vices.

CHAPTER NINE

The Prime

Bithia was tired and worried about her recent revelation with Pollando, but duty still bound her to the throne. She had, however, perked up somewhat, despite presiding over meetings with her realm's administrators. Hope crept slowly back into her and she expected her father and friends might return any day now... and with them, she thought even Zabe might return at any moment.

Shjikara had also been hovering about, taking care of some business on the castle grounds and making himself generally available to both the crown and the populace. It had been unlike him to be useful up until now.

Since Zabe's disappearance, the High Priest had been coming around much more frequently and volunteering to take on the ever-increasing duties required. Until a week ago, Pollando had been the go between that connected the Veritas and the Castle, even if the High Priest's office had always filled that role under previous rulers.

"I believe that I am close to being able to restore the statue garden... or at least some of them," Shjikara told her.

Bithia nodded as the Priest concluded his report.

Tay-lore watched him from the side of the room.

"You will recall the refugee situation that we once had in our cloister? In the resulting peace that you've helped bring to the realm, the monastery helped resettle and re-home all of those displaced by Nitthogr's failed invasion."

"That is good news," the princess said.

"With your permission," Shjikara continued, "I'd like to similarly assist with whoever we are capable of reviving from the statue collection. They will, no doubt, require a certain amount of re-education in order so they may be reintegrated back into our society. Some have been frozen in stone for hundreds of years. It seems likely that there will be need of therapeutic services which the Veritas could provide."

Bithia nodded, agreeing to his proposal.

Tay-lore would never voice an objection in royal chambers, but he did not like the idea at all. He'd made many efforts to experience the full depths of human emotion, and he believed that he had just felt his skin crawl. He did not have skin, but it crawled all the same. He did not like or trust Shjikara and drew closer so he could better follow the exchange.

"When do you think you might see some results? When might you revert the first of them to flesh?"

"I, uh, still have some things to test and read up on. It may also require some elements from the Sacristy vault," Shjikara claimed. "The process takes much out of me, so I must take it slow, you understand. Much testing. Many late hours."

"I understand," Bithia said, looking towards the next order of business and excusing the High Priest to go about his work.

"Yes, Shjikara," Tay-lore said. He understood that Shjikara had used many words to tell her absolutely nothing—another point of suspicion. He added, "best of luck in your endeavors."

Desolation

"All will be new," Gerjha said. "Maetha will restore Edenya. He has shown me this," he claimed to those gathered around him. The prophet's back was turned to a roaring fire and cinders rose on hot eddies like swirling fireflies. "For the first time I bring you a new prophecy that He has revealed: He has promised that I will live to see this thing happen."

Trenzlr sat next to the tribe's chief, Klewdahar, the father of the vyrm with a broken mind. Klyrtan, his son, sat on the other side of him. Chief Klewdahar had yet to make an introduction of the person on his other side, but Trenzlr had learned from the crowd that the scarred vyrm's name was Chartarra.

He found himself assuming Chartarra's past. The newcomer carried himself like a soldier, but he did not appear to be tarkhūn; whichever of the five tribes he might belong to was anybody's guess. Vyrm of the Black were difficult to guess as far as political alliances, but his presence here meant that he either had none, or was looking for a new one. His scars looked like they should have been fatal, and the way Gerjha the prophet held his interest, it was clear to see that Chartarra had come to believe in the coming Maetha—the one who would re-make the vyrm as they were intended before the Sh'logath cult fractured the vyrm's racial identity.

Chief Klewdahar had asked them both to meet at his tent whenever Gerjha finished addressing the crowd.

"You all know me," the prophet exclaimed. Every vyrm young and old gave him their full attention. "Some of you thought me crazy; I was another zealot confined to a circle drawn in the sand, where I waited for many years. Some of you joined me for a time or fed me, and I thank you. Some believed my words and others mocked—but we are all vyrm. *We are all Seekers of Maetha and nothing can divide us!*"

A ripple of energy circulated through the crowd as they murmured assents, stirred to passion by the prophet.

Gerjha held up a hand to keep them quiet. "I have had a vision."

The crowd held its breath, waiting for the prophet's revelation.

"We have each waited patiently for the coming of Maetha. That day is drawing near, and soon—and I do not mean that in a philosophical sense. We can rest in that promise."

Trenzlr's scales practically puckered at the words. There had not been a divine word for generations, and now, as faith had begun to falter, Gerjha revived their hopes.

"Maetha is not what we make him to be. Perhaps Maetha is not a *He* at all. We too often rely on what we think we know and memories from revelations we may have misheard. I only caution you so that your hearts are prepared for Maetha's coming—so you will not lose faith if the chosen one turns out to look less like Chief Klewdahar and more like whatever form Maetha has chosen."

A voice called out, "What will he look like?" More voices yelled the same request.

Gerjha continued, "In my dream, I looked to the sky, a sky free of that obscene monstrosity—this was a clear indication that Maetha had come. And in the sky I saw the moon, but the moon was not a moon at all, rather it was a sun: fiery and bright. And the sun had consumed the moon. Together they became something else greater. This new moon-sun both scorched and relieved all of those who waited for it at dawn." He turned and looked directly at Chartarra. "Only with the light of this sun could those seeds planted for generation after generation finally germinate and bloom. Their fields covered all the wastelands until it revived Edenya."

Trenzlr's brows knit in thought and he whispered to Klewdahar, who also functioned as a member of their tribe's priestly caste. "What does he mean?"

The chief cocked his head. "I thought you knew the stories from your lessons as a child?"

A voice teased him in a matching whisper. "I thought you knew," Klyrtan said with condescension. Hirdac, seated nearby, shushed the simple-minded vyrm.

Klewdahar looked at him. "The sun and moon? Symbols for mankind and vyrm. He's implying Maetha could be a Dunnischktet." The Seeker stood as the group had begun to disperse in order to ponder the prophet's words. "Now come. I value your input on a council I am forming."

"M-me? A council?" Trenzlr stammered. "But I am not qualified to be a leader or..."

Chief Klewdahar waved away his protests. "You are the last of your house and you have spent much time in the Prime. Surely you have gained valuable insights during your travels. I won't accept your refusal."

Trenzlr did not protest further. "Thank you, Chief Klewdahar. I am honored," and he followed him to the tent of meeting.

The Prime

Shjikara remained behind the closed doors of his chamber where he communed with his dark agod. Never before had he experienced such closeness with the Devourer, except when he was trapped in the void: present with Sh'logath and in an eternal state of everlasting digestion. Now, he walked reality again in that same state; his soul burned and his skin flayed from the inside as the Devourer's spirit wormed through him like acidic, larval tendrils.

He stood and looked in the mirror. His face had begun to melt and gravity slid his flesh downward in sheafs as Sh'logath's touch decayed Shjikara's corpulent form.

Nitthogr drew on his connection to that dark power and exerted control over his body. His visage reformed into that of the Veritas High Priest. He smiled at his reflection. "We are not yet ready to be revealed," he told the man whose body he'd hijacked.

Ready to be seen publicly again, he exited the private cell and walked the warm stone halls of the Veritas monastery. After a short journey through the corridors, he arrived at the massive door to the sacristy. The impenetrable vault was much like the Chamber of Mysteries in the royal castle; here, the Veritas kept its holy relics and items of arcane power.

As the High Priest, he was the only one who could open it of his own accord. Its mystic wards were not quite as specific or potent as the spell guarding the royal chamber. *This body still remains necessary.*

The circle-shaped door had five halo shaped ports in its center. In the middle bowl, the crest of the Veritas was emblazoned proudly. Surrounding it were four similar sigils for the heads of the four orders: Wax, Flame, the Mystics, and the Merciful Hammer.

Nitthogr stuck his fist into the center and the door clicked open with a slight hum of vibration. Within the sacristy towered several shelves that housed a variety of artifacts. A long table with items that were still being examined and cataloged spanned the length of the room. At the far end of the table sat an over-sized codex, an inkwell, and a single chair.

The undead sorcerer took a seat and opened the book as he scoured it for information. Entries in the book were recorded and cross-referenced each with a detailed drawing and description. Much of the book was penned in Shjikara's patient script, but large, earlier sections were known to Nitthogr and were even recorded into the Grimmorium Nitthogr, his ancient book which he'd kept since before he'd become a dunnischktet, and which now lay in the possession of the Heptobscurantum.

One page he tore out and set aside for later. Its drawing depicted a mechanical box inlaid with astronomical symbols. The instruction sheet detailed its usage and location within the vault. He'd locate it another time—it was a necessary component for much later in his plans.

He smiled for a moment, recognizing his own loose script. A few of the entries in this book were his, even; Nitthogr had once been next in line to assume leadership over The Flame Order, which studied the arcane and magical arts. Familiarity encouraged a smile, which Sh'logath stymied with a jolt of pain that coursed through the sorcerer's mind. The agod refused to allow anything less than total devotion in Nitthogr, and nostalgia threatened that.

He flipped another page and found the first item he'd been searching for. The second was cataloged a few pages afterward. Nitthogr went to the shelves and withdrew a gnarled crown of color-shifting, glassine material. The crystals ensconced veins of darquematter that permeated and gilded them; this item had been secreted away within the sacristy since before the Veritas had come to understand the potent nature of the stuff and how it was keyed to the multi-verse. He polished the crown with the folds of his robes and then placed it on the table near the tome. He picked up the second item: a twisted, cage-like enclosure.

The High Priest turned it over and examined it. Looking much like a fisherman's crustacean trap, this blasted wreckage was not an artifact and didn't have any powers worth noting. It was, however, made of pure darquematter. The material had been cast in an odd, criss-crossing shape during the first battle with Vangandra so long ago when the vyrm first encroached upon the Prime. This piece had been blasted off the vyrm champion's armor and recast in random fashion.

Nitthogr placed the twisted shape into the sack and exited the sacristy, sealing it tightly. The bag and item within were rather unassuming except for those familiar with the other-worldly material. Likely only Minas, the current head of The Flame Order, would find the contents of the cleric's sack suspicious.

Skulking through the corridors, Nitthogr did not encounter any of the four leaders of the Veritas disciplines, and the other adherents bowed so low at his passing that they barely noticed what he carried. He exited the monastery and passed through the outer cloister, where preparations were being made to receive and care for any poor souls who Shjikara might free from stone form. Night had drawn long, and the work had already stopped for the evening, allowing the thief to descend the mountain slope by the monastery trail without being spotted.

After a short trip, Nitthogr arrived at the castle. He passed the gates with ease in his current persona. These last few days had made the guards familiar with him. They also had a Veritas cleric with them, stationed at the gates, in order to detect and prevent magic users from any sort of obfuscation.

He passed them, citing his business as private, and headed for the courtyard. It was quiet and empty at this late hour except for the statues reclaimed from Limbus. Nonetheless, Nitthogr stretched out with his senses in order to detect any life forms who might be present.

Detecting none, Nitthogr threw the bag aside and removed the twisted cage. He worked his stone fist into the interwoven mesh of arcane metal, placing it over the source of his power: the rune his brother had unwittingly delivered before his escape from the void.

Nitthogr meandered through the neatly arranged rows of the statue collection. He summoned the dark energies that coursed through his body; they had gone undetected by the Veritas clerics so far. Power emanated from the rune, spreading out like a corona of eldritch light, but tainted by black clouds. The darklight permeated the garden like a flashing thunderhead and the darquematter cage filtered the raw power as if it were a mesh designed to restrain the rune's power from effecting the human members of the Prime. Only the vyrm spies and enemies that had been sent to infiltrate Basilisk over the years had been affected by the Rune of Return.

A thin veneer of rocky coating broke away like eggshells as those trapped within emerged. They shook off the chunks of chitinous debris as the cloud of power retracted back within the sorcerer's stone fist. Double lidded, reptilian eyes blinked back at him, ready to pounce on the High Priest.

Looking like Shjikara, Nitthogr addressed them in the royal vyrmic tongue. [Greetings, faithful soldiers—friends, all. I recognize so many of your faces. Each one of you was sent on missions throughout the ages and were discovered by Basilisk. You each paid a penalty for his sins. It has been revealed that *he has betrayed Sh'logath*.]

The suddenly awakened army relaxed their aggressive postures, but many still remained skeptical, still uncertain of what events had occurred during their petrification. Each one of the three hundred warriors, a full third of the statue collection, let down their defenses, revealing themselves to be vyrm shades who had been turned to stone while shape-shifted into various disguises.

[Look around, brothers,] the High Priest insisted. [We have finally breached the castle of the Prime, and I have released you back into service of almighty Sh'logath.]

One of the nearest shades cocked his head in a lizard-like fashion. He sought clarification. [Who are you?]

Pushing power through the flesh that encased the sorcerer's filthy spirit, Shjikara's features melted away and reformed into that of the Herald of the Apocalypse. "I am Nitthogr—the true servant and heir of Sh'logath. I have returned to fulfill the Awakening in a way never before imagined." He held aloft his arm of flesh and it split apart, oozing blood and slime that dripped like thick honey as it formed into a writhing mass of Sh'logathian tendrils. "I am here to institute something new—the Awakening cannot happen without first enduring this new and chaotic event: the Birthing."

Nitthogr's baleful, yellow eyes surveyed his secret army, which gathered closely around him. "I am the child of Sh'logath, more than any mere dunnischktet. I am the Acolyte of the Great Devourer. I am Sh'logath incarnate."

All around him, the shades began to bow, taking one knee as they pledged their fealty to the sorcerer once again.

Nitthogr opened his mouth to direct them back to the monastery when his eyes caught a glint of light on the terrace above. Only briefly, he spotted the distinct form of Tay-lore as the android slinked backwards and into the shadows near the overlook leading to Respan's lab, where he could usually be found.

A homo diurnus is not alive—of course I could not sense him!

Nitthogr returned to the vyrmic high speech. [We will move out and resume our glorious mission as soon as I return. I have a simple task to perform at once.]

His body exploded in a cloud of mist so that he could not be seen by recording devices that were stationed along various sections of the hallway leading to the lab. The cloud moved swiftly and disappeared through a door, leaving behind an army of three hundred shades, milling about in the courtyard.

The shades flexed their distinct muscles and returned to those faces that they had each worn before being trapped in stone.

[Soon,] the secret army hissed. [Soon our true purpose will be revealed.]

Chapter Ten

Tay-lore hurried into the lab he shared with Respan. He moved both as quickly and as quietly as he could, hoping that he hadn't been seen.

I knew it! I knew it all along—something has been wrong with Shjikara all this time. He validated his suspicions with his self talk. Accusing the High Priest without some kind of evidence would not have gone over well... and the sorcerer returned was a formidable foe. Outing him early and without evidence would have proven disastrous.

A message flashed on his console and he accessed it quickly. A simple text thread sent by Vikrum Wiltshire who asked for assistance on a case. Tay-lore almost dismissed it, but he glanced briefly at the attached images and the result made him pause for thought—as much as the analogy worked for an android with such incredible processing power. The "pause" was almost immeasurable by human standards.

He directed some of his computing ability to run facial recognition on the face, which he thought seemed familiar. *The subroutine picked up key genetic trait markers with high probabilities... could that be a relative of Zabe's?*

Tay-lore didn't dare to hope that it might have been Zurrah. The android, along with the other members of the werewolf's inner circle, knew that the boy had been freed from Caivev's forces when they controlled a time-stasis chamber. Zurrah had been lost in the Darque, forcing Zabe to choose between rescuing the princess or his brother. Bound by duty, Zabe had to leave Zurrah behind in order to stop Sh'logath... but this person's age did not appear correct for the story's details.

Facial recognition completed and confirmed the identity of Zurrah with a high probability of accuracy. If Tay-lore had been human, he would have groaned and sighed about the bad timing for good news.

He computed the likelihood of various outcomes; given the resurgence of Nitthogr and the army of shades now hiding within the Prime. His circuits sank when he got the odds and he risked a moment to run the chances of survival against various outcomes from his immediate actions.

The results failed to encourage him.

Tay-lore snatched a hover drone from Respan's shelf and stuffed it with a few items. He glanced at the star chart and determined the next open portal time and location. Tay-lore programed the drone quickly and then placed it back on the shelf, knowing that it would automate and fulfill its mission without any further assistance.

He composed a brief response to Vikrum Wiltshire and then sent it. The remote relay system he'd set up to communicate with the Earth dimension, and to scan the various planes of the multi-verse, would deliver the message at the next available planeswalking window, which would open a few hours from now.

Tay-lore turned his head to face the monitor from the nearest security checkpoint in the hallway. The video feed revealed nothing except an eerie fog that crawled across the floor like a cloud rolling down the face of a mountain. Such a phenomenon sometimes happened in those halls exposed to the elements, such as the terrace where he'd spied Nitthogr from. He checked the atmospheric data to determine if the weather was right for fog. It was certainly not a natural occurrence; Tay-lore stood straight.

A moment later, a familiar figure darkened his doorway. "Tay-lore, my friend and loyal servant of the crown," a voice called. "You and I must have a chat."

Tay-lore did not have emotions per se, but he had a bad feeling about what lurked outside his door.

With the early morning sun about to crest the distant mountain vista, Nitthogr wiped the black oil and hydraulic fluid from his forearms and face. He returned to his minions, who awaited in the courtyard. As a reminder of his power, he resumed Shjikara's form. The impostor led his human-looking army from the castle gates and up the hill to the monastic cloister.

Members of the Merciful Hammer, the warrior caste, were typically responsible for watching the walls. Upon their leader's triumphal return, they pointed and shouted, rousing their fellow adherents to welcome the disguised victims into the make-shift encampment they'd assembled to reintegrate and acclimate the un-petrified to their new lives in the future. One of the guards ran to wake Master Druen, the head of the order.

Members of the Merciful Hammer strived for mastery over the physical body, and Druen was a true specimen of perfection with a tight beard, a shoulder length ponytail, and bulging muscles that defied his age. Druen gathered his cohort, so they were ready to serve the wave of incoming refugees. Many of those under his directorship also acted as healers and herbalists; those ones he sent to check the health of the men and women Shjikara led through the gates.

The High Priest clapped grips with Druen and flashed him a fake, weary smile.

"What... how..." Druen found himself at a loss for words.

Nitthogr made up a greasy, self aggrandizing lie about a sudden urge to visit the statue grove and attempt a turning. "I felt inspired in the middle of the night, as if the Architect King himself appointed me to go down and release these captives. But it does take a lot out of me—despite the holy power that I channel. I must return to rest." He put a heavy hand on Druen's shoulder and the big man nodded, pledging to oversee the new wards.

A few minutes later, Nitthogr locked himself within the sacristy vault, the safest place in the whole of the monastery. He tossed aside the scepter that represented his authority in the halls of the Veritas—it held no meaning to him. It only mattered to the fools he was deceiving. Shjikara's form melted away; fat boiled down into muscle and bones shifted as the lithe figure of the dunnischktet formed from the base materials.

Nitthogr felt more comfortable in this state, and he knew the next task would truly tax him. He disrobed and lifted the crown, setting it upon his brow. The sorcerer seated himself upon the cool floor and reached out with his astral senses, sending out dreams and feelings, altering moods and sentiments much as he had done before with Claire Jones, before Zabe had interfered with Nitthogr's original plans.

Already he could feel the temperature incrementally rising within the room. It had been rather simple when he'd meddled with the disposition of one girl from Earth... it strained him to connect minds to so many at once.

The crown amplified his power as it connected him to the minds of the Black vyrm, the faction that remained mostly loyal to him. Nitthogr had never connected to quite so many before. They were spread across more than thirty planes of reality, and the mystic headpiece connected to them by the power of the tesseract.

His dark dreams spread out from him like black, invisible tentacles; they festered in the heart of the lesser reality gems. Their power permeated the substance of the multi-verse and touched Nitthogr's loyal subjects. His commands echoed through the ether like pinpoints of blackness, rebounding back to signal their allegiance as if it was a kind of arcane transponder.

Hours passed and the temperature within the sacristy sweltered, making Nitthogr wish that he had bent a tarkhūn icelord to his will. He wiped away the sweat from his face and pressed into the connections he formed. Nitthogr ignored the fact that his scales had revealed themselves and separated to let out additional heat and act as cooling fins. His internal body temperature rose beyond the normal tolerance limits of any vyrm or man... but he was no longer either. Nitthogr was dunnischktet—but he was even more: he'd become the Acolyte of Sh'logath.

He growled and shoved his will into the dreams and thoughts of any remaining vyrm minds not genetically aligned to the tarkhūn caste. He sent a siren call to whatever forgotten tribes, mostly made up by the rover clans, could hear him. His final push exhausted him and Nitthogr slumped to his side, falling into a deep slumber. The crown rolled from his brow and came to a rest at the base of the racks that lined the sacristy walls.

Desolation

Down the mountain slope from where Gerjha had his visions, Chartarra awoke from a vision of his own. He wiped away the cold chill that clung to his scales and sat up. The scars across his neck and torso burned as if they contained fire and the simple sheet provided by the Maethans had soaked through with Chartarra's sweat.

The memory of the dream clung to him like a bad taste in his mouth. The vision felt more like an experience than a dream. In it, Chartarra cheered on Nitthogr as he led an overwhelming horde of the Black alongside the sorcerer. Together, they overthrew the tarkhūn and completed the Awakening in the heart of the Prime:

they loosed the blood of the Architect King's daughter between the wide-flung doors of the Chamber of Mysteries. Their profane act shattered the Tesseract, and brought about the end of all, finally sating the hunger of Sh'logath.

Chartarra put his feet upon the broken soil beneath his tent and argued with his vision. *I am no longer a follower of Sh'logath,* he insisted, reassuring himself. *I seek Maetha...*

His knees buckled below him and he fell back upon the cot. Chartarra tried again, slowly and more cautiously this time. He stumbled on weak legs as he fought off the impulse to seek out other members of the Black and form ranks. The last thing he recalled from the vision was Nitthogr looking directly into his eyes, a personal and empathetic gaze, and the sorcerer insisted in the vyrmic common tongue, [The time of Sh'logath is at hand. I draw near; prepare yourself for the Awakening. The Birthing is complete, and I am made new as the incarnate Acolyte of the Devourer! *You* will lead His revolt. The Black needs you, Chartarra. I go now to awaken our other brothers, long trapped in darkness and ready to make war.]

Chartarra shook off the villainous premonition and emerged from his tent. He spit, trying to get the taste of bile off of his tongue. So late in the night, the village path was clear of rovers; aisles between the tents of the nomadic maethans would typically remain clear into the early morning. He turned his head and locked eyes with the only other figure to emerge after the sorcerer's siren call: Klyrtan, the simpleton. The chief's son did not appear as equally sickened by the vision. He searched the trails for others and Chartarra slunk back into his dwelling unseen. Eventually, he heard the rustle of fabrics as Klyrtan did likewise.

What does it mean? Chartarra asked himself. Deep down, he felt sure of the portent's implications. *Nitthogr is alive... and something wicked is coming.*

Earth

Like a wraith, Sisyphus stalked through the house. It was an enormous and mostly empty place. He paused at a window and glanced out at the overlook featuring the expansive Lake Superior. White caps roiled upon the dark and distant water.

He sensed the two residents of the house, heard their muffled voices and felt the slight vibrations of old floors as they creaked. They were in a distant wing and down one flight of steps.

Sisyphus ran a finger through the accumulated dust upon a stair rail. Many things appeared untouched in years, at least on the top level of the two story home. He grinned and assumed the owners were elderly. *Probably don't do stairs well—this should be an easy job,* he thought. The home-owner's profile, according to property records in the Heptobscurantum's files, seemed to agree with that assumption.

Treading lightly, he descended the stairs as quietly as his bulk allowed and listened for the voices. They laughed and spoke in tones that indicated a belief that their privacy was secure.

Sisyphus paused at the bottom step. The voices were stronger than he expected from a geriatric resident: a woman's laughter sounded strong and confident. He cocked his head to get a better read. *Maybe the lady is the old man's nurse or a Meals on Wheels driver or something?*

A man's voice echoed two rooms down the hallway. He sounded young as well—if not young, certainly not elderly.

Sisyphus scowled. He was capable of taking on the Scholomance; two surprised opponents did not worry him, but it had been a while since he'd replenished his energies and he'd come here straight from interrogating Bwbych the Boggart. The big man hadn't come to fight, but rather to steal the amulets he'd heard might be here.

He prepared himself for the inevitable conflict and began walking towards the voices. Stacks of books reached waist high as they lined the hall. Curio cabinets and decorative shelves boasted knick-knacks from across the world and an oval picture frame displayed a photo of the elderly couple he'd expected to encounter: a black man with stubby white hair and a khaki vest hugged a white woman with silver hair and deep laugh lines. Another framed photo below that one had been taken at an archaeological dig site many years prior to the circular photo; the black man linked arms with a teenage Claire Jones and her father Sam.

Miles Jecima. Sisyphus put a name to the home-owner, though he was unsure who occupied the adjacent room.

Sisyphus wrapped his hands around the handle of his kophesh and prepared for the slaughter. He took a step towards the door and he paused. His footfall creaked beneath his weight on the old hardwood floors. Something caught his eye, and he looked downward at a buffet table next to the doorway.

An opened puzzle box rested atop the counter. Within it rested a collection of darquematter pendants.

Sisyphus grinned and snatched them up. He heard the stranger's footsteps approach from the other room and the wrestler headed into an adjacent one. He fingered the ear piece he wore, and it connected him to his partner.

"Hello? Is someone there?" the resident asked into the hall—the woman with a strong voice.

Sisyphus spoke quietly and moved swiftly. "Hey Doc. Get me a portal out of here."

The woman's steps approached with a cadence that indicated cautious suspicion. Sisyphus estimated she would not arrive in time. A triangular portal ripped open, and he stepped through, letting it wink out of existence again before he could be found.

He heard the lady's voice as it trailed off with the connection to that portal severed.

"Hello? Who's there—is that you, Mister Rath?"

The Prime

Nitthogr walked through the ancient tunnels of Vangandra; moving helped him shake off the fatigue his most recent act had thrust upon him. The tunnels wormed their way through the mountain that the monastery resided upon. He had access to Shjikara's memories, and so he knew how Zabe had met his grandfather, Shardai, in these tunnels.

He knew that the old Vangandran had died during a skirmish in one of his prison camps before the Battle of Nebraska. Shardai had caused the diversion that enabled Zabe and Claire to survive their attempted rescue of Bithia. The princess's sacrifice let them escape, but not before she murdered his Tarkhūn general, Regorik.

What Nitthogr hadn't known until he took Shjikara's body was that Shardai and his family kept a secret. They, along with the High Priest, knew that a hidden dimensional gate existed within the Vangandran catacombs.

Not even the vaunted dunnischktet explorer had known of that one. Zabe had used it to sneak back into the Prime after Nitthogr had placed guards at every portal site to prevent his access.

Nitthogr hadn't given much thought to Zabe's seeming disappearance. He hadn't even bothered to search for him beyond sending out feelers to locate him on the Prime. The sorcerer couldn't find him in this dimension—and the fact that Claire hadn't been able to reach him seemed to indicate he had planeswalked beyond his home. If so, it worked perfectly into Nitthogr's plans; this time he would do more than guard the dimensional doors—he would shut them down entirely—he'd bend them to his will so only he could use them.

For now, Nitthogr had a different purpose. Basilisk was always known as the Great Games-keeper, a master strategist who could not be beaten... but Nitthogr would bring pieces to the table that his brother did not know were in play.

He stepped onto the secret portal site. The sorcerer could feel the attunement hum within his spirit; the activation point called out to him and he felt the runic carvings on the rocky platform.

Nitthogr cut Shjikara's flesh and spilled a trickle of blood to power the arcane device. The subsequent portal split him to shreds at a molecular level, filling him with a cold, familiar lance of electric ice and simultaneously rebuilt him inside the Desolation realm.

He smelled ancient dust in the chamber. This place was familiar. The first time and last time he had seen it was before the merging—his name had been Keldric and the place had been glorious... and then Keldric died to birth Nitthogr—just like existence had to die in order to awaken Sh'logath.

The air was thick inside the old atrium, even though a section of the roof had been broken away; rubble littered the floor of the tomb-like facility. A breeze swirled through the ancient place where stony podiums rose above the sand-strewn floor. Many aisles of altars had been placed with the mummified bodies of the Thousand Elders laid to rest in torpor upon them.

Nitthogr looked down at the metal chair where the corrupted form of The Voice, or what was left of him, sat in cadaverous repose. The Voice was an honorary title—a kind of hold-over for the prophet role that the Sh'logath cult stole from the ancient religion that existed prior to them, and which the rovers still practiced. Nitthogr remembered the old vyrm; The Voice, who had been a part of his dunnischkte ceremony, his and Basilisk's both.

There was no longer meaning in this. *Sentiment was not the vyrm way*, he told himself.

Exiting the ceremonial chamber, he strolled out and into the streets of Straruck. The long dead city that become infested with carrion worms. Nitthogr let his terrifying aura extend as a ward to the vermin nearby to keep the lesser ones away, and then he called out to one nearby: a queen.

Rumbling towards him in the loose sand and scree, the massive beast answered his summons and crawled from the shadows, carried along by thousands of cilia-like legs. Nitthogr enslaved her mind with a burst of black sorcery. Docile to his touch, he leapt upon her chitinous, multi-segmented hide and stood upon the flat section of her head, taking a seat as if it were a saddle.

His worm surged forward and cleared the edge of the Straruck, dashing into the Plains of Neggath at speeds faster than most land vehicles were capable of producing in these badlands.

They rolled across jagged, glassine scree and copses of razorbrush shrubs. A short while later, Nitthogr arrived by wormback at the ghostly city of Sharonash: one more ruined town that suffered a total and catastrophic loss during the Syzygyc War. His mount stopped at the outskirts of Sharonash. Another territorial worm screeched a challenge in the distance and the ground rumbled as it charged for them, unseen except by worm senses.

Finally, it crested the soil and gave a blood-curdling screech.

Nitthogr shrieked a warning of his own in a language that the beast would understand. It halted dead in its tracks. The sorcerer howled again and the enemy vermin retreated to cower in the dark, afraid of whatever stronger predator it had dared challenge.

Beyond the edge of the Sharonash ruins, a vale sloped away; stone bodies littered the landscape where thousands of vyrm warriors had fallen to the Architect King and his Stone Glaive, the mythic blade now wielded by Zabe—wherever he may have gone.

This was the place where the war had ended so long ago. This was where Sh'logath's entry into reality had been halted. It was fitting that his return to this site would hasten his agod's arrival.

The sorcerer's mount ambled down into the midst of the petrified army and Nitthogr stood tall upon the creature's crest. He held high his stone fist.

"Hear me, brothers, sisters, loyal servants of the dark! You were each preserved for this very hour... a dark moment that our enemies do not even know is upon them."

He growled and exerted the power of the rune stone. Skin cracked and peeled. His sleeping army awoke, numbering thousands strong.

One vyrm in particular bore Nitthogr's face and dress. The impostor approached the true sorcerer and allowed his flesh to revert to its actual shape.

"Ah, Krenyr," Nitthogr welcomed him. "my loyal hunter. You were not destroyed in the war, after all." The talented shade had been sent on a diversion mission during the final battle.

"I was successful in the first task, my lord... I failed in the second." Krenyr bowed. He was supposed to have lured the Architect King in with the promise of peace talks. Once he was close enough, Krenyr was supposed to have plunged his dagger into the heart of their enemy.

"Do not worry, my friend. There will be more opportunities to strike from the shadows—especially for a shade as talented and irreplaceable as you. I have rescued you for this very purpose, and you alone possess the power to redeem yourself in the eyes of Sh'logath."

The sorcerer conjured a shape out of light and molded it into the face of Respan the scientist. "This man must die, secretly. Make sure none are suspicious of the death, not for several days, at least. We shall need some time to prepare without more prying eyes." He figured he should explain, "Respan has developed a technology that allows its wearers to see auras from darque-born creatures, including vyrm. He could potentially unmask every shade with its use, and we are not yet ready to step out from the shadows."

Krenyr's face took the shape of Respan. "I think I would like to take a holiday... perhaps visit the crystal sea and reflect upon the grandeur of the universe. I'll be gone for some time... hold all my packages, please," he spoke with a slightly foppish tone.

Nitthogr smiled. "Perfect. As usual."

Krenyr took a knee and bowed, the first among the reclaimed vyrm. "For the sake of my own redemption in the eyes of the

Devourer, you have my allegiance. Krenyr the Hunter is at your service," he hissed.

Earth

Wiltshire yawned to reset the pressure building between his ears as the private jet descended towards the small, regional airport. He re-examined the short message from his contact, Tay-lore. The detective silently thanked both the Hepobscurantum and the Canon Foundation, which had made him rich enough to afford things like last minute private jets to Duluth, Minnesota, even if he'd had to blackmail them to get the cash they owed him for services rendered.

Tay-lore's last line bothered him. *Get to the coordinates immediately; I am sending a package with a followup message and more details. Life or death importance!*

He'd never heard Tay-lore speak so forcefully or urgently. *This might be the only time I've ever seen him use an exclamation mark,* Wiltshire thought, and they'd been communicating for years off and on.

The detective felt the weighty bulge of his sidearm and absent-mindedly checked that all of his magazines were in their place. He had known Tay-lore long enough to guess that, whatever he was, he was not a human. Wiltshire never breached etiquette and asked. He merely prepared for the situation to turn foul.

He scrolled back up and read the digital message. Tay-lore had laid out a map for a system of astral gates and alternate dimensions. The whole network was mind boggling, but the individual pieces of the puzzle lined up with things that Wiltshire already knew to be true, even if they each seemed far-fetched enough to sound crazy to any folk not wearing tinfoil hats.

The plane touched down with expert ease as he continued reading and a few minutes later, Wiltshire found his rental car and sped downtown, where he found an abandoned church at Tay-lore's coordinates. The old cathedral had been boarded up and scraps of police tape still fluttered against the door, though the brittleness of the plastic suggested they'd been out in the elements for well-over a year.

Wiltshire stood atop the stairs in the entry and fingered the yellow plastic barrier. A scrap of tape broke easily and fell to the concrete when a tiny symbol engraved there caught the detective's eye: a seven-pointed star.

"The Heptobscurantum... I should have known," he said, pushing his way through the doors. The fall chill was brisk and so he shut the way behind him.

His footsteps echoed through the sanctuary. Pews were scattered and left in disarray. Forensic markers lay where they'd been forgotten, circling brown stains and indicating bullet holes and angles of shots.

Wiltshire remembered reading about the church massacre a few years back. The crime had never been solved. Guessing that with the Seven's involvement, it never would be.

He continued his walk up to the lectern; Wiltshire shoved aside a podium and found what Tay-lore had sent him after: some kind of drone. Two pincer-like vices were mounted on its undercarriage and one of them clutched a busted flute of glass.

Besides the clamp-like grips, it had a compartment hatch that he had to force open. He disconnected and removed a display device that was internally affixed to the drone.

"Huh. Looks like a small iPad or something," Wiltshire said aloud. He took a seat on a derelict pew and activated the display.

A blank humanoid face greeted him. It looked more like a mannequin than a person. "Greetings," the recording said, "I am Tay-lore. I apologize for the hastiness and nature of my message and hope that my appearance does not startle you... I would assume that by now you had suspected that I was not entirely like you..."

"Understatement of the year there, buddy," Wiltshire mumbled.

He nodded along as Tay-lore explained the network of astronomically linked portal projectors that tied to the lunar and solar phases through a series of complicated algorithms. Wiltshire noted that Tay-lore's body never moved aside from his face. *It's some kind of video simulation with a manufactured voice transmitting data... more like one of those auto-readers for the blind than an actual video recording.*

"So this isn't even a recording," Wiltshire sighed.

"Not exactly," Tay-lore responded.

Wiltshire blinked. "Wait. What?"

"I am a limited but interactive AI interface that Tay-lore quickly encoded for you. My name is Beta-lore, an extension of Tay-lore's mind, and all that now remains of him."

"Huh? What do you mean—what happened to Tay-lore?"

"The video of his fate is what follows. I represent a limited subset of data that he chose to send to you in the final seconds before his demise," Beta-lore said. "He certainly would have helped you locate your thief, and the stolen page. The page's thief is not unknown to us."

"I don't understand," Wiltshire said, dragging a hand through his shaggy hair. "Why did he send all of this to me, of all people?"

"You two had history," said the program. "Tay-lore knew that you could find anything, given the right resources. You are tenacious, committed, and loyal. He'd hoped that these combinations of traits which he, too, admired, would mean you would help stop the great and coming destruction."

"What do you mean—the Solomonari? This wizard who attacked the Scholomance? The Heptobscurantums' Seven?"

Beta-Lore merely stared. He issued a beeping noise. "Unfamiliar terms," he reported.

"Ok, then, what did he mean?" Wiltshire asked.

"An evil far greater than what is known on Earth, except from scholars of obscure works. Sh'logath rises and his Acolyte has returned from the void. Nitthogr."

Wiltshire drew his lips together thinly. He'd heard both names before, but knew only scraps of lore. He was sure that the program could fill in the gaps. After all, it was part of Tay-lore's purpose in sending the carrier drone, right? *The purpose... the purpose... what am I forgetting?*

He remembered. "Tay-lore needed me to find something; what is it?"

"There is a device left inside of the drone. It will help you find the only person who we believe can stop Nitthogr from wiping out all life from each of the thirty-three dimensions of the multi-verse," Beta-lore stated. The screen filled with a series of still images of a man.

"He looks suspiciously like the kid I am chasing... the guy who stole a Codex Gigas page from Old Man Wainsmith's sealed vault," Wiltshire stated.

"Tay-lore believed that your quarry is this man's wayward brother. He was lost some time ago and may have fallen in with malefactors, since. You must find Zabe, the older brother. Zabe can help you find Zurrah and help you retrieve your lost page, after you stop Nitthogr, that is."

Wiltshire raised a brow. "Hold up. Tay-lore was always better at finding stuff than I was... why can't he find this Zabe guy? I've got a lot on my plate already between ancient strigoi, my parter's murder, and some kind of wizard interfering with his triangle-based portal magic."

"Because Tay-lore is dead," Beta-lore said with a hint of snark. "Surely your species also stops functioning when your life ceases to—"

Wiltshire interrupted the cheeky AI. "That's not what I meant. I mean, *why did this Zabe guy leave—where did he go?*"

"Zabe left on his own terms and in mourning after his father was murdered by one of his apprentices. Much has transpired in a matter of so few weeks. Zabe does not know that the Tesseract is again in peril—or that the woman he loves is in grave danger. If he knew..."

"Yeah, yeah," Wiltshire grumbled. "Alright. I'll look into it, but I don't know where to begin."

A schematic came on screen with a picture of an eyepiece scanner that appeared like something from a Google tech lab. Beta-lore explained that the device could help locate and track individuals that gave off a Darque aura.

"It will only work when Zabe is shape-shifted into his lycan form. He otherwise looks like he does in his photos and reads as normal through the sensor," Beta-lore instructed.

"Of course he's got to be a werewolf," Wiltshire muttered, mounting the sensor over his brow and activating it.

Beta-lore continued, "Tay-lore knew it would be a long shot, but strongly felt that you were all of reality's best hope to find Zabe and warn him of the High Priest's betrayal."

"What betrayal?" Wiltshire asked. Not all the pieces had come together for him yet. He looked up and got a very strong reading on Respan's scanner.

"Did you not watch all the materials yet?"

Wiltshire clicked to lock onto the aura's location. It was not far, and he hoped he'd gotten lucky—he did just fly halfway across the country, after all, and would love for the mission to be a short one. "Of course I didn't. You should know that. I only turned you on like ten minutes ago."

"Shall I show you the final footage Tay-lore attached?"

"Go ahead."

Video played from the drone's point of view. It sat silent and inert, motionless on the shelf as a secret observer not tied to any main systems.

The occult detective watched the monitor for several minutes. Wiltshire blanched at what he saw. He'd just finally learned his long-distance friend's face and then watched as it was violently ruined.

Video captured the whole grisly scene and the attempted cover up as Tay-lore's murderer erased any surveillance footage in the security files and then destroyed most of the tech connected to the central computer where Tay-lore had operated from before his killer had entered. The drone had been left on a shelf across the room, neatly tucked away.

At the end, the motion lights eventually went dark in the room and the drone lifted from its perch. Using its pincer hands, it snatched a vial of blood from one of the science labs many sample bays and flew to a portal location several miles away. The drone descended rapidly and shook as it bounced off the ground with an intentionally bad landing to bust the glass tube and activate the portal with the blood it carried. The video flashed and then ended with a glitchy shot of graphics as the device planeswalked.

"I've got to find this Zabe guy," Wiltshire said breathlessly, the footage of the murder still fresh in his mind.

Chapter Eleven

Desolation

Caivev strolled through the Limbus streets. She felt something that bordered on contentment as she walked, flanked by her guards from both the Black and Tarkhūn factions.

Skrom kept near as he always did.

"The Dead City," Caivev said with bewilderment.

Skrom looked down at her. "Huh?"

She shook her head. "Nothing... just something they say about Limbus in the Prime." Rows and rows of trimmed houses packed neat within the grid-work of streets and culverts. The Limbus she'd come to know was entirely different from the one folks thought they knew in the Prime dimension.

True, something had killed the human life in this plane long ago, maybe even the vyrm were responsible for that, but old Edenya had welcomed the foreigners from the Darque. And she knew that Limbus was anything but dead.

Things grew quieter as they walked deeper down the hillside and towards the edges of town. The uppermost layers of Limbus belonged mostly to Tarkhūn families. House size shrank and styles became less artistic as they meandered further from the center. Homes became more uniform as they went further down the slope; they'd passed into quadrants where citizens of the Black were the majority.

In the proletariat districts, a noticeable silence blanketed the neighborhoods. The Black, as a people, were less boisterous than their tarkhūn brothers and sisters. Though the houses were smaller and tended to be single story as earthen hut-like dwellings, light poured from windows and modern conveniences were easily spotted if you knew where to look.

Heads popped up in windows. A child waved with big eyes and a scaly grin. Caivev waved back. The district was casted such that visitors of any renown were uncommon in it.

All heads turned to the noise at a nearby intersection. A group of Black vyrm dragged a woman and her child through the streets.

"Stop," Caivev commanded.

They either did not hear her or refused her order. Skrom stepped into their midst. His size and booming voice finally got their attention, "Lady Caivev said stop!"

One of the vyrm hissed. "We are on a mission of law," he said. The ruffians finally spotted Caivev and recognized her. They bowed briefly and remained at one knee, still holding their prey in clutches of hair and flesh.

"Apologies, we did not recognize you," claimed another. "The heir apparent of Nitthogr will always be obeyed by the Black."

Caivev nodded and signaled for them to stand, even if something distasteful about her past allegiances lingered in her mouth. She recognized that her zeal for the old ways had lessened since her marriage, but especially so in the last couple of weeks. "What do you have here? What is your mission?"

Their leader stood. "I am Jeerzha, leader of the Limbus Hunters Guild," he stated proudly.

"I have not heard of you. Do you often hunt women and children?" Caivev asked with a disguised disdain.

Jeerzha's lips curled to reveal his sharp teeth. "No. We hunt Seekers of Maetha! It is known that you have done the same in the past. It is more than sport to us... we do this in honor and service to Sh'logath!"

Caivev watched Jeerzha; she'd once possessed similar fanaticism. Turning her eyes to the woman, she asked, "How do you know she is a Seeker? She does not look like a rover."

"We are not *all* rovers, my lady," the woman admitted. "I have lived all my life in Limbus."

"You say *we*, so what... you just decided to change your beliefs?" Caivev asked.

The woman nodded measuredly. "I was raised in a lie. Truth *discovered me*, and I chose to accept it. He can verify." She looked at one of the vyrm males who held her captive.

He snarled, "My wife is no liar—whatever else she may be. But heresy cannot stand."

Jeerzha turned his attention back to Caivev. "The heretics must be purged. The law commands it. We only await the order... we were on our way to see High Priest Charsk and fulfill our commission... but *you* are the leader of the Black—you could grant it?"

"Must we kill them?" Caivev asked.

"The writings are clear." Jeerzha stiffened. "Death sentences are common, but not demanded as punishment." He looked at Caivev's honor guard and sized them up.

Caivev gave them each a glance from the corner of her eyes. The Tarkhūn seemed indifferent, but members of the Black clearly sympathized with Jeerzha. She *had* noticed that the lesser faction had grown unruly these last couple of days, but she couldn't reason why.

Jeerzha continued, "What do you say that we should do with them? We are one vyrmkind now, but these Tarkhūn have been content to dwell in Limbus for generations and have refused to stamp them out from the outlier lands. Basilisk's apathy has been the same as leniency! But what do *you* say, leader of the Black?" He stared at her, awaiting an answer.

Caivev looked into the eyes of the woman prisoner and her child, who clearly shared his mother's beliefs. She felt compassion for her and remembered being rescued by rovers at Sharonash; she had hoped she could repay that debt in some small part. "Woman. Would you forsake Maetha in return for sparing your life?"

Her voice trembled, and she hugged her young son to her side. "I am sorry, my lady, but I cannot."

Caivev looked from face to face in the small mob. She could tell that something was brewing—something larger than this mere encounter. Bloodlust had already set in the eyes of Jeerzha and his peers; they were ready to break free at a moment's notice. Only violence would abate them.

"Then your judgment is pronounced," Caivev said. "Jeerzha, do as you wish with her."

"Kill her!" howled the woman's husband.

Jeerzha yelled, "For Sh'logath! Hail the mighty Devourer!"

The Maethan woman and child barely uttered a peep as the mob tore them to pieces. Caivev walked stoically past, turning at the intersection to a path that rose back towards the center of Limbus.

She could not shake the foreboding feeling that something significant stirred in her people: something that she did not yet know or understand.

Earth

Sisyphus smiled as if returning home after a long time away. The groggy bodies of sedated men and women barely responded as he triumphantly entered the room.

A row of them stood along the wall, propped up by the restraints and arranged like mummies. They looked shaggy and downtrodden, like homeless vagrants stolen from off the street; nobody ever asked Doctor Walther where he collected his subjects that supplied power to the portal device. Thin tubes connected to their arms and drew blood away as needed to operate the dimensional splitter.

The blood donors barely stirred as Sisyphus entered the room; he passed through their chamber and into the adjacent room. Sisyphus wasn't there for them, anyhow. He was there for the scrawny man chained to the bed in the center of a private room.

"My guest of honor," Sisyphus roused him. "I'm glad you're awake to see what we're accomplishing.

Sisyphus's doppelganger looked up at him and his eyes barely focused. The restrained man looked like the wrestler's identical twin, except that his muscles had atrophied and he was unshaven.

"Lookie here," said the hulking brute. Sisyphus brandished the collection of darquematter amulets. "Soon I will be the most powerful creature on the planet. Ain't nothing can stop me—especially as long as I have your blood to keep me going strong, Jarfig."

Professor Jarfig met his gaze, keenly aware of the pain in his arm where the bleeder contraption harvested his life energies. "I... I won't let you do this."

"Heh. You're in no condition to stop me, weakling." Sisyphus looked down at the withered version of himself. Even before being captured from the Prime dimension, the wrestler had scorned his Prime version. Deep down he condescended any who didn't strive for peak physical perfection—at least he loathed his own dimensional variant.

"Nobody's coming to save you, Professor. You're mine... and you're too weak to do anything about it."

Jarfig looked into Sisyphus's eyes. The wrestler found the connection unnerving.

"I'm stronger than you realize," Jarfig insisted.

"You're the weakest version of us," Sisyphus argued, more loudly than necessary.

A glimmer formed in Jarfig's eye; he knew he'd rattled the big man. "Not all strength comes from the human muscle," he insisted.

Sisyphus scowled and then hit a button on the bleeder machine, ordering it to draw an unsafe amount.

Jarfig gasped and then lost consciousness.

The Desolation

Chartarra sat in the leadership circle along with a few others. Something weighty about the responsibility of being in the assembly pressed against his thoughts.

Klewdahar, who had organized this council, was there, along with Trenzlr and Gerjha. "Much is happening," Klewdahar said. "Brothers, we are in the midst of the greatest days. I expect that, based on Gerjha's prophesies, we shall be the generation that sees the dawn of Maetha and the restoration of Edenya."

A murmur of assent rippled through the room.

Klewdahar continued, "We are here, each picked because of our unique background, experience, or knowledge, to make sure that we guide our people into the truth as effectively and as strategically as possible. We know that Maetha uses individuals for his purposes, like how he has spoken through Gerjha."

Trenzlr piped up. "I am honored that you thought of me for your council," he said, "but I do not feel worthy to..."

Klewdahar interrupted him. "Duly noted. You and every other one here has issued that same objection. I would not accept your resignation if it was offered. If you are here, now, it is from a basis of responsibility—not because of vanity."

Trenzlr nodded and relaxed into his seated posture.

Chartarra sat forward. "I have an issue we should discuss."

All eyes looked at him.

"You all know my story. I was a soldier of the Black before Maetha found me; working directly below Caivev, I had great influence and authority, and I should have died in the refuse pits beyond Limbus. Like so many others, I followed Caivev's leadership as a fanatical loyalist of Sh'logath... until everything changed.

This has never happened to me before, but two nights ago I had a vision while I slept."

"A dream?" one of the older Seekers asked.

"This was not a dream," Chartarra said. "I wonder if anyone else reported a vision? Based on its nature, I believe I am not alone in receiving it, and that it foretells a great evil that is calling out, trying to seduce soldiers for its cause."

"What do you mean?" Klewdahar asked for clarification.

"Nitthogr has returned, at least in this vision. I fear it may be more than a metaphor—he might actually be back. He claimed to be the incarnate Acolyte of Sh'logath and is rallying for war." Chartarra swallowed audibly. "I felt compelled to muster with his other agents. Before I was fully awake and could resist the impulse, I found myself outside in the morning dawn. Based on that, I do think I represent a liability to this circle and hope you will reconsider my resignation."

Klewdahar frowned. "You resisted?"

Chartarra nodded.

"Then you belong to Maetha and not Sh'logath. I will not release you from service."

Chartarra bobbed his head and spoke with measured words. "There is one more thing, Chief Klewdahar." He chose his words carefully as all hung on each one. "In the streets, there was one other person. I saw the madness in his eyes, his devotion to the agod."

"Who was it?" an older member of the tribe asked.

"Klyrtan was there."

All eyes moved to Klewdahar.

"Well... I'm sure that was a mere coincidence," Klewdahar stammered. "He was probably up early looking for Hirdac. He sometimes does that. He's a good kid. I'm sure anyone who's spent time with him would attest that he's a good Maethan, right Trenzlr?"

Trenzlr stiffened, somehow called on to provide character witness for the boy he'd wronged decades ago. Klewdahar looked at him in such a way that he felt dread and guilt for his part in Klyrtan's stupefying as a child. "Klyrtan is simple," he said. "It must be as Chief Klewdahar says."

Reluctant nods circulated the room, all except for Gerjha the Prophet, who took everything in with cold indifference.

"What I am most interested in discussing is the prophecy that Maetha may come to us as a dunnischktet," Klewdahar said.

"It cannot possibly be Basilisk, and Nitthogr is dead," said the Seeker on the far side of the circle.

Another asked, "What of the new one, the third dunnischktet, this Caivev?"

Chartarra perked up. "Excuse me, what? Caivev is dunnischkte?"

Nods answered him. "Even I had heard that," said Trenzlr, "and I spent most of these last couple of years hiding in the Prime."

Chartarra looked from face to face, trying to guess at the accuracy of such a rumor. The nomadic rovers did not have a clear supply of information. "If this is true, then I must visit her," he insisted.

Klewdahar furrowed his brow. "I'm not sure that it is a good idea to..."

"But if there is a prophecy saying that she could become a tool of Maetha, someone must go. Perhaps this is how it happens—how she is turned away from evil."

Other faces from the circle looked at Klewdahar, daring to hope that Chartarra could be right.

Klewdahar's face softened. "You are still so new to us, Chartarra. You may be right, but..."

"But nothing. It has to be me. I was loyal to her for years, and now, out of our number, only I have a chance of getting through to her. This is why Maetha spared me from these fatal wounds—it is my purpose; He has been preparing me for this task."

The others looked at him. None spoke, but they all clearly thought the same outcome was likely.

Trenzlr finally spoke up. "You will almost certainly die. She is married to Basilisk, now. The task is insurmountable... but the rewards could be that much greater."

"Even if I die," said Chartarra, "I will be like a seed going into the ground. Perhaps it will bloom into something far better."

"Fine," said Klewdahar. "But take a team with you. If you die, we will want a report of it so we know how to proceed in regard to the Empress."

Chartarra nodded.

"I will go with him," said Trenzlr. "We will find two others and form a company of secret travelers." He turned and embraced his cousin.

"Maetha's blessings," Gerjha said.

Klewdahar bit his lip, but nodded in agreement.

Trenzlr and Chartarra rose and departed at once.

Earth

Shandra took a step backwards to the door and motioned for Sam to hand her the hammer she'd left in the room. He recognized the worried look on her face and tip-toed over with the weapon.

He marveled at its weight as he hefted it, but knew that she'd learned to wield it expertly under Master Druen. Sam followed her down the hall as she called out, stalking whoever had invaded their privacy. "Is that you Mister Rath?"

She stepped past the threshold of the room where she suspected an intruder might have retreated, but found nothing. Shandra walked a circle and checked any potential hiding places before returning to the hall.

"I'm not going crazy, am I? Did you hear it?"

He looked down to avoid eye contact. *Maybe a little crazy.* He hadn't heard a thing. "Um, Shandra," he asked, "you didn't move the amulets that Miles had been collecting for Claire, did you?"

She shook her head and joined him at the buffet table where the puzzle box sat empty. Someone *had* been there and he or she had stolen the artifacts.

Sam believed her intruder theory and whirled, startled when someone knocked at the door, making him jump. He rested a hand on his chest to calm his rapid heart and motioned for Shandra to lower her weapon, or at least hold it out of sight.

He walked to the door and checked the peephole before opening it. "Can I help you?"

The man outside barged into the house at the first opportunity. "Where is he? I'm looking for someone named Zabe."

Sam tilted his head and took stock of the new invader. He was a slightly unkempt man, average build but with a strong frame; his haggard appearance looked more like the product of over-productive, sleepless nights than poor hygiene. The archaeologist recognized Respan's darque scanner mounted above his brow. "Who are you? How do you know Zabe and Respan?"

The man paused to meet Sam's gaze. He stated flatly, "I don't know them. Tay-lore sent me to stop the end of the world, or something like that."

"Tay-lore?" Shandra asked. "Is something wrong at home? How is he?"

"Tay-lore's dead," he said with a cold edge. "He was my friend and now he's gone." He stuck out a hand and introduced himself. "I'm Vikrum Wiltshire."

Sam wiggled a finger near his face to indicate the wearable tech. "A mutual friend of mine and Tay-lore's built this; his name was Respan. How did you get it?"

"Tay-lore sent it to me. He said I needed to find a werewolf named Zabe or Nitthogr would rise."

Both Sam and Shandra froze when he named the enemy. They looked at him like a deer in the headlights and so Wiltshire continued talking.

He tapped the side of the lensed reticle. "This thing indicated a strong signal here, and it was close from the place where Tay-lore sent it…"

"The gate at the old church?" Shandra clarified.

Wiltshire nodded. "I had hoped that the signal might have been this Zabe…"

Sam interrupted this time. "He is my daughter's fiance; Zabe disappeared a little while ago. He needed some time to himself—some space—and we allowed him to have it."

"I'm sure she must be so happy," Wiltshire snarked, trying to complete his thoughts. "It was only a few minutes ago when I activated this thing. Right before I got to the house, the signal disappeared completely. It just blipped out of existence."

Shandra and Sam turned to each other. "The thief," she growled.

Wiltshire leaned in conspiratorially. "I'm chasing a thief as well. Yours doesn't happen to travel through a high-tech triangle portal that can create doors through the fabric of time and space?"

Sam gave him a wild-eyed look. "Space."

"Excuse me?" Wiltshire said.

"Just space. It doesn't time travel."

"So you know the guy? Tay-lore told me he was Zabe's younger brother," Wiltshire said.

"Zurrah is alive?" Sam exclaimed; he and Shandra exchanged optimistic glances. "Maybe it's a clue to Zabe's whereabouts!"

Shandra calmed him down and told their new companion, "Zurrah is not *our* thief. There is a man, a member of a group called the Heptobscurantum…"

"I'm familiar with them," Wiltshire interjected.

"Their leader, a wizard named Jacob Sisyphus, controls one of these machines. They can open holes between places, even between dimensions, but they come at a terrible cost," she nodded to Sam.

Sam bobbed his head. "I was hooked up to one of the earliest versions, connected to a bleeder contraption. Much like the dimensional gates that power the planeswalking portals that brought that device to you from our mutual friend, it requires blood magic to activate. I can't imagine the constant supply required for Sisyphus's continued use of it."

Shandra shrugged, "Although Respan once hypothesized that it needs less if you have a more potent source, like a prisoner taken from the Prime."

"Jenner's father... Professor Jarfig?" Sam speculated.

Shandra nodded.

Wiltshire looked back and forth, not really following the conversation or those names he failed to recognize.

"One thing is certain," Sam said. "If Sisyphus stole the amulets from our house, they must be reclaimed. If he wants them, it can only be for ill purposes."

"But *after* we find Zabe and return to the Prime," Shandra insisted.

"There might not be a Prime left, if Tay-lore was right," Wiltshire interrupted what began to feel like a private side conversation.

Sam grimaced. "He must have been wrong. Tay-lore is smart, but not infallible. He can be tricked into certain routines—he's almost *more* fallible in that regard."

"He's also dead," Wiltshire reminded him.

"I'm sure you must be mistaken," Sam stated. Besides, we know that Nitthogr is dead, annihilated by Sh'logath the Devourer. He's not just dead and gone—he was pulled into a void that lies beyond existence."

Shandra explained the reluctance to take Wiltshire at his word, "Tay-lore is the last member of *homo diurnus*, a race that almost defeated humanity in a great war two generations ago. Surely, he could fend off an enemy. In that era, it took three of my order, highly trained members of the Merciful Hammer, to take down just one android."

Wiltshire swallowed the dryness in his throat and turned over the reader. "Beta-lore, play video," was all he said.

Tay-lore only glanced once at the camera that recorded him, as if to say goodbye to those watching his final moments. He turned and began working at Respan's computer terminal. He composed a message when the mist crept in from the hallway.

The android stood straight and turned to meet the individual who lurked beyond. Shjikara entered the room. "I see you're reporting on me."

"No. I was just working on a report to..."

"You're lying. I can read the message from here. You're a terrible liar." The High Priest strolled into the room and read the message aloud. "'Do not trust Shjikara. He is not what he seems. He is actually...'" He turned to face the automaton. "You did not finish your message. What am I?"

Tay-lore struggled to put his words together. His fear seemed very real, even if he wasn't supposed to have had emotions. "I was merely..."

"What am I!" Shjikara shut him up with an angry shout.

Tay-lore slumped and admitted. "I saw you. You are Nitthogr."

No sooner did he say the name than the man's flesh shifted and took the form of the long-gone sorcerer. Only his one fist remained stone, and he leapt for Tay-lore in a rage.

The robot whirled to his side and unfurled twin laser cannons from each forearm. They blasted with brilliant bolts of energy that passed through the sorcerer, who exploded into a mist and instantly reformed into solid mass behind him.

Nitthogr grabbed and hurled Tay-lore across the room with uncanny speed and strength. Tay-lore crashed through a bank of lab equipment. He tried to right himself, but Nitthogr was already upon him, smashing him with his stone fist and driving massive dents into the armored sections of his body.

Tay-lore scrambled and tried to get away, but his enemy tore one of his arms free and chucked it across the room where it toppled a tray full of tech gadgets. "Guards! Someone help," his monotone voice elevated to broadcast at maximum volume.

"Fool," Nitthogr laughed as he grappled with him. "I have already cast a spell of silence over this area. None outside this room will hear you."

The monster leaned in close and gloated. "You all think you are so smart. I broke the Guardian Corps with a simple traitor—and you locked up the wrong one as soon as you suspected him. How it made my heart sing to watch the hope dying in poor Jenner's eyes… and to know that the traitor was his lover all along? The irony is delicious—even the true Shjikara, as self-centered as he was, would have noticed the shade's marking and prevented this madness," the beast cackled as he wrenched on his prisoner's mechanical joints.

"You did not fool us all," the automaton insisted. Tay-lore's servos whined as he tried to break free from Nitthogr's grasp. With his one remaining arm, he grabbed a loose cord and lassoed it around the sorcerer's neck.

Nitthogr could not free himself without releasing his prey, and Tay-lore tightened the cable and began to strangle the villain. The enemy's arm suddenly burst into a writhing mass of tentacles; they coiled around Tay-lore's head and each of his knees as they pulled, meeting force with greater force.

Tay-lore actually yelled, cried out with pain simulated by his subroutines. His shriek twisted in pitch and warbled and then suddenly went silent. His chassis gave way and the sorcerer, who was now more a mass of prehensile appendages than anything else, cackled, strewing broken parts of the loyal automaton through the room. Whitish effluence bled from his synthetic internal organs and blackened hydraulic fluid sprayed from his limbs in spurts.

Nitthogr drew himself back together and sank to his knees, mounted over Tay-lore's severed head. The victim's body laid nearby, ripped open and separated into pieces. Returning to Shjikara's form, the attacker brought his stone fist down like a club and crushed Tay-lore's head with a resounding thud.

After wiping himself mostly clean, he composed himself as if nothing had happened. Shjikara wiped all the data banks clean in the lab's computer terminals. He deleted everything in the system and then smashed it with surprising ease.

The monster looked across the contents of the room to take the final measure of it. His eyes swept over the shelves where the drone rested in what looked to be a deactivated mode. They passed over and took no note of the recording device. Finally, Shjikara turned and left.

A long pause followed. Several minutes passed on the video feed. The lights went out, and then the drone awakened into a fully active mode. It hovered over to the far wall where several vials of blood were racked in a cryosuite; it used a grappler to retrieve one, and then it fled into the night, bearing the last record of Tay-lore and the extinction of *homo diurnus*.

Vikrum Wiltshire ended the replay mode. Nobody could speak for a few moments after witnessing such violence that the sorcerer had visited upon their friend.

Shandra's face twisted into a mask of rage. "We've got to stop him... that *liar!* Shjikara is bad enough, but we've been dealing with an impostor for who knows how long now?"

"Yes. We'll stop him, alright," Wiltshire insisted, "but let's do it like he asked. Tay-lore said we've got to find Zabe. You saw him, this Nitthogr guy is crazy powerful. We're going to need all the help we can get."

"We have a whole army at our disposal," Shandra insisted, hefting her hammer. "We must planeswalk at the first available portal," she said.

"Three armies, actually," Sam said, agreeing with her. He snatched a notebook where he kept a chart detailing the astral alignments.

"You don't think Tay-lore knew all that? He still insisted I find Zabe. Tay-lore sacrificed himself to make sure I got that message."

Sam looked Wiltshire in the eyes. They burned with unmatched urgency. "You don't think I know that? That... that... thing has access to my daughter. Right now, she's trapped in another dimension and doesn't know the danger she's in! I'm going with Shandra, and we're going to stop that thing. You can come or you can stay—but if Zabe's not around to protect her, then *I will*. That's what fathers do!"

Wiltshire stared Sam down long and hard. Finally, he cursed and looked away. "Fine." He took out and checked his hand gun before re-holstering it. "But you're going to need all the help you can get."

Shandra flung open the door. "And then you can help us take down the Heptobscurantum after we stop the sorcerer. I don't know what part they play in all of this, but I'm pretty tired of this whole damned Sh'logath cult. First we exile Nitthogr, and then we burn them to the ground."

Wiltshire followed the others outside. "Sounds like a tall order. How bout after that we kill some strigoi? You guys are going to owe me one after all this."

Chapter Twelve

The Prime

  Oh, Zabe... where are you? Bithia wondered, *Everything is falling apart without you!*

She stood next to Shjikara at the edge of the carnage in Respan's lab. The poor scientist had found his friend shortly after dawn. He'd already spent the bulk of the morning with a grief counselor; the savageness of the murder had emotionally ruined the poor inventor.

Several investigators from the military peacekeepers scoured the room, buzzing around Chira, their chief. Tahnak was also on site and Gita had followed as well. The short girl had given Bithia a tearful hug. She shrank back slightly when she spotted Shjikara.

The high priest turned about the room, his face twisted with grief.

Confronted with the barbarity of the murder, the princess teetered between rage and a fugue. She only seemed to catch snippets of conversation between bouts of sheer terror. *The murder happened just down the hall from the royal keep. Who could get in here and do this?* She glanced sidelong at Shjikara and wondered if Tay-lore's Veritas sympathies were part of the reason... *Tay-lore had accompanied her to that AVA rally—maybe he'd been marked for death because of it?*

Tahnak pulled Chira aside and mentioned that the security footage and all logs surrounding the time of death had been deleted. "It may have been someone with rank who is responsible... someone who has system access killed our friend."

Shjikara leaned in close to Bithia and Claire and speculated, "We can really only trust us three."

"What about Chira and Tahnak?" Bithia asked, eyeing the two as they talked in the corner of the room, trying to determine motive and method for the murder.

"How well do you really know them?" Shjikara wondered, keeping his voice low. "Tahnak *did* try to kill you on at least one prior occasion, and Chira's background is... interesting," he said, as if he had access to secret information.

He knows about Chira's family, Claire thought.

Shjikara continued, "Were it not for the heavy losses our forces took during Nitthogr's invasion some time back, he never would have climbed the ranks or even been allowed into the Guardian Corps. His mother and father were excommunicated as heretics by my predecessor."

Bithia surreptitiously watched Chira. She'd read the dossiers and knew that the part about Chira's parents was true. He might have been overlooked for service otherwise, but Nitthogr's invasion *did* happen, and he was the best they had—battle tested and approved.

"My dear princess," Shjikara said with words dripping both honey and caution in a grandfatherly way, "You must take care to always guard yourself. There are many who would seek to take advantage of this opportune moment with Zabe's absence. Keep your friends close."

I need you, Zabe... and you too, Claire...

Chira interrupted her thoughts. "What are we discussing over here?"

"Oh, uh..." Bithia jumbled her words.

Shjikara stepped in for the save. "Tay-lore was a true friend and faithful servant: loyal beyond all doubt. This is a true tragedy," he said. "I'm wondering if we've looked into the domestic terrorism angle. I've heard of some anti-Veritas talk in the past," he eyed Chira knowingly.

Chira stiffened, guessing from the High Priest's tone that he wondered if Chira had some inside information given his family's sordid history concerning the AVA. "I promise to look into it," he stated flatly.

"You know," Shjikara continued, "Tay-lore had worked closely with us and our agent Shandra on the Trenzlr situation. The AVA is opposed to any vyrm alliances; our kind treatment of the displaced Seeker of Maetha was met with hostility from them ever since news of it leaked to the public."

"I'm not sure how this connects to—"

Shjikara talked over Chira, directing his words to the princess. "I would feel more comfortable if we could get a member of the Guardian Corps appointed as a liaison between the Veritas and the military? It would help handle these kinds of concerns in a timely fashion? I fear the violence will only increase after... all this," he nodded his head to the dismembered remains of Tay-lore.

Tahnak had joined them by now. "I think I can make some arrangements."

"Would you consider Gita, Princess?" Shjikara asked. "Since our meeting, I have come to trust her completely."

Gita bristled at the request. Standing around the gory scene, nobody noticed.

Bithia barely heard the cleric. She'd been staring at the ruined face of her friend, half-crushed by some blunt object. Bithia waved her hand, absentmindedly granting his simple request.

I know you must have a good reason to remain away for so long, Zabe, but it's the worst possible timing.

Jenner sat on the cot in his cell. The walls were plain. His sheets were drab. Even his prisoner jumpsuit was gray.

He stared at his hands and flexed them, seething with anger. Jenner knew he was innocent—he'd been set up, and now his commanding officer, a man who he looked up to like a brother, believed he was a traitor and a murderer. His eye twitched, and he heard the clanking of steel gates down the hall.

Jenner looked up when the door opened. Gita walked in. As soon as their eyes met, she turned them to the floor.

She still couldn't look at him. Gita took her seat in the lone chair in the aisle outside of his cell. Only Jenner occupied this wing.

"Gita. Gita, look at me," Jenner said. "Gita, I'm innocent. You've got to believe me."

She finally swallowed the lump in her throat and reluctantly met his gaze. "I know you're innocent. I never doubted that."

Jenner breathed a sigh of relief. "Thank you—thank you for believing in me. I've just... I need *someone* to believe that I'm innocent. The statue—whoever was in there was a vyrm shade. I saw the marking clear as day. I don't know why it disappeared or what happened to it, but I saw it. *I know I saw it.*"

He looked up and tried to change the subject. "How is everyone... I mean, I assume that Zabe hates me and wants me executed, but everyone else? Our friends?"

Gita looked away again. "Everyone has moved on. Other things have happened. Things have only gotten more insane since you killed Zaha... since you killed the vyrm impostor."

"What do you mean?"

She looked back again. "Zabe has disappeared. Tay-lore was murdered. Basilisk and Caivev have walked freely inside the castle walls. The AVA has caused riots." She ticked off names on her hand, "Wulftone, Jackie, Sam, and Shandra are all away from the Prime and have been for weeks, and Princess Claire is... I don't even know. Things are just... wrong."

Jenner furrowed his brows. Something didn't fit right, and he mentally repositioned the pieces; they began to fit right, but only when he entertained ideas he previously thought were impossible. "That sounds like the perfect storm—like a scenario engineered so someone could try to take the crown from Claire."

"There's more." Gita's voice warbled. "I'm stuck. Someone is making me..."

"Making you what? Who is it? Who's hurting you?" Fire lit in his belly; Jenner knew he had to protect her—she was all he had left.

"I can't. I'm sorry." Gita got up and rushed out of the hallway.

A few seconds passed, and the door clanked open again. "It's okay, Gita. I want to help—just tell me how," Jenner called, assuming she'd returned.

It was not Gita who entered, but Shjikara. The Veritas leader surprised him for a moment, but it made a certain amount of sense. The nature of his crime made it unlikely Gita could have come to him for a visit... unless someone with power and influence helped make it happen.

As soon as Jenner met Shjikara's gaze, the final piece fell into place; things suddenly made sense. "It was *you*, wasn't it? The marking on the shade was there all along and you hid it!"

Shjikara smiled deviously and made a symbol with his hand to complete a simple, silent spell. The air shimmered briefly and the mysterious incantation took hold.

"You have begun to figure things out, I see. But it is too little too late." Shjikara's face looked pained as he spoke, and the cleric massaged his temples.

Jenner howled for the guards. Shjikara watched for several bouts and let the younger man scream himself hoarse. "My spell is quite unbreakable. No sound will pass beyond this room unless I release it."

"You're the one behind all of this. You want the throne—you've always been an ambitious little pretender."

"Oh, it's worse than that," Shjikara said. His features melted away and revealed his true form.

"Nitthogr," Jenner hissed. "Are you here to kill me?"

He rubbed his temple again and resumed Shjikara's form. "No. Sh'logath does not wish it—I am here for my own pleasure alone." He met Jenner's eyes and drank in the prisoner's anguish. "I am here because your suffering brings me joy, and once the Awakening begins, all will be burned away, including even that joy." He massaged his forehead again, trying to stave off the punishment Sh'logath inflicted upon him for taking personal pleasure in something outside of his direct commands.

"We'll stop you. I'll get out of here and I'll put an end to this madness once and for all!" Jenner howled at the sorcerer, who'd begun to leave.

Shjikara turned and spoke over his shoulder. "How will you do that? Besides me, you've only had one visitor this whole time. You think little Gita can help you? She's your only outside connection."

"She's stronger than you know. She is fierce and she is loyal."

The fake priest laughed so hard he had to put a hand on the wall to prevent collapsing. He looked Jenner in the eyes. "You haven't figured it out yet? The identity of the traitor? It was Gita all along."

Panic and despair shocked Jenner into silence. It destroyed his remaining defiance and any spirit of hope he clung to.

Shjikara turned and left. Shutting the door behind him, he addressed the two guards posted by his hall. "He is quite mad, I think. Raving about conspiracies. I think the boy has lost his mind."

The guards shrugged. Neither had formed an opinion; it was beyond the scope of their jobs.

"Are you both faithful adherents?"

"Yes sir," they both responded. Shjikara was the most recognizable figure in the Prime's religious field.

"Excellent. You are both doing good work here. I shall praise you to the crown." He shot a skeptical look backwards at the door to

Jenner's hall. "The murderer's connections may go deeper than we suspect; he could be in league with terrorists, such as the AVA. Make sure you keep him in isolation unless I send word otherwise."

Both guards nodded and snapped to attention.

Shjikara returned the nod, bid them farewell, and departed.

The Desolation

Chartarra and Trenzlr plus two other rovers walked along the barren wasteland ridge. They did not need to carry much for supplies, but Klewdahar had insisted that they take a churdachk.

The rat-like beast carried their packs with ease. Churdachk had adapted to the harsh climate of the realm and thrived where so many other creatures had failed; many vyrm had domesticated them and even used them as mounts. As excellent climbers, the creatures could go where few others could.

The vyrmic party had made excellent time, due in part to their relative youth and tenacity. In the hazy distance, Limbus loomed before them.

Chartarra asked, "Have any of you been to Limbus before?"

None of them had ever gone beyond its outskirts, past the refuse holes where they sometimes scavenged. Even then, they were always fearful in the shadow of the city.

"You should all follow my lead," Chartarra said. He swallowed hard, hoping he fared better this time than the last. He'd only been to Limbus once before and it had cost him his life... but also had it given back to him.

The travelers kept to themselves and bartered in the lower districts to swap out their clothes for something less readily identifiable as Maethan garb. Their mission demanded some level of secrecy.

Each day for two days, they swapped watchers and camped near the main road into the Imperial Citadel, where Basilisk and Caivev lived. After two day's worth of watching, they finally ascertained which of the rooms belonged to Caivev.

They watched a commotion around them on the far side of the citadel's gated wall with curiosity. A large, wheeled platform carried Basilisk's most prized possession away from his home. The statue of the Architect King was being returned to the Prime as part of an arrangement with Princess Claire. They'd heard some buzz about it as they purchased new clothes in the proletariat sector at the edge of town. Most of the population felt indifferent, either way regarding the statue, but some of the Black were upset that it might demonstrate weakness on the part of the vyrm. They also seemed to resent Basilsk for his role in representing their voice at all.

With Caivev's window identified, Chartarra got to work. He used a laser signal and aimed it at her window. He tapped a message out, repeating the pulse signal with a code used by the Black Army since before Nitthogr had taken the Prime. He knew that she would recognize it instantly.

Your loyal servant and soldier of The Black Army has returned from the dead. Meet me outside the servant gate. Come alone.

After repeating the loop for what seemed like ages, they finally spotted the Empress sneaking out of the castle. She looked over her shoulder repeatedly and made her way past the gates unnoticed.

Trenzlr waved to her and Caivev pulled up her hood, trying to remain inconspicuous. Chartarra pulled Trenzlr's arm down.

"Not like that. You draw too much attention. She would have found us. We are already out of place here in the Tarkhūn district."

Trenzlr shrugged an apology as Caivev wandered over to their cluster.

She took stock of each of their faces. None were familiar until she came to Chartarra's.

He nodded when she recognized him. "It is I, the son of Charobv."

She greeted him. "You live, despite your mission."

Chartarra lowered his head. He'd previously been an assassin, trained by his father, who had been a general in her army. During one foray, he'd been sent to murder Basilisk. "I failed in my mission," he admitted, "and there was a cost." He pulled aside his tunic to display the wounds he'd taken after Basilisk had discovered him. "I assume that, given current politics, the mission has ended."

Caivev nodded curtly.

"How is my father? He was always opposed to working with Tarkhūn."

"He died in my service," Caivev said flatly.

Chartarra nodded, thin lipped. He tried to hide his disappointment. "Then there is no risk in my coming to you, and you'll know that nobody has leveraged me into this."

She raised an eyebrow. "You have a purpose in coming now, or is this mere devotion?"

Chartarra agreed. "Devotion, yes, but not to the Black or to Sh'logath. My devotion is to you... Empress." The word felt odd coming from his lips. The Black had always served a ruler, appointed by the heads of the five Black vyrm tribes, but only the Tarkhūn had ever had an emperor and empress.

Caivev stood waiting for the message. She was no nonsense, a trait valued by the Black.

"I have abandoned the service of Sh'logath," he confessed. "I've found new meaning and purpose—a new god to serve, one who spared me and sent me to you." Chartarra expressed his uneasiness with the Great Devourer and his uncertainty that the Awakening was the right path. "The Seekers have told me older legends and they tell older tales than even those told by Kadrist the prophet. Rasthakka, Kadrist's philosophical opponent, always said that the Maetha would come from a royal line."

Caivev crossed her arms. "I know some of the old tales. What are you getting at?"

"You are now royalty, Caivev. You are Empress," Chartarra said. "There is another prophecy, a new prophecy given by the rovers' prophet, this one's cousin," he pulled Trenzlr forward to vouch. "The new prophecy is that a Maetha will be dunnischkte."

She bit her lip. "You think I am going to be this Maetha, the one who paves the way for the restoration of Edenya? I've been no friend to the rovers; I have hunted and killed them for sport."

Chartarra cocked his head. "Is there cause to hate the Seekers? They only *seek*. They... *we only want to see restoration* rather than annihilation. It's been said that you and Basilisk have sought to unify the race. Kadrist's teachings would say that unification is achieved by purification: destroying all but one line, the Black or the Tarkhūn. You can't follow Kadrist's teachings if you merged the two. But Rasthakka..."

She held up a hand to talk him down. "I do not hate the Seekers," she admitted with a sigh and looked around to make sure no one else could hear. "I have my own reasons. But I, too, have reevaluated my loyalty to Sh'logath."

Before Chartarra could excitedly continue, she stayed him with a hand. "But know that I am no Maetha. Your prophet could be wrong. Prophesies are rarely exact in their symbolism."

"How do you plan to stop Nitthogr if you now oppose Sh'logath?" Trenzlr interjected.

Caivev met him with a blank stare. "Nitthogr is dead," she finally spat, looking from face to face.

Chartarra shook his head solemnly. "He has returned and is raising an army. He sent dreams and visions to the Black in order to muster his forces for war. Have you not experienced them too?"

She shook her head. "I am not a blackborne. I am a dunnischktet and I have never been vyrm."

The others nodded, understanding. Mostly, the rovers had not had them either, only Chartarra, who was once a loyal follower.

Caivev's mouth twisted, "But it certainly explains why my Black have been..." A loud voice interrupted her.

"Halt! We have you surrounded," yelled Skrom. He and a contingent of mixed vyrm rushed to prevent any escape.

Chartarra and his company froze.

Caivev whirled in a panic and identified herself.

Skrom straightened. Next to him stood Jeerzha from the Hunters Guild. "My apologies, Empress. Jeerzha and his guild identified four rovers in the city two days ago... Chartarra? Is that you?" The massive soldier recognized his former peer.

Chartarra nodded and nearly spoke up to acknowledge his role in the group. Caivev pulled him away from the other three. "Yes. It is Chartarra, son of Charobv. He has been on a secret mission from me for a long time."

"Yes," said Jeerzha, scanning Trenzlr and his companions for confirmation. "Yes. These are the ones. I am sure of it—they have a rover look about them. But there was another." He turned his gaze back to the last member of the party.

Caivev eyed the wounds on Chartarra's neck again. "There was a fourth, but he has died," she stated truthfully, though in another manner of speaking.

Jeerzha shrugged and withdrew a knife. The zealot was intent on killing their captives.

"Hold your blade," Caivev said forcefully enough to stop the radical vyrm in his tracks.

The guilder looked at her wild-eyed.

"I gave you the kill the other day because you had captured them. *These ones* are mine and so their punishment is mine to deal and not yours."

Jeerzha hissed slightly, but turned the handle of his blade to her so that she might carry out the execution.

"The law does not demand their deaths. You admitted this yourself?"

He scowled, but nodded.

"Skrom, take them to the dungeon until further notice."

He bowed and dutifully began escorting them towards the citadel. Jeerzha scowled and Caivev noted how the Black in Skrom's party of hunters bristled at the command, but they obeyed, for now.

Caivev felt exposed with the tension running high. She bowed to Chartarra, understanding his new path more than she let on. "Chartarra, I release you from my service. Your mission has ended."

The Empress returned to the safety of her walls and left him behind.

Chartarra had nothing left he could do, but he was inspired by the discovery that Caivev, too, had reservations about Sh'logath. Chartarra climbed aboard the back of his company's abandoned churdachk to make as much speed as he could. He had to report the news to Klewdahar.

Caivev claimed she was not Maetha... but she *was* dunnischkte, and she was no longer a follower of Sh'logath.

The Prime

Shjikara looked up from his studies when a young monk knocked on his door. He recognized the woman as a relatively new adherent to the order and a member of the Mystic order; he made sure that he maintained his psychic defenses. Shjikara did not think such a low-level Mystic could scan his psyche, but if anyone was foolish enough to try, it would be someone completely unqualified to attempt it.

He grasped for her name. "Yes, Veranna, is it?"

A smile twitched at her lips and she closed the door behind them for privacy. "Not quite." Veranna's shapely figure smoothed out and her skin peeled back, taking the shape of scales.

Shjikara smiled. Krenyr was good, very good.

"My mission has been accomplished," the hunter said. "Your meddlesome scientist will only be found by the flesh gnawers at the bottom of the great Muck-a-waa Swamp, two hours north of the Crystal Sea. None will suspect a thing. Before the doctor announced a temporary leave for mental health reasons, I gathered and destroyed whatever scanners I could find."

Shjikara nodded. "Perfect. I have your next assignment for you. Surveil and disrupt my enemies on earth. You will need to planeswalk for this task." He gave him brief instructions of the process. "This may be a one-way trip, my friend. It is not likely you will be capable of returning, but if you are capable of eliminating all the targets I mark for you, you might find a man called Jacob Sisyphus. If you impersonate him, you could use his men to return you here. You might find him a *difficult* target to eliminate... the same could be said for these other four targets." He slid a collection of graphics over to Krenyr for him to look at.

The assassin's eyes locked on Wulftone. "This one wears the Vangandran bracer," he grinned. "I will get to kill another of the werewolves."

Shjikara bobbed his head. "I could think of none more suited to the task. Go to earth, now. Remember, surveil and disrupt... they may have enlisted the aid of others, so tread with caution and strike when you can do the most damage." He remembered back to the first time he'd pursued Claire Jones as Nitthogr. The net had closed around her multiple times, and in each instance, she seemed to slip away with the aid of others.

Krenyr bowed low, gave his lord a vyrm salute, and then departed.

Chapter Thirteen

Nitthogr sat naked in the chamber, as he had each night for the last few days. The darque-crown rested upon his head. This time, he only had one message for his minions spread throughout the multi-verse. "It is time."

He removed the circlet and placed it on the table before pulling his robe back over his body. Nitthogr wore his own face, now. He no longer hid; his time had finally arrived.

Grabbing his communicator, he fired a simple text message to summon his spy. He had need of Gita soon. Nitthogr patted the statue of the child, Shara, on the head. She had been placed inside the Sacristy vault for safekeeping until now, when he needed leverage most. He tossed the communicator device aside.

Unfolding the sheet he'd torn from the inventory codex more than a week ago, the sorcerer picked up a magical box that sat atop the table in the sacristy. It was the last piece he would need to complete the Birthing.

Nitthogr looked down at it; the box's dial bore the image of the royal crest and internal clock-gears connected the working mechanisms together so that it rotated to keep track of the astral alignments of the realms at all times. Two movable pieces indicated the sun and the moon in their astronomic positions and the different, surrounding nodes that represented the thirty-two other dimensions turned in tandem.

It was such a small thing. Then again, the most powerful artifacts were always the tiniest. He tucked the box underneath an arm and summoned an intense blast of eldritch energy that burst the Sacristy door's hinges free. The vault access fell outward and smashed to the hallway floor in a smoldering heap.

Nitthogr stepped into the hall. Screams echoed down the corridor and he smiled when he watched a shade slide his blade into the back of a Veritas monk and then steal his face.

The monk turned and bowed. "It is time," he repeated back to the sorcerer, and then he turned a corner and went to the main courtyard. Bloody splatters were all that remained of the sentries that normally watched the doors. None of the Merciful Hammer manned the walls any longer and the tent city that had sprung up barely two days ago had emptied since sending his psychic three word command.

Nitthogr sank to his knees beneath the white light of the full moon and set the box down before him. The lid clicked open when he released the tiny tabs that held it shut.

Inside the box was a round mirror mounted onto positioning brackets; they let it turn in any direction. The sorcerer knew this device; as a previous ranking member of the Order of the Flame, the arcanist class, he had intimate knowledge. He slowly, methodically, positioned the focusing mirror until it was centered on the moon and then calibrated the device using two small wheels at the outermost corners.

The box seemed to hum and glow with the energies it collected as he synced it to the fabric of space and the astral bodies.

Nitthogr looked skyward. "I have all that you required, my lord. Your people are ready for the Birthing!"

He glanced aside and saw Gita coming up the hill. Nitthogr had already trained her in use of the device, which had only needed to be activated and attuned. In full view of her, he closed the lid and rotated the knob to realign the solar and lunar positions. All dimensional gates would be simultaneously flung wide, as they had been during the Syzygyc War. He depressed the central knob, which functioned as a button and the new settings went into effect.

Nitthogr screamed into the sky as it rumbled with ominous power. "A new Birthing is at hand!" The air shuddered and the very fabric of reality jittered under the stress of the shifts.

Gita arrived just in time to see the change in Nitthogr. She gasped and her face drained pale. She could barely bring herself to keep walking towards the monstrosity that Nitthogr had become, but for her sister's sake, she pushed forward and towards the squirming, inky black mass of tendrils and quivering flesh that molded and reformed back into Nitthogr's shape as he handed her the box.

"You will carry this, now," he insisted. "In one hour, close all the gates—it will be enough time for my army to have mobilized through the portals."

Gita hung her head and obeyed.

Earth

Sisyphus *felt* the rumbling of the explosion more than he heard it. He opened the door to the panic room area of the floor he cohabitated with Doctor Pietro Walther.

Walther's side of the top floor of the German high-rise was more suited to scientific and technological pursuits, while Sisyphus's was geared to the arcane. The wizard walked towards the door, guessing that some kind of experiment of his partner's had gone awry. Sometimes those things happened. It's why Sisyphus had engraved mystic sigils of binding on each of his walls to contain any potential gremlins that might act up in an errant summoning spell or what not. He didn't worry much about the adjacent laboratory; Walther was always very cautious.

The separating wall between them was thick and well insulated. Sisyphus was surprised he'd noticed anything at all, but figured he should check in on Walther.

He opened the door to total anarchy. Sirens blared around the corner and he heard the crackling of fire as well as the distinct sounds of things being smashed. Voices shrieked somewhere in the distance. He dashed around the corner and sprang into action.

The twisted bodies of three female interns, all Heptobscurantum members, lay draped over furniture in the receiving room. As a legitimate business office for one of the Seven's shell companies, they employed a half-dozen people, all who could assist the scientist when he needed it—though perhaps not as ably as Cerci Heiderscheidt had..

Sisyphus stepped up to the corner; enemies cackled on the other side. He suddenly realized he'd left all his magic items back in his section of the building, and Walther had been researching his newly acquired darquematter amulets. *No kophesh, no mystic trinkets, no bags of Primal fuel... it's just me—and ain't that enough?* His blood boiled.

He heard distinctly vyrm voices, and a woman screamed, louder than the sound of a sickly thud that had probably ended her life. *Another intern.*

Sisyphus didn't dash in blindly—he had to find out what he faced, first.

"This! This is what they are hunting—the one who is killing our kind! It must be cleansed!" The creatures howled, followed by more crashing noises as they smashed and destroyed things.

Judging by their noises and voices, he figured there were three of them. The wrestler steeled himself and then stepped around the edge in time to watch one of them cut down the last employee he could spot on site, their resident fixer: a man skilled at combat and responsible for collecting the homeless transients they Walther sometimes needed for his experiments.

"This will show your boss not to mess with the vyrm!"

The fixer cried out as the scaly enemy slashed him across the face with his jagged claws; a talon opened the victim's jugular.

"What do you think you're doing in my home?" Sisyphus demanded.

One of the vyrm looked up, caught red-handed. He clutched the collection of darquematter amulets that Sisyphus had recently stolen. The vyrm shook them in the air. "This is why you are killing us? Rooting us out and murdering us one by one—you seek the mystic metals?"

The Doctor had hoped to learn more about the odd material from a scientific perspective. Perhaps they would lead to new breakthroughs.

"Put those down!" Sisyphus howled a spell and blasted the speaker with a fierce bolt of arcane fire. It incinerated him in an instant. The amulets clattered to the floor.

The other two creatures altered form, both of them grew in size and shape to match Sisyphus, becoming near-perfect copies. He grinned, knowing that would not be enough to stop him.

A set of glass vacuum tubes connected to the portal machine's internals had been destroyed—Sisyphus didn't know what exactly was in them, but he knew that if they were ever opened or if the glass cracked, they would cause instant explosions. The state of the machine had proved that true.

Its ruins lay busted and blackened where it had caught fire. The invading vyrm stopped smashing remaining equipment around the portal generator and charged at him.

"Shades," Sisyphus hissed, taking a defensive stance. He leapt forward and flared his arms wide, clotheslining them both. They had his form, but not his bulk.

Sisyphus snatched one of them and lifted him overhead, before smashing him to the ground. He whirled just in time to dodge the other assailant and then he lifted his hands to blast the attacker.

The vyrm pulled off his charge and spun to his side to avoid the eldritch blast. He scrambled off behind a bank of equipment to get a better attack angle. His partner rushed for the wrestler.

Sisyphus spotted him in the nick of time and lifted the man overhead in a gorilla press. He hurled the copy of his own likeness across the room using the creature's momentum and then flashed a mystic shield up just in time to block the trio of bullets the other shade snapped off from behind cover.

With his free hand, Sisyphus made a sign and growled a spell that lit his fist on fire. He blasted the cover with a wave of black fire that sent the vyrm scrambling.

Pressing both wrists together and aiming, he launched another spell. A dark orb sought out the creature before he could escape and smashed into him. The vyrm exploded into a cloud of ash and his charred skeleton clattered to the floor.

The wrestler growled a pained yelp as the remaining, wounded vyrm wrapped an arm around his neck from behind and slipped him into a choke hold.

Sisyphus's last spell had drained too much out of him for such an impromptu battle. Without his artifacts to aid him, he could only rely on brute force at this point.

Darkness crept in at the edges of his vision. The scaly enemy had locked in the grapple and stopped his airflow.

"You will die, too. Just like your friend," the scaly opponent hissed as his skin melted back into his vyrmic shape.

Sisyphus moved his eyes and spotted the bloody figure in the corner. Doctor Walther laid against the machine, as broken as the contraption, and just as destroyed. His head was bowed and his neck ran red with blood. The man would never watch another wrestling match or invent another machine to push the bounds of science.

Sisyphus howled and jammed a massive elbow into the ribs of the creature behind him. He pivoted and turned his hips out so he could grapple with the vyrm and he dug his fingers into the attacker's neck, picked him up and then smashed him down overtop of his knee.

The vyrm cracked like a brittle plank. His spine and bony bits poked out at chaotic, wrong angles and the creature lay twisted in a gnarled and broken repose with a surprised look froze upon his face.

Scrambling to his feet, the big man hurried over to Walther. He checked for a pulse and confirmed his fear. Walther was beyond medical attention.

Sisyphus paused, standing over the body of his fallen friend and greatest fan. He was confused. "What did they mean? Someone was killing them because of the amulets? I don't understand…"

Walther was dead, and the machine was ruined. The scientist and his contraption were critical to his plans. Without it, Sisyphus had no idea how he would be able to maneuver as freely as he had in the past or position himself to take want he wanted. Sisyphus could no longer come and go unseen, easily killing any who got in his way.

The question bothered him… *who is killing random vyrm shades on Earth, and why?* He only knew he could not ask them because he'd just killed the only three who could answer his questions. *Someone… some thing is rooting out those cells hiding in this dimension and the shades believe it's tied to the amulets.*

The Desolation

Chartarra's churdachk earned him incredible speed. It had been a brisk two-day journey for the small cohort and it had taken less than a day for one rider to cross the plains and return to the rovers' camp. The creature's versatility allowed him to ride through areas that the small group had to detour around, and at quick speeds.

Churdachk's feet and ankles were covered in thick hide that even copses of knee-high razorbrush couldn't harm.

His mount scampered into the cavalcade's edges, where Klewdahar and Gerjha rushed out to meet him. Hirdac breathlessly chased after Klyrtan who followed them, eager to see who had returned.

"News... what news from Limbus?" Klewdahar called out.

Chartarra handed the reins of the churdachk off to a local who took it to be refreshed.

"Is Caivev our Maetha?" the chieftain asked. Hope welled in his eyes—he wanted to believe it was true.

Chartarra admitted that he could not say either way. "Caivev is... different. Something in her has changed. Her rage is tempered. She is not the same, but I cannot say that she has become a Seeker... only that she is no longer a tool of Sh'logath."

Gerjha listened in on them and noted, "All can be used by Maetha, sometimes even despite themselves. It is not unknown for bad persons to be moved to do good things by a higher power."

"Do you think that she could be the chosen one despite herself?" Chartarra asked.

"I only know what is possible and what Maetha tells me."

A ripple of murmurs zigzagged through the growing crowd. With equal parts excitement and worry, some of them pointed skyward. "A sign!" someone shouted.

Night had nearly come on, but the daylight had actually brightened. The pall that normally painted everything in the Desolation with shades of sepia had suddenly disappeared, like some world-wide filter had been removed from the light spectrum. Seekers squinted against the unfamiliar light as they shielded their eyes and stared into the sky.

"A sign—a sign." Others repeated.

No matter where they searched on the horizon, they could not spot the lurking dread of the Great Devourer. Sh'logath's presence on the threshold of reality had disappeared.

"Is it true? Is it really a sign?" Klewdahar asked. He looked around for Gerjha, but the prophet had already left his side. "If it is a sign, then should we move towards Limbus? It is where Caivev lives."

He moved out from the swelling horde of bodies, looking for Gerjha. People were already proclaiming the day of Maetha had arrived. Klewdahar looked out and saw that Gerjha had already begun heading towards the capital city on foot and with nothing but the clothes on his back.

The crowd began to follow after him, chasing the Maethan prophet on his journey into the wilderness.

Seekers began journeying down from the cliffs and emerged from various nooks and crannys where they'd been hidden. They moved as one people, a disjointed parade with one purpose: a pilgrimage to Limbus to see if a dunnischktet was the prophesied one.

"That one is crazy, I think," Klewdahar pointed to the prophet and noted when Chartarra caught up to him.

"Isn't that the way of faith?" Chartarra asked as he departed, heading for the suddenly mobile caravan. He did not yet know what to make of the disappearance of the Lurker, but he understood why the people thought as they did. Sh'logath's presence had departed. The agod's presence was the single greatest blight upon the realm of Desolation—old Edenya. So long as it remained, they could never hope for restoration.

Chartarra wanted to believe Sh'logath's disappearance was a divine encouragement, but could not shake a seed of worry that coiled through his heart. His worry only strengthened when he looked at Klyrtan.

He remembered the look of glee on the simpleton's face several mornings ago when the visions began. The way Klyrtan looked around expectantly only reinforced Chartarra's dread.

Klyrtan knew something the rest of them did not, Chartarra felt certain of it.

Basilisk looked up to the sky from his home in Limbus. Many things had changed in his garden retreat. The game tables were gone; he no longer endured the endless stalemates. But the change of scenery was not the only shift. Something intangible had altered the light.

He looked around and then spotted the difference. The sky had cleared. Sh'logath was gone. Basilisk recognized the laughter nearby and found Charsk, the High Priest of the Sh'logath cult.

Charsk was drunk, not an uncommon occurrence for him, especially given the hour.

"What do you think?" Basilisk asked him. "An omen? What does it mean? Is Sh'logath gone... destroyed, perhaps? Or maybe he's finally been restored to eternal slumber..."

"Gone?" Charsk laughed some more and took a heavy swig from his bottle. "No. You cannot simply remove something like the mighty agod." He rose to leave and see to whatever other business he might need to attend to. Something significant to the cultic faith had happened for the first time in many years; he might be needed. Charsk almost fell over in a stupor and he barely caught himself on a door frame to keep from stumbling.

"Then what about his disappearance?" Basilisk tried to mask any optimism from his voice. He'd already made the decision to politely decline following through on any future plans to unleash Sh'logath from the Nihil prison; that decision was partly what prompted his engagement to Caivev and the efforts to unify the vyrm as one. The writings of Rasthakka had suddenly made sense to him.

Charsk chuckled and wiped the drool from his reddened face. "Disappearance? Ha. That is not the vyrm way—and Sh'logath is our patron deity. Sh'logath is not gone... he is only hidden. And in the dark, he grows more powerful than ever. He stirs, but is no longer trapped between the parting veils... he might now walk among us."

The high priest staggered off towards the road back into the heart of Limbus beyond the Imperial Keep. Charsk left Basilisk staring at the evening sky.

Sure that he no longer had shades stationed nearby to protect him... or to overhear his startling admission, Basilisk muttered, "This is not good."

CHAPTER FOURTEEN

*E*arth

Sam paced back and forth through the front of the old church. Shandra scowled as she watched him practically wear a hole through the path that he repeatedly walked.

Wiltshire lounged on a pew, waiting more patiently than the others. "So, to get this straight, we're going to travel to a different dimension and rescue a princess while possibly starting a kind of civil war?"

"Don't tell me you're one of those types who doesn't believe in that kind of stuff?" Sam asked. "I used to be one myself. I thought multi-verses and magic were all clever fictions."

"Oh, I believe," Wiltshire admitted. "I just wanted to be clear on the plan... it doesn't seem like a very good one, is all. I mean, you saw how easily this enemy killed Tay-lore."

"We just need to notify our friends," Shandra insisted. "As soon as everyone discovers Nitthogr's return, all factions of the military will turn out against him. Enough of the populace harbors a grudge after the last takeover that I expect civilians will show up with pitchforks and farming tools to help fight him."

Wiltshire nodded thoughtfully and checked the time. "Are we ready?"

Shandra checked her own timepiece and nodded; she'd already explained that they had to wait for a certain time window for the portals to line up so they could travel where they needed. The group moved to the portal location. Sam joined her, and Wiltshire stood behind them both. The cleric cut herself across the forearm and splattered the activator. She stared forward vacantly.

After a few moments, Wiltshire asked, "Should I be feeling something yet? How long does this normally take?"

Shandra turned to the others. Worry contracted her eyes. "It's not working."

"What do you mean, it's not working?" Sam asked, consulting his notes on the portal charts. He read and re-read them. "But this is right—the equations match. The portal should work!"

Sam cut his own arm and tried the passage again, but he did not planeswalk. He looked up and glanced from Shandra to Wiltshire. "Something is wrong, you guys... the portal no longer works! We can not return to the Prime."

Zabe could feel the urban vibrations of the city above him as he stalked through the dark tunnels. His lycan eyes allowed him to see capably in the dark and his senses reported that he was close. Even in the subterranean black he could read the graffiti. *Hadyuka*. The word, and a spray-painted snake, marked that he'd been following the right trail.

He wore one of Respan's scanner gadgets. Before leaving the Prime weeks ago, he'd had just enough wits about him to grab a few supplies, the scanner among them. Using the device, he had tracked down any lead he could find, and there was a heavy concentration of leads in the Odessa catacombs. He'd had to rely on his keen lycan sense of smell while in his wolf form. The scanner showed the location and distance to the brightly glowing blip, but the Ukranian tunnels beneath the city of Odessa created the largest labyrinth on the planet. Tracking his prey through it required more than a heading and distance.

Zabe sniffed the ground near the marker. It smelled strongly of vyrm scents. The odor from the air near the next turn had grown to its strongest yet. *Maybe two turns until I find the nest?*

He growled in the dark and hurried through the catacombs. Zabe twisted around one corner and turned the next. He met the surprised faces of a vyrm cell.

The wolf roared and leapt upon the first one. The next two put up a little resistance, but Zabe easily overpowered them in his massive werewolf shape. He whirled in the dark and turned to a group of six shades. They wore the disguises of local politsiya and had their firearms trained on him.

Zabe did not want to kill innocent folk who might be caught up in extra-dimensional affairs they knew nothing about.

They shouted orders for him to stop in the local language and stiffened their gun arms as the werewolf growled and slowly turned to face them. Their smell filled his nose and confirmed their vyrmic identities to Zabe. *Definitely shades.*

He roared and ducked as the police opened fire. The werewolf shrugged off the marginal small arms fire that bit his hide and he leapt into their midst, slashing with his claws. It was over within moments and the chamber again laid quiet, reeking of vyrm blood and gun smoke.

The battery operated lights provided enough light to see by here, and Zabe melted back into his human shape. A table in the middle of the room was filled with materials and several maps had been hung on a wall. Pins on the map marked locations across a couple nearby countries.

Zabe paused when he realized that he'd already been to many of those places. He looked closer at the world map. There were roughly fifty pins across the planet and they had heads of two different colors.

He traced his finger backwards across the line he'd cut across Europe and traced his route backwards. This was the seventh vyrm cell he'd wiped out since embarking on his quest.

Each of the previous six was circled on the map: three of each color.

"They were tracking me."

He realized that seven of the different pins had stars drawn around them and they were all yellow pins. Odessa's pin was red. "What does it mean?" he wondered aloud.

Zabe looked down at the table and sorted through their documents. He didn't speak a lick of Ukranian, but luckily they were mostly in vyrmic, which he knew enough of to struggle through.

He grinned when he scanned the hasty vyrm scrawls. The red pins were looking for him and they'd drawn up a map for every cell of shade sleepers they knew about. Zabe had just found a map to direct him to all of his targets if he could just decipher the clues.

Since coming to Earth by the first available portal, which dumped him in Russia, he'd been using the scanner to track down any signals displaying darquematter auras. It was the best lead he had on finding Sisyphus without attacking the Heptobscurantum head-on. One of the last things Jenner had said before being hauled off to prison had deeply bothered Zabe.

My father was taken from me by those psycho cultists—Nitthogr's minions from Earth, and we still haven't done a damned thing to get him back.

Zabe was angry with Jenner—furious! The kid was a killer... but he'd been right about that one thing: they had barely looked into recovering Professor Jarfig.

Jenner's comment stung and Zabe figured he could at least do this one thing; Jarfig deserved to be rescued, whether or not his son was a murderer. Zabe was still his father's son, whether Zahaben was alive or not, and rescuing Jarfig was the right thing to do.

More than anything, Zabe wanted to make Jenner tell Jarfig what he had done to Zabe's father. That was the punishment Zabe wanted for the murderer: to endure his father's disappointment, and he would do it if he had to track down every darquematter scrap on Earth until he eventually found the wizard and forced him to surrender the professor. He assumed Sisyphus had collected at least a few of the alien items.

Zabe clutched the notes and turned his attention back to the map and its seven stars around yellow pins. *What are there seven of?*

The three yellow pins were locations that he'd raided and all of them had heptobscurantum icons and items in their lairs. It had not surprised him; the Heptobscurantum frequently used shades to plant new factions of their cult across the globe. It was how they'd spread so rapidly since their near eradication after the defeat at Mullen, Nebraska.

Zabe looked around. The *Hadyuka* site had none of that. As he thought of it, neither did the other three locations with red pins... they were not aligned with Illuminati and their Seven leaders.

It clicked into place. *That's where the Heptobscurantum leaders are located!*

He scanned the notes again. The Red pins knew that *something* was wiping out their nests and had deduced that it was something targeting the Heptobscurantum—that the cult must've done something to make a deadly enemy who the red-pinned Shades knew nothing about.

Zabe traced a finger to the nearest star on the map. "Germany."

The pin was several countries away, and he'd have to sneak in and out of each one since he had no passport or transportation. His eyes burned as he stared at the yellow pin within the starred dot. In as few as a couple of days, he expected he'd collect his prize.

"Jarfig is coming home to see his son's trial," he promised aloud.

The Prime

Nitthogr looked across the grassy fields of the cloister. They had been cleared out now that the shades were stationed inside the monastery.

The sorcerer sniffed disdainfully at the weakness of the human olfactory gland. He could smell the blood from here. Most of it had been scrubbed clean or hidden behind closed doors in the barracks section where they had piled the bodies like cord wood.

Down the road, he could see the hoverskiffs approaching. They were filled with Guardian Corpsmen; their distinct armor flashed brilliantly in the daylight. His army excelled at disguise and subterfuge; none in the royal army or guardian corps were aware of his take over yet... aside from his servant, Gita.

Nitthogr reformed his body into the shape of Shjikara. It felt doubly unfamiliar now. Every cell of the sorcerer's body was filled to the brim with dark energy. They practically vibrated with the power of his ravenous agod who now lived in and through him. Nitthogr was no longer *also Shjikara*... he was Sh'logath and *also Nitthogr!* And nothing could stop him now. Nothing remained of Shjikara but a fading image used when it became convenient.

Still, he felt compelled to reveal his true form and devour the Guardian Corps troops as soon as they entered the soiled grounds, but he knew that the time had not yet arrived. Shjikara looked over to his minion.

Gita held the box in both hands. Her eyes indicated that her total despair had been made complete.

The skiffs settled down in the courtyard and Tahnak exited. Two dozen of his guards walked across the lawn to meet Gita. "I got your message, Gita." He gave a secret hand sign to indicate that he'd understood the coded words she'd inserted and understood that she'd thought a situation was urgent and potentially violent.

Tahnak did a double take at the empty grounds and spotted Shjikara as he headed inside the monastery. "The un-petrified men and women are gone already? I would have thought it'd be months, and not mere days, before they were moved on."

"That's what I wanted to show you," Gita said. "Follow me. It's easier if you see it, rather than let me describe the problem."

Tahnak raised an eyebrow, but went where she led. The Corpsmen, both men and women who Gita knew by name, followed them in. They were on high alert and expected some kind of trouble; the soldiers did a poor job of hiding their edginess.

The halls of the Veritas' home were as warm and inviting as ever. Monks passed them with friendly smiles and nods.

Gita arrived at the door to the Sacristy vault. It had been blown off its hinges. At the center of the vault, a statue of a small child had been placed. The young girl had a broken hand clinging to her arm.

"What... I don't understand," one of the Corpsmen said.

Tahnak whirled around. A vein in his forehead twitched. Tahnak had become attuned to the nature of the Darque during his time trapped there and he could sense things others could not. "Shades! They are everywhere," he shouted. "Form up!" Tahnak didn't understand the statue, but who else would have broken the Sacristy's barrier?

The leader of the Corps stepped in front of Gita to guard her from the noises coming up the hall. "There are vyrm in the Vangandran tunnels—I can feel them there—*hrrk!*"

"I'm sorry... I'm so sorry," Gita said through the tears that rolled down her face. She pulled the knife out of the Tahnak's back. She'd slid it in between armor plates, where only a corpsman would know to strike. "*He made me...*"

Her fellow soldiers could not react to the murder before the overwhelming force of vyrm rushed upon them and began the slaughter. An elite unit slipped out from their hiding places in the Sacristy and gunned the others down while they fought the vyrm pouring forth from the tunnels.

Shjikara shuddered, and he became Nitthogr again. One of the shades howled from the courtyard. "They're getting away. They're getting a—*ackk!*"

Gita and the shades closest to her sprinted outside. Pollando, Druen, Perribelle, and Minas all climbed aboard one of the skiffs and slammed the throttle forward.

Nitthogr glanced aside at the four shades who had taken the forms of those heads of the order after they'd killed them. "I thought you murdered them in their sleep?" the sorcerer hissed.

The shades nodded, just as confused as their leader. Catching Minas's eye as they sped away, the sorcerer growled, "Of course they used magic. The head of The Flame Order must have seen you coming. You killed illusions, you fools. They were just waiting for an opportunity to escape!"

Nitthogr turned to the small army that had gathered and awaited his commands. "Well, don't just stand there! Shades, overtake them!"

The shape-shifting vyrm hurriedly stripped and dressed in the armor of those they'd just killed. They scrambled towards the remaining two skiffs and piled in. Spotting the four heads down the mountain path, the vyrm raiders blasted over the edge of the road and cut an angle to intercept them.

In the pilot's chair, Druen spotted them taking the dangerous maneuver and tried to game the angles. The two pursuing craft slid in behind them and the four leaders shouted when the first one rubbed fenders with it.

Druen kept the craft from fishtailing and righted it on a straight course. With fewer passengers, they pulled away and put some distance between them.

Perribelle of the Wax order snatched the gun from Druen's holster. "I'll hold them off," she said and then crawled to the rear of the open-air flying platform. She snapped off a few shots and the first craft veered away. It quickly corrected itself and then resumed the chase.

The hover skiffs were designed for use by the Guardian Corps. Their armor would hold against a small blaster.

Perribelle screamed as the fake soldiers behind her returned fire. Chunks of plating scorched and sizzled with a heavy volley of laser blasts. The enemy had bigger guns at their disposal.

Druen spotted the Guardian Corps barracks up ahead at the group's main compound, only a short jaunt from the castle walls. He angled for the outpost and heard Perribelle's high-pitch wail. She crawled back towards the driver's seat, moaning.

The leader of the Merciful Hammer smelled the burned flesh and could tell she'd been shot without needing to look. "Almost there, Belle... hold in there. The Corps will set things straight!"

Voices squawked on the communicator that opened to the Guardian Corps' private channel. "Incoming, incoming—GCHQ. We are in pursuit of four rogue vyrm shades. They've stolen a skiff at the monastery and are inbound!"

"No, no, no!" Druen shouted as he spotted the turrets on the outpost wall angling to acquire *them* as targets.

"A little help, Pollando... Pollando?" Druen called to the psychic head of the Mystic Order. He remained stoic and mute as ever. He stared off to the distance and Druen knew that he was not present—he'd departed for some other mission—hopefully one that would help them stay alive.

Minas looked up from tending Perribelle's wound and he flung his hands skyward just in time to throw up a force field as Druen swerved. Their skiff evaded the first laser battery, and the force-field caught the second burst. It slammed into the magic bubble and shook the air, thundering with shimmering azure intensity.

Druen's skiff darted around to the far side of the outpost and they were nearly clear when a third battery fired. It hit directly on center for a kill shot and Minas's protection splintered into shards of pure force that smashed into them and nearly derailed the skiff from its destination.

Perribelle panted from the floor of the vehicle. "So much for help from the Corps—and our Veritas are out of commission, too."

"We can't be certain the Military is safe either," Minas said.

Druen knew what had to be done. "We've got to rescue the Princess before we are overrun from within." He didn't take his eyes from the road, but could feel their nods of agreement.

The enemy skiffs closed behind them again. They spotted even more as their allies bought into the lies of the enemy—the four would be dead before they had a chance to correct their peers.

Druen maxed out the thruster and arced a tight corner and angled for the main gate of the castle. He spotted the guards at the door's control; their eyes had turned a milky white as Pollando held them in psychic stasis. Controlling them only slightly, he made his thralls slam the door shut as they coasted through and then they threw the keys over the edge of the protective walls to buy the four fugitives a couple of extra minutes.

Nearly crashing the skiff through the statue garden, Druen did his best to minimize casualties. He apologized profusely as the vehicle clipped a few of the petrified warriors, breaking some and toppling others. Their craft's hoverfield failed as the engines crumpled under the damage and it skidded to a halt in the main courtyard.

Curious onlookers said nothing, but all eyes were fixed upon them.

Druen scooped up Perribelle, and he dashed into the hallway. Minas and Pollando followed.

"I can walk. The wound is superficial," Perribelle insisted, and he released her. They sprinted as a team towards the royal hall. This time of day, Princess Claire would be holding court in the throne room. They'd just gotten inside when the alarms sounded at the gates, barely audible within the buildings.

"They're inside the castle if the alarm is up," Druen said. "We don't have much time!"

A few steps later, they rounded a corner and found the entrance to the throne room. The main chamber was filled with citizens of every stripe as the court conducted its regular business.

The four comrades pushed their way through and emerged before the throne where Claire sat. A strange moment of awkwardness passed through the crowd as the four religious leaders shoved their way to the center. All eyes fell on them within seconds.

"Princess, you've got to come with us," Perribelle insisted, looking beaten and bedraggled. A scorched wound seeped blood at her shoulder.

A siren split the air and startled the crowd. Voices came from the speaker a moment after. "Intruders. Intruder alert—four vyrm shades disguised as the heads of the Veritas factions have accessed the castle..."

The princess stood to her feet, ready to flee. The crowd stiffened, ready to finally enact their revenge upon an enemy that had caused so much hurt in the past. They outnumbered them at least thirty to one.

Minas growled, "We don't have time for this!" He raised his hands as he shouted and used a blast of wind to shove all the crowds out of the doors. With a telekinetic bump, he slammed the doors shut and locked them with cross braces.

Claire looked up with panic in her eyes.

Pollando rushed to her side. "My princess. My princess, it is I. I know that only you will recognize the sound of my voice," his words came out raspy from his unused voice box.

She stopped in her tracks. "Pollando?"

He nodded enthusiastically. "You are in danger. Nitthogr has returned, my lady. He is stronger than ever and he has infiltrated the Veritas *and* the Guardian Corps. We must get you out of here before it is too late."

She nodded as the others joined them.

"Those doors won't hold forever," Minas insisted. The only way out from here was up. They could retreat up the rear stair, which led to the private residences of the royal family, but the mirror room, which had historically been their best escape option, had been destroyed during the conflict with Akko Soggathoth. The soldiers would likely look for them there and they would have no other escape routes.

"Here," Bithia said, uncovering a secret compartment where they could escape into the subterranean tunnels. "It is connected to the Vangandran caves." Bithia no longer had access to all of Claire's mind, but she remembered this part—the memories were too vivid to forget.

They scrambled down and into the secret paths before resetting the hidden access. The leaders followed their princess as she led them through a grotto and into a dark and winding trail. Minas conjured an arcane light to guide them.

None of them knew these caves. "Where does this lead?" Druen asked, wishing Perribelle had not lost their only weapon in the chase.

"It leads to the tunnels that belonged to Zabe's ancestors," she said. "They connect to the monastery..." she trailed off, realizing they had just come from there and were now going full circle. "There is a gate there. We can open a portal in the depths of the monastery and escape. Nobody but Zabe's family knows about it... and, well, just a few others. It's a secret gate," she insisted.

Many in the Veritas and Guardian Corps knew of the Vangandran tunnels that burrowed beneath the monastery grounds. The tunnel connecting them to the throne room, however, was a better guarded secret than the complete contents of the Chamber of Mysteries.

A short while later, they rounded a corner and spilled out of the tight quarters and into the main caverns. The cluster of vyrm soldiers hiding there whirled as they spotted the intruders.

Druen charged forward and slammed into the cluster of enemy soldiers guarding the gate. He knocked them back and began smashing them with his fists and feet.

Bithia looked up just in time to see it: the statue of the Architect King, guarded by a whole contingent of Black vyrm. *Basilisk had made good on his promise to send the sacred statue back to the Prime by the hidden portal. Why didn't Shjikara inform me that it had been delivered? How deep can this conspiracy possibly go?* Below the statue, Bithia's eyes met with Gita's. She held some kind of box and wore a mask of shame.

"I'm so sorry," Gita said, and Nitthogr stepped out from behind the statue.

Bithia hissed a curse as she berated herself. She'd told Gita and Respan about the tunnel during their foray into the AVA gathering.

Druen continued fighting and refused to budge an inch. He would not allow an enemy to get past him.

Minas grappled with Nitthogr on the arcane sphere. He was grossly over-matched, and the dunnischktet threw him around the room.

Pollando yelled to Claire, completely forsaking his vows. "Claire, get to the portal," he reached into Gita's mind and foresaw the enemy's plan. "The box! The box has shut down the portals!"

Perribelle launched herself towards Gita and knocked the arcane box out of her hands. It skittered across the floor and into Pollando's hands. He cranked the dial as Perribelle shrieked. Nitthogr tore Perribelle apart and Druen finally fell as the vyrm overwhelmed him with massive numbers.

Bithia howled as a blaster fired and split open Pollando. The psychic's hot blood splattered across her face and upon the ground, activating the portal.

Before she planeswalked to a different realm, Bithia watched helplessly as a vyrm shade took her face. The creature's brows and chin reset as her skin smoothed to take a mirror-like visage.

As the cold bolt of energy lanced her body and flung her through the multi-verse, Bithia gasped with shock. Nitthogr smashed the statue of the Architect King. She saw the look of terror on Gita's face as the regal figure collapsed in busted heaps.

Bitha winked out of existence and the vyrm howled. They tore the defiant Druen's arms from his body and ripped Minas to shreds.

Nitthogr ground the statue to dust beneath his heels and then snatched the box from the ground. He turned the dial and closed all gates between the dimensions. "Now, nobody in this realm is capable of stopping us... of stopping me! I am the physical incarnation of Sh'logath!" The halls had filled with bloodthirsty vyrm; they cheered at the announcement.

He placed the gate box back into Gita's hands. "Do not lose this again or I'll extract a toll from your sister. I'll take one piece at a time until you learn to take your role in this seriously."

Gita nodded soberly and wiped her tears away. Her hopes were as dashed as the broken form of the Architect King, and she could only obey.

Chapter Fifteen

E^{*arth*}

After his peers spent an entire frustrating hour of trying to activate the portal, Vikrum Wiltshire finally stood from the pew he'd waited in. He knew he had to let his new companions at least attempt activating it by every means possible, but he'd grown impatient.

"Can we go now?" The detective asked bluntly.

"The portal's still not working," Sam said.

"That's been painfully obvious," Wiltshire said. "And I don't think it's going to spark up anytime soon. I'm sure that, given what we know from Tay-lore, something in your dimension has drastically changed..."

"Which is why we must get back." Sam's eyes burned with worry.

"Which is why we should go. *We cannot use this gate.* You're a scientist, Doctor Jones. Use your head. I know you want to rescue your daughter, but you can't get there from here." Wiltshire spoke firmly, but not rudely.

Shandra put a hand on Sam's arm. "He's right. We're wasting time here that could be better spent trying to find Zabe."

"We haven't been able to find him from the Prime and we had all the resources possible at our disposal, there. Tay-lore was working on it," Sam argued.

"You didn't have me," Wiltshire stated. "I don't mean to sound cocky, but remember that I was Tay-lore's plan. Tay-lore sent me after Zabe and you were the first stop—I found a lead within minutes of my assignment."

Shandra nodded. "You have a plan for where to go next?"

He shrugged. "The key is the brother, Zurrah. I was already searching for him when I stumbled onto you."

Sam took a deep breath and acknowledged the hard truth: this portal was no good to them... Wiltshire's alternate plan was the next best thing. They had to find another way to help the princess, and right now, this was the only option they could move forward with. Sam bobbed his head and sighed. "Yeah. I've never actually met the kid and don't know much about him except that he was taken hostage as a child and locked away by the sorcerer Nitthogr. Zabe doesn't talk much about it, so I only have hearsay from my daughter."

Shandra corroborated the data for him. "They said he hasn't aged and was trapped in a time-stasis chamber in Central America. Trenzlr called the place the Lost Temple." She realized he wouldn't know who Trenzlr was. "He is a vyrm we are friendly with—so was Tay-lore."

Wiltshire didn't know what the vyrm were, but it wasn't an imperative detail at the moment. "So let's lay out what we know. Zabe hasn't seen Zurrah in years, and he's basically just a teenager. He's got a partner who looked to be a cute young woman, and he's got access to a teleportation machine. His last known whereabouts were Central America."

"Chiriqui, to be precise," said Sam.

"Great." Wiltshire raked his fingers through his hair. "A war-torn country with no direct access from America except by U.S. Diplomats."

Shandra suggested, "We could sneak in from a neighboring country?"

Wiltshire shook his head. "What else do we know? I mean, we don't expect to actually find Zurrah there. We're just gathering clues right now. We will leave it on the table, but let's exhaust local options first."

"The portal!" Sam exclaimed. Both of the others looked at him. "We know the vyrm have used it because of their alliances with the Heptobscurantum."

Shandra corrected him, "Caivev owned that alliance and her relationship with the Seven seems tenuous now. We can't contact her anyway, so I don't think it's…"

"That's not it," Sam said. "The machine is powered by blood. And it's huge—not easily portable."

Wiltshire nodded. "That's logical if it's an arcane device."

"I was once hooked up to one of them," Sam said. "The earliest version."

"There's more than one?" Wiltshire asked.

Sam shrugged. "I couldn't tell you. I only know it was in some underground, top secret R and D lab in a warehouse district outside of Detroit."

Wiltshire stroked his chin. "That's just a couple hour flight," he mused. "We're not gonna get a closer clue, I think." He took the keys from his pocket. "I've got a private flight already chartered. Cost me an arm and a leg, but Michigan is on the way back. It can't cost me much extra. Let's go—we can keep brainstorming on the way."

Lost

The first thing Bithia noticed was the smell. Something putrid decayed nearby; it fouled the air with a wet, filthy odor like stagnant water. She wrinkled her nose and guessed that something large had gotten trapped in the mire and died.

Bithia looked around for clues and found herself in a swamp. Brackish water surrounded most sides of her location. Bald cypress and towering tupelo hemmed in the edges of her little island where shawls of Spanish moss screened in the portal site like a burial shroud. Something about the bayou gave her a chill as she stood on the engraved stone outcropping. Clusters of sticks and bones bundled together hung from tree branches along with other voodoo trinkets. They lay next to black candles that had burnt down to their wicks where they surrounded the location.

The princess bit back her worry and crept away from the portal. The sun would go down soon and she did not want to be trapped in this swamp with whoever used this place for his or her evil ceremonies. She shuddered at the thought and remembered that the portal locations were often revered as places of power because of their natural magics; power attracted the worst sort of person just as often as it called to good ones—sometimes more often.

A small trail led her away from the isolated area and her heart caught in her throat. Bithia had no idea where she was. It could have been any of thirty two planes of existence, and of those dimensions she could have been anywhere within them. Panic rose within her and drove her heart rate even higher.

She moved down the trail with more urgency than ever. Bithia had to find something, someone—and not whoever had been conjuring dark spells nearby. The small footpath opened up into a broader trail a few hundred meters down the way, and Bithia sucked in a breath of relief. She followed the new trail and kept walking.

As Bithia moved, her anxiety rose with each new footstep. The sun crawled towards the horizon and eventually went down. Bithia quickened her pace. She still hadn't spotted another living soul and could barely hear anything over sounds of her roaring pulse as it echoed in her own ears.

Something made a sound behind her. A twig snapped, and she froze. She heard it again, followed by a splashing noise. A jolt of fear shot through her and she bolted ahead, paused, and listened. The sounds had either stopped or whatever had been behind her, real or imaginary, fell further away and into the distance. She turned to resume her journey and realized that she'd somehow left the trail when she'd sprinted blindly.

Bithia turned a circle and tried to backtrack, to no avail. Finally, she sank to her knees and began to weep. She was hopelessly lost and in the dark.

Where are you, Zabe... where are you, Claire?

The Prime

Beneath the green-ringed moon, Gita still clutched the gate box. She looked up at the sky. New waves of terror gripped her heart by the hour.

An eerie, murky ring of color encircled the moon like the corona of an eclipse. Tendrils of the fell hue crawled towards the lunar body as if they had reached around its edge and grappled with it, holding it in place. Her eyes returned to the contraption in her hands. She was both powerful and powerless to stop the thing.

Gita went inside the monastery, sickened by the night sky and her involvement in shutting down the portal gates. In the hallways she heard the sounds of vyrm rejoicing, celebrating the coming day of Sh'logath—the great Awakening.

She walked deeper inside to get away from the voices. The open door to the sacristy revealed the disturbing sight of Nitthogr. He'd become more tentacle and blackened, other-worldly flesh than anything else. She might not have recognized him had it not been for the crown upon his head as he communed with his loyal minions across the multi-verse. One errant limb remained capped by his stone fist and another tendril wrapped around the petrified body of Shara, her kid sister.

Gita felt sickened by the sight and so she delved deeper into the monastery, eventually finding her way into the secret warrens and the caves of Vangandra. She walked until she could not hear or smell any vyrm, and then she wandered some more, until darkness and silence swallowed her.

Arriving at a dead end, she could go no further, at least not without knowing how to access the hidden tunnels connecting the caves to the royal keep.

"Gita?"

She jumped and searched for the sound. Nobody was there, but she felt certain that she'd heard her name spoken as plain as day. She looked down and saw the shattered, crumbled stone where Nitthogr had destroyed the Architect King.

Gita sank to her knees and wept over the wreckage.

"Gita... what are you going to do?" But this time, the words were hers. "The vyrm have put a stranglehold on the Prime. They've infiltrated the castle and put an impostor on the throne."

She looked down again at the box and felt tempted to smash it to a million pieces. "Don't do that Gita. Your sister's life depends on it." She wasn't sure if the words belonged to her, or another. She knew she couldn't do it, but she also knew she had to do *something*. As long as the gates were shut, no help could arrive and Claire was trapped wherever she'd been flung off to.

Earth

Zabe stood adjacent to two homeless men. He raised his hands to the fire that glowed within the steel garbage barrel. Traffic noises from the bridge overhead intermittently drowned out the crackle of the fire and the burning trash bothered Zabe's nose with pungent odors. Smells were different in this part of the world, he'd noticed, but homelessness was a universal problem.

The two vagrants could have been from any country. They'd recognized Zabe as one of their own and welcomed him immediately with the kind of generosity marked by men who'd rarely experienced it. Zabe gladly received it; it was not the first time he'd flown under the radar by acting as a transient. It helped him remain incognito; polite civilization rarely dared to look poverty in the face.

Night had drawn on and the temperatures dropped. Since stamping out the Ukranian hive, he'd cut a straight line for Germany on foot, but the trip would take him several days. Zabe rubbed his hands and held them to the flames again. Soon, he could return home in triumph.

As he watched the yellow tongues lick the air, Zabe felt his consciousness fade; a vision overtook him.

He saw only blackness and a flicker of light, barely in focus. A chanting, pleasant voice called from the light—a song Zabe knew as the *Lament of J'v-Ellah*. Most children born since the Syzygc Wars knew the song that described the sacrifice of the Architect King.

Like a mantra, those words rolled over and over as the flames began to come into focus.

Serpent, dragon, wizard-beast
flung wide the gates to hon'r void,
The Prime's caught daughter, most beloved;
captors of the princess toyed,
Her blood to free agod Sh'logath;
salvation all his ransom brings,
Turned to stone at Sharonash,
Lord J'v-Ellah, th'Architect King.

Within the fire, explosions became clearer and clearer. Mud and debris flew as lasers bit the air and steel clashed against steel. Zabe knew he was not on Earth, at least this vision was not from Earth.

"I'm in the war," he realized, surveying the pitched battle around him. *The Syzygyc War.*

A sudden quiet fell over the chaos and Zabe walked through the darkness that formed as the flames dissipated. In the center of it he found a statue that he'd seen once before in Limbus: the Architect King.

The statue's hands were opened, just as they'd been after Claire had claimed the Stone Glaive, his mythic sword which Zabe now wore across his back, attached to a baldric sheath and wrapped like a bedroll. He reached over his back to check that it was still there; he felt the familiar weight of it. When he returned his gaze, the Architect King was looking at him.

"Zabe, son of Zahaben," he said.

"You... you can talk?"

"Of course I can talk. No power can confine or destroy the Architect King."

Zabe said, "But you are stone... a statue."

"Do you think that stones can not talk... even if I will it?"

Zabe bit his tongue. He bowed, instead, embarrassed by his lack of faith. "I am honored that you would speak with me."

"There are things you must know, child of the Prime, in order that you will not lose heart." He looked at Zabe. "You are on a mission of revenge and you have called it justice."

Zabe's heart wavered. He knew the Architect King was right, and he felt the sting of his king's words that struck far more sharply than his anger against Jenner.

The statue surprised him. "I am giving you secret knowledge so that you will know a thing is true when it comes to pass. You must not give up your current quest, but understand that the mission will succeed: *a son will have his vengeance—but it will not be you. Your vengeance is false. Your father made his final sacrifice long ago.*"

Mists around them transformed into the walls of the Prime's royal castle and Zabe vividly relived the memory. Zahaben gave him the bracelet emblazoned with the family crest: the lupine symbol of Vangandra. Then, he ran into the hall and drew off the attackers so that his son could fulfill their family's oath and protect the throne. Behind him, Zabe heard the report of blasters; they had the sharp crack of a kill setting and not the softer *blat* of a stun blast.

Zabe realized that his hope had been false: it was something engineered to twist him and distract from his true calling. As the walls transformed back into fog and that haze dissipated, Zabe realized he was in the Caves of Vangandra, where he had taken Claire for refuge with his grandfather Shardai.

He did a double take. Nitthogr was already there, standing over the corpses of the Veritas leaders and cackling madly as he cowed a cohort of vyrm soldiers behind him. The Architect King was there, too, frozen in his form; the vyrm warriors had all turned and bowed to the statue. Though the Architect King was no longer animated, he still spoke directly into Zabe's mind.

"The Spirit of the Architect King will always exist. It *has* always and *will* always lead the men and women of the tesseract. Once you and my daughter are joined, you must help fight for my people. *All* of my people, until my chosen one is declared. It will require the strength of two in order to succeed—the new king I have chosen for the children of the Prime has this dual nature: someone who can be what is required to lead."

Nitthogr could not see Zabe, but he clearly locked eyes upon the statue and he brandished a long scepter, an ornate piece Zabe knew intimately. Shjikara owned it: the scepter of the High Priest's authority. The vile sorcerer stepped towards the figure and brandished the club.

"No!" Zabe screamed, trying to insert himself between Nitthogr and the Architect King. He was one step too late.

Nitthogr wielded the scepter like a club. It struck and shattered the Architect King with brute force; the famous statue exploded in a cloud of shrapnel. A jagged chunk glanced off of Zabe's head and he sank to the floor over the pile of debris. The sorcerer laughed and departed as Zabe ran his fingers through the sharp, broken pieces; tears ran down his face as he sifted through the wreckage of the petrified king.

"It's only a dream. It's only a dream," he kept repeating.

The vision faded when one of the homeless men at his fire grabbed him and shook him from the reverie. Zabe met his eyes and realized the man had been talking to him.

"Vous saignez... vous saignez." He pointed excitedly and Zabe touched the hot, wet spot forming on his forehead. His haggard companion stated in halting English. "You are bleeding."

Zabe's eyes widened at the implication even as the Architect King's words rang hollow in his mind. *The spirit of the Architect King will always exist.* But he knew in that moment that the statue had truly been destroyed... his head wound convinced Zabe of the truth of his vision, just as the Architect King had promised him.

Turning to the night, Zabe sprinted into the darkness. He knew where another portal location was, one of many he'd committed to memory. Zabe shifted into his lycan form in order to increase his speed, he did not care about whoever might spot him as much as he cared about getting home to protect the kingdom, guard the throne and his fiance, and stop Nitthogr from destroying the Veritas and the statue they all revered so highly. *Maybe it wasn't too late.*

He'd reached the portal by early morning and he glanced at the stars, which had nearly disappeared with the advent of dawn. Zabe did the mental calculations. He would have to pass through two other dimensions to find his path, but he could be back at the castle within an hour.

Zabe bit his hand and drew a bead of blood that he wiped upon the portal site to activate. He stood in the circle. Nothing happened. He walked around within it. Drew some more blood and tried again, to no avail.

Panic wormed through his heart and he knew that something had fundamentally changed following his vision.

The portals no longer worked. Zabe's heart plunged into his gut; he was trapped here.

CHAPTER SIXTEEN

*E***arth**

Half of the old warehouse lay ripped open, exposed to the sky. In the years since Sam's imprisonment, something had torn free a section of wall, floor, and roof. The rubble of it laid in a pile near the edge of the building. It would have looked excessively run down and decayed, except that this was Detroit and par for the course, considering its location.

Wiltshire closed the driver's side door and locked the vehicle after the others got out.

"Yes. This is it. I'm sure of it," Sam said. "I remember crawling out of that hole right there. They'd tied me up and I was in and out of consciousness, but I remember a flurry of movement. People came and went, running off with whatever they could salvage."

They stood on the edge of the gaping hole and looked down. Several lengths of knobby corrugated tubing descended into the pit.

"They used some kind of heavy machinery and tore all this away. The Heptobscurantum didn't care whatever else they wrecked, they just needed to make sure they got the machine out. I wriggled free several days after they abandoned the location," Sam explained. "They left in such a hurry that maybe they left some clues behind?"

Shandra nodded optimistically and pulled a trio of flashlights from the plastic bag. She loaded them with batteries and handed them off to the others. The cleric looked at the scraps of trash, wondering where to put it. Finally, she dropped it down the hole and followed the others down. At the bottom, she retrieved her trash and placed it into an overturned wastebasket.

"Ya know, you could just leave it," said Wiltshire. "It's not like anyone's gonna notice."

Shandra stated flatly, "But I would still know."

Wiltshire shrugged and then delved into the laboratory. Leftover racks of equipment lined the walls. Safety gear hung from hooks and loose papers were scattered about and deposited wherever the winds had occasionally whipped up and blown them. He leafed through some of it, but nothing had any significant value. A few steel trash cans contained old ashes at the bottom. Wiltshire surmised that anything of importance had been shredded and burned.

"Over here," Sam's voice echoed through the shadows.

The trio gathered in the largest open space.

"Right here is where the machine was," he pointed off to the side. "And that must be where they opened the portals. They needed plenty of space,"

Wiltshire shuddered when he walked through the area. Sam raised an eyebrow when he did so.

"Shandra got goosebumps in that spot, too," the archaeologist said.

Wiltshire bent to the ground and began looking for seals, runes, or mystic signs. "You think it's a coincidence?"

Sam walked into that same spot. The hair on the back of his neck prickled. "No. I think there's a kind of arcane energy... maybe a residual impact of some sort." He thought about it for a moment. "Do you have Respan's scanner that Tay-lore sent you?"

The detective handed it to Sam.

"You think there might be some kind of dark power here?" Shandra asked.

"Not really." Sam put it over his eye and activated it. None of the settings revealed anything. "But I do think that if there is some kind of errant energy signal, it could be detected. The scanners only highlight a few certain readings on the spectrum." He made a grabbing motion to Wiltshire. "Let me see that data unit Tay-lore sent, too. They should be able to interface."

Wiltshire turned it over and gave him a skeptical look. The detective didn't have a head for technology, but he did have a nose for clues. "You got a hunch?"

Sam nodded and began connecting the scanner apparatus to the processor.

"I'll leave you to it, then. I'll look around for other clues." Wiltshire wandered off and into a few office rooms nearby where it looked like some kind of science team had stationed their desks.

Sam looked up and down at the energy readings and isolated the data. "Beta-lore, can you create a new setting on the eyepiece for me?" He punched in a wide, new frequency range for the energies he suspected were present.

"Affirmative," the AI said, making it so.

"Wow," Sam said, looking through the eyeglass at the strange location. He handed Shandra the headset.

She put it on. "Whoa. It looks like a giant tear."

Sam nodded. "That's exactly what it is, I think. The fabric of space was torn open here repeatedly. It's created a kind of soft spot in the dimensional planes: a rift from the fabric being stretched and opened so many times... kind of like rubbing a friction hole through the knees of your blue jeans."

"What are blue jeans?" Shandra asked.

"Nevermind," his mouth kiltered into a grin. "I would bet that this kind of tear has a very specific kind of reading. Beta-lore, can you scan for this kind of anomaly on a planet-wide scale?"

"Affirmative. Tay-lore installed certain protocols that will allow it. The process will take a considerable amount of time."

"Is there any way to speed it up?"

Beta-lore responded, "I can scan locally with an effective range of one thousand, five hundred miles."

"That's local?" Shandra scoffed.

"Earth is about two hundred million miles around, so in the big scale of things, I guess it is," Sam said.

"You will need to get above ground," Beta-lore said. "Slowly rotate the scanner three hundred and sixty degrees."

Sam crawled out of the hole with the device. It was easier this time; before he had been dehydrated, fatigued, and nearly bled dry.

Wiltshire poked around at the desks in the room adjacent to the section with weird readings. He took a printed picture from his pocket and stared at a photo frame on one of the desks. Wiltshire compared the two, and then he tapped the photo enthusiastically with a hunch of his own.

Tossing the picture frame aside, he emerged from the offices and clambered out of the wreckage of the old lab. "I got something," he told them. His peers had crawled back out of the hole.

"Calculating data," Beta-lore said. "One moment. Comparing coordinates to satellite grid."

"You've got a hit, too?" the detective asked.

Sam and Shandra nodded. They looked down as Beta-lore announced an exact reading for a set of coordinates that matched the energy signature.

"Let me guess," ventured Wiltshire, "It's in Houston?"

"How did you know?" Shandra exclaimed.

Wiltshire twirled the keys around his finger. "I'm a detective... I detect things. It's what I do," he grinned. "Come on. Let's get back to the plane. We can get there in about five hours if we hurry."

They climbed into the low-grade rental vehicle and began their drive towards the airstrip. A fancy, black town car passed them, heading the opposite direction as Sam thumbed buttons on the prepaid cell phone he'd purchased when they bought the flashlights.

"That's a pretty fancy rig," Wiltshire said, watching the rear-view mirror as the expensive automobile turned off in the distance. It didn't belong in this part of town, unless some drug kingpin owned it; the detective assumed they had just dodged a potentially messy encounter by their quick departure.

"Who are you calling?" Shandra asked Sam.

"Just a number I've had committed to memory for a very long time... ever since a nasty bit of business with my local PTA group."

"PTA?" she sounded confused.

Wiltshire interjected, "Like Parent Teacher Association?"

Sam nodded. "I'm playing a hunch. We might not have found Zabe, but if we're hunting his brother, we might need the help of another wolf."

"And what... you just happen to know a bunch of werewolves serving on your hometown school board?" Wiltshire laughed. He'd heard of stranger things in his line of work, actually.

"Something like that." He put the phone to his ear. "Yes, hello Archie... by any chance, is your daughter there?"

The Desolation

Caivev stood at Basilisk's side on the overlook of their stronghold. They could watch the majority of Limbus from here. Though they couldn't see much for detail, they got the general overview of a situation below. The Black were rioting again in Jeerzha's district; the social organizer had already formed his own militia. Caivev suspected the trouble went deeper than her husband let on.

Basilisk didn't watch the anarchy below. He looked worried, but he stared into the sky in silence instead. The horizon was still unfamiliar and empty—and that worried him more than a few unruly vyrm.

Something about that clear skyline made Caivev infinitely more fearful than knowing where the Devourer lurked upon the veil of existence. At least then she felt certain that the threshold of reality still constrained him. Now... who knew?

Caivev's scowl matched her husband's. Together, they had finally made a new and strong alliance and put actual thoughts towards building something. Both had finally chosen, and their choices led them away from the vyrms' old order of things. Caivev and Basilisk had re-aligned their warring people and established a proper kingdom... and now an unstoppable evil chose to finally rise from its slumber.

She sighed at the implications.

"You have thoughts?" Basilisk asked, his eyes remained locked on the skyline.

"Yes," she said curtly.

Basilisk turned his gaze to her. A smile tugged at the corner of his lip; they had not been together very long, but she had already learned how to needle him in all the best ways. "Will you share?"

"I am upset," she admitted. "Until recently, I don't believe I knew what I really wanted. After your proposal, I finally realized what that was: to create, thrive, and prosper. I was once the servant of your brother, Nitthogr—*more so* I was the servant of Sh'logath. That path may have brought me here, but I would have never found purpose inside of that road... it led only to destruction and disappointment."

Caivev stared down at her feet and pushed a few pebbles over the ledge with her toe. "I keep wondering what *you* want? You were a Herald of Sh'logath once—one of the two Brothers of the Apocalypse: the Thinker and the Beast. Wasn't it your role to release the Devourer? There was a prophecy, you know."

Basilisk nodded slowly. "I feel much the same way as you, though I had the secret words of the Architect King as my anchor. At first, I thought those whispered words crippled me, forced me into indecision and waiting. In the end, they freed me. They caused my proposal to you. I used to think about the old prophecies… but time passed and they became just that. Old… nothing more than words meant to steer me. Not all 'prophecies' foretell. Eventually, I yearned for something new."

Caivev met his eyes. She spoke tenderly, not demanding an answer. "What did the Architect King say to you?"

Basilisk lowered his voice, but spoke freely with his wife. "'You will not destroy me because you can not destroy me. You know the nature of eternity. Some day you will choose new allegiances and forsake Sh'logath. It shall come to pass because of a girl who changes everything.'"

"Claire Jones," Caivev stated, recognizing her part in starting this revolution.

Basilisk took his wife by the chin and made her look into his eyes. "Perhaps. But perhaps it was *you*."

Caivev's eyes sparkled, and she smiled warmly at his unexpected words. She mulled the implications over in her mind and decided that the vyrmic prophecy must have been wrong. Sometimes prophecies were just as Basilisk said: words spoken by fools and addicts.

"Sh'logath is gone," Basilisk returned his eyes to the empty spot in the sky. "The only way for that to happen, short of his banishment from the multi-verse by the Architect King, would be for him to be unleashed—and that would require some kind of herald. *I am not that herald.*"

"*Could something else have banished him?* You sent the Architect King to the Prime and we know that the vyrm shade Vylar, who was disguised as General Zahaben, was freed from petrification before his death. Perhaps they found a way? And if the Architect King had access to the Tesseract…"

Basilisk shook his head. "Perhaps the Tesseract caused it, but not likely. If the humans learned to channel its power to that end, they would have released all the others as well. My spies say that is not the case… and then there is the matter of Shjikara. The priest is alive and well—my last act of obedience before forsaking the Devourer was to petrify that man."

He had not shared every secret with his wife. "I played many angles over the years and kept many stratagems available to play. There is only one way Vylar was released: an enchanted rune of return, stolen from a Veritas cleric many generations ago. He claimed a secret knowledge in crafting them. He'd sneaked into the Desolation in the hopes of freeing his lord, the Architect King."

"Can he make more?" Caivev asked excitedly.

He shook his head. "He died before surrendering the secret. I possessed only the one rune. At the direct command of Sh'logath, I put this rune stone into the hand of Shjikara as I petrified him. It is still trapped within the High Priest's hand."

Caivev swallowed. "Is he the Herald?"

Basilisk nodded slowly. "I believe so."

"Chartarra was right, then... Nitthogr is alive," Caivev whispered. "In spirit, at least."

Basilisk shot her a surprised look. "Chartarra is dead. I killed your general when we were still at war—he tried to kill me, you know."

"Those were certainly his orders," Caivev shrugged playfully. "He is returned. Chartarra sought me out... he become a Seeker of Maetha after his first death." She pointed to the civil unrest below them. "He tells me that the Black have been stirred to violence because of visions and dreams... they come with the return of your brother, who is calling them again to prepare for war."

Basilisk bit his lower lip. He had not foreseen this move and was put in an odd position: he had to play a game with rules he did not understand and could not exploit. "Shjikara... is... Nitthogr?" Voicing the question only determined his answer.

He focused on his own words for a few moments. A melancholy smile stretched upon his lips. The sorcerer's return meant that Basilisk's final moments of obedience to the agod weren't somehow responsible for whatever had happened... at least not directly. Basilisk had not accidentally freed the agod.

"If Sh'logath has been loosed upon the multi-verse, he could destroy everything we have been working towards," Caivev said. "If he has been somehow conjured, whether by your brother or by another, there is no force in existence that can stop him. Well... there *might* be one, but I do not know the Maethan prophecies well enough; only the Seekers remember them."

Basilisk always knew everything that happened within his walls and knew the reports from his dungeons. "We do have a few prisoners in our dungeon right now who claim to be Seekers of Maetha." He gave his wife a knowing look, certain she was already aware of them.

Caivev had kept as much of that under the radar as possible. She weighed the options and then told Basilisk everything: how she was rescued by a rover at Sharonash, how Jeerzha and his allies murdered a woman and child and how it bothered her, and about the Maethan's new belief that Maetha was dunnischkte.

He had been the Herald of Sh'logath for many lifetimes before she had been born—and Caivev worried that his first instinct might have been to kill her. The stakes were large. He listened to her words and at the end of them, Basilisk nodded slowly and thoughtfully.

"Then we must go and hear from these prisoners below the keep." He took her hand in his and they walked towards the door.

Approaching them stomped Charsk, the leader and High Priest of the Sh'logath Cult. Some new zeal burned in the vyrm's eyes; it was a change from the glassy, drunken shine that usually characterized him. Some new purpose had sobered him.

Both emperor and empress knew that Charsk was Blackborn.

Charsk passed by the two guards at the entrance and closed the door. "I assume you have both heard the news?"

Neither of the royal couple indicated one way or the other.

Charsk continued, "The Awakening might well be at hand. Your servant Jeerzha, a member of the Black nonetheless, is organizing his countrymen. Sh'logath has called and Limbus shall answer!" He rubbed his hands greedily. "And what have you planned to do with those rovers he says are in your dungeon? I hear they are a part of a larger company that is even now moving towards the capital."

Basilisk cocked his head at the news. "I plan to go now and speak to them."

"Speak to them? Their words are poison! You must execute them immediately," Charsk insisted. "If word gets out that you entertained them, you might well risk a civil war..."

The emperor's claws flashed out, and he cut Charsk's jugular in one smooth motion. "I do not seek your permission," Basilisk stated.

Grabbing his throat, the vyrm priest coughed and spluttered once, and then collapsed to the tiled floor of the royal chamber with surprise frozen on his face.

"Idrakka?" Basilisk called.

The door opened and one of the tarkhūn stationed outside his door entered. Normally, Caivev would have bristled at Idrakka's presence, but not this time. Idrakka the frostmancer had once betrayed her for his secret allegiance to Basilisk, but now was the time when such devotion became convenient.

"My lord?" Idrakka asked. His eyes met Caivev's and silently pleaded for a chance to demonstrate his loyalty to her as well as her husband.

Until now, she had avoided him. At best, she'd tolerated the tarkhūn who could summon intense cold and kept him off of her personal retinue when possible. She'd always favored the fiercely loyal Skrom, who she knew would gladly die for her.

Basilisk bobbed his head towards the body. "Charsk has had an accident. For the time being, no one must know."

Idrakka nodded. "I'll see to it at once. Only the carrion birds shall know."

Caivev conjured a mental picture of the ice-lord freezing and shattering the corpse before scattering the busted pieces for the vermin and carrion-wings to devour.

Basilisk wiped the blood from his talons and then gripped his wife's hand again. Together, they departed for the dungeons.

Earth

Jacob Sisyphus exited the black town car and instructed the driver to keep it running. The old building, once owned by Bruce Cannon, was a mess. Huge sections of wall, floor, and roof were torn away. Sisyphus knew why; he had been there when they'd extracted Walther and his equipment. He touched his side momentarily, remembering the broken ribs and old injuries he'd sustained in Nebraska shortly before moving the equipment to a safer location.

The pro wrestler remembered the way down. He walked through the dilapidated remains of industrial equipment and a massive, decommissioned turbine housing. With the power deactivated, the hidden stairwell could not be accessed by throwing a switch, so the wizard used the power of his kophesh. The turbine shuddered as Sisyphus grabbed it with his mind and pushed it aside with concentrated effort. Enough of the stairs revealed itself that he could pass by.

At the bottom of the psuedoscience lab, Sisyphus found the place exactly as he expected it. He rummaged through the shelves and overturned, mostly empty bins. He looked for any kind of data or spare parts for the destroyed teleportation contraption that the rogue vyrm had destroyed in his German penthouse suite.

Caivev and the Heptobscurantum cleaners had done a thorough job of eliminating any trace of the old lab's purpose, he realized. Sisyphus frowned. He had already secured a new corps of prospects to take over Pietro Walther's work. They could not, however, recreate it all from scratch.

Though they had most of the strange doctor's work and notes, the researchers didn't understand key pieces of it. They needed to see it in action or study existing pieces of the contraption that had not been annihilated by the scaly invaders. They were missing critical components.

Sisyphus meandered through the underground construction and entered the research pod. He found a couple of desks littered with stacks of paper and other discarded items that were nonessential to the project. The wizard grinned when he spotted a desk decorated with pro wrestling paraphernalia. Sisyphus picked up an action figure bearing his likeness. He posed it a few different ways and then set it off to the side, leaving it behind as a small monument to Dr. Pietro Walther.

Wandering to the next desk over, Sisyphus found Cerci Heiderscheidt's workstation. Not nearly as well adorned as Walther's, she had only a simple post card to adorn it. A framed picture of the old Astrodome in Texas and a team photo of the players lay on the desk. He picked up a picture frame. By the looks of it, it seemed recently disturbed.

Sisyphus examined the piece. The photo was of a little girl in an Astro's cap sitting in the seats with someone who looked like her father; she looked to be about five years old. The ticket stubs, from a 1999 game, were behind the glass making a kind of shadowbox.

Doing the mental math, he guessed at the little girl's age and surmised the identities of the girl and her father. Sisyphus knew from Walther that Heiderscheidt was something of a genius in applied metaphysics. Although the old scientist hadn't really understood where she had disappeared to or why, he did know that she was orphaned at a young age and had very few ties to any people or places.

Sisyphus also knew that the old stadium had sat empty since the nineteen ninety-nine season. An old sports stadium made a perfect hiding place. He smashed the frame and slid the ticket stubs into his pocket.

He grinned and headed for the stairs. The wizard had already planned his next move.

Chapter Seventeen

The Prime

"Do it now," Nitthogr demanded as he playfully toed through the shattered remains of the Architect King. He made sure to grind to dust any piece larger than half his fist.

Gita frowned and turned the dial on the box. Her master cut her across the arm with a shard of the broken statue and then used the jagged piece to flick the blood against the portal's activator.

Nitthogr had already selected settings that would direct the destination to the Eternal Sky, a dimension with an overly optimistic name. The irony drew a smile upon the Herald's lips. He dug a taloned grip into Gita's shoulder with his non-petrified hand.

Together they went to the portal and planeswalked to the other realm.

Awaiting them on the other side, an army of the Black stood arrayed and waiting for their arrival. A well-muscled, but lithe vyrm with piercing eyes stood at the helm of the gathering.

Nitthogr raised his arms and beckoned them to a roaring cheer. They complied, and the cacophony shook the trees surrounding the forest glade where they'd met. Flocks of a kind of bird Gita had never seen before leapt into the sky.

"The Awakening is at hand!" the sorcerer shouted, eliciting more cheers.

Gita stood behind the monster, stoic. She'd already cried out all of her tears and her hopes had fully evaporated. Even this ceremony did not move her as the leader of this faction of vyrm approached his master. She had seen this same thing happen already to the other four leaders of the vyrm tribes.

Nitthogr made his claim, screaming it to the sky, defying the Architect King and challenging him to send a hero to stop him. "I am Sh'logath incarnate! None can stand before the power of the vyrm. I am Herald. I am the Beast of the Apocalypse—and I demand your fealty."

The wave of reptilian invaders bowed in unison. Their tribal chief sank to his knees before the dread lord's acolyte.

Nitthogr melted further into his Sh'logathian form. Arms split into tendrils and he became a writhing mass of fleshy terror. Amid the tentacles, an ebon proboscis raised high overhead and crashed down, stabbing into the chief's skull like a nail piercing a grape.

The crowd gasped but remained steadfast. Their chief writhed against the pain and Nitthogr's appendages held him firm as he injected something dark deep within the tribal leader.

Slowly, the vyrm's eyes turned jet black, as if he'd been injected with ink. Finally, he blinked his obsidian eyes and Nitthogr removed the claw from the wound.

The tentacle monster reformed into the sorcerer's shape. "You are now filled with my spirit," he hissed. "You will know my will and my thoughts at all times." He turned to address the gathered army. "Prepare for war, my loyal children! You will know when the time has come to launch the attack." He took Gita by the arm and headed back for the portal.

"It will come much sooner than any dare to think."

Still Lost

Bithia wandered through the forest for a while longer, becoming so hopelessly lost that despair set in deeper yet. She plopped down and wailed, giving a deep, snotty cry.

Although she'd gone as bravely as possible into the Darque, she'd felt confident in her abilities then—she knew her powers. This... this was different. Bithia was out of her depth and had never really been in this sort of position before. She had no powers, no resources, nowhere to go, and no hope to keep her going. *Claire had, though... she'd continued on and kept us alive after our first fusion. Maybe she's really the stronger one?*

Bithia was desperate to have Claire's presence again. Through her tears, she noticed a glint of moonlight reflecting off something in the soil. A shiny piece of metal had been half buried in the sod ahead of her; some kind of windswept trash must have brought it to that spot ages ago.

She reached for it and cleaned it as best as she could with her spit and a sleeve. Bithia stared into her dim reflection and wiped her tears away. She dragged her fingers through her hair as best as she could, a natural and feminine response to seeing her bedraggled visage.

In her mind, Bithia called out for Claire, even knowing she'd lost the ability and the right to do so. Finally, hearing no response, Bithia turned away—but she wasn't in the forest anymore.

Bithia recognized the place where she found herself: it was her apartment in the Prime. It was decorated just as it had been before Claire had ever come on the scene and Bithia felt as much herself as she ever had.

She sensed others in the room with her with a kind of shadow-memory of her powers. Bithia turned and located the minds that she'd felt. Thirty-two children occupied the room with her.

"So many kids," she said. They were well behaved, as much as youngsters could manage to be, that is.

As Bithia looked closer, one of the children felt distinctly non-human. One nearby child, a little girl, shied away from another child: a young boy who pestered her. When the boy turned, Bithia noticed the scales. He was vyrm.

The princess swallowed, and she saw the symbolism in her vision. Each of the children represented one of the dimensions of the Tesseract which she governed and protected—but she was responsible for all of them as the daughter of the Architect King.

A sense of darkness crept into the room like a chill wind: a distinctly astral kind of dread that Bithia had felt before. One of the children screamed when something banged on the door and demanded entry.

Bithia's senses had returned, and she felt the full terror of *him*. Nitthogr was on the other side of the door and he felt stronger than he ever had before.

"You will let me in!" he shrieked from the outside. "Let me in so I may devour the children."

The kids screamed and clung to her legs, pressing in against her for safety. The closest child who had scrambled to her for protection was the scaley boy. He buried his face into her hip as if it could hide him.

More pounding. Boots echoed in the hall beyond as so many of the enemy's shock troopers stomped towards the door that it shook the floor.

Bithia was trapped. There was nothing more she could do, but she knew that she had to protect the children by whatever means possible. She glanced back at the mirror and announced, "I can sense you there, Claire Jones. I have only a scrap of my abilities right now—and I'm sure you must have allowed me access to them. That means you've got to be close."

There was no response. Bithia waddled over towards the mirror as best as she could with the children in tow. It did not provide a reflection.

"Come on Claire. I know you're in there—I may have lost my powers, but I can sense that you're still in there. I can't initiate contact because you blocked my powers last time."

The door cracked loudly as the banging intensified. Someone smashed it with a battering ram. Children screamed, and the door splintered. Vyrm strode into the apartment on Nitthogr's heels.

Bithia pleaded with the mirror. "We've got to stop fighting and work together." She swallowed hard and admitted to her reflection, "You are the stronger one, Claire... and I need you."

Claire appeared in the mirror and time seemed to stop. The vyrm froze—even Nitthogr became time locked.

From the other side of the mirror, she asked, "Do you really need me?"

Bithia nodded, bleary eyed.

Claire looked at her other self with a pained look on her face. "I... I'm sorry. Sometimes I forget that I'm supposed to be calm and collected and some grand example of royalty... and then I just smash it all. I guess I'm not you. I'm no princess."

Bithia nodded enthusiastically. "But that is *why* you are strong! You are *different*, Claire. We complement each other. We need each other like two halves of a whole."

Claire shook her head. "No. That's not quite it. We are both our own wholes... but we are so much more than that when we are together." She looked Bithia up and down and then looked at the children. "I... I'm sorry I tried to hurt you. I thought I was taking away the thing that you valued most, your abilities. I can see now that you value *these* more."

Bithia agreed and then ventured, "What can we do now? Where do we go from here?"

"I've had lots of time to think," Claire admitted. "Do you remember the last time we spoke like this?"

"It was in a school," Bithia said. "We fused until we were hit with the vyrm's psychic poison."

Claire nodded. "We fused. We were like one, then, but still in both our bodies. That poison's effects have haunted us this whole time, even though it was long ago purged. Now we share one body, one soul and two minds..." she reached inside her chest with a hand

and pulled a glowing orb out from where her heart would have been if she was flesh and blood.

Bithia raised her eyebrows. Psionic merger was an advanced psychic skill. Claire had truly grown in that very silence which had made Bithia more fragile.

The brilliant orb blazed with chaotic ripples of illumination as it passed beyond the glass of the mirror; it pulsed as their heartbeats synced. Claire's hand pushed through and she offered up the orb.

"If you accept it," Claire said, "there is no more Claire or Bithia. We are Claire *and* Bithia... we are one, and we are so much more." She looked into Bithia's eyes. "We stop fighting because there is no more you and I. There is only *us.*"

Bithia took the orb and pressed it into her breast. The glowing ball melted through her and when the princess opened her eyes again, the two were merged. They had become something new.

Time resumed in that moment and Nitthogr held his ground as the vyrm warriors surrounded them. The sorcerer locked eyes with Claire and walked a cautious circle around the children like a wary predator facing down a lioness who guarded her cubs.

"Something has changed inside you," Nitthogr hissed.

"You have no idea," she said, reaching out a hand of warning. "Leave now—return to the void of Nihil or I will destroy you."

Something glinted in Nitthogr's eyes. The dark light in them was both devious and deadly—but they also recognized that this prey was more well guarded than anticipated.

"Surrender a single child and we will leave," he bartered.

She looked down at the terrified children and her eyes locked on the vyrm one.

"Yes," Nitthogr said. "Leave us with *that one* and we shall depart." His voice dripped with evil.

The princess glared at him with her fiery gaze. "No." She reached out with her mind before the enemy could react and she melted them all with a blaze of psychic fury. Nitthogr and his vyrm boiled down to their base elements and bubbled like toxic soup in wax-like puddles.

Her children clung to her, praising her and thanking her for protecting them.

The vyrm child looked up at her. He said, "You're finally here. We've been waiting for you for so long."

Looking at him, the child evaporated like mist with the rest of the vision and the princess found herself in the forest. She stood with renewed vigor and saw what looked like a straight line breaking through the trees.

"That has got to be man made," she mused and walked towards it. After arriving on the long, straight trail, she recognized it as an ATV path. The trail markers, written in English, indicated it was a state trail—that meant she was on Earth, and in the United States.

She started walking, knowing that it wouldn't be long before she would be able to find her way out, and then, hopefully, call for help.

Chapter Eighteen

*E*arth

"You're sure this is the place?" Shandra asked, looking through the scanner. She and the others sat across a vacant parking lot inside a rental vehicle while they surveyed the old stadium.

Wiltshire held up the security system photo of their targets and compared it to the decades-old signage. "I am."

"You said you'd buy supper if you were wrong," Sam said. "But what if you're right?"

"I'm not wrong," Wiltshire insisted, and handed Sam the photo. *n Astrod.* It fit perfectly against the colorful letters spelling *Houston Astrodome.*

"The background," Sam said, "it looks like maybe a loading dock or something?"

"Exactly my thoughts," Wiltshire said. He retrieved the duffel bag from their rental car and slung it over his shoulder.

They stalked around the perimeter for a short while, looking for any indicators of forced entry or easy access. The doors they'd checked proved mostly secure. One access in the rear-most secluded part of the stadium boasted a shiny chain and a new padlock.

"They're in this part," Wiltshire said matter-of-factly.

"How do you know?" asked Shandra, who turned on the scanner to check for signals.

"The chain is new. Probably locked it from the outside. Remember, they've got a teleportation rig. Once they're inside, they could lock it and never bother with another door again."

Sam called from a nearby electrical hub. "Someone's jacked into the power grid over here." He wiggled the security panel to show that it had been tampered with.

Shandra readjusted the eyepiece over her brow. "I have a reading," she said. "It's not as strong as the one in Detroit, but it's there. They are probably using it for very small, limited jumps, so it has not left behind as much of a dimensional echo, yet."

Wiltshire set his duffel down and began rummaging through his tools. "You're probably right. About how far away is the signal?" He withdrew a heavy bolt cutter to deal with the lock and chain.

"Do you think we should wait for our backup to arrive?" Sam asked. He'd already made arrangements for help.

Wiltshire barely responded. "They'll get here when they get here." Before he had a chance to clip the chain, Shandra smashed it free with her hammer.

She shrugged defensively. "I thought time was of the essence."

The detective kept his face neutral. He both hated and loved the banter—but mostly it reminded him why he was on this mission to begin with: his partner. The Scholomance had either killed or abducted Atticus, and Wiltshire needed to know his friend's fate. From what he'd learned of the strigoi, death was more merciful than the alternative.

They breached the door and kept their voices down. The loading access met a hallway junction, and they identified the power cable tying them into the grid; the entire corridor descended lower as they followed the cord and the distance and depths made any noise from the surface extremely hard to hear.

The group ventured deeper and further into the dark. Wiltshire held his gun firm and Shandra gripped her hammer. Sam brought up the rear.

They turned a corner and discovered a loading and staging zone that was lit by freestanding lights. A massive contraption sat in the middle of the area, surrounded by sleeping bags, discarded food wrappers, assorted trash, and sacks of cash, coin, and other valuables.

Wiltshire and the others pulled back into the hall. Barely discernible voices could be heard near the machine.

Shandra confirmed it was one of the gate devices. At this range, the signal was easily read. She peeked back at it; the terminal looked more like a cobbled-together collection of old parts, each interconnected to a fancy briefcase by a web of cables. The case bore the property markings of the Heptobscurantum cult.

"Let me try something," Sam said. Before the others could argue, he stepped around the corner, put his hands up in case their targets were armed. "Hello? Are you there? I'm looking for Zurrah, Son of Zahaben, and Cerci Heiderscheidt."

Feet scrambled somewhere in the distance, hidden behind the contraption. A flutter of intense whispers, both from Sam's targets and from his partners around the corner, rippled through the shadowy room.

"Miss Heiderscheidt, I don't know if you remember me, but the folks you used to work for once hooked me up to one of these things."

"Stop right there," a feminine voice called out.

Sam complied.

"Are you armed?" Cerci asked.

Sam turned his hands over both ways. "No," he admitted. "But I have friends nearby, and they are. But right now, it's just me."

"You know I could slice you all to pieces with this machine, right? It's stronger than a laser and nothing known to man could stop it."

Sam casually sank into a seated position. "I'm well aware of that—remember, I've seen it before. But I'm just here to talk," he spoke with a warm, fatherly tone. "I'm not here to stop you, rob you, or whatever you might think. I actually came to you for help. My daughter is in trouble, and I'm hoping you might be willing to help me."

"I don't exactly have a long track record with benevolence," she answered back. "I've done nothing but hurt your family in the past... or at least help others who did."

Sam bobbed his head. "But they aren't here now, and I'm not asking them. I'm asking *you*. I also think your friend will want to help. Zurrah, your brother might be in some kind of trouble, too. Zabe has gone missing... and my daughter is his fiance."

The heads of the two young people poked out from behind the machine. They pulled back and whispered fiercely. Finally, they both came out, but Cerci carried the device's controls with her.

They sat next to him and Sam asked, "Why the Astrodome?"

"Her father was an Astros fan," Wiltshire said, coming out from behind the corner and holstering his weapon. He kept his distance, but made himself visible. "He took you to a game here when you were little, right?"

Cerci nodded. "How did you know?"

"I found the ticket stub and photo. Plus, I pulled a file from your history—I didn't have much else to go on. But your boyfriend here is another story."

Wiltshire caught Cerci off-guard with the romantic label. "Oh, uh. We're not officially..."

Zurrah grabbed her hand and interlocked his fingers with hers. "I'm not from around here," he explained.

"Indeed not," Shandra came closer and sat down. She laid her hammer in front of her, knowing that Zurrah would recognize it and understand that she was of the Veritas. "We all have different missions, but we're here because of Tay-lore."

Cerci looked at Zurrah and then shook her head. "We don't know anyone named Tay-lore."

Sam locked eyes with Zurrah. "He's a friend of my daughter's and your brother. He died helping us find you. Android in service of the throne ring any bells?"

Zurrah vaguely recollected and nodded slowly. His path with the android had not crossed as often as Zabe's had, and he was taken by Nitthogr when he was still very young.

By now, even Wiltshire took a seat in the conversation circle. He laid out everything that they'd learned in the last couple of days. "We're not here to stop what you guys are doing or make you give back any of the loot, except that page you took from the Heptobscurantum vault. Honestly, you can keep all of it—on some level I can respect what you've managed to accomplish with your machine. We just need your help. Without it," he punctuated his final words with a snap that echoed in the darkness beyond the light racks, "all of reality as we know it might stop."

"It's Claire," she spoke into the pay phone in the truck stop in a remote part of Louisiana on Interstate ten. She'd decided in that moment what to call herself after the princess finally merged into a complete version of herself. "Do you have Jackie's phone number? I assume she has a cell number after..." She began scribbling the digits on a napkin.

She thanked Jackie's parents, Archie and Janet, and hung up. Claire had never been so grateful to see a pay phone in her life; most places had ditched them long ago. Luckily, this one hadn't been phased out yet.

Claire stacked up the coins along the counter near where the phone was attached to a cinder block wall. The campers she'd stumbled upon had been kind enough to furnish her with a quick meal, a ride to the truck stop, and whatever change they could scrounge together from the cup holders in their Volkswagen bus. It was enough for a couple of phone calls.

She punched in the number Jackie's mother had given her and waited as it dialed.

"Hello?" Jackie answered in an odd voice she reserved for using with telemarketers.

"Jackie! Jackie, it's Claire..."

"Claire? Ohmygodforreal? Wait... Claire or Bithia?"

"Claire," she said. "Bithia and I are... I'll explain later, but we're all good again. Better than good. So much has happened in the last couple of weeks. Where are you guys? I'm stuck at a Louisiana truck stop, of all places, and the portal gates won't work."

"Yeah," Jackie said. "I talked to your dad just a little while ago. Wulftone and I are on our way to meet him and Shandra in Houston—our plane just landed, in fact. Let me get you the number for the burner phone he's using here on earth. Let me know when you're ready."

Claire grabbed her pen and napkin. "I'm ready. Go." She jotted the digits down and then her eyes caught a familiar face leaning against the wall near her, watching her. He wore a ball cap and looked like he'd just come from a county fair where he operated the tilt-a-whirl. But she'd recognize him anywhere.

Zabe!

"I... uh... I've got to go. I'll see you soon." Claire hung up the receiver and turned to her fiance. "Zabe?"

The man shook his head. He put a finger to his lips to insist she remained quiet as he pulled up his shirt to reveal the handgun in his waistband. "I'm Rob," he told her.

Claire frowned. She saw the startling difference in the man's eyes. He was Zabe's Earth copy, just as Claire had been Bithia's. The last time she'd seen Rob was before the Mullen Nebraska incident; he was Heptobscurantum, and he'd kidnapped Claire and turned her over to Nitthogr.

"I'm sorry, mister, you must have me mistaken for someone else," she tried to play coy and hoped he'd fall for it. Claire started to move past him, but he pushed her against the wall with just enough force to move her without any true violence.

"You don't think I could ever forget you, do you, Claire Jones? I know we're a long way from high school in Minnesota, but I remember." He winked. "Besides, I overheard your phone calls. Talk about irony, or dumb luck, or whatever… maybe it's kismet. I dunno." Rob put a hand on the butt of his concealed firearm and motioned for her to head towards the door. "Now let's go."

She growled and left for the door. Claire was smart enough to see the writing on the wall, but knew she couldn't fall into the hands of the Heptobscurantum cult. Right before she was prepared to bolt and hope Rob had terrible aim, he put a hand on her from behind and twisted a fistful of cloth to keep a handle on her.

"I remember how fiery you were last time, and you're not getting away from me unless I say so," Rob whispered.

Claire sighed. She'd have to wait for an opportunity she could exploit later. Claire hung her head and walked grudgingly towards the familiar semi-truck cab where she'd been held hostage once before.

Wulftone and Jackie came down the tunnel with Shandra while Cerci and Zurrah explained how Cerci had come up with the plan to steal resources from the Heptobscurantum's suppliers. "She called it a Robin Hood thing," Zurrah said with a confused lilt to his voice.

"I had a hunch that Caivev and her, uh, people, were just going to leave Zurrah in that other dimension. We'd become friends while at the temple and I couldn't just leave him there." Cerci shrugged. "So I stole the first gen model of the machine that Doctor Walther and I built. I didn't have all the know-how to actually *build* the thing from scratch. Some of the data he'd always refused to share, but I knew if I had the central control node I could cobble together the rest with pretty common parts." She indicated the briefcase that had clearly been taken from her previous employers. A system of vacuum tubes unlike anything else they'd ever seen lay nestled in the center amid warning labels reading *Danger: Wundrefluvium.*

Next to a wheeled IV pole where a sack of red fluid hanged, Cerci sheepishly tried to hide a cooler behind the bulk of the contraption. A large sticker on it read *Property of Houston Area Blood Bank.* "Once I got Zurrah out, we just kept raiding them and going after bigger and bigger targets." she flashed a subtle smile for their accomplishments.

Once Jackie was close enough, she rushed over to give Sam a hug. She'd already been brought up to speed on the situation, as had Wulftone. "I'm so happy to see you guys." She pulled away. "How's the reception down here? Did you get Claire's call?"

Sam shot her an incredulous look. "Claire called? She's here?"

Jackie nodded. "Yes. And it was *Claire,*" she insisted, cluing in only those aware of the situation that there had been any issues.

Sam checked his phone. No messages or missed calls, even though he had full service down here. "How long ago?"

Jackie shrugged. "Ninety minutes ago. Maybe more?"

Zurrah spotted his cousin, and Wulftone walked over and gave him a huge bear hug. He looked over the youth who had grown so much since their last encounter. He took off the leather cuff from around his arm. It bore the Vangandran wolf sigil. Wulftone latched it around the young man's wrist. "I think this belongs to you," he said.

The youngest son of Zahaben choked up at the gesture. He knew what it meant. It was a family heirloom that had once belonged to his father.

Sam, Shandra, and Wiltshire had already brought Zurrah up to speed on his family situation, or what they knew of it since his capture as a child.

"Don't you need it to shape-shift?" Jackie asked.

Wulftone shook his head, as if unsure. "It's time to take off the training wheels, I think. Zabe was able to do it without the bracer after he'd worn it a while... I think I'll be able to as well." He clutched arms with his cousin. "We are Vangandra. It's in our blood." He clapped the lad on the back and turned to Sam and Shandra.

Sam had begun another worry spiral since he hadn't gotten a call yet from Claire. Wulftone noticed and gave him something to focus on. "Hey Sam, what have you got on our over-all situation?"

The archaeologist shook away his anxiety and put a marker to the free standing dry erase board near Cerci's machine. He began drawing up names of those he thought the survivors could trust and their allegiances. "Let's map out a plan," he said.

Shandra - Veritas, Earth
Sam Jones - Earth
Zabe - missing
Wulftone - GC, Earth
Jackie - GC, Earth
Jenner - GC, Prison/Prime
Shjikara - Enemy/Prime
Gita - Enemy/Prime

"Whoa, hold on," Wulftone said. "Gita is with the enemy and Jenner is with us... do we know that?"

Sam continued making his list, mostly so he could make sense of their situation and their resources. "You haven't seen the video yet. It's not pretty, but it explains a lot." He waved to the detective, who stood and activated Beta-lore.

Wiltshire introduced himself. "My name is Vikrum Wiltshire and Tay-lore was my friend. That makes it hard for me to replay this, but the details probably mean more to you than they do to me."

As he cued up the video, Sam pulled Cerci aside and conferred privately. He flipped the marker board and used its back. Together, they completed some kind of complex equation.

Wiltshire activated the video and let it run its course. They saw everything: the murder, the gloating confession, the details about Jenner and Gita that Nitthogr intended to remain secret.

Those who hadn't seen it yet watched appalled. They stood as if in shock and Wulftone asked, "What do we do next... where do we go from here, besides search for Zabe?"

Sam announced, "We might be unable to find Zabe; we'll need to hope that *he* finds *us*. But I think we're going to need every ally we can get right now. I'm hoping and praying we get a call any minute from my daughter, but we have a small window to get at least one more corpsman."

Cerci added the last couple of notes from the equation and finished punching in data to the machine's central array. Sam flipped the board and circled Jenner's name. "We can't leave the kid behind."

Heads bobbed and then a triangular gate split the air. Its seams rippled with crimson energy like chain lightning and then it expanded to reveal the inside of the prison where Jenner remained incarcerated. The equations had been close enough to open the rift in the hallway outside of the cell.

Behind bars, Jenner stared at the menacing shape that had haunted him for years—ever since his father's abduction. Finally, he noticed the faces of friends on the other side. His face turned from rage to surprise and relief.

"Um... hey guys," Jenner said. "It's about time you all came to my rescue."

"Yeah," Wulftone said, "Sorry about that. It was a delicate situation, and it took some doing. We're basically moving heaven and earth to get you out."

"It's that bad already?" Jenner asked, still blocked by the bars of his cell door. He guessed, "You found out about Nitthogr."

"It's worse than anyone realizes," Wulftone agreed.

Jenner noticed, "I don't see Zabe with you."

Wulftone shook his head gravely. "He's been missing ever since the... incident."

Jenner scowled. "He'll turn up. When he does, he and I are gonna have some words—him of all people shouldda known I was innocent."

"Understood," Wulftone said. He turned his head to something on the other side of the gate. All the earth-side heroes ran to something Jenner could not see from within his cell.

"So get me out of here already," Jenner howled. He shook the door and roared, trapped with a row of bars between the portal and his cell. Confinement forced him to watch as his friends battled against something in another dimension—something he couldn't see that had taken them by surprise.

Eldritch blasts zipped by like comets with telltale streaks of energy trailing behind. Jenner only had a glimpse and could not see the full picture.

Finally he saw it: the face of his hated enemy, Jacob Sisyphus. The man who had taken his father now attacked his friends and Jenner was powerless to help.

He could hear the screams and noises of battle on the other side. Suddenly, the gate began moving towards Jenner. The young corpsman backpedaled, knowing how dangerous the fiery edges of the portal were.

The triangle cut through the bars as if they weren't even there. They snapped and fell to the floor inside of the gate, clanking onto the ground on Earth.

Jenner growled, loosing all his rage; he charged forward and launched himself through the portal. The Corpsman tucked and rolled to the ground. A fraction of a second later, the portal blinked out of existence. The machine opening the rift broke apart with a loud ripping noise and a small burst of flames.

Cerci screamed as Sisyphus batted her aside. She flew several feet and skidded across the floor, knocking over one of the light sources. It erupted in a shower of sparks and darkness.

The wizard produced the ticket stubs he'd collected in Detroit and tossed them after the woman. "You forgot these," he said as he wrenched the machine's central control unit free—the part that was the proprietary secret of Dr. Pietro Walther. It was the only piece that Cerci could not reconstruct on her own. He tucked it under his arm and began heading for the exit.

"Stop him!" Screamed Sam.

Wiltshire rolled to his side and tried to get to his feet, himself punch drunk and his firearm lost somewhere in the shadows after the initial assault.

Both Wulftone and Zurrah shifted into their Lycan forms. They looked at each other, both surprised that they'd summoned whatever internal grit was necessary to make such a transformation. The werewolves launched themselves at their enemy.

Shandra picked herself up off the floor and roared as she joined their charge, hefting her battle-hammer.

Sisyphus threw a bolt of energy at her, but she deflected it with her mystic hammer. It splashed against the mallet head like a ball of water and she continued charging after him.

The wizard gripped his kophesh and both of the werewolves flew off their feet, flung into the distance at opposite ninety-degree angles, each smashed aside by a wall of force. Sisyphus used his blade to block the Veritas soldier just in time; he caught her hammer against the ancient blade.

They traded blows. Either would have been lethal had one of them connected.

Whap! The wet impact of steel on flesh echoed in the shadows.

Sisyphus screamed and stood erect. One of the steel bars cut from Jenner's cell protruded from his torso. Carved sharply from the angle it was trimmed to, it penetrated the wizard's shoulder where the young man had thrown it like a javelin.

Shandra wound up and smashed her hammer at Sisyphus, intending a killing stroke. It recoiled off an arcane force-field that Sisyphus threw up just in time. The hammer hit so hard that it shattered the energy wall and flung the hammer aside, knocking Shandra backward.

The werewolves howled in the distance as they righted themselves. Wiltshire spotted his nine millimeter and scrambled for it. Panic washed over the invading wizard as he realized his enemies stood a chance to win.

Sisyphus returned a blow for a blow and blasted Jenner with a bolt of pure energy. It sent him reeling off his feet.

Summoning arcane powers, and feeling the distinct drain on his energy caused by his wounded shoulder, Sisyphus poured all his remaining energy into one final blast. The shock-wave of pure force knocked everyone from their feet and a crest of fire blasted behind it, emanating off the thaumaturge like an expanding ring of fire.

Everything near and behind the heroes burst into flames.

Jenner coughed and rolled to his knees, ignoring the smoldering mark that charred his chest. "After him! We can defeat him!" He got to his feet and realized that most of his comrades were still down.

Wulftone and Zurrah were the first to rally to Jenner. "We'll catch him if we can. Get everyone out!" They sprinted towards the tunnel where Sisyphus had escaped.

Sam was up next. He scooped up Cerci and helped her up.

Cerci's eyes widened when they focused enough for her to see the destruction. "No—he can't get away! That part he stole is the only way anybody can create one of these without Doctor Walther's help."

Sam put her arm around his shoulder and helped her move away from the flames.

Wiltshire snatched the page from the Codex Gigas before the fire could destroy it. He rolled it up and tucked it away within his jacket and then hefted two of the sacks stuffed with cash.

"Really?" Sam spat. "You're saving the *money*, of all things?"

Wiltshire scowled, ignoring the billowing smoke. "Lots of things this money can buy, like parts to rebuild the machine and travel to steal that part back. The kid was right. We can totally take this guy—but we're gonna have to catch him first."

Cerci coughed on a lungful of sooty air. "He's right... and I don't need the part... I just need Walther's notes. I know where his lab is now, and I also know the password he uses for everything. The guy was a pro wrestling nut: *Tombstone Piledriver*. Just sneak in, get the notes, and get out."

Jenner picked up a bag of cash in each hand and headed towards the tunnel. "No." His voice burned as fierce as the flames behind them. "We've got to finish it. Sisyphus has to die."

None argued with him.

Shandra grabbed the remaining bag of valuables and headed after them.

Together they cleared the tunnel and found the lycans staring at the distant helicopter in the sky. Their shapes melted back into their human forms.

"He got away," Wulftone said. "Probably on his way to the airport. He could be anywhere in the world in a few hours."

"No," Cerci insisted. "I think I know where he's going."

"You're all gonna go after him, right?" Wiltshire asked.

Shandra nodded. The others agreed.

"I'll have to catch up with you all, then." Wiltshire turned over one of the sacks of money he'd rescued. "I think you're all better equipped to locate your friend now, but if you haven't found your missing werewolf in a week or so, feel free to call me; I'm in the New York City phone book. I'll get an Uber to drop me at the airport. I've got to finish my other mission first and play another angle or I'll have more strigoi showing up in my apartment."

Sirens blared in the distance as the fire took hold of the building and crept up the side of the dome. Wiltshire thumbed his phone and summoned a ride.

"Your truck is different," Claire said from the passenger seat of the Peterbilt.

Rob gave her a thin lipped scowl. The make and model were the same, but little differences stood out to her. She'd silently cataloged all the details of the truck's interior the last time she'd been taken hostage inside it.

"Yeah," he muttered. "Right after handing you off a couple of years ago, someone stole my truck." He put a hand on the shifter and changed gears. "I had to get a new one."

She took small pleasure in that fact and knew it had been destroyed in Nebraska. "So you're still with the Heptobscurantum?"

Rob nodded.

"And they still want to kill me in order to cause some kind of Armageddon?"

He shook his head and relaxed as he talked with her. "You know, the same old guys that used to be in control of the organization are having something of a power struggle. I don't think they know what they really want, even. There is more energy and guidance coming from the ground level these days."

Claire gave him a skeptical look. "And what level are *you* a part of?"

He winked. "I'm all in on the grass roots side, baby." He explained as he guided the truck around a slower patch of west-bound traffic. "I think the brass was a little miffed at being left out of the whole Pyramid, Kith-Koth Awakening thing with the goat-man. I dunno. Details are light... I really only get rumors, but there hasn't been much news from the Seven lately. Heck, I don't even know *who's a member anymore.* I do know that Jacob Sisyphus has been mostly MIA, with him working on personal projects. And the new guy, Percival Wainsmith, has been hard to pin down, too."

"You think the whole cult is fragmenting?" Claire asked.

He nodded, but did not look at her. "Big schism. Lots of in-fighting. I think they're more content to snipe each other and posture against this Red Order group that has been harassing them lately… some kind of Vatican influenced enemy or something." He shrugged. "It's about time the Church figured out their war was real."

Claire nodded slowly. "And you think that turning me over to them will somehow bring peace in the midst of that? *Peace through destruction,* right?"

Rob finally turned to look at her. "No. I do not." He trailed off and then stared ahead. "The Seven have left the true path, and there will be a reckoning. Their devotion to the agod has soured as they've each been consumed with private pursuits rather than the mission."

Claire sat in silence and waited for more information. Rob didn't seem like he planned to hurt her, but she didn't want to press her luck. She ventured a direct question. "Are you going to give me to them?"

Rob said nothing for almost a minute as he drove. Claire could tell that he was deep in thought, weighing his own desires against the goals of the Heptobscurantum's cause.

The semi braked slightly and Rob switched lanes, letting the truck slow for an exit that read Houston. Rob tossed Claire his cell phone. "Call your father and get a location. I'm dropping you off once you have a location."

"Thank you," she said, dialing his number on the verge of tears. "You won't regret this, I promise."

"I just hope I never hear about it, Claire. To be clear, this never happened. Got it? I'm doing this one for old time's sake, not because I've been thinking about quitting the Heptobscurantum or anything like that."

Claire nodded, certain that Rob was probably lying—he wouldn't likely go back to the cult after a betrayal like this. She pushed the button and dialed. "Dad?" she said after hearing his voice.

"Clairebear?" She heard sirens in the background. "Claire, where are you?"

"On my way to Houston. I'll be there soon. I just need to know where I can meet you."

Chapter Nineteen

The private jet carrying Jacob Sisyphus had gotten the wizard airborne as quickly as he had arrived. Limitless money and cultic devotion afforded him many sorts of luxuries, such as prompt take off and departure times.

Sisyphus sipped an expensive scotch while the medic he'd arranged for tended to his wounds. The doctor, pulled straight off the emergency room floor for an obscene amount of cash, stitched the wound and promised him he'd be healed up soon and would retain full mobility.

"Thanks, Doc," Sisyphus said. "It'll probably be even quicker than you expect. I have certain... factors that will speed up recovery. Now just kick back and watch an in-flight movie. Staff will get you a bottle of Cristal and a wagyu steak. You won't arrive home till this time tomorrow, but I'll take care of you."

A stewardess escorted the medic to a private part of the plane so Sisyphus could conduct his business away from public eyes. He checked the clock on his cell phone and groaned. As comfortable as the private jet was, he'd really become accustomed to the instant travel speeds afforded by Walther's rift generator.

Sisyphus hooked up a battery supply to the data box nestled within the heart of the contraption he'd just stolen. He sent whatever information he could gather, including a full array of photos, to his science team waiting for him back in Germany.

The wizard removed a piece of red dyed wool that had been woven into a strand of yarn. He tied it around his finger and let it dangle straight down, using it as a medium to detect falsehood.

Taking another sip of scotch after the task completed, he dialed a phone number. There was one man Sisyphus thought might have access to secret knowledge of the Venus Oculus—the mirror he sought above all else. He knew that other members of the Seven were collectors, like himself.

The other line opened. "Good afternoon, Mister Sisyphus," Percival Wainsmith said. "It is so good to hear from you."

Sisyphus grinned as the red strand bent to the side, as if a breeze had moved it. He knew the divination was working; Percival had lied. The string returned to normal as Wainsmith continued talking. "Word is, you are jet-setting around the world as of late. I did not think that you took so crude a form of travel."

"Har, har, Wainsmith," Sisyphus said to his fellow Illuminati member: the ruling council of the Heptobscurantum. "I need some help finding an arcane item I am interested in obtaining."

"Ah! Have you become a fellow collector, then?" Wainsmith asked.

"Something like that. The artifacts I chase tend to have a greater purpose beyond mere pride of acquisition."

"I can understand that, and would assume nothing more," Wainsmith stated.

Sisyphus wasn't sure if the fop was trying to insult him or not. He never really could—but it didn't matter... it *wouldn't* matter as long as Sisyphus got his mirror. "The item I seek was held for many years by the Scholomance. A magic mirror."

Wainsmith spoke with a lilt that indicated he was smiling. The man took particular joy in knowing more than someone else or in being needed by another—especially if the needy person was powerful. "There are many magic mirrors in the world, my friend, and a group as revered and long lived as the school of Solomonari are likely to have possessed many magic mirrors."

Sisyphus tried to play coy. He wanted to hedge his bets that whatever information he could glean would help him acquire the mirror and do it faster than Wainsmith. He assumed Wainsmith might try to find it before Sisyphus had the chance—collectors were like that: knowing an object was desired increased their need to own it. "They possessed a mirror that would grant a single wish to any who possessed it, but only once every one hundred years."

"Ah!" Wainsmith said, "The Venus Oculus. I have read of the mirror and know much about it."

"Do you know where it is?" Sisyphus asked. He would know if the slippery Wainsmith lied or not, so long as he answered directly.

"I *do*. After the Scholomance released it, the piece was taken in a raid by the Red Order. That was nearly two hundred years ago. They whisked it away to one of their holding facilities for powerful, arcane artifacts where it was locked away yet deeper after the object proved too tempting for some of their poor detectives."

Sisyphus hissed at the mention of the Red Order. He noticed that his red string had not moved since the beginning of the conversation. "Where is it now? It would bring me extra pleasure to pillage one of their stockrooms."

Wainsmith chuckled. "They no longer possess it. A few years ago, the facility holding it met an untimely end. The piece was sold at auction to a man who purchased it for a bargain; few knew that it had gone up for sale. The Red Order simply failed to send someone to retrieve the mirror... or to warn the new owner that the item could extract a steep toll if used. These things happen, sometimes. You know how it is... personnel shortages and what not. Pretty common when the job consumes life and death in a struggle against the paranormal. Would you like an address for the new owner?"

Sisyphus snorted. He was afraid that he'd just put the item on his peer's radar, not that he feared Wainsmith at all—he could always let his fellow Heptobscurantum member collect it and then steal it from him before it could be used. "You're not going to try to scoop this one out from under me, are you, Wainsmith?"

The other Illuminati member laughed. "No, no. I do not want that particular piece. Already, I have more power than is good for me. I would not even accept it as a gift."

"You sound like you're scared of it," Sisyphus scoffed. The string remained vertical.

"More like a healthy respect. That much power comes with too hefty a price."

"All power comes with a price," Sisyphus noted.

Wainsmith paused. "That is an accurate and fair statement. The Oculus was purchased by a Mister Miles Jecima. A sometimes-retired archaeologist who got into collecting arcane artifacts a couple years ago after a lively meeting with Claire Jones. Jecima was a colleague of her father's."

"Bloody Hell," Sisyphus spat. "You've got to be kidding me."

"The address... do you need it?"

"No! I don't need the address." Sisyphus was certain the well-connected member of The Seven already knew why.

"As always, old friend, it was good talking to..."

Sisyphus noted that the string bent again, and he hung up on Wainsmith. He knew he needed to get that mirror at any cost. The object of his obsession would grant him anything... *everything*. He only needed to claim it before another could use it, but he had to *find it* first.

He checked the clock again. Nine more hours until they touched down in Germany.

His new team of occult scientists promised they'd be able to make the machine work so long as Sisyphus brought them the missing piece. Sisyphus tossed his glass tumbler aside and bit the cork off the mouth of his whiskey bottle. He'd bring them the piece. He'd already given his team ten hours' notice to comb through Walther's data and prepare for his arrival.

And they'd damn well better make the machine work as soon as I get there. I've got a ticking clock.

"I'm pretty sure that I know where Walther's lab is... well, what *was* his lab, anyhow," Cerci confirmed. All eyes turned to her. "He was a 'Beautiful Mind' kind of genius. But he had his *things*. The man was obsessively devoted to Jacob Sisyphus. I guess he grew up enamored with pro wrestling as a kid."

The group's two rental sedans were parked a few blocks from the Astrodome, where they could watch it burn. With the doors open, the Earth-stuck rebels tried to develop a battle plan that wouldn't be a total flop. *They needed to reclaim the stolen part from Sisyphus.*

"Where is the lab?" Sam asked.

"Germany. The Heptobscurantum bought a building and put us in it after Detroit. Walther and I started this. We robbed some government vaults to make sure we'd have a slush fund before the cult was strong again. He was paranoid about being shut down over operations costs... then he got close to Sisyphus and the point became moot. He was sure his hero would let him conduct the research on his own terms... I didn't think Sisyphus could find his way out of a paper sack. It might've been my attitude that got me sent to Central America," Cerci wondered.

"But how can we get there?" Jackie asked.

Cerci pulled out a huge sack of money. "It's amazing what a person can buy with a big stack of cash... we can just charter a private jet."

Jackie's eyes bulged when she spotted the cash in the back of the rental car. Then she noticed a few more bags just like it.

Sam sighed and stated the obvious. "With Wiltshire off running errands in New York, we're down a man, but we've got to get that device back—at almost any cost."

"Swiping the control module from Germany is the best-case scenario," Cerci interjected. "If nothing else, Walther's laptop or his notes should do fine. I think I can recreate the thing if I had his notes."

"No," said Jenner. "Sisyphus has to die. No mercy this time—he abducted my father. He ruined our machine. He's helped to try destroying the known universe on at least two occasions *that we know about*." He turned his head to meet everyone's gazes. None gave him any disagreement.

Shandra swallowed hard. She sympathized with Jenner and agreed that the Wizard had to be stopped; lethal force was likely the only way to accomplish that. However, assassination was not their primary mission. They couldn't sacrifice the greater good for the sake of a grudge. "At the very least, we've got to destroy his machine. If he came all this way to steal that part, it must mean that his is broken, and as Cerci said, Walther either *will not* or *can not* repair it. I'm not opposed to putting this madman down, but let's remember the prize."

None gave voice to why Walther couldn't effect repairs. It didn't take any stretch of the imagination to assume that he'd met an untimely demise.

Heads nodded around the circle. Every other time they'd faced the spell caster, he had fled. Even though they were planning to invade Sisyphus's home, their track record indicated he would flee yet again when confronted.

When a massive Peterbilt rumbled to a stop right next to the gas station, all heads turned. Claire opened the door and hopped out.

"Wait a minute... is that Zabe?" Jackie asked, catching a glimpse of the driver.

"No," Claire said somberly. She looked back into the cab and gave a little wave. The driver goosed the engine and released the brakes with a metal on metal creak. A few seconds later, the truck was gone.

Claire turned to the group and added herself as the seventh member. "Where do we stand? What's the plan?"

They brought her up to speed in as little time as possible.

"I'm going to take Cerci and Claire back with me to Duluth," Sam said. "It's someplace that most of you know... Jecima's old house. We'll do our best to get the parts ready so Cerci can build a new version of the machine."

Claire hesitantly bobbed her head. Clearly she wanted to be a part of the strike team, but understood her father's reluctance to let her rush directly into danger right after thinking he'd lost her. Family or not, the rest of the others had combat training.

"If we can get that portal machine working, not even Nitthogr will be able to stop us from getting back to the Prime." Claire looked at each of them in turn. Hope chimed in her voice. "We can do this. We can save the multi-verse from the Devourer."

"Again!" Jackie exclaimed her reminder. "Three-Peat!"

Claire hugged her friend. "Be safe."

"Of course I'll be safe," she said excitedly. "I just got married like a week ago. I can't die until I've had time to annoy my husband a million ways. I can't wait to put my cold feet on his back in the winter time. I've got too many life goals to accomplish before I can die."

Cerci put a flash drive into Zurrah's hands. "Take this, too. It'll uplink a connection to my computer that I can use to remotely connect to Walther's system; it'll allow me to pull the data that I need."

Her friends shot her awkward glances, which she shrugged off. "Yeah. So I've dabbled in a little cyber-crime in my past... but it's coming in handy now," she admitted.

The young man looked at the flash drive awkwardly, not totally certain he knew how to use it. He handed it to Wulftone, who looked only marginally more confident in its use. Jackie rolled her eyes, took the drive, and pocketed it.

The team heading for Germany crammed into one car. Sam, Claire, and Cerci piled into the other.

Jackie prattled on with the window down. "I want to go on record that, out of all of us here, I'll be the only one with three confirmed 'Sh'logath shut-downs.' I want a medal when this is over, Princess. Don't leave me hanging like Chewbacca! At least get me a bumper-sticker." She wookie roared as the cars drove apart.

Claire smiled sadly as they drifted away from each other. A stroke of melancholy hit, and she hoped this wasn't the last time she would see her friend alive.

The Desolation

Basilisk came down the hill wearing his battle armor. It shined with a flat, chrome-like breast plate that had been mirror polished. Caivev walked alongside of him in a new custom set designed to match. Together, they shined with a dangerous glint.

The tarkhūn stood straighter as they noticed Basilisk in his armor. Their emperor had not suited up for battle since the Syzygyc War. Both his presence and his appearance meant something significant.

Skrom and Idrakka stood at the head of the gathered knot of soldiers. The mighty Skrom headed up a crew of equally large tarkhūn berserkers. Idrakka commanded a company of firelords and frostmancers.

The military shifted nervously on its feet. The Black had been growing antsy in the lower quarters of Limbus and they outnumbered the Tarkhūn by a large margin, hence the increase in military activity.

"Report, Skrom?"

Skrom didn't mince words. "There's talk of revolt. The Black do not like the rumors that have been spreading."

"Which one?" Basilisk asked.

"The one that you and the Empress have been visiting the Maethan heretics in the prison."

Caivev met the gazes of all the tarkhūn forces and spoke frankly. "So what if I have? What good has Sh'logath ever done for us? I don't care if you believe in this Maetha or not—some kind of promised rescuer of the vyrm people, a kind of herald for a redeemer just like there is a prophecy of a herald that will unleash Sh'logath. Maetha or otherwise, I think each vyrm should have the right to choose... and to choose wisely. We've endured generation upon generation of devotion to Sh'logath. And for what?"

The vyrm soldiers around her looked anxious for her to answer the question. Even Basilisk hung on her words.

"What real and genuine blessing has it ever brought any of us? None... I have chosen something else. I've chosen *hope*—and done so even when the night looks bleakest. The time of Sh'logath appears to have arrived at last, and I knowingly turn my back on the very evil I once served. Look around you... we have thrived in the Desolation and built our homes in the darkness. Imagine what greatness we could accomplish in the light."

Basilisk couldn't help but smile. He had come to similar conclusions, but his wife had a certain elegance when she put it into words. His hackles rose slightly when Skrom lumbered a couple of steps towards her, a grim look set upon his face.

The army stiffened and waited for the massive vyrm's actions.

Skrom took a knee. "You know I would follow you anywhere, Caivev. I followed you into the hopeless darque and I would follow you into the service of this strange Maetha if you order it."

Caivev caught his eye and drank in his gaze. "My friend... I would never order you to such a thing. I am merely *asking* you to consider each person free to decide."

Skrom nodded repeatedly. "And that is why my answer to all your questions is always yes."

The others around them all sank to a knee and declared their fealty. The royal leaders knew they meant it, too. They had asked Skrom and Idrakka to gather those troops who they knew could be counted on to remain absolutely loyal in the face of a Black revolt.

Idrakka offered an additional report. "Lots of bad info going around the lower ranks," he said. "I suspect that Jeerzha has been intentionally trying to stir up dissension. He might be trying to stage a coup. He certainly hates the rovers with an unmatched zeal... but after getting his pride wounded by the Lady's refusal to execute the Maethans, he may hate the royal house even more."

Basilisk stroked his chin. "Misinformation, eh?" He waved to some servants near the royal grounds and bid them to retrieve some broadcasting equipment. "Then let's give the people the correct data and force his hand."

"Is that wise?" asked Skrom. "His pride will not let him back down if you call out his lies. And look," the big vyrm pointed towards the looming people group on the horizon. A massive caravan of Seekers plodded towards Limbus, mostly on foot.

Skrom pointed out his tarkhūn variation. "I am an apex—and a good one, too; I know predators. Jeerzha is unhinged, and he has an army. He will attack the weak points first, but he will come for *you*, my lord. Never overlook a lack of breeding for talent: tenacity goes a long way towards victory."

Basilisk grinned as the communicators were set up. He would use the device to broadcast into the homes of every citizen in Limbus and all those connected vyrm across the Desolation. "Good," he told Skrom. "I put on my armor for a reason."

He did not beat around the bush, but got straight to the point within mere seconds of his broadcast. Basilisk pointed out the merger between the Black and the tarkhūn. "We have come to a tipping point and decided our people need a new way forward. The same old failed ideas have never been enough. Our Tarkhūn and Black castes were once at war—new thinking ended that. We found common ground. The thing that has always united the black and tarkhūn has been our loyalty to Sh'logath, but something has changed. What is it?" Basilisk pointed the camera to his wife, surprising Caivev.

"Everything is different," Caivev stammered. "But don't take my word for it."

Trenzlr stepped out from the shadows at Caivev's signal to join her. He briefly introduced himself and then began. "What if generation after generation of vyrm since the Thousand Elders' sacrifice has made mistake after mistake? What if our way of life was based on a lie?"

Earth

Wiltshire could feel the plane begin its descent towards the airstrip. The lights of New York City were off in the distance. Between the flight time and time zone change, it put his landing at shortly after dusk.

The detective made sure that his package was secure and then buckled his seat belt. As soon as they were airborne he had let Theera know by text message that he was on his way and then taken extensive photos of the page for his own records before returning it.

Researching and translating the page had given him something to do during the flight, at least. Thoughts of the page's contents consumed him. The vellum sheet cataloged a few arcane items. Among them was a detailed drawing of a magic mirror named the Venus Oculus.

The Codex Gigas page promised that the Venus Oculus had the power to even raise the dead, grant eternal life, or give any other sort of limitless wish. Wiltshire stared at the detailed drawing; something about it looked familiar from his days with the Red Order.

He hacked into the Order's archives using Atticus Sexton's password. As Wiltshire had guessed, the maintenance division had not scrubbed the dead man's password from the system. The corner of his lips quirked; the Order had deactivated *his* within hours of his excommunication.

Wiltshire navigated the Red Order's listings of occult materials. They had amassed huge inventories over the centuries and removed them from circulation for the good of the public. He scrolled the digital files and found a sub page for arcane mirrors and looking glass entries. The mirror was there, the Venus Oculus, and it had a high-level rating for its power and danger ratings. A location entry listed it as stored inside an Italian depot belonging to the Red Order... a site Wiltshire knew had been destroyed ten years ago.

Something still bothered him about it... the pieces finally clicked. *Strigoi can't use magic mirrors because they have a silver base! The Weathermaker said it was a magic mirror! This is what Sisyphus is killing Solomonari for—that must mean it's still out there.*

He popped the saved image from the archive into an Internet image search and got a hit. Several looked close, but one of the results was a dead ringer. He clicked it.

An archival system link listed the item as up for auction on an antiquities site. When Wiltshire clicked the date, he found it had been sold a couple of years ago to one *Miles Jecima*. He clicked the broker's info link and peeked at the company's data in the Whois Directory. It read, "A Wainsmith Company."

Wiltshire cursed a hot streak and called down a thousand plagues upon Percival Wainsmith, who he knew was Illuminati, and his undying servant Theera. The detective couldn't do anything but wait until they'd landed. Once the plane finally touched down, Wiltshire looked out the window and spotted Theera waiting for him on the tarmac.

He punched in a search for an address on Miles Jecima. The address popped up on his mobile phone's GPS—the same home where he'd met Sam and Shandra during the initial search for Zabe.

"Hey Captain," Wiltshire knocked on the cabin door. Since it was a private commission, and they were taxiing, the flight crew opened the door, expecting some sort of *thank-you* from their guest for such a smooth flight.

Wiltshire looked at them gravely. "I need an immediate turn-around. We've got to get airborne again right away and get this bird back to Minnesota."

The co-pilot groused, "We've got regulations. Mandatory downtime and whatnot; I'm afraid that's impossible."

Wiltshire shook his head. "Fill the plane back up and get us back in the air straight away. You guys can rest when we get there—it'll be one way and Percival Wainsmith will foot the bill... plus five grand each as a bonus," he promised.

The co-pilot opened his mouth to argue. Wiltshire tossed a stack of bills to each of them, a fraction of the haul he'd rescued from the Astrodome. The pilot overruled his junior officer. "Yes sir. It'll take us twenty to thirty minutes to refuel once we've stopped, and we'll get back up straight away."

"Good man," Wiltshire said, and the plane jostled as it came to a rest and the door opened to an airstair. The detective quickly descended and the flight crew exited behind him so they could freshen up and order the maintenance crew to set them up for a quick turn around.

Wiltshire clutched the rolled up page from the Codex Gigas. "Do you have my files?"

Theera handed over a memory card which Wiltshire popped into a mobile device to double check them. Once he saw the extensive scans, he turned over the vellum sheet.

As soon as Theera had it, Wiltshire decked him in the mouth with a closed fist. Theera reeled and clutched his bleeding face. Through bloody teeth and gums, Wainsmith's majordomo laughed heartily.

"I figured it out, you snake," Wiltshire growled. "I guess it was convenient that I was already on the trail of the Gigas pages in order to find the Scholomance?"

Theera grinned and laughed. "So you realized I sent the strigoi your way?"

Wiltshire yanked his gun from its holster and aimed it at Theera's head. "I just don't know why you did it?" His gun hand wavered, and he put the weapon away. Wiltshire knew it would do him no good. The strange creature would just regenerate within a few minutes anyway, guessing by the last time he'd seen Theera shot in the head.

Theera smirked. "My master and I keep many contacts. The Scholomance had asked for the address." He cocked his head. "Do not worry. You were in no danger; the strigoi promised to leave you unharmed."

Great. Now I've got to move again, he realized.

"Mister Wainsmith thought it might motivate you to work more quickly. Time is certainly important," Theera said. "Jacob Sisyphus has been chasing the mirror for some time now and he is hot on its trail. You will need to hurry if you are going to stop him from acquiring it."

"*That's not the job!*" Wiltshire shouted. "I don't care about magic mirrors and Sh'logaths. I just want the page you promised me. I don't owe anyone anything—except the Scholomance. I owe those guys a heavy dose of retribution on behalf of Atticus Sexton and his dead wife and kids."

Theera merely leered at him. Both of them already knew Wiltshire had no choice. He would protect the mirror because Sexton would have wanted it that way. Atticus had always been the level-headed one; he'd been Wiltshire's moral compass.

"I'm sure you understand Mister Wainsmith's position," Theera explained. "He could not take any direct action against Sisyphus because of their mutual business and, uh, professional interests. And besides, you would not have taken the job had we simply told you about the mirror."

Wiltshire set his jaw and exhaled sharply through his nose, trying to keep his cool. He hated being manipulated. "On second thought," Wiltshire spat. He yanked his nine millimeter from its holster and put a bullet through Theera's brain-pan.

The hollow point's exit wound blasted a chunk of skull and flesh free in a chunky spray of crimson. Theera crumpled. It might have been ultimately futile, but it made Wiltshire feel better.

He holstered his weapon again and turned his thoughts inward. Wiltshire knew the Venus Oculus would command a heavy toll if used—but it could potentially restore Atticus... and using the power of the Oculus *would* prevent Sisyphus from commanding it to something far more evil. Certainly, the wizard had his own foul intentions.

Wiltshire began clomping up the stairs to the cabin. By his estimate, Theera should be recovered before the pilots returned. He checked his timepiece. It would take another five hours to get back to Duluth. As long as he didn't run into further troubles, he'd be able to arrive in Minnesota before the rest of Jecima's weird friends attacked the Heptobscurantum building in Germany.

He twisted his mouth with worry. Sisyphus had a sizable head start on them. The real question was whether or not Sisyphus could make his rift machine work right away. Wiltshire didn't know if he could beat the Wizard to the Mirror.

Jacob Sisyphus answered his phone. He noted that the incoming call came from a number listed as Walther's workshop.

"You got something to report?" he asked curtly, without so much as a greeting.

"Uh, yes," said the flustered voice on the other end of the line. "We feel confident that we understand the late Doctor Walther's notes. We are certain we can get the machine working within one or two days if you bring us the part."

"I'm touching down in just a couple more hours. You've got one hour to make it happen, so have your act together." Sisyphus spoke with ultimate authority.

"But sir! We've never even seen this thing operate... the science is purely metaphysical and we barely understand its nature."

Sisyphus growled, "Then you better re-read those notes; you don't need to understand the science, you just gotta make the machine work. I'll stretch my time line to ninety minutes," he agreed, as if he were acting benevolent. "After time expires, I'm killing one of your family members every ten minutes until you get the thing operating. Do we have an understanding?"

He could practically hear the scientist gulp.

"Y-yes sir. Ninety minutes."

Sisyphus heard him scrambling in the background, hissing demands to the men and women of his team as he tried to get everything ready for the wizard's arrival. They would need to make optimal use of their time. "Good," Sisyphus told his minion. "Get ready to fire it up right away... I've already got the next location picked out and I'm not willing to delay. Ninety minutes." He pressed the red button and ended the call.

CHAPTER TWENTY

As they traveled, Cerci Heiderscheidt worked feverishly on the designs for her new machine. She'd barely looked up from her sketchbook, spending most of the time drawing diagrams and jotting notes. She wrote down the necessary supplies on a separate sheet.

Sam and Claire put an X next to each item on her list as they researched supplies and called in orders from local vendors around Duluth's bay area. They paid a premium to have them delivered and left on their doorstop. Everything they could think they needed would be ready and prepared for them once they arrived.

Cerci could begin work immediately upon arrival. Luckily, she'd helped build three of these machines in the past—*if Walther is dead, that makes me the foremost expert in the world,* Cerci thought.

She had promised them a quick turnaround, especially if Sam and Claire could take direction and help with the assembly. Cerci finally clapped the notebook shut with only a few minutes left before the plane's planned descent. "It won't be pretty, but we'll get it constructed fast... and it will work. Shouldn't take us more than a few hours if we hurry and don't screw it up the first time."

Claire raised an eyebrow. "You're telling me that a machine capable of piercing the fabric of reality can be built in a few hours and from hardware store parts?"

Cerci grit her teeth. "Not quite," she admitted. "The *machine* will be ready; the rift machine is actually fairly simple. The program that runs it, however, took years to develop, but it doesn't require anything special to run—any modern laptop should be able to handle it... that and one other key ingredient."

"And you can just whip that software up?" Clarie asked. "I guessed you were a genius, but..."

Cerci held up a flash drive. "I'm not *that kind* of genius, but I'm smart enough that I *did make a copy of the software*. We're still going to need Walther's notes. Calibrating the machine is the tricky part. There is a complex algorithm tied to the Earth's magnetic field, solar constants, and lunar positioning. Without those things, we have no point of reference and activating the machine could have disastrous consequences."

"Such as?" Sam asked.

Cerci bit her lip. "The rift could open inaccurately and flare wide open in the middle of you or me, eviscerating one of us and leaving chunks of our flesh in another dimension. Alternatively, it could tear open in the center of the Earth's core and destabilize our planet's travel, sending us hurtling out into the galaxy, flash freezing the population or burning us to a crisp if Earth falls into the sun."

Both Sam and Claire stared at her wild eyed, surprised she and Doctor Walther had even experimented with this thing to begin with.

"Don't worry," Cerci said. "The former is much more likely than the latter."

Sam only blinked, still wild eyed. He couldn't help the sarcasm in his voice. "Oh, don't worry? Okay."

"As long as they can get me those notes, everything will be fine," Cerci reassured him.

"But we have everything else we need, then, aside from them?" Claire confirmed.

Their scientist set her jaw and shook her head. "Almost." She wrote a final item on the list. *Wundrefluvium. "*There's a reactionary agent that is necessary to instigate the quantum equlibrator... it's what keeps people stable as they pass through the dimensions—without wundrefluvium. The rift-gate is just a fancy way to smash yourself into atoms."

Sam raised his eyebrows. "I read about this stuff. Super volatile and very expensive. There has been lots of recent research on it... some kind of new lab-created element with strange properties?"

Cerci nodded slowly. "There's a small vial of it at one of the research labs at UMD. Stuff's expensive to make and can be explosive. It is really not much more than a curiosity at the moment, but it resonates at the right frequency to filter out the harmonic resonance that all matter vibrates at."

Claire nodded along, trying to track with the sciencey talk that followed, but her mind latched on to the harmonic resonance part. "Are you saying all reality vibrates to a set pattern or frequency?"

Cerci shrugged. "Something like that. Almost like everything that exists was sung into existence by some higher power. It could be the sound caused by the big bang, or maybe there was a divine song that sang the world into being..."

Sam grinned at the skeptical note in her voice. He'd been equally skeptical before his time in the Prime and his exposure to the teachings of the Veritas. "Like the Jews and Christians believe?"

"Whatever floats your boat." Cerci crooked her jaw. "I was referring to the ancient Pythagoreans or the Ainulindalë, the creation song from Lord of the Rings." She shrugged again. "Maybe they're all correct in their own ways."

Sam nodded and steered the conversation back to the matter at hand. "I can get it for you: the wundrefluvium. I spotted a set of keys last time we were at Jecima's house. I should be able to sneak into the labs and get it for you."

Cerci nodded and their jet touched down with only a slight bump and squeak of the tires. "Just don't open the tube. If it's exposed to oxygen, the stuff will explode… not as violently as nukes or anything, but it'll be bad—bad enough that the military stopped exploring it for weapon related purposes due to instability concerns."

"Got it. Don't blow up," Sam confirmed.

Several minutes later, they arrived at the Jecima estate and left the motor running. Cerci began setting up and bossed Claire around as Sam hustled towards the house. *That's not going to last real long, I think.* He grinned and hurried inside.

He hustled through a long hall and into one of the many rooms stuffed with antiques and obscure mementos which Miles had collected through his many years. He stopped in front of a large, ornate mirror on the second level. The white drop cloth that covered it provided a perfect backdrop for the fancy end table where Professor Jecima's identification lanyard, pass, and university keys had been left.

Sam glanced at the white sheet. He momentarily wondered about the mirror beneath it, and then he turned and left. Time was critical, and he needed every advantage he could get.

The Desolation

Klewdahar walked at the front of the line, leading his rovers. The cracked, barren ground of the Neggath Plains had begun to slope up and into a gentle rise, capped by Basilisk's city. Limbus was only a short distance away now, and it loomed tall before them. The city had no walls, but many structures ringed the edge like teeth.

Tension rippled through the burgeoning cluster of Seekers. They numbered several thousand, but possessed barely a dozen weapons between them, not that they needed them. "Maetha will provide safe passage," Klewdahar had insisted.

Unprotected and uncounted, the mass of vyrm approached from the wasteland. Each step had become one of faith.

Beside Klewdahar walked Gerjha and Chartarra with Hirdac and Klyrtan behind them. The simple-minded vyrm had been eager to walk towards the front, though Hirdac struggled to keep the same pace as the others.

"Oh good," Klewdahar said, noticing movement in the city. "They are sending a committee to welcome us."

Before them, a murky line of bodies bled out from between the buildings and approached like a swarm of glrg-worms. It writhed and moved towards them with the speed of a rested churdachk.

Chartarra put a spyglass to his eye and scanned the horde. He focused on the vyrm leading the charge. "Hold!" he ordered, overriding even Klewdahar's desire to reach the city. The group stopped. "It's Jeerzha, the one who has been rallying the Black for our blood."

"Blood," Klyrtan repeated behind him with a giggly kind of voice.

"He got his army and they're coming this way—fast and angry!"

A collective gasp rippled through the Seekers behind them. They formed a tight cluster and packed together instinctively.

Klewdahar turned to their prophet. "Did we choose rightly?"

Gerjha grimaced. "Right choice rarely means the chooser shall be spared from harm... obedience seldom equates safety..."

Klewdahar cursed. "Speak plainly! Will we survive?"

The prophet only shrugged. "I do not know." Despite his ignorance, Gerjha's eyes looked as if he felt peace.

As Jeerzha and his army thundered towards them, the rocks trembled from the shaking of the baked tiles underfoot. Chartarra withdrew an old, rusted sword from beneath his cloak, an item he'd picked up before leaving Limbus once Caivev had freed him.

Hirdac chuffed, "Will that do any good here?"

Chartarra responded over his shoulder, "I only know what I was prepared for. I am formerly of the Black and was made for battle.

It makes me no less a Seeker if I have different strengths than the rest... but I was bred for war and will defend Maetha's people with whatever I have within me."

Klyrtan stared at the blade as if transfixed.

Jeerzha and his hunters howled war cries as they surged ahead and closed the gap. Raising their weapons high, they had nearly fallen upon the defenseless enemy when sirens blared from Limbus, an official call to battle.

Klewdahar's posture sank. "So this is it, then? All of Limbus turns out against us?"

Barreling down from the edge of Limbus came a host of tarkhūn riding tyradons; the soldiers carried weapons from the backs of their battle-bred lizard creatures. From both sides, speedy skiffs arced around the edge of the city, approaching with uncanny velocity.

Rovers cried out for Maetha to save them. Such an enemy would easily wipe them out.

"I cannot believe this is the end," Chartarra insisted. "I refuse to believe that we are abandoned!"

Right before Jeerzha and his crew could smash into them with brutal force, the skiffs tore through the guilds-men's flanks and opened fire. The air filled with scents of blood and smoke and with the sounds of screams and hate as the tarkhūn turned on Jeerzha's hunters.

Earth

Sam got back to the house only a short while after committing a low-key larceny and identity theft. The first room off the entryway had been haphazardly cleared of its contents, which were strewn through the main hall. Jecima's old belongings had been deposited wherever they could be stacked, with no thought given to value or purpose. Space was a premium.

Piles of machinery and items were stacked around the edges of the chamber and connected by layers and layers of cable and cords. He watched as his daughter and Cerci worked in feverish silence—he thought it probable that they'd had some sort of blow-up in his absence, as he suspected two strong women might have. The resulting quiet had helped establish new boundaries.

He held aloft the vial of mysterious wundrefluvium. "So, uh, how's it going in here?"

"Good," Claire said curtly as she connected cables and checked them against Cerci's notes. The length of cord failed to reach, and so she pulled out a wire stripper and cable crimp to connect a new set of ends for a longer one.

"We are right on schedule," Cerci assured him, snatching the vial and placing it some place safe where she could remember to hook it into the contraption. The machine looked like an exploded view schematic as it lay in interlinked parts around the room. "Now be a dear and bring in the rest of the stuff from outside.

He began the arduous task of hauling in the remaining spools of cable and pieces of equipment that had been delivered by his suppliers. Sam had no idea what most of the items were, except that they looked like set pieces from Frankenstein's lab. He set the final bank of scientific machinery down. Between labored pants of breath, he groused, "You'd think I would have ordered a wheeled dolly or a cart or something, too."

Sam stood and pushed his hands against his hips, cracking his spine. He overheard the girls talking in the adjacent room. "We've got to get to Gita. She is the key," Claire insisted. "We still don't know where Zabe is and I've got to assume he's tried to get back to the Prime to find us by now. Without the gates opened, he'll never be able to get back and we'll never find him-and they won't open without Gita." Claire said sorrowfully, "The universe is a big place, and I'll never be the same without him."

Cerci worked in silence a little while longer. "I only know his brother, Zurrah." She seemed to blush as she spoke. "Tell me about Zabe; I wonder if he's anything like his younger brother."

Claire began listing the things she liked about her fiance and gave examples. "He's loyal and kind. He takes his duty seriously, but knows how to have fun when the opportunities present themselves... like when he surprised me in the middle of the day and proposed at a picnic—which Jackie crashed, in fact. It didn't bother him when she did." She trailed off after a few more examples and then started listing other things. "His skin is so hot—it's great to snuggle against. He's super cute..."

Cerci laughed. "Yeah, sounds just like Zurrah."

The door behind Sam suddenly flew open, slamming loudly against the threshold. Wiltshire charged into the house with his gun drawn.

Sam stood straight. "Geez, man, is this always how you make your entry?"

Wiltshire stalked through the hall with his weapon ready. He walked past Sam, "Usually... at least with this house, I guess." A smile tugged at the edge of his mouth, suggesting he'd made a joke, but his mission was deadly serious.

Sam watched Wiltshire move through the home and check each room. "Is there something I can help you with, Vikrum?"

"Where is it?" Wiltshire asked, eyes burning with deadly purpose. "Tell me where the mirror is."

The Desolation

At the back of the battle, Basilisk's loyal tarkhūn soldiers fell upon the rear of Jeerzha's army. They struck from atop their tyradon mounts. A handful of frostmancers encased enemy vyrm in ice, freezing them solid; the lizard-mounted warriors crashed through the rebels and dashed them to pieces across the Plains of Neggath.

A firelord washed a contingent of Jeerzha's snarling followers with a tidal blast of flame. They collapsed in blackened heaps of melted scale and cinder that puckered and crumbled in the heat.

Blaster fire bounced off of Caivev and Basilisk's skiff as it plowed into battle. They cut a sharp line through the Black, targeting Jeerzha, the would-be leader of a mob that had turned out nearly a quarter of Limbus's population, including more than a third of its warrior class. Jeerzha snarled, defiant, "These rovers are parasites and should be destroyed. It is our way!"

Caivev and Basilisk leapt off of the skiff and crossed blades with the Black, who surrounded Jeerzha.

Her countrymen screamed at Caivev, "You were supposed to be one of us, traitor," and "You are unworthy of the dunnischkte!"

She shrugged off their insults. Slashing with her blade and putting blasts of deadly laserfire through those who defied her, she pressed further into the fray.

Basilisk's skiff turned away and began strafing the enemy; its mounted weapons fired into the crowd of Black with merciless precision. The emperor activated his deadly stare as Jeerzha and his most capable generals tried to swarm him.

"Do not meet his gaze!" Jeerzha ordered, too late. Most of those surrounding him had already been petrified by Basilisk's arcane ability.

Jeerzha roared and crossed blades with the emperor. He shrieked his accusation, "You have joined the heretics and turned your heart away from Sh'logath!"

The game master lost a step against Jeerzha and thought about how long it had been since he had actually trained for martial combat. He wondered about how much his prowess had declined with his lack of focused training.

"I did not begin this game with any intention of losing," Basilisk fired back, slashing and blocking Jeerzha's jagged sword. He did not know where Jeerzha had learned to fight, but he proved himself a capable warrior, doubtlessly trained by one of the martial masters of the Black before settling in Limbus with the merger of the Black and the tarkhūn.

"You cannot defeat Sh'logath!" Jeerzha howled. "Sh'logath is hunger—Sh'logath is eternal!" He hacked with ruthless abandon, coming at the emperor like a tornado of blades and fury. Jeerzha kept his eyes fixed upon Basilisk's plated chest so that he would not meet the deadly eyes of his enemy.

Basilisk grinned, knowing that this soldier stood a very real possibility of beating him. *The most exhilarating games are the ones with a chance of losing.* "I always win," Basilisk argued with himself. He would not have risked his wife had he not thought through the battle plan and weighed the odds.

Jeerzha pressed in again and Basilisk looked down into the mirror finish of his breastplate and locked eyes with Jeerzha's reflection. The vyrm stopped, startled by meeting the amber eyes of his deadly enemy. The opening was enough that Basilisk plunged his blade into the enemy's belly. As he pulled it free, he locked eyes with the stunned Jeerzha.

The mutineers' leader gasped and his skin petrified, encasing him in his final moments of shock and pain.

Basilisk's tarkhūn and other faithful soldiers mopped up the rest of the mob with barely a casualty, and the emperor ended his use of the terrible gaze. He strode over and found Chartarra next to Klewdahar and Gerjha, guarding them with a blunt sword that should have been melted for scrap rather than pressed into service.

"So we meet again, Chartarra." His eyes lingered on the scars across the vyrm's neck and chest—wounds which were supposed to have been fatal.

Chartarra bowed. "Lord Basilisk," he greeted without any hint of a grudge. "It appears you've just freed up several homes for occupancy. May we make an inquiry?"

Basilisk noted Caivev's approach from the rear. He turned to the prophet and the leader of the rovers. "Welcome to Limbus."

The Prime

Nitthogr's face slid to one side as if the bone structure below had lost integrity. His troops stood around the parapets that ringed the wall of the royal castle. A hovering holo-broadcaster captured his likeness and sent it out to all receivers—into the homes and communicators of all those living in the Prime.

He hissed, "You all know who I am." He raised the petrified hand to the camera, "I came to you as Shjikara Stonefist, but I have assumed my true name: Nitthogr, Herald and Acolyte of Sh'logath."

Nitthogr made a spectacle of brandishing the scepter of the Veritas and placing the darque crown upon his head. He whirled and clubbed the closest half dozen stone figures still frozen within the statue garden of the royal court. "As his growing incarnation, I am ushering in a new age of Sh'logath. *The Prime is His*," he hissed, nodding to Gita.

Tears streamed down her face and her cheeks burned crimson as she tried to refuse his order. The sorcerer's voice dripped with villainy as she shook her head. "Do it or your sister dies."

With a whimper, Gita turned the knob all the way on the mystic box she had been saddled with.

Nitthogr put a hand to his brow and spoke to all his loyal Black wherever they were scattered across the multi-verse. "Now is the time, my chosen ones. Come to me... enter the Prime with all hatred and force. Eviscerate its people and give to them the gift of death."

He grinned as if punch-drunk and then dropped the crown. He had no more need of it. Everywhere that there was a portal, vyrm poured into the realm, bringing with their weapons and bloodlust for the pleasure of Sh'logath.

The camera followed Nitthogr as he strode through the corridor and entered the throne room, where his impostor princess sat upon the throne. "I feel your fear, residents of the Prime. It nourishes me, sustains me. I can sense the slaughter beginning even now and I feed upon it." His voice warbled and shifted, hearkening something even more wicked that lived within him.

He approached the throne and the shade, still in Claire's form; she bowed low to him. "The Prime is yours, my lord and king."

Nitthogr grinned and passed by her, ripping the throne from its moorings and flinging it across the room. His eyes clouded black. Nitthogr's body began to roil and bubble as the tentacles emerged once more, writhing, black and menacing. His voice lowered a full octave and dripped with evil. He was more Sh'logath than anything else now.

"I consume your spiritual essences at the point of death. They invigorate me. Welcome to my new era of darkness... and this realm is a mere appetizer. I shall graze over it one morsel at a time rather than consume it wholesale." He turned to address the remote audience. "This existing quite agrees with me, and I take pleasure in the act of devouring each of you."

His demeanor changed, and he reverted back to the form of the sorcerer; the birthing had not yet fully completed, even if the pangs had begun. Nitthogr snarled at Gita. "Enough time has passed. Close the gates."

She cranked the dial back all the way to the other side, sealing the dimensional portals once again and locking out any who hoped to use them. Gita choked back her sobs. With blood-thirsty vyrm pouring in through every gate, she knew that there was no chance that any of her friends could have sneaked in with so short of a window.

Nitthogr stood in front of the massive doors of the Chamber of Mysteries. With his back to the camera, he declared, "I am

Nitthogr, Herald and Acolyte of Sh'logath, and I will have my prize!"

CHAPTER TWENTY-ONE

E^{arth} Wiltshire tromped through the house and slipped out of sight. He didn't even pause to check out the progress on the dimensional rift generator.

"You girls keep working on that machine," Sam said. "I'll see if I can figure out whatever our friend needs." He foraged deeper into the mansion, looking for Wiltshire. "Hey!" he called, "Where are you at?"

"Up here," Wiltshire called down the stairs.

Sam hurried up the steps and found him in one of the rooms. Wiltshire stood in front of the wooden stand where he'd grabbed Jecima's keys only a couple of hours earlier. Sam found him in the old professor's "work room." His active projects were the ones left in this room, either relics in need of research or stacks of papers in need of sorting.

"There it is," Wiltshire said, waving a hand towards the draped mirror. "The Venus Oculus."

"The what?"

Wiltshire shook his head, dispelling any notion that the archaeologist should know it. "It's a magic mirror... the very one that Sisyphus is looking for."

Sam stepped towards it curiously. "What does it do?"

"It can grant one limitless wish to a mortal once every one hundred years," Wiltshire explained as Sam picked up a manila folder leaning against the artifact's base.

Sam leafed through its contents and laid the loose pages out on a table. They were mostly photocopies of older manuscripts and they bore Miles' distinct scrawl in the margins. He scrunched his forehead as he read the ancient works; they were mostly accounts of the mirror's usage. Many passages had text underlined, highlighted, or marked with an asterisk.

Before he could translate the writings, a triangular shaped rift split the air nearby. Wiltshire and Sam both turned to confront the monster on the other side.

The detective fired a trio of shots through the opening. Shouts came from the floor below them while Sisyphus flashed a defensive ward up to block the bullets.

"Open it wider," Sisyphus snapped to his new science crew. "I don't want you idiots to cut me off at the knees."

The portal widened, and Sisyphus jumped through it.

Sam snatched a nearby hat rack and charged at the big man. Sisyphus smashed through the furniture and clubbed the archaeologist with an elbow. Sam went down with a bloody nose as Wiltshire dropped the mag out of his gun and ejected the round in the barrel.

Slamming in a new magazine and racking the slide, Wiltshire took aim again. He fired off another flurry of rounds. They busted through his arcane defenses and the flat nosed slugs slammed into his flesh. *Thwap, thwap, thwap!* As they hit, one of the amulets hanging around Sisyphus's neck glowed brilliantly.

Sisyphus roared, understanding that the bullets had been each inscribed with mystic runes to break through his arcane shield. Luckily, one of the stolen darquematter shards provided additional defense and slowed the bullets on impact. Still, they left a trio of ugly welts that stung and bled like he'd been shot at close-range with a barrage of paintballs.

The wrestler snarled and flung his hands out, trying to catch his enemy with a blast of eldritch fire.

Wiltshire ducked and rolled.

Sisyphus pulled off when the detective cut in front of the mirror—he couldn't risk damaging it.

Sam scrambled to his feet and tried to tackle Sisyphus from behind. The wizard was too strong. He grabbed Sam and threw him over the banister railing; Sam howled as he tumbled over the edge and clattered down the stairs.

Sisyphus turned back to Wiltshire even as he heard the shouts from the women below; he heard footsteps as they rushed to help. Wiltshire fired another set of bullets into the big wizard; the arrow-head shaped amulet in the necklace cluster glowed again as it absorbed the bullet's kinetic energy. Sisyphus charged towards Wiltshire and they locked into a grapple, knocking the detective's gun to the floor.

As strong as Wiltshire was, the roid and sorcery fueled professional wrestler easily overpowered him. "My gun," Wiltshire yelled, pressing through the grapple.Claire and Cerci had rushed up the steps to render aid. "He must not get the mirror or he could become more powerful than Nitthogr! As soon as I snatch his amulet, *shoot him!*"

Wiltshire surged forward with all his might while his enemy steered his head in another direction. Wiltshire blindly grasped and yanked a necklace free.

Claire aimed and fired until the gun ran out of bullets.

Sisyphus stood straight with pain, but he remained alive. He looked down and saw that Wiltshire had ripped free the wrong amulet. The detective clutched the baked tile rune that Sisyphus had taken from bwbych the boggart. He snapped a quick jab forward and busted the rune in Wiltshire's hands.

Wiltshire looked up, suddenly confused and worried, and then he blinked out of existence with a puff of smoke and a flash of light. Its freed magic ensnared him and shot him off to the Feylands before he could even think.

Sisyphus grabbed his kophesh by the handle and harnessed its telekinetic abilities. From across the room, he flung the sheet aside and exposed the Venus Oculus.

"At last," he cackled and with a flick of the wrist, commanded the magic device to move across the room and follow him. He grabbed the mirror by its frame and turned towards the triangular rift. Terrified faces of curious scientists looked on from Germany.

Suddenly, Sisyphus fell to his knees. He dropped his weapon and clutched his head, reeling in horror. Jacob Sisyphus was only twelve years old and nursed a black eye and bloody nose as his father yelled obscenities at him. He could smell the beer on his father's breath again. The child broke down tearfully, trying to protect himself from another punch to the face.

"No... no... get out of my head," Sisyphus yelled, keenly aware that he'd been flung into a dream state. He peered through the fog, barely able to see past it and locate the woman who had summoned this hated memory. She exposed him to the total recall of his abuse and weakness in the face of an abuser's strength. "No! Stop it! I won't let you..."

Sisyphus charged towards her but lost her in the mists of visions. Every memory, every bad thought, all his life's self talk crashed into him over and over in what felt like eternity—he was under Claire's microscope and injected with weakness and impotence.

Clutching his skull, Sisyphus finally struggled to his feet and threw himself through the fiery gateway. On the other side, he screamed. "Close it. Close it... shut it down!"

The rift snapped shut, leaving only Sam, Claire, and Cerci in the mansion. All was suddenly quiet. Sam finally shambled up the steps, nursing his cracked ribs. He found the girls examining the mirror.

"Where's Wiltshire?"

Claire shook her head sadly and her father scowled.

Sam insisted, "Sisyphus can not get that mirror. I'm still researching Jecima's notes, but it's some kind of magic... I guess Jecima had become quite the collector after his first meeting with you and Zabe."

Claire hugged her arms to herself. "Wiltshire said we can't let him get it or he'll become just as bad as Nitthogr. I barely stopped Sisyphus this time, but he'll be prepared next time."

Sam picked up the mystic, ancient kophesh and gave it to Claire.

"No place is safe," Cerci insisted. "He's already gotten his machine working and we're still waiting on the data from the others. It's the only thing we still need."

Sam and Claire nodded slowly. She said, "They'd better hurry. I have a terrible feeling that we are running out of time."

The group of five crept up in the dark and double checked the address against the one provided them by Cerci. The German streets had filled with shadow as Jenner, Shandra, Jackie, Zurrah, and Wulftone stalked through them.

"This is it," Jackie whispered, checking the clock. It was nearly three o'clock in the morning, German time and they'd made as quick a trip as possible. She and Wulftone each wore their Guardian Corps armor. It went everywhere with them—even on their honeymoon. She peered around the corner and through the glass front of the locked building. "I see three armed guards stationed in the lobby." She squinted, "Lapel pins... I see the seven-pointed star of the Hepobscurantum?"

Shandra, wearing her Veritas armor and wielding her hammer, whistled from near a discreet, locked service door on the side of the building. She tapped the hammer against the doorknob and it busted off. She tried to open it, but the lock still held firm. "Nevermind," she said sheepishly. "I thought I had a solution."

Wulftone approached and grew into his hulking lycan form. He dug his talons into the steel door and ripped it off its hinges before tossing it into the shrubs.

"That works, too," Shandra whispered.

"Follow me and pray that this didn't trigger a silent alarm," Jackie said. "Everyone stick close to the Earth-girl just in case... and let's hurry."

She clutched her laser rifle and slipped inside. After turning a sharp corner, she found the west elevator lobby. It required a key fob to call a carrier. She headed through the door and up the stairs. Leaning over the rail, she looked up and at the dizzying heights they'd need to climb. "Good thing I lost all that weight," she sighed and started pumping her legs. "I better get me a whole box of donuts after this."

Wulftone whispered after her, "Can I get some of those, too?"

"Get your own," she teased. "Now pipe down. These stairwells tend to echo."

They climbed seemingly endless levels of steps until they found the upper most level. Flush and slick with sweat, they tried the door. It, too, was locked.

Jackie stepped back and Wulftone pried the door open, tearing out part of the steel framed threshold with it. The barrier twisted free. An alarm blared and trouble lights came on in the stairwell. It pulsed through the hallway before them.

"Time to get busy," Jackie yelled, charging ahead.

Her comrades trailed after her. They hustled through the corridors and pushed their way into a research pod where a bunch of confused scientists shouted angry words at them with thick German accents. Wulftone and Zurrah, both in lycan forms, splayed their claws and roared at them. The men and women in lab coats panicked and fled.

Outside of the room, a larger chamber spread out where the Heptobscurantum's portal generator had been reconstructed.

"We should expect trouble any minute, now," Shandra said as they hurriedly searched the research stations

"There," Jackie pointed to a desk adorned with stacks of notes and decorated with professional wrestling memorabilia. She hurried to it, slid into the seat, and opened the laptop. A password screen popped up, and she typed in *Tombstone Piledriver.*

The computer granted her access. "This is it," Jackie said. I got it!"

Voices exploded in the lobby, past the main room. The scientists escaped as the security team entered. Shandra grabbed Zurrah. "Let's go, kid—we've got to keep them busy."

The lycan nodded as Shandra hefted her weapon and they rushed off to battle.

Jackie plugged in a USB drive that Cerci had given her earlier. It ran a simple, automated program that uplinked Walther's laptop to Cerci's.

A few seconds later, Jackie's phone rang. She answered it.

Cerci offered no greeting or useless chit-chat. "I got the data we needed. Destroy Walther's laptop. We can't allow the Heptobscurantum, or anyone else, to have access to this kind of stuff."

Jackie severed the line, pocketed her phone, and then snapped her pulse rifle to her shoulder. She blasted the computer into useless debris and the laser fire melted the hard drives to slag.

Wulftone looked up, "Alright, Jenner, let's go find this Sisyphus guy and beat some answers out of him—he might know where your father..." He looked around but couldn't locate the young soldier. "Dang it, Jenner!"

He grabbed Jackie and rushed towards the lobby. Shandra and Zurrah guarded the door where a pile of bodies had fallen to form a partial blockade. Shandra saw the others coming. "Jenner went that way," she thumbed down the hall.

Jackie grimaced at the carnage near the elevators. "You'd think the Hepobscurantum would run out of minions at some point, right?"

In response, the elevator dinged down the hall and black-clad special-ops types poured into the hallway. "You just had to say something, didn't you?" Zurrah growled as Wulftone and Jackie rushed past the door in pursuit of Jenner.

The new soldiers proved to be a whole class above the others and raised their riot shields. They shouted commands to each other and worked the hall to get close enough to try to deal some actual damage against the lab's intruders. One of the mercenaries barked, "These ones are different from the last. No scales... but we'll show them no mercy!"

Wulftone looked over his shoulder and watched Shandra and Zurrah maintain their defensive position. "Well, that explains why they have all these soldiers at the ready—some rogue vyrm faction already hit them, for some reason. Caivev must be on the outs with Seven."

Jackie and her husband found the panic-room door. Jenner had already used his blaster pistol to burn through the locking mechanism and forced it open. They rushed forward and into a macabre sort of study, where Sisyphus performed arcane rituals required by dark arts.

A table on the far side of the room sat opposite an open door; it held glass alembic vials and alchemy reagents at the ready for potion brewing. A collection of apothecary tools and texts had been stacked neatly. Jenner's body flew through the air suddenly and smashed the table, shattering glass in every direction and throwing the loose pages into the air like leaves in a gust.

Sisyphus's distinct voice howled from within the room. "You think you can challenge me *in my home... where I am most powerful?*"

A weak voice croaked from within, "Run, Jenner..."

Wulftone and Jackie sprinted past their fallen comrade while he growled and tried to right himself. The werewolf launched himself over a fixed gurney and attacked. Wulftone's eyes widened when he realized the man strapped to the table was Professor Jarfig—Jenner's father.

Sisyphus snatched Wulftone by the throat and looked into his eyes. Blood dripped down the wizard's chin. He practically radiated power as he held the lycan against his will and smashed him against the wall. With his free hand, Sisyphus held up a wall of pure force and deflected the shots from both Jenner and Jackie as they opened fire at him.

The wrestler snarled as he stared into Wulftone's face. "You come in here and attack me? None of you can harm me—not here—not so close to my prize! Not even that little girl who stole my kophesh!" Sisyphus hurled Wulftone towards the sheet of glass that stretched from floor to ceiling: the penthouse window.

Wulftone crashed into it, but the industrial strength material did not break. It cracked and splintered like a smashed windshield, but didn't yield against the force of impact. The high-strength, laminated pane could stop anything short of a sustained spray of bullets.

The lycan heard a thud, like a bird hitting glass behind him and he looked behind. Someone had clawed all the way up the side of the skyscraper and slapped a blinking wad of plastic explosives against the window where they'd stuck with LEDs blinking their warning.

Wulftone leapt forward, darting past the wizard, and shielding Jarfig. The room erupted a split second later and covered the room with glass, shrapnel, and fire. From outside, Zabe leapt into the room with a snarl and pounced upon Sisyphus in his lycan form.

Sisyphus was a big man and barely managed to hold his own against the massive lycan. Wulftone whirled and shook his thick hide, dislodging whatever glass shards had pierced his skin. He leapt into the fray and aided his cousin. They hacked and slashed, but Sisyphus somehow mustered the power to repel them. He'd barely moved from the central spot in the room.

The wizard blasted Zabe and Wulftone with fiery eldritch bursts. They flung the rebels to the far side and smashed them against the wall. Jenner and Jackie fired laser blasts against Sisyphus, but they simply deflected off him. Errant energy bolts splashed harmlessly against the floor and ceiling as one of the strange stones around Sisyphus's neck flashed with brilliant color.

Wulftone was simply glad that Sisyphus didn't have his kophesh any longer. He might've simply thrown them all out the busted window if he'd had access to telekinetic abilities. He crawled to his feet and looked at Zabe. "I've never seen him so powerful before!" And then he cocked his head at him. "Welcome back, by the way. Glad to see your timing hasn't improved."

Zabe flashed him a grin and yanked the Stone Glaive free from his baldric. "That may be true, but I've never seen something capable of resisting this weapon." He roared, leaping back into combat. He hacked and slashed, while the wizard deflected blow after blow with a shield and blade he drew out of thin air; he'd composed them of fire and pure eldritch energy.

With only a simple glare at the doorway, he flung back Jenner and Jackie. He snorted like a bull and ripped the entire wall free, collapsing it around them and entrenching them within rubble and debris.

Screams came down the hall as more and more soldiers came at their rear guard, threatening to overwhelm the defenders. They suddenly stopped and Wulftone's heart sank at the implications.

Zabe sniffed, catching a whiff of a familiar scent. He turned and looked past the rubble and their fallen friends. "Claire?"

Sisyphus seized the opportunity and smashed the lycan with his energy shield, knocking Zabe prone. Wulftone jumped to his defense, keeping the wizard from immediately dispatching him. *"How is he so strong?"* Wulftone spat.

Claire walked across the rubble and into view, kophesh in hand. Her eyes burned white, and she glared at the enemy.

"Not again," Sisyphus snarled. "Not here in my seat of power—not even *you* can get to me here."

A magic, psychic energy rippled in the air between them. The hair on the lycan's hides tingled as if taken with static energy.

Zabe looked up and noticed the intravenous tubes connecting Sisyphus to a supply of harvested blood from Jarfig. Another tube created a direct lead to the restrained victim, giving the wizard a constant supply. He pulled the Stone Glaive to his side and used it to cut the line between Jarfig and Sisyphus.

The Wizard looked down at Zabe. For the first time since the assault began, panic took the big man. "What have you done?"

With a connection of flesh to flesh through the line of primal blood, the magic of the Glaive took hold. The cut line filled with stone and transformed the blood. It petrified and turned gray and solid as it raced up both sides of the catheter.

Sisyphus screamed and yanked the IVs free from his body before the Architect King's power transmuted him. Wulftone had already leapt into action and yanked the tubes out of Jarfig's arm. While he was close, he snapped the man's restraints and pulled him to freedom, rushing towards the safety offered by Claire.

Zabe also leapt clear as his fiance held aloft the kophesh and hurled all the debris at the howling wizard, uncovering her friends and burying her enemy in rubble. For good measure, she ripped the other two walls free of their moorings and smashed them together, clapping Jacob Sisyphus between them.

"I'm so glad to see you," Zabe said, embracing her, but uncertain what to call her. When he'd last seen her, only Bithia remained—and this move was unlike the sort of thing she would do. He looked into her eyes and saw that she was different. "Claire?"

She nodded. "We are Claire. I'll explain later." Claire hugged him tightly once more. "It's a long story. But we've got to get out of here. I already knocked out and wiped the minds of the Heptobscurantum's science corps."

Helping Jenner and Jackie to their feet, Jenner threw his weapon away; the power source had already depleted. The boy embraced his father, who swayed on his feet, barely able to stand between the muscle atrophy and the low blood supply.

"We've got a gate of our own waiting for us—it's how I got here." None of them questioned Claire; they hurried back towards the main chamber where she had come from.

Shandra and Zurrah fell in with the rest. Minor scrapes and bruises indicated that the battle had been fierce before Claire arrived to aid them; unconscious soldiers lay strewn about, lives also saved by the psychic. Zurrah walked in lockstep with his brother. "Zabe? It is good to see you."

"Likewise," Zabe said. They'd both been trained by the same warriors and knew better than to stand around and talk shop in the middle of battle. As soon as they'd cleared the hall, all three elevators dinged and belched out more troops. Further behind, they heard Sisyphus roar again as he freed himself from the rubble; he may have been separated from the Primal energies, but he was still a powerful sorcerer.

Half of the mercenaries chased them through the corridor and the others split off, going the other direction. Wulftone slammed the doors behind them to block the mercenaries and wrapped a steel chair leg around the knobs to prevent them from following.

As soon as they got to the room where their escape portal waited for them, the far wall crumbled as Sisyphus opened a new path. He strode through the hole, dusty, bruised, and with trickles of blood streaming down his face. "You will all regret that! Each of you Primes will be hooked up to supply me with raw energy—the rest of you will be killed," he hissed with snake-like vigor.

The security team busted in behind him with guns blazing.

Jarfig and his rescuers ducked behind tables and whatever else they could find to provide cover. They tried to work their way closer to the waiting portal. Right behind it, the wizard's portal generating equipment had been stationed.

Sisyphus howled for his men to stop. "Cease fire—cease fire! I can't risk you destroying my machine!" They'd already drawn a bead on their targets and attacked like sharks with blood in the water. Ignoring Sisyphus, they took shots anyway, aiming carefully.

Weaponless, Jenner tried to dash to safety and slid to a stop near the portal. On the other side, Cerci screamed as stray shots came through and bullets fired halfway across the world bit the walls and floor of a house in Duluth, Minnesota.

"Father, come on! We have to run for it." Jenner darted out from behind his cover and made a line for the portal.

A nearby guard led his target and pulled the trigger with deadly precision, aiming for Jenner's heart. At the last moment, Professor Jarfig launched himself at his son and took a bullet to the chest, protecting him.

Sisyphus screamed with rage. He hurled a blast of pure force and snapped the necks of his own security team as he growled with animalistic fury. The source of all his amplified power laid dying in a pool of his own blood and he did not truly know if any other blood except that of his own Prime would give him the same potency.

Claire shouted through the portal leading to Duluth. "Cerci, I need to know how to operate the other rift generator. I need a portal from *here* to the Prime, and I need it *now*!"

"Where to, in the Prime?" Cerci shouted.

"I don't care... anywhere—*but it has to be the Prime.*"

Cerci stammered, "You need to... you just have to... watch out!" She hurled herself through the portal and somersaulted to a stop. She kept her head down and crept towards the German contraption's controls. "Cover me!"

More guards came in and Jackie peppered them with blaster fire. Jenner sat on the floor, holding his father. Jarfig's chest heaved as he struggled to draw successive breaths. Blood leaked everywhere from his wounds.

"No! No, father, I can't lose you—I've done so much to save you from that monster," he sobbed, holding Jarfig's head. The light began going out behind his eyes as soon as the rift opened to a dark and starless night filled with foreign constellations.

The three werewolves continued to harass the wizard when he suddenly stiffened, as if he'd been struck by a jolt of electricity. He groaned and levitated slightly as Claire stood, kophesh in hand. She seized him with telekinetic force. Her eyes blazed and frosted milky white.

Cerci spread wider across the area of the second portal.

Jarfig convulsed once and then fell limp. Jenner wailed, his cries matched the wind coming from the Prime's sky as it whipped through the new energy gate and chilled the room.

Jackie pushed ahead and blasted the remaining guards. She secured the room with the help of Wulftone and Zurrah, who took up points on either side of the space in case more intruders arrived. Zabe stood adjacent to Claire and guarded her with his life.

Claire asked, "Do you feel that, Sisyphus? That's a spectacular and specific kind of pain coursing through you. I'm not causing it—I'm only holding you still. What you're enduring happens only in the Prime and when the death of one of its own occurs while a dimensional variant is present. His or her soul is slammed into a foreign body. It is a very rare occurrence—something I once endured."

Sisyphus grunted through the shock and the pain. He blinked back the sudden thoughts that began rambling through his mind—Jarfig's thoughts and emotions clouded his brain. "I'm... not... in the... Prime," he growled through clenched teeth.

"As long as that portal is open, the metaphysical rules of the Prime exist here," Claire said. She released the wizard, and he curled up on the floor, too weak and distracted by the battle inside his mind to even stand.

"No! get outta my head..."

His voice seemed to shift, and he spoke more like Jarfig. "I *told* you that not all strength is physical…" The big man turned his face to Jenner. "S-son? You did it. You freed me!"

Jenner scrambled over to him and hugged the doppelganger who had become his father, only in a much sturdier frame.

The wrestler shook his head. "Nnnnneerrgh! No! I must not… rrrrrr." He stiffened and convulsed with a seizure as the wills contended with each other over and over again.

Claire's eyes went white, and she reached out with her psychic abilities. She breathed heavily for a few long moments, and then her eyes returned to normal. Jarfig, the new Jarfig, opened his eyes with a flutter and they locked on to Jenner. He returned the big hug.

"What did you do?" Shandra asked.

"I recently learned a great many new psychic tricks as a result of my own struggles. I locked Sisyphus away deep inside, someplace where he'll never be able to bother the Professor again."

Shandra nodded. She'd not taken any studies with Pollando, but she'd understood what they might entail. "Let's get out of here," she said as more gunfire erupted beyond Jackie and the lycans.

A group of bewildered homeless vagrants emerged from a nearby room and scrambled over the rubble. Bloody catheter tubes dragged behind them where the homeless victims who powered the rift machine had torn themselves free.

Claire and the others dove through the gateway and back into their home base in Minnesota. Cerci snatched the roller-ball controls and spun their triangular door on its access so that it faced the front of the Heptobscurantum's machine. As the opening shifted, she caught sight of new research drawn on the walls of the lab; Walther's distinct scrawls identified what he had been working on: *whole other planes of existence outside of the Tesseract!* She didn't have time to identify what looked more like a rune with numbers attached to it than a scientific equation. German voices belonging to international Heptobscurantum cultists echoed as they pushed their way inside. They would arrive in seconds.

"They can't keep that machine," Claire said. "It's far too dangerous!"

Jackie leveled her pulse rifle at the glass bulb containing the wundrefluvium and pulled the trigger. The machine exploded into flaming pieces, obliterating any chance of rebuilding it.

Cerci hit the kill switch and severed their link to Germany before the flames could reach them.

CHAPTER TWENTY-TWO

Dawn had only just begun to break, and Sam walked through the halls of the Duluth estate. The frost of the morning had just begun to burn off the autumn air with the sun's first rays, giving Sam a subtle boost of optimism.

The wooden floors creaked slightly beneath his weight and he noticed the little accoutrements and decorative flourishes all around the place. In the eerie quiet of the cold Minnesota morning, things focused into crystal clarity for Sam.

"This house needs a name. *The Miles Mansion?*" Sam spoke aloud to himself.

He hit the brew button on the coffee pot and shivered slightly. The house's heat hadn't been turned on yet since temperatures hadn't yet dipped below freezing, but that didn't mean it was warm. He knew folks from southern climes would balk at what northerners considered acceptable levels of cold inside a home. Sam yawned and untucked his shirt from the pajama bottoms he'd swiped from one of the many dressers on the property.

The crisp, autumn air rolled off of the nearby Lake Superior and rustled the orange and ochre leaves beyond the large windows. Gentle snores came from many of the rooms attached to the hallway. They had all been so tired upon the return from Germany that nobody had even bothered shutting doors. People had fallen into beds and couches wherever they could find them.

Sam poured a cup of coffee and looked up to see one very tired and bleary-eyed Shandra approaching. He took a sip as she yawned and said, "The Miles Mansion sounds stupid."

He chuckled, spluttering a laugh into his coffee. Something about it tasted wrong. "You have a better suggestion?"

"Yes," she said, carrying the pot to the nearby closet bath and dumping it out. "Don't make decaf. Your brain doesn't work right on that stuff."

Sam picked up the can of cheap coffee grounds and shrugged. He'd been so tired he hadn't noticed.

Shandra reset the machine and began to brew a proper pot with some beans from the local roaster. The smaller bag was old, but couldn't be more stale than the blue tin he'd been using.

"*The Jecima House? The Miles Jecima Mansion?*"

"I'm partial to the Jecima Estate," he offered.

"I can get behind that," Shandra said, finally pouring a cup of black coffee for herself. She wandered into the portal room where the rift generator had been set up. It was perhaps the best place for the early risers to talk and plan without disturbing the others. "I'm still a little confused about what Sisyphus wanted—I mean, besides the parts for his portal generator; he had to have a grander scheme... and whatever happened to Vikrum Wiltshire?"

Sam tightened his mouth. "He's, uh, gone. I don't know where—heck, *Wiltshire* probably doesn't even know where. We can search for him later. *After* we deal with Nitthogr." He sipped from his hot mug. "He and the rest of us here stopped Sisyhphus from getting his hands on some kind of powerful artifact that could've turned him into an even bigger threat than Nitthogr. Something Jecima collected... Wiltshire called it the Venus Oculus."

Shandra stopped mid-sip. "The Oculus? It is here?"

"You know the Venus Oculus?"

"We know of it on the Prime. An arcane mirror. It was originally built in our dimension, as were so many of the magic items that found their way to Earth, but it was lost long ago."

"What does it do? I haven't had a chance to read Jecima's notes yet," Sam asked.

Shandra didn't answer immediately, and footsteps shuffled down the hall. Claire walked in, raccoon-eyed and clutching a coffee mug with both hands. She shambled into the room and sat, taking several long sips, until she was ready to talk. "We need to come up with a plan. I know we're all still recovering, but we need to strike soon. We don't have the option of cooling our heels too long... not with Nitthogr released." She took another long sip. "We do have one advantage: nobody else knows that we have the gate generator. With the Tesseract's portal system shut down, we'll have the element of surprise."

One by one, the rest of their party began to filter in. The last two in were Zabe and Zurrah. They'd stayed awake well past everyone else talking through the last several years that had passed with the younger brother lost or in captivity. Once the last of the lycans had taken a seat, Sam stood and wrote a question at the top of their white board.

What do we know?

"We need to account for as many variables as we can if this mission is going to be successful. I am not a warrior, I'm a scientist. I make hypotheses. We'll need as much data as possible if we are going to succeed."

He drew a few numbers one by one and listed the top items. *1. We might all die. 2. Unchecked, Nitthogr will destroy the universe. 3. We have the element of surprise.*

"What else do we know?"

They started calling out items to add to the list.

Gita is a traitor (probably unwilling).

The vyrm are at odds with Heptobscurantum.

Some vyrm reject Sh'logath.

The Veritas, Guardian Corps, and military are likely destroyed.
We have no trustworthy allies on the Prime.
Claire is stronger than ever.

Sam twisted his lips at the list. It was not overwhelmingly positive. "Now let's list what resources we have and what we need if we're going to launch a full scale assault on the Prime, which we can safely assume is under Nitthogr's full control."

Resources:
A third werewolf.
Rift generator.
The Stone glaive.
Jarfig can pretend he's Sisyphus.
Telekinetic kophesh.
The Venus Oculus.
Chamber of Mysteries is impenetrable.
Needs:
An army.
A diversion.
A miracle.

Together, they stared at the list. Cerci blinked at it. "It's official… we're all gonna die. But at least we have a name for the house." She winked at Shandra and Sam. "I overheard you earlier… We're going with the Miles Mansion, right?"

Everybody groaned, but they were glad for the moment of humor to break the serious tone. "She's joking everybody," Shandra said. "It's the Jecima Estate."

Claire broke the burgeoning silence that followed after the humor petered out. "I think I have an idea, but we might not all like it."

Sam and Shandra stole up the stairs to continue research on the Venus Oculus. Below them, Cerci operated the machine, helping the others pilfer resources from the Prime. Using as much stealth as possible, the thieves raided the Guardian Corps' armory to steal armor and weapons.

In Jecima's project room, Shandra stared at the shapely form of the mirror. She traced her fingers over its curving, ornate lines as Sam sat on the floor with Jecima's research spread out before him. Shandra whistled as she touched the gilded edges of the frame. It looked much like the enchanted mirrors that the royal family had previously kept in the royal keep of the Prime.

"This is really it," she said reverently, "the Venus Oculus."

Sam raised an eyebrow as he translated the texts in his head and grumbled about how slow he was at this part; Miles had always been the linguistic genius between them. "It says something here about trading values... I'm not sure what that means."

He chuckled as he sorted through his old friend's notes. "That old huckster... all this time, he sounded like he didn't believe in magic." He scanned some notes written in the margins. "But I think he was trying to bring his wife back." He felt a little sheepish about reading Jecima's private thoughts, as if he'd sneaked a peek into Miles's diary.

Could Wanda's return help me bring Jared home? Miles had written. It seemed obvious Jecima used every option at his disposal to try to fix whatever rift had transpired with his son—he even entertained necromancy... Sam could sympathize with his deceased friend.

Sam read aloud from Jecima's other notes scribbled lengthwise down the page, those notes relevant to the mirror—and whether or not they could or should use it in their quest. "For every gift granted, there is an enormous toll... how much is too great a cost?"

"It is known that the mirror takes something of value to use," Shandra said. "There is a high cost—a form of a curse, depending on the situation. What do your ancient writings say?"

He sighed and summarized the texts. "There are some very sad tales. One features a man named Tarquin. I think that's an ancient Roman name," he muttered. "Tarquin used the mirror to bring back his dead lover. She was restored to beauty and perfection, but she now despised him."

Picking up another photocopy, he summarized again. "A man returns to life his child claimed by a plague. At the same moment, the child's healthy mother dies of the same illness." He set the sheets down. "There are others, each like the rest."

Shandra touched the inscription in the mirror. It was written in the secret code of the Veritas Order. "'The mirror of gifts gives when it takes, lest what's held dear reciprocates, what's old is new and powers break, truth revealed unmasked annihilates.'"

Sam looked up and recognized she was reading some deep message, which he lacked the context to understand. "What does that mean?"

"It means those stories are probably more than simple folklore," Shandra sighed. "We cannot use the Oculus without making a terrible trade."

Sam asked, "And what do you desire most... your 'what's held dear?'"

"My allegiance is to the Architect King, like all Veritas... like *most Veritas*," she corrected to account for the ones like Shjikara. "That is what I hold most dear."

"I don't know how that could be transformed into a curse."

Shandra grimaced. She could envision a few situations similar to the lore in Jecima's copies. Mostly they involved martyrdom and sacrifice—and not all were of her.

She didn't ask Sam his. He answered anyway. "Mine would have to be my daughter. I would move heaven and earth to keep her safe." He trailed off, knowing that he was incapable of assuring her safety under any circumstance given the nature of their enemies.

"We have to do this," said Claire as she cinched the straps on her combat uniform. "It's the only way I can think of to get the army we need." Light glimmered off of Zurrah's old armor which Claire had previously claimed; it no longer fit the third lycan, anyway.

Seeing her in it, the youngest of the Vangandrans nodded his approval. He and his girlfriend had managed to swipe a new set from a raided armory, which better fit Zurrah, anyway.

Among the armor, they'd scored crates of artillery, weapons and supplies, and a massive stack of heavy shield generators, which had been piled symmetrically against the far wall. Together, they stood against them in a neat row so that they could all rush through the portal quickly if necessary.

Cerci hit the button and activated the energy gate. A triangular rift split the sky somewhere over top of Basilisk's Desolation stronghold. The fiery geometry slowly descended and expanded to meet the eyes of a startled tarkhūn soldier.

Speaking in the vyrmic high-speech, Claire demanded, [Summon your masters. Tell him and her that Claire Jones has arrived.]

The large, reptilian guard hurried away. A few minutes later, Basilisk and Caivev approached the gate. Two vyrm of the Black followed behind them.

Shandra recognized one of them. "Trenzlr, is that you? But... how?"

The skinny vyrm bowed. "Only have I recently come to Limbus," he said. "The Emperor and his wife have welcomed the Seekers of Maetha back into vyrmkind."

Caivev waved a hand. "Please, enter Limbus. We will guarantee your safety." Caivev did a double take when she spotted Jarfig, but relaxed a moment later; Jarfig's compassionate eyes told the large man's story. He was no longer Sisyphus, and any who had known the wrestler would recognize that in an instant.

The group walked through. Last to follow, Sam turned to Cerci, who had to stay behind with their machine. "Give us a couple of hours and then check on us. I trust Trenzlr... but not any of these others. Not yet."

She nodded, and the portal zipped shut.

Basilisk led them through to the gardens that Zabe and Claire were already familiar with. Now, however, the statues were gone. Only a few of the gaming tables remained, and these looked to be actually used, rather than left in stalemates. "Refreshments will arrive shortly," he said, scooping up a handful of pieces from a game board as he walked past. "Allow me to tell you why you have come," he said.

Claire's mouth smirked. The tarkhūn emperor had always been one step ahead of everyone else—even when he didn't have access to his renowned spy network. She nodded.

Basilisk held out his hands with two fists full of pieces.

Claire cupped her hands and Basilisk dumped a whole load of pawns into them.

"You need an army."

She nodded. "I assume you know what has happened in the Prime?"

He nodded. "I knew the instant I saw you bow to my brother on his broadcast. I was certain that he'd replaced you with a shade."

Claire scowled, but nodded. "Will you help us?"

"I suppose I must add some moral credit to my ledger," Basilisk said slyly. "The rovers think that I or my wife have some kind of intrinsic connection to their Maetha. I can't be a villain and a savior both, can I?" He smirked and then whispered, "We've joined with them for our own purposes... that they think we might be some kind of god because of our dual nature linked to old prophecies works to our advantage. Together, however, we can defeat my brother."

Claire cocked her head and stared at the Maethans and then at Basilisk and Caivev. If *he* thought they could defeat Nitthogr, then perhaps they still stood a chance. "Do you believe them? Are you Maetha?" Her words sounded skeptical.

He and Caivev both shook their heads.

"We've never claimed to be such, and both deny it could be possible," she said. "However, we've both come to believe in much of those teachings they have followed for generations... certain proofs have come to light, things that neither of us could deny."

Basilisk slowly nodded. "Chief among them is that Sh'logath must be stopped."

Zabe pointed up and the rest of them realized that the unspeakable horror no longer blotted out the sky. The weather was actually pleasant on Desolation. "Where is he?"

"My brother has returned only to become Sh'logath's living incarnation. A different sort of Awakening has happened than what you stopped at the Nebraska World Gate. For my part in it, I apologize. Sh'logath used me for his own purposes and then cast me aside... though it is not for petty revenge that I defy him now. I made an unbreakable vow to your Architect King long ago. Whatever else I am guilty of, falsehood is not among my crimes... that would be like *cheating* and that is a crime I can not condone."

Zabe looked at Claire as if to ask her, *do you trust him?* She nodded. They both believed him to be sincere, and for the first time, they didn't sense ulterior motives in him.

A line of servants entered the garden courtyard carrying food and drink. Caivev motioned for them to sit and Basilisk summarized the events of their last few days for them.

"So you will help us?" Claire asked optimistically.

Basilisk tilted his brow. "If you will open the gates," he promised, "we will bring our army and fight for our right to exist. Nitthogr may have most of the Black, but those who remain with me, and any of our tarkhūn, are worth ten of them."

Claire leveled a conspiratorial gaze at her newfound ally. "We must move *soon*. Can you have your troops ready by the morning?"

He nodded with severe resolution.

Claire gripped Zabe's hand. "There is one more request I have."

The Desolation

A red sky drew across the vista beyond Limbus. It swirled with shades of fuschia and purple that cast everything with a cerise tint.

Trenzlr stood off to the side and brought his cousin Gerjha to a ceremonial altar of stacked stones he'd helped create. Sam and Shandra stood alongside Basilisk and Caivev. Wulftone and Jackie clustered together with Zurrah in their midst; Jenner and Jarfig watched from the rear.

Claire and Zabe approached the altar, where the Maethan cleric waited for them. Gerjha bowed to them both. He turned to the red sky and stared into the distance for a long time—almost uncomfortably long.

"I have stared at the evening sky every night of my life," he said. "Never have I seen such a sunset... until mere days ago, there was no beauty in the sky. The red horizon is an omen." He turned back to the couple, not telling them if it was a good one or bad.

"You are joined, wed together. There is no special magic in this ceremony except what already resides in each of you, and the fact that the Almighty One sanctions it. But your magic is a jealous thing that becomes one whole which is greater than the two. Protect each other. Love each other." He winked. "Make babies and prosper. Live long and enjoy laughter for as long as the world still remains."

Zabe leaned forwards and put a finger under Claire's chin to turn her face up to his. "In the morning, I will earn your kingdom back for you."

She responded, "Even if you can not, I would be satisfied with only you."

He kissed her.

Shandra smiled as the newlyweds led them back to earth so they could make final preparations for an early assault against the devourer god. "It was no Veritas ceremony," she whispered to Sam. "But it will do."

Earth

The old house on the Minnesota coast creaked as the heat finally pumped through the home with the sounds of a shuddering air filter that shook into place for the first time that year. Cerci rubbed her bare arms to quell the gooseflesh.

"Thanks," she told Sam. "I know it's barely halfway through October, but I've gotten used to that Texas weather."

"Don't worry about it," Sam said, emerging from the utility room with a flashlight. It amused him that the girl was capable of constructing a machine that could tear holes through the dimensional fabric of space and reality but couldn't figure out how to start a natural gas furnace. He grinned... it might have had more to do with her need to see a father do fatherly things.

Cerci threw a blanket over herself and bundled up like some kind of monk beneath a fleece prayer shawl. She shuffled back towards the center of the house and Sam wandered the hallways in search of Shandra.

He'd had much on his mind. His daughter had just wed, and all of reality might soon end—not that he'd be around to see it if they failed to stop the nigh omnipotent forces of evil that had entrenched itself in their home.

Sam knew Claire wanted to bravely rush towards their possible end as a married woman. He had toyed with the possibility of a similar proposal and wedding from the last Veritas cleric. There might not be much more time; ticking clocks surrounded him as they waited for Armageddon in a dead man's home.

He didn't find Shandra on the main level and so he began climbing the steps. He rubbed his sore ribs from where he'd been thrown down those stairs only recently. *How long ago was that... two days, maybe three?* Time had mostly stopped passing in noticeable increments for them.

Sam spotted Shandra in the mirror room. Her back was turned, and she didn't know he was there. They'd already agreed that the Venus Oculus would prove too dangerous to use.

He walked in, planning to come up with some kind of impromptu romantic gesture on the fly. Instead, his heart sank. Shandra appeared to be sobbing.

"Hey... what's wrong?"

Shandra whirled, startled. "I... I'm so sorry." Tears steamed down her cheeks and collected on her angular chin before falling in hot splashes.

Sam noticed another; crimson drops fell from her finger tip. He looked up and saw a smear of blood across the mirror frame where the mysterious letters had been engraved; *she's already activated it!*

Catching his own eyes in his reflection, Sam stood transfixed. Rooted in place by the magic, he whirled to look at her, panicked by whatever magic had been unleashed by the Oculus. His reflection no longer moved in tandem with his own.

"What... what did you wish for?"

Shandra wiped the tears away. Her voice cracked. "My heart's desire." She looked down. "You told me what *yours* was. You would do *anything* to protect Claire, *pay any price?*"

Sam wanted to be mad. Instead, he gave her a melancholy smile. In his heart, he knew it had to be this way; he understood what toll the mirror would extract... and he was happy to be a sacrifice for something as valuable as what Shandra might wish for.

"Tell Claire that I have always loved her... and that I always will."

Shandra sank to her knees, bawling. She'd hoped the high cost of this magic could have been anything else.

Sam turned back and faced the mirror. He cocked his head at his reflection. It looked so much like him, but with slight differences.

His eyes radiated a kind of power and charisma and the reflection wore a circlet upon his brow.

"Is it possible to refuse the magic? Do I have a choice in the matter?"

The reflection nodded solemnly.

Sam paused for only a moment to look back at Shandra and meet her gaze one final time. *Her eyes are so bright when she's crying.* He nodded and turned back, accepting the aid of the mirror.

Crumbling, Sam collapsed like a pillar of ash and disintegrated, leaving behind only a puff of evaporate and a small pile of salt.

Shandra burst into fresh tears and Sam's reflection stepped out of the mirror, adorned with kingly robes. He glowed ever so slightly and he knelt at Shandra's side, wiping away her tears exactly as Sam might have. She looked into his eyes. He looked every bit of Sam Jones, but Shandra knew this was no man: he was so much more.

"Do not worry, loyal one." He lifted Shandra to her feet. "It was always meant to be this way—his sacrifice was necessary for my return, and though it pained him to do it, the father gladly made his sacrifice for his child and for *you*."

Red eyed, and tear streaked, Shandra bowed. Choking on her words, she said, "Welcome back, my Lord, Architect of the Universe: my King."

Chapter Twenty-Three

Claire watched the rising sun burn off the morning haze as it peeked above the horizon of the great lake, covering Duluth in a blood red dawn. She hit the button on her coffee maker and looked around for her father. He was usually up before anyone else and brewed the pot. She appreciated the sentiment, even if the coffee was rarely any good.

Cerci shambled out from a side room with Zurrah ambling behind her. Both of their hair was matted and clumped from their awkward sleeping arrangements.

The scientist rubbed the crust from her eyes and poured the second cup, which she clutched with both hands. Cerci watched out the window with a grimace. "I'm not big on omens," she said, "But you know what they say, 'Red sky in the morning...'"

Zurrah shook his head. "I do not know the saying. What does it mean?"

Claire stared out at the waves. "'Take Warning.'"

Shandra came down the steps. Her skin looked paler than usual and her eyes seemed puffy and grayed.

Claire took another slug of coffee. "Is my father up?"

The cleric swallowed hard. "Can I talk to you for a moment in the other room?"

Claire followed her out of the hallway and into the kitchen.

Cerci clutched her hot mug and leaned into Zurrah's arm as they watched the growing dawn. She sipped the hot drink and sighed. "I have a bad feeling about today."

A scream split the air, coming from the room with Claire and Shandra. The entire house turned out within seconds; everyone crowded around the door frame.

Claire had sank to her knees. Her coffee mug lay tipped and broken with its coffee spilling across the floor. "What do you mean he's gone—like he's *just dead*? Where is he? I want to see him—if he died, there would be a body!"

"The mirror has claimed him: the Venus Oculus." Shandra stood, her posture remained straight, but her face revealed much anguish. She shook her head. Tears streamed down her face. "He is not dead... not exactly. He was a sacrifice. Sam knew it was the only way to stop evil from winning—Nitthogr would have beaten us if he hadn't..."

Claire beat the floor, refusing to believe her father was gone. "No! No, there has to be another way. Take it back... undo whatever it is that you did to him." She knew it had been a very *Claire* thing to say, and she felt her mind twist momentarily into two halves; her *Bithia* half understood what Sam had done. The princess knew of the Oculus and she wondered, *what did we get in exchange?* Even as she felt the hot emotions bubble and boil over.

"We could have fought him," Claire insisted. "We've done it before... you didn't even let us try to defeat him again."

A deep, familiar voice radiated its warmth through the room as it spoke. "There was no other way."

All eyes turned to the man standing before them. *The Architect King.*

"Father?" Clarie's words leapt to her lips. Then she realized it only *looked* like Sam... this was something else—more than Sam Jones. This man was much more than human.

He wore a circlet crown and royal robes flowed as he picked Claire up off the floor. "Daughter," he said. "I am not him."

She buried her face in his shoulders. "I-I know," she cried, re-signing herself to what had happened, understanding that it could not be changed.

The Architect King said, "You would have all died this day." He looked far off and away, as if peering into a potential future. "Sam would have died first. Followed by the rest of you, one at a time." He led them into the room across the hall where the machine was and looked at Cerci. "Even you would be dead, gatekeeper."

Cerci looked hesitant. "I don't see how that…"

"You would have kept the rift open, waiting for Zurrah's return, keeping hope—but a hope that would not arrive. Running low on power, you use your own blood until you drift off into eternal sleep."

The Architect King took a syringe from a medical bag lying among the rest of their emergency supplies and plunged the needle into his arm. Cerci watched him fill the tube with royal blood.

"What do we call you?" she asked. "I mean, the others seem pretty familiar, but I don't know you."

He turned and offered her the vial. "You will. My name is not pronounceable in your tongue, but you may call me what the ancient Veritas did when a name was required, J'v-Ellah."

"It's not enough," Cerci said, looking at the syringe.

J'v-Ellah smiled. "You will find it is more than enough. My blood is not like yours." He turned to address them all, looking them each in the eyes.

Zabe heard the King's words in his mind from the vision he'd had before being reunited with Claire. *The Prime needed a King.* He left for a moment and returned with the Stone Glaive. "This belongs to you. Claire had claim to it when she received it years ago in Limbus. I have no right to keep it."

J'v-Ellah pushed it back towards Zabe. "You are Claire's husband now. You have become my son… you have that same right. Keep it. The coming battle will require tools of war, but I will fight it in another manner… the way that Sam would have fought."

He bowed to them. "I will meet you all there. I do not require the machine. The Tesseract obeys my commands, even from afar. I must go now and speak with all my other children."

As silently and instantaneously as the Architect King appeared came his sudden and mysterious exit.

They stood in the stark silence for a moment and looked at each other. Claire. Zabe. Wulftone. Jackie. Shandra. Jenner. Jarfig. Cerci. Zurrah.

Nine men and women, about to fling themselves against an unstoppable god of nothingness in an alternate dimension.

Claire wiped away any residual hints of her sadness, compartmentalizing her feelings. She asked, "Are we ready?"

Cerci plugged the new tube of blood into the system and pressed a button. "Let's hit it."

The Prime

Laying flat, the Triangle portal opened in the sky outside of the capital. Small at first, it glided over the armies camped around the walls of the Prime's castle and surveyed the scene like a tiny drone. The city surrounding the castle walls had already been annihilated, razed to the ground. A horde of the Black clustered around it.

Finally finding a spot, the rift widened and descended to a reasonable level and poured out the warriors from Earth. Shandra leapt through first with her hammer raised high.

Vyrm looked up just in time to see the Veritas Cleric smashing down at them with her mystic, blunt weapon. Three werewolves followed, raking enemies with claw and fang; Zabe slashed through swaths of enemies who were still too surprised to evade the massive blade. The glaive left behind faces eternally frozen in surprise and the fractured rubble of busted statues.

Claire clutched her kophesh. She and Jackie dropped through in their midst. Jackie was strapped with as much ordinance as any human could carry and her pulse rifle spat shot after shot into the enemy, mowing them down with deadly precision.

The scaly enemy snarled in opposition, but none were prepared for the daughter of the Architect King. She wielded her hooked blade, hacking first through the vyrm nearest her and then used its telekinetic abilities to wipe the area free of enemies, flinging them into the distance like children's toys.

Claire's eyes frosted white and her hair and skin crackled with power. A shock-wave seemed to pulse off of her and the battlefield cleared. Every vyrm within visible distance collapsed with blank eyes; blood dribbled from their noses and ears, but they still drew breath. They'd been reduced to husks, void of conscious thought or motor skills.

Zabe caught her as she staggered after the extreme effort. Such a blatant use of raw power winded the princess. The castle gates cracked with a thud and then began to open. Enemies hurried along the parapets of the walls as they prepared to belch out another wave of the vyrm that had taken the castle.

Shandra looked up to the mountains and spotted the Veritas's stronghold. Dark lines of movement roiled in the distance as the army stationed there deployed to engage them.

"Looks like everyone knows we're here and is coming to kill us," Zabe said. "Objective one is a wild success."

Claire reached out with her mind and located the target. They needed to pinpoint her perfectly for their plan to work. "I've got it," Claire told her peers. "We need that army."

From the other side of the energy gate, Jenner and Jarfig dropped large boxes through the hole, followed by the shield generators. The werewolves snatched them and broke them open so they could pull out the stolen equipment within.

Claire looked up to Cerci, who watched through the portal with awestruck eyes, impressed by her friends' battle prowess. Claire put a location of their next target directly into Cerci's mind.

The rift shrank to something the size of a bird and then flew off into the distance as the diversion team set up the equipment and powered up the shields. The energy barrier would prevent snipers from picking them off or an army from mowing them over with pulse rifles and normal ordinance. In order to engage them, the enemy would have to walk through the protective bubble roughly one hundred fifty meters in diameter.

Zabe, Shandra, and Claire brandished their melee weapons, and the other werewolves flashed their claws. "We'll force this battle down to hand to hand."

The triple sided portal flared open and the two men fell from overhead, landing on top of the diminutive Gita. She screamed as they crushed her to the ground and the arcane gate-box tumbled across the floor.

Jenner leapt to his feet first, leaving his father to restrain the poor girl who howled and flailed against his bulky mass; Gita was small, but she was fierce. Were it not for Jarfig's newly acquired form and its stronger muscles, he may have been unable to contain her.

Snap firing, Jenner dropped the vyrm soldiers who provided Gita's escort. He sprang towards the remaining guard that fled to call for backup.

Jenner rounded a corner around the cluster of statues in an alcove adjacent to the royal courtyard. He aimed and burned a hole between the enemy's shoulder blades. Another vyrm leapt out of the shadows and sank his claws and teeth into the warrior.

His Guardian Corps armor protected most of his body, but the creature's teeth lodged in the back of his neck.

"Jenner!" Jarfig released Gita and crashed into the vyrm. The professor had never been a man of violence, but with his son threatened, he beat the vyrm to death with his bare hands.

Jenner rolled away and scrambled after the arcane box that controlled the portals.

Gita did the same, and they crashed into each other, both grasping for it. Fighting with a ferocity born of desperation, Gita shoved him aside and snatched the device.

She rolled to her hip and found Jenner seated, but with a blaster pistol in his hands. He aimed it directly at her. Gita froze, her expression torn between anguish and shame.

"How could you, Gita? You betrayed me—betrayed *us*. I thought that what we had was... well, I don't know what I thought." Jenner's aim never wavered. "I don't want to pull this trigger, but you've got to hand that box over."

"I... I..." Gita broke down in tears, a wailing mess.

Thinking she might be manipulating him, Jenner did not lower his weapon.

Between ragged breaths, Gita tried to explain. "It... it was always a lie... the whole thing. First Basilisk forced me to join the corps as his spy. He froze my whole family, but promised to restore them with a rune if I did what he ordered." She sobbed and wiped away the tears and snot as Jarfig took the box from her.

The professor turned it over in his hands, studying it with great interest.

Gita continued, "And... and then Nitthogr came... disguised as Shjikara. He... he..." The tears sprang freshly anew. She blubbered, "I didn't want to do any of it. He smashed my family, Jenner. Nitthogr killed them all except for my sister, Shara. He's holding her hostage."

Jenner had known and loved her for a long time. Only now did he finally lower his weapon. Still, his gut warned him, internally acknowledging that she had fooled him once before. Jenner chose to trust her. "Where is she—your sister?"

Gita pointed to the small child standing in the row of petrified bodies. "They recently put her back with the others when Nitthogr took the castle." She looked around and noted, "Something has drawn off all the vyrm who claimed the castle?"

"You're welcome," Jenner replied. "Claire, Zabe, Jackie, and the others are beyond the wall, luring the enemy out."

Jarfig shot his son a glance. For all his smarts, his area of studies had been history; arcane arts were not an area of gifting for him. He didn't understand how to use the gate box.

"But there's so many of them," Gita began. "They can't last long out there... Jackie and Zabe are *both* back?"

Jenner nodded. "That's why we need the box. There's a whole army waiting for the gates to open. Trenzlr got to Basilisk and Caivev. They are on our side, now... but if those gates don't open, our friends will all die beyond that wall."

Gita slowly, painfully reached for the gate box while her eyes remained fixed on the stone form of her sister. She cranked a dial and opened all the gates; every portal site across the prime opened to the Desolation. "I'm sorry, Shara," she whispered.

"Hey, hey." Jenner took her by the face. "This isn't over. We'll find a way to rescue her."

"But only Nitthogr has the ability to turn her back. He has the only rune."

Jenner put a pistol into her hand and wiped the mud and dirt off of her armor, revealing the Guardian Corps' crest again. "Then we will force him to turn her back."

Claire growled as the wave of jade and olive scales continued surging towards them. The force-field deflected the projectile and energy weapons, but the army of the Black would push through it any second now and engage them.

She and her companions defended the shield generators, baiting as much of the armored enemy into their proximity as possible. She crossed blades with them as her lycan defenders hacked them apart.

Jackie leapt atop the equipment and picked her targets. She blasted the enemy with her pulse rifle and pushed back the vyrm who'd pressed in against her best friend. "Hit em again, Claire!"

Groaning, Claire's eyes misted over and melted the minds of her enemies again, albeit with less range or effect. Many of the vyrm still stood, staggering and stumbling through the field with bloody noses, as if punch drunk. "I don't know how many of those I have left in me," she called out, surveying the scene. The gathered enemy remained huge: hundreds of thousands strong at least—and that was just the ones surrounding them.

The tail end of the massive occupation force pouring from the castle gates formed a picket line. They encamped the castle and trained weapons on them so the Princess and her guards could not leave their protective bubble without being gunned down.

Claire could see them smiling as they watched through scopes and binocs. Another wave of vyrm soldiers kicked up dust as they sped towards their position; the troops from the Veritas's monastic stronghold would arrive any second. The vyrm would keep coming, smashing themselves against the heroes until they finally overwhelmed them.

"We can't stay here—the endgame is in the castle," Zabe said, wishing that the Architect King would have given them the battle plan. "We have to get to Nitthogr."

Zabe steeled himself at the edge of the force-field, ready to make a run for it and draw as much fire as possible. There were many of them, and they were all armed. Still, with his strong hide and fast healing, it was remotely possible he could survive.

"Wait," said Claire as she looked at the castle. The doors towered over the enemy. In all the Prime's history, they had only been breached once before, and that had been by an army of the Black very much like this one. "I've got them," she panted, tightening her grip around the handle of her kophesh.

"You can not over exert yourself," Shandra cautioned her. "What if you deplete your psychic energies and…"

Claire cut her off with a wave of her hand. "I'm not using my mind. I'll use this." She held up the blade that she'd claimed from Sisyphus and concentrated on it, routing her will through it.

The doors rumbled and jittered slightly and then they broke free from their hinges and slammed down, smashing the vyrm beneath them.

"Come on!" Wulftone yelled, slinging a pulse rifle over his shoulder.

Claire dragged the huge doors to them and tented them together to create a protective barrier. They only had to gun down the few remaining vyrm on the far side of the impromptu tunnel.

The others followed, chasing after Claire and Zabe, slowing only to lay down cover-fire or take pot shots at the vyrm who tried to snipe them on their approach. Jackie was a crack shot and took out most of those on the walls. Any that she missed, Claire pushed over the edge with her telekinetic abilities and they fell to their doom.

They sped past the main entry of the castle and found themselves fighting again, this time on familiar footing. They cut a line away from the curtain wall and angled for the main facility.

Bursting into the castle's interior corridors, they quickly cleared out the vyrm within. Panting for breath, Shandra estimated, "The army from the monastery should be here any second."

Claire nodded. "Let's pray that Jenner got those gates open."

A vyrm patrol spotted them from the far end of the hall, forcing them back into action.

Zabe and his family drew the enemy fire, shrugging off the vyrm's singeing shots. Jackie and Shandra mowed them down from behind whatever cover they could find and utilized every distraction. Any they didn't pick off fell to the claws of the enraged lycans.

Finally, they reached and cleared the corridor leading to the main chamber of the castle: the throne room. Claire walked up to the gilded double doors of the royal hall and kicked them in. Flicking them with a burst of telekinetic power, they flew apart under the act.

She hissed as she found her enemy standing where the throne had once stood. The scepter of the Veritas lay cast off, bent and mangled, much like the state of the clerics.

"Nitthogr," Claire met his gaze; only one eye still remained, black and vile: the same single eye that she'd seen amid the horrific bone halo of the Darque dimension's Nihil gate. His other eye had slid behind the elastic, mutable flesh as the sorcerer lost more and more of himself to his ghastly agod.

He greeted them, "Claire Jones and company," his voice warbled and sounded an octave too low. He chuckled. "You have finally come to grant me access to the Chamber of Mysteries."

Claire and her companions cautiously entered the throne room, keeping a healthy distance from the thing that Nitthogr had become. Zabe brandished the sword that J'v-Ellah had given him. "We finally finish this, Nitthogr... once and for all."

"On that score, we can agree," he hissed, raising his stone fist defiantly. "Though you use a name and a logic that no longer applies here." Becoming pure nightmare fuel, his spine snapped and shifted into a posture that shouldn't be possible for any humanoid with a central nervous system; they could hear his spine break as he shifted forms.

Sprouting two more tentacles, the beast's jaws seemed to unhinge and brandish jagged, yellow, and bloody teeth. He shrieked and belched black smoke as he launched himself towards the heroes of the Prime.

The ground shook beneath them. "This is it, men and women," Yardi shouted as he walked through the hidden battalion of soldiers. They'd stayed on the move and hidden beneath whatever camouflage they could find.

Servos on his cybernetic leg whined, and he hadn't slept more than a few hours straight in days. "It's what we've been waiting for since the vyrm showed up a week ago—no more hit and runs!" He dragged a set of armor over his chest and stepped aside. Other soldiers scrambled to get ready and report to their duty stations.

Tahnak crawled to his feet and likewise readied himself. Yardi watched him. The brave soldier twitched and convulsed more and more every day, as if plagued by micro seizures. He'd gained the condition while trapped in the Darque with Zabe and Claire.

"Are you okay to go?" Yardi asked for confirmation.

"Yes," he insisted, certain that a nod would go unnoticed amongst his tremors. "The shakes have gotten worse ever since Shjikara revealed himself as a traitor, but I'm not missing the chance for a little pay back."

Yardi looked at the shaky man as he laid armor over his shoulders and turned. A knife wound ran the length of clavicle to waist where Gita had sliced him open. Medical staples held him together, and luckily, the wound had missed his vital organs. Tahnak had managed to crawl from the monastery when the shade army pursued the Veritas leaders.

Tahnak's efforts had allowed them to rally a few loyalists and escape before the shade's assassinations could penetrate their entire force. They'd killed a shade assassin, leaving their commander's private quarters after knifing Chira in his sleep.

Chira struggled to rise from a nearby medical pallet. His face was covered with bruises. The rosy, puckered skin of freshly stitched wounds stretched and burned as he clambered to his feet like a young drakoise, still in its protective shell.

Yardi tried to stop him. That Chira lived at all had been a miracle.

"Get off of me. There's no way I'm staying out of it—contrary to how you two have been acting. That Shade did *not* kill me back in the barracks."

Yardi tried to urge their leader back down, "You're in not in any condition too…"

"Tahnak?" Chira barked.

"Yes?"

"If he tries to put me down again, have one of your sudden 'convulsions' and kill him," Chira ordered.

"Yes, sir." Tanak knew his friend's urge to fight, despite the pain. He shared those feelings.

"Fine," Yardi growled at both of his friends. "But at least let me help you get your armor on properly."

Chira nodded, resolute, but thankful. "What do we have?" he asked as his friend helped dress him.

Tahnak reported, rubbing the sore area where his armor rubbed against the seeping wounds on his back. "Thirteen operational skiffs. All of them have guns, most are poorly armored. Our numbers are small, but the population is mobilizing. The citizens are coming out from hiding: they are saying they've had visions of the Architect King. They say that he's commanded them to fight—and *if he's ordered it*, then we too must obey."

Chira nodded and pointed to the screen displaying aerial footage of a battle that their drones were broadcasting. "And what is this?"

Vyrm were fighting vyrm. Flashes of ice and fire scorched and froze the massive army of the Black as the tarkhūn arrived to harass the armies gathered outside the busted gates of the castle.

"It looks like Basilisk and his troops have come to our aid," Tahnak said. Only a sliver of hope permeated his voice.

Yardi looked at the footage as it zoomed in and spotted a familiar face fighting alongside Caivev and Basilisk. "Is that Trenzlr—the rover who the Veritas once harbored? I thought he'd disappeared? He somehow did it… he's rallied the Tarkhūn."

Chira hurried as best as he could towards the vehicle-pool. All around him, engines fired up and crafts began to hover at the ready. "Everyone, ready to move out! At our skiffs' top speed, we can be on the field of battle in about five minutes."

CHAPTER TWENTY-FOUR

Jarfig towered over Jenner and Gita. Both of the two younger soldiers wore Guardian Corps armor. He only knew what his son had told him about this girl. Jarfig admired that Jenner believed in her despite her betrayals, and he hoped that his son would be proved right for it.

"You two go on ahead." He said. "I'm not a soldier—I never was. I will stay and guard Shara." Jarfig produced a blaster pistol that had come with him through the invasion portal.

Gita handed him the gate box and then nodded with gratitude. He returned the gesture with a stiff wave and the two warriors dashed down the hallway. Blaster fire erupted around the corner and deeper in the corridor as the younger warriors engaged the enemy.

Jarfig clutched a pain in his side and then examined his hand. *Blood.* He'd been injured in the initial encounter; it was apparently more serious than he'd first suspected. The professor grimaced.

"You're hurt," said a woman's voice.

Startled, Jarfig looked up. The angular rift had shrunk, but remained open, and he spotted Cerci watching him with concern. He'd nearly forgotten she was there. "I'm okay," he assured her, and then tried to move. A resulting jolt of pain nearly toppled him. Much of pain management was mind over matter—at least in that, Sisyphus had the professor bested and Jarfig lacked the same pain tolerance.

"Let me get you a medical kit," she said. "I see one across the room. It'll just take a moment."

The facade of pride on Jarfig's face cracked, and he thanked her. "That would be prudent," he agreed, re-examining the wound. "I'm not certain how deep this goes."

She disappeared for a couple of seconds. He expected to see her face any moment, but she did not return.

The small box of medical supplies tumbled through the rift, and then he heard Cerci's voice.

"Oh, it's you; you scared me. What are you doing here? I thought you were..." Something crashed. Cerci screamed, and then a tongue of flames and a rush of heat from an explosion flashed through the gate from the other side and the portal winked out of existence.

Trenzlr swung the weapon in his grip, a kind of bladed club, and helped push against the Black army. Many of the Maethans had volunteered when Caivev asked them for troops to save their species by fighting against their greatest enemy: themselves... the vyrm army about to destroy the multi-verse.

Along with several others who volunteered, he had stepped forward. There were so few who volunteered... until Gerjha, his cousin, pledged himself. With the prophet attending, many others finally stepped up as well.

Near Trenzlr, Basilisk and Caivev used blaster and blade as they fought the overwhelming vyrm army from the front lines. Nitthogr's forces swarmed and whelmed. More came from around the walls of the castle where they'd been waiting for orders to mobilize.

"Where did my brother get so many troops?" Basilisk growled as his skiff stopped. Soldiers rappelled over the sides and a hydraulic arm deposited another self-enclosed laser artillery unit to beat back the enemy.

"He's been secreting them away within the different dimensions for years now," Caivev explained. "Had he actually intended to cause the first Awakening before his first gambit with Claire Jones, he might have been successful—though he'd never before shown much skill at negotiating with the heads of the five tribes. He lacked your diplomacy and tact, sweetheart."

As if cued, five different and distinct trumpet signals sounded. The tribal leaders approached from the horizon. Basilisk could see their eyes, fully black like wet ink and driven mad with the spirit of Sh'logath. They would hem Basilisk in within a few moments.

"Evasive maneuvers," he yelled, clambering back aboard. The royal battle barge had crushed its way forward, blazing a path through the much larger forces that had come down from the Veritas's cliff-side home. Basilisk refused to be overwhelmed by the endless sea of the Black, but the Tarkhūn could not face the fury of *all five* tribes at once.

Before the distinct and very noticeable flagship could re-orient itself, the artillery from all five of the surging armies opened fire. Brilliant illumination flashed and heat from the deadly lasers ricocheted off the shields. They sizzled and crackled, super-heating enough that they could have boiled elements.

Basilisk pushed the helmsman from his seat and cried, "Evacuate starboard!" He punched the thrusters and began spinning the craft with one side's thrusters at max. The shields began to fail.

Heavy laser fire sheared away armor and the skiff's port engines erupted in flames, as Basilisk expected they would. He'd already sprinted for the side deck and hurled himself overboard as the starboard thrusters rammed the vehicle into the ground and created a barrier to hedge them safely against the five armies, leaving only two flanks as the direct methods of attack.

Gerjha and Skrom were the first to snatch the Emperor back to his feet. Caivev and Trenzlr followed close behind him.

Basilisk looked up, saw more incoming troops, and then flung himself towards the battle. "We must not slow—our allies will win the day! Keep fighting!"

His battle-cry bolstered the tarkhūn and they beat back the opposition, securing the area behind their crashed skiff. Trenzlr shoved an enemy vyrm and struck him down. A familiar cry howled at his side, and he glanced over. Hirdac fell as an enemy sword pierced him.

Klyrtan screamed with blind rage. He hacked the enemy apart with unseen ferocity and then moved on to the next target in a berserker rage.

Basilisk pointed to a canyon just around the edge of the castle. "If we can take that position, we will be better defended, especially if we can get a shield generator inside."

"Already on that," Skrom barked. He and another massive Tarkhūn picked up a couple pieces of equipment that had been left on the battlefield a little way near the crash site. The generators laid in front of the castle's main gates where the doors had been ripped from their moorings.

"First, we've got to punch through that army coming around the castle wall." The army had come from down from Shjikara's keep and snuck in from the blindside to enact a pincer maneuver. If they turned to face them, they would leave their rear flank exposed to the other half of the army.

A dozen or so Prime skiffs suddenly pulled out of the canyon's mouth with lasers firing. They outflanked the pincer and ripped open the Black's defenses. As the vyrm's morale broke into sudden chaos, the tarkhūn capitalized on the opening and charged, cutting them down. Basilisk and his forces advanced as quickly as they could manage.

One of the smaller vehicles picked up the Emperor and Caivev to speed them to the mouth of the canyon. Another whisked Skrom away to set up their defensive shield. The others lagged behind, making their way as quickly as possible given the relative safety of their position and sudden lack of enemies.

The Maethans trickled to the rear. Unused to the rigors of battle, they moved more slowly, but fought with no less heart. Trenzlr rested his hands on his knees momentarily, planting his back to the wall of the castle. Gaping sections had been blasted away and massive fissures large enough to hide man or vyrm had been cut away.

Gerjha paused next to him, equally winded. "Did you ever think you would be in the Prime, fighting against the black and killing your countrymen?" he asked his cousin.

"Never," admitted Trenzlr, breathing hard. "The Seekers have always been passive. We had always expected Maetha to win our battles for us."

"He will; I am certain of it. But sometimes we are called as participants in his work... and quite honestly, history reveals that too many Seekers have said whatever they want about Maetha and expected their own interpretations of holy writ to be followed. What if Maetha is more than the culture we've allowed ourselves to become in his name?"

Trenzlr raised a brow and looked at Klyrtan, who stood nearby, seemingly untired by the battle. He simply stood there, clutching a short sword and splattered with the blood of friend and foe.

Chira grasped hands with Chartarra as their skiffs abutted each other. "Thank you for the assistance," the vyrm told him. "I am Chartarra, Caivev's commander of the advanced scouts," he shared the titled he'd been recently given.

Grimacing as he shook the hand, he gave his name. "Chira. Leader of the Royal military... or what's left of it. This is Yardi and Tahnak," he introduced.

Caivev and Basilisk came alongside their rescuers' skiff a moment later and thanked them again.

"You have Maethan's fighting alongside your tarkhūn?" Chira asked.

"Some, yes," Caivev told him. "You know of them?"

"They are not unfamiliar to us." Chira pointed to Trenzlr in the distance. "I know that one..."

Tahnak twitched some more, drawing odd looks from the Tarkhūn leaders. "Who is that with him?"

Chartarra looked back. "Next to Trenzlr... that is Gerjha, the prophet of the Maethans. He is Trenzlr's cousin and the..."

"No." Tahnak twitched. "The other one with the black eyes. There is something wrong with him."

Basilisk gasped. That same inky darkness he'd seen in the tribal leaders' eyes was also in Klyrtan's.

As soon as they all looked back, Klyrtan plunged his weapon into Gerjha. Trenzlr rushed to grab his kin as the prophet collapsed in a bloody mess. Before anyone could train a gun on the traitor, Klyrtan had fled through the cracks of the castle walls.

Chartarra cried out with shock and berated himself for not realizing something like this could happen—he'd seen Klyrtan's reaction to Nitthogr's dream-call. He already had his skiff turned around when he saw Trenzlr lay his cousin prone. The grieving rover crossed his cousin's arms, respectfully closed the victim's eyes, and then retreated from the advancing armies.

Trenzlr sprinted towards the mouth of the canyon. There, Chartarra sped in order to pick him up.

The enemy had nearly closed the distance, and they needed to hold the line until Claire and the others could defeat their primary adversary: Nitthogr. Suddenly, the enemy army stopped advancing. Some of it even turned aside and refocused their attentions.

"What is happening?" Basilisk shouted, when they refused to engage. He called for a report from his troops.

Chira waved to the emperor on the adjacent skiff. "I'll beam over our feed. We have a few aerial drones on the far side of the battle."

A video feed showed a massive, tangled swarm of humans, citizens of the Prime. They charged ahead on foot and drove civilian vehicles. Their improvised army crashed into the rear flank of the vyrm forces. Each of the five tribal armies, commanded by leaders of the Black, suffered the same harassment. The humans fought valiantly and with whatever tools they had at hand, invigorated by the call of their King and their distaste with the constant invasions and schemes of the enemy.

Citizens of the Prime had finally had enough. Casting off fear and inspired by visions of the Architect King, they turned on their assailants and shifted the winds of war.

Chira grinned. "Our reinforcements, the army of the Architect King, has arrived."

Earth

Hearing the exterior door to the Duluth mansion click shut, Cerci looked up, startled by the intrusion. "Who's there?" she called.

Sam Jones stepped around the corner.

Cerci had been rummaging through a medical bag and held a compact first aid kit in her hands. She put it behind her so Sam could not see it and then tossed it behind her with a flick of the wrist so that it fell through the portal.

"Oh, it's you; you scared me." Cerci stepped further away from the dimensional rift and tried to keep herself calm. All the twisting and changing due to the magic messed with things. She didn't know what was happening—but something felt off... Sam was gone. She'd been sure of it, replaced by J'v-Ellah. "What are you doing here? I thought you were..."

"I had to slip away," Sam said. "It was a kind of secret mission. Nobody could know about it... not even Shandra."

Cerci nodded slowly as she backed casually up against the portal machine, trying not to give away the fact that she was not convinced by his performance. "Well, welcome back to the *Miles Mansion*. They'll all be glad you are back."

She watched his eyes. Sam nodded without any recognition for the inside joke. "It's good to be back."

Cerci turned her head and looked past the suspicious Sam and at an empty room. "Oh, hey there, Claire," she said, fooling the impostor.

He turned his head, and Cerci used the momentary distraction to her advantage. She snatched a hand gun she kept loaded and hidden atop the portal machine.

Fake Sam snarled and let his disguise fall. Scales revealed themselves as Krenyr the Hunter leapt for Cerci. She fired off a few shots, but none were even close to the trained assassin. He ducked and weaved as he drew her fire in the wrong directions while he rushed for her.

Krenyr snatched her by the wrist and wrenched her hands upwards, so she pointed the gun away. They struggled for a moment, though she was far over-matched.

Fighting for the gun, they did an odd kind of tango across the floor and Cerci noticed they'd moved precariously close to the portal which hovered in the middle of the room, flat and fiery. It hung in stasis just above the floor.

She yielded the gun and put all her efforts into kicking his leg. Krenyr's foot flailed and clipped the edge of the portal. The laser-cut edge burned Krenyr across the ankle and he yelped, losing the gun somewhere behind him.

The shade turned and bared his fangs while drawing a wicked dagger from his belt. He hissed with murderous intent.

Cerci panicked; her options had run out. She snatched the vial of the Architect King's blood and pocketed it to keep it safe. The limited supply of regular blood they'd secured from a local blood bank kicked in as an automatic backup. She tried to escape, but the enemy sidestepped and prevented any movement except backing her up against the wall around the bulky edges of her equipment banks.

Krenyr wrapped his talons around her throat and brandished his knife.

Cerci reached for a weapon, whatever her hands could find. Her fingers seized upon the grip of a familiar instrument of death and destruction. She brought it to bear in front of her. The flyswatter was little more than a flimsy wire with a plastic slapper—but it would have to do.

The scientist gulped and Krenyr laughed in her face as she tried to fend him off with the wiry whip. Cerci momentarily wondered how many annoying insects it had killed in its day. *What's one more, then?*

She slapped the glass cylinder containing the wundrefluvium and caused a massive explosion. It mushroomed out from the wall while the machine's bulkhead shielded her from the blast. The flames engulfed the surprised assassin and fried him to a crisp. Damaged beyond immediate repair, the machine went offline.

Cerci hissed and stared at the mess in the long silence that followed. The portal was gone, but the laptop across the room had sustained only minimal damage, and it still operated. She had plenty of cash and easy access to the parts, wundrefluvium aside; Cerci could rebuild the machine, but knew it would take her weeks all by herself.

She sank to the floor, certain she could have no impact in whatever battles raged within the Prime. For now, she had to hope and pray that Zurrah would make it out alive.

The Prime

Gita and Jenner dashed through the halls. Bodies of fallen vyrm littered the corridors, and they stepped over them with footsteps echoing as they tromped through.

Jenner grabbed her and they climbed a flight of steps. "There's a back way to the throne room. Maybe we'll get an angle on Nitthogr. It's a good sniper position."

Up ahead, they cleared the edge of the stairwell. At the end of the corridor, a trio of vyrm stood at a large picture window.

Gita raised her pistol and put three precise shots into the enemy, one for each of them. Jenner caught up to her and they looked out beyond the castle walls. Vyrm fought against vyrm, but the men and women of the Prime had arrived to join the battle as well. Blue flashes of ice and red waves of fire glimmered below and beyond them, near the fraying edges of the tarkhūn force.

"I wonder if this is what the Syzygyc war looked like?" Gita asked. Dread reverence quieted her voice.

"I hope not," Jenner put a hand on her shoulder. "That was the final breaking point for the vyrm... when the Edenya realm truly became the Desolation. What would become of the Prime if all that death and destruction came here?"

Gita turned and headed the opposite direction. "Come on," she finally said, with malice in her voice. "We've got a monster to kill."

Jenner hurried on ahead of her and led Gita to a bank of doors with a keypad. "I did a sentry post here once shortly after joining the Corps."

"And you just happen to remember the password?"

He smiled. "By coincidence, the number is my birthday. It's hard to forget something like that." He entered a code, and a door clicked open.

They sneaked into a balcony with booth seats that overlooked the royal court. Below them, they found their friends squaring off against the writhing mass of tentacles and teeth that Nitthogr had become. The horrific incarnation of Sh'logth surged towards Claire and Zabe.

Jenner pulled his rifle to his shoulder and opened fire. Gita raised her pistol as well. Laser bursts splashed off the monster from the rear. They did not hurt the beast, but he whirled and snarled.

Sh'logath crab-walked nearer with incredible speed and lashed out with an elongating tentacle. He ripped the balcony free from the wall and sent it crashing to the floor.

Gita and Jenner crawled from the rubble, coughing on dust and bleeding.

Sh'logath smiled, licking his giant jagged teeth. "Slave," he commanded her, "Turn your weapon on your friends and kill them."

"No!" she screamed, finally loosing her pent up rage. "*You can't control me anymore!*"

"Fool. Your sister will die—and I will not give her the courtesy of leaving her petrified during the act. I will restore her to life and flesh before I devour her, alive and conscious, and she will know that *you* could have saved her."

Gita opened fire on the monster, mainly so that she wouldn't have to listen to any more of his threats. She had already made her choice.

The others pressed their attack, and the monster met each one, tracking their attacks with his one monstrous eye and multitude of tentacles. As soon as he'd knock back one, another fighter took his or her place.

A tentacle snatched Claire and threatened to squeeze the life out of her when Zabe slashed it with the Stone Glaive. He hacked a chunk of Sh'logathian flesh away, but it did not turn to stone.

They all gasped at the discovery.

"Fools—I have grown beyond the power of your petty, mystical tools. I have transcended the rules that bind your reality—*I am born of the void* and you cannot stop me! I am Birthed and I am Awake!"

CHAPTER TWENTY-FIVE

Klyrtan fled into the cracks and squeezed through the fissures that twisted like jagged pumice tunnels between the walls. Laser blasts sparked and snapped behind him as he wriggled through the gaps. Fear and dread gripped him to the core and radiated out from his spine.

He barely knew what had come over him. A feeling of intense joy and manic power had overwhelmed him only minutes ago; his emotions seemed to dictate his movements as if he was not in control. Klyrtan could still feel where the hot blood had splattered across his face and a sort of primal frenzy had over-ruled his mind and heart.

As soon as he'd wriggled through the winding passage, the memories washed over him. His entire life poured out in his mind's eye. Klyrtan remembered staring at the stupefying face of madness and living a life as a cripple. He remembered the siren call of Nitthogr's dream and knew where the dark lord was; even now it was connected to him.

Klyrtan stumbled to his knees and collapsed within the confines of the castle walls. "H-he used me," Klyrtan groaned, understanding that he'd been set up. He had acted as an unwitting agent of the enemy—groomed since childhood for this very role.

Even now, the dark whispers called to him. Evil thoughts nibbled at the raggedy edges of his consciousness. Voices of the vile one reached for Klyrtan. All one thousand of them cooed, cajoled, and cried out for him, trying to wrap his sudden clarity up within psychic fetters.

He looked up towards the inner buildings and dashed across the near-emptied royal grounds. Klyrtan knew exactly where the agod lurked. The vyrm's hate consumed him, but this time it burned against Sh'logath.

Klyrtan did not know how long he could resist the lure of those siren voices. He was barely sure of which voice was *his*, even; the others grew with swelling volume. Klyrtan dragged the sharp edge of his blade across his skin. His own mouth cried out in pain. With it, he found his voice, hidden among the others, but burning intensely hot.

Locking onto the sound of it, Klyrtan made sure to remember which of the voices belonged to him. The only thing Klyrtan was sure of was the sharpness of the short sword in his grip; it was covered in the prophet's blood. He looked up and then sprinted across the courtyard, searching for the agod and inexplicably drawn to him.

Sh'logath contorted as he moved, evading the weapons of the arrayed heroes. Gita and Jackie both peppered him from the flanks with their blasters as Jenner readied an explosive device. Their shots did little more than annoy the fiend.

Jenner hurled the cluster of bombs and his friends leapt aside as it detonated. Flames and jagged shrapnel washed over the beast.

The monster shrieked. Weapons of the humans scorched and shredded Sh'logath's adaptable skin, but none of them did significant enough damage.

Jenner's face soured—he realized that they could not win this fight. He picked his gun back up and opened fire. "I don't think all the ammo charges in our entire armory could take this thing down," he told Gita.

Sh'logath whirled his tentacles above Claire and the others and then snapped them back like a whip. Jenner caught a wicked glint in the monster's bulbous eye; he grabbed Gita and shoved her out of the way.

The tentacles smashed into the ground where Gita and Jenner had just stood. Sh'logath's appendages moved like whips but hit like clubs.

Gita and Jenner scrambled back to their friends, who covered them. A writhing arm tried to ensnare them before they could reach safety. Zurrah shredded the tendril with his razor claws. Sh'logath ignored the scratches and wrapped the limb around the werewolf like it was a python.

Zabe leapt to his brother's aid and slashed cleanly through the curl of monster flesh. The severed arm fell to the floor, and Sh'logath growled. Although a splatter of nearly black blood fouled the floor, his lost extremity crawled back to Sh'logath like a snake and reformed into his inky mass.

"We can hurt it!" Wulftone cried. As a group, they all surged forward, drawing attacks and recoiling as others assaulted him.

Sh'logath seemed to loom larger and larger with every swing and shot they took. Claire wielded her kophesh, but the magic of her telekinetic power had no inherent effect against it—Sh'logath seemed a blind spot on the magical spectrum, and she feared touching him psychically too much to try anything with those abilities. She had tried it in the past and it had never ended with anything but pain... and they could not chance distractions. Especially not now.

A vyrm berserker suddenly bust in from a side door, too fast for any to react to. The blood-soaked vyrm wielding a short sword leapt into the fray, screaming, "You will never use me again!" Klyrtan slashed and cut cleanly through one of Sh'logath's arms, and then whirled and hacked apart another writhing appendage. He struck and attacked with reckless abandon, not caring if he lived or died—just that the voices plaguing him ceased.

Sh'logath roared at the minor annoyance and recoiled so that he had a space cushion to move in. With more room to operate, one of his tendrils wrapped around Klyrtan and crushed him limp; the pressure of Sh'logath's grip broke shoulders, femurs, forearms, and spine with horrific cracking sounds.

The beast opened his mouth and chomped down on the rogue vyrm. He could have swallowed a person whole, but he took pleasure in the chewing as Klyrtan shrieked, powerless to stop the grinding, stomping teeth as they smashed down upon him over and over.

One of the tendrils Klyrtan had severed lay limp upon the chamber's tile. It bore the stone fist of Shjikara at its tip.

Gita stared at the cursed hand of the High Priest where it lay a meter away from her. When Sh'logath roared, his severed chunks of flesh writhed and squirmed, moving back towards the monster.

"No! Stop it," Gita cried, lunging for the writhing, snakey thing. It slipped just beyond her grip.

Shandra stepped forward and smashed it with her hammer. The black flesh splattered and smeared into something like an ink stain across the floor. The force of her blow cracked the fist-like shape.

Gita scooped it up and pushed against the cracks that had formed after Shandra's attack. She pried it open like a nut at Christmas time and found, nestled within it, an onyx runestone etched with a mystic sigil. Gita clutched it to her chest and tears streamed down her face—she finally had what she needed to rescue her sister... now she had to keep it safe.

Sh'logath roared as the heroes formed up against him again. He cackled, laughing off such inconsequential damage as they'd caused. "You can not beat me—not all of you combined—not if you had a million years to prepare." He grinned wickedly. 'And you have much, much less time than that."

A loud click *throom-boomed* behind both Sh'logath and the heroes. Slowly and on creaking hinges, the doors to the Chamber of Mysteries opened to reveal the Architect King. He stood in the middle of the vault and stared at the beast who had drawn precariously close to the arcanely locked barrier.

Gita stared, squinting slightly at the glowing man within. "Doctor Jones... Sam Jones?" She shut her mouth and gasped when she realized who it really was.

"Maybe *they* cannot stand," he said. "But I stand with them."

Sh'logath drew himself up to twice the height of J'v-Ellah. The agod practically trembled with rage. He shouted and screeched accusations and traded barbs with J'v-Ellah in some unknown language. Sh'logath began to approach the doors of the sanctum where the Architect King stood.

"Quickly," Zabe ordered. "It must be a trick or a trap of some kind—we must not let him reach the Chamber!"

J'v-Ellah held up a hand as his princess-daughter led the charge. "Stay where you are. None of us can stop this now."

Their faces fell, crestfallen. The Prime's mortal enemy, an insidious sorcerer who had birthed a nega-god within him, had finally breached the royal chamber and was about to profane the most holy sanctum of the realm.

Sh'logath sneered as he walked past the ancient barriers that Nitthogr had long tried to breech. He could have annihilated the entire realm—all of it and still been unable to bypass the magic that held those doors shut. His destruction would have created a paradox, one that allowed existence to continue for all eternity—even in Sh'logath's realm of Awakened void.

"He is certainly no Nitthogr," J'v-Ellah told them, stepping aside to let the beast pass. "The sorcerer is gone. Burned away. Devoured. This is something entirely *other*. It is Sh'logath incarnate."

"Have none of you believed me?" the agod hissed, only tenuously stepping within the doors. Light, arcane and holy, shone throughout the chamber. Only the most valuable and rare items were stored within. Most of them had passed out of remembrance, but one item had lived large and in pure legend.

Even Claire had never actually seen the Tesseract; though she could open the Chamber, she was too fearful and reverential to do so. The Tesseract rested upon a decorative plinth in the center of the vault. The lights that rippled around the room came from light generated by the holy jewel.

"No!" Claire cried out. "You cannot let him have it—we cannot simply surrender." Tears welled in her eyes.

J'v-Ellah gave Claire a compassionate look, and then he winked. "No, my daughter. I never said I would surrender."

Claire traded confused glances with Zabe. They both looked at Shandra, the religious expert. Worry lined *her* face, too, but she was as confused as the rest.

"I will give you one chance, Sh'logath," the Architect King insisted. "Because I created where there was once void—though you had not even yet lived, I will allow you to leave this place. I will even construct a new void for you, something outside the confines of reality—much like this chamber—a place where creation will never again intersect with the silence of your rule." He stared at the monstrosity with a flinty edge to his gaze. "I suggest you take my offer."

Sh'logath hissed. "Your offer sounds like a prison—I quite enjoy existing, now that I am made real. And if you are bartering, then you must be desperate—*you cannot defeat me...* I have grown too strong to contend with."

"Do not confuse compassion for weakness." There was a stern edge to J'v-Ellah's voice.

"False! I will show you the true, eternal power of the void!" Sh'logath lunged for his enemy with god-like speed and attacked with a force like an eternal, brutal tide.

Sh'logath lunged and struck with scary speed. He struck and lashed at J'v-Ellah, but the Architect King seemed to disappear every time, like a blur. So fast, J'v-Ellah became momentarily unbound by time and evaded each attack.

"We must help him!" Clarie cried out again, motivated by her feelings more than common sense.

"We cannot enter *that*," Shandra insisted. The center of the Chamber had become a maw of teeth and violence, a whirlwind of daggers and malice. "We'd never survive."

"The whole realm might perish if we refuse," Claire spat. She readied her grip on the kophesh and prepared to launch herself into the storm.

Zabe growled, but decided he would follow his wife anywhere.

Shandra could see on the faces of her friends that Cerci had been right, *We're all going to die... but at least we go down together!*

Claire cried out, leading the charge with her weapon held high. As soon as she stepped a toe over the threshold, the Architect King stopped flashing from one place to the next and stopped her, placing both arms on her shoulders in a fatherly gesture.

"I told you, Claire Jones... you must *trust me*. This is the way it must be in order to ensure your future... a future for *all* my children." J'v-Ellah turned aside to glace knowingly at Zabe, who felt sure he'd heard those words before.

A sharp, ebon spear penetrated the Architect King's chest as the beast lanced him directly through from behind. Blood splattered onto his daughter and dribbled from the wound where Sh'logath had gored him.

Claire and the rest screamed. Time seemed to have slowed as the horror of the situation overrode the way their central nervous systems processed data.

A trickle of blood leaked from J'v-Ellah's lips, bubbling up from within. Behind him, the agod had used his other appendages to snatch the reality gem.

Sh'logath held the Tesseract high above the melty lump that passed for his head. He pulled the jagged spike from his enemy's back and it made a horrific *slurking* noise.

The agod locked his dread gaze upon them all and roared, "Now, you will each understand the torment of a thousand years spent in agony! I will dismantle you each, devouring you alive, tasting your fear and anguish one morsel at a time..."

Chapter Twenty-Six

J'v-Ellah put a hand to his wound. He stood straighter, wiped his mouth, and laughed. The Architect King turned and looked directly into the face of the abomination. "*You?* You really think that you could kill me... or even stop me?"

Sh'logath screeched, confused and angry to see that J'v-Ellah still stood.

The Architect King looked down his nose at the enemy. "*Nothing* cannot possess *everything*, or even *anything*. *You are nothing*, Sh'logath, in a quite literal sense. Nothing except for a greedy void which can never be fulfilled." J'v-Ellah turned back to look at his daughter and the others and flashed her a wink as if to say, *I told you... I knew how this would play out all along.*

Sh'logath vibrated with rage and coiled his tendrils around the crystal he held. The center of the Tesseract clouded within his grip. Something deep within the central, glowing light seemed to crack and turn dark as it reacted to the demon's attempts to control it. The energy within roiled between the facets.

In that moment, the Prime cracked; they could all feel it. Tectonic plates broke and shattered, grinding over the top of each other. Volcanic activity long dormant erupted fresh, and the planetary crust splintered, releasing ground lightning and eldritch energy.

"You should have taken my deal," J'v-Ellah told him. By now, the wound upon the King had healed completely.

Sh'logath tried to release the jewel, but his slimy appendage would not obey. He panicked, looking for a way to escape from the power of the Tesseract. The agod's form began to melt away like drips of black rain; the reality gem began consuming him like dust into a cleaning tube.

He shrieked, "No—no, this can not be!" The power of the Tesseract sucked at him like loose silica pulled toward a vacuum—the inescapable crack in the multi-faceted gem had become an unstable black hole specifically keyed to the dark one. In a split second reversal, the Devourer became the devoured.

With a final, gasping shriek, the Tesseract collapsed Sh'logath and pulled him within the roiling black spot. The crystal healed itself and quenched the scattered darkness blooming within it.

J'v-Ellah picked up the jewel and set it back on its resting spot. Beneath them, the ground quaked, and the sky rumbled as the fabric of the realm itself groaned and screamed.

"Entropy and decay have entered the Prime," J'v-Ellah said. "It will continue unabated until the realm is fully dismantled."

Zabe looked at the Architect King with hopeful eyes. "But you can stop it, right? Surely you will set things right?"

J'v-Ellah cocked his head. "All will be set right in the end," he said. "But the Prime was never my only priority. This," we waved his hands to indicate all the created stuff: castles, tapestries, busted thrones, "none of this was ever my priority. *Things* were never crucial to my plan."

Another quake struck. This one was strong enough that some of the stones set upon the castle's foundation shifted.

"But *we don't know the plan*," Zabe spat.

The Architect King put a reassuring hand on his shoulder. "If you follow me, you won't need to know every step. You only need the general heading." Even his rebuke felt kind and warm.

Zabe closed his mouth and bowed his head. He didn't like the answer, but he knew it was a deep truth, the kind that could guide a life's pursuit. *The King is in charge... and I am not.*

"But what about the Tesseract?" Claire asked, already hedging away from the Chamber of Mysteries as the ground rumbled again. Somewhere outside, a creaking noise reverberated as if structural beams had given way within some nearby, massive structure. It became increasingly clear that they could not stay here—neither in the castle, nor in the Prime.

"The Tesseract is safest where it is," J'v-Ellah said. "However, you are not."

He bowed with a smile and watched Claire and the others flee. The Architect King closed and sealed the massive doors behind him, certain that the Tesseract could never again be loosed upon reality. It could never be spoken of again except as a legend.

Claire and company dashed from the hallways. Support beams and pylons rattled and collapsed behind them. They spilled out and into the courtyard and nearly ran over Jarfig, who wore a collection of fresh bandages.

"Where is our portal?" yelled Wulftone as he frantically searched for it. Cerci's primary job had been to hold the gate for them.

Jarfig shook his head. "I do not know. There was... some kind of accident. I did not see—but I heard something attack her."

Zurrah's eyes widened, and he joined the frantic search.

As Gita rushed to the statue of her sister. Another quake toppled a number of statues. They broke as they hit the ground, but Jenner caught the figure of Shara, refusing to let it tip.

Gita clutched the rune stone in her fist. "I... I don't know how to use one of these," she wailed, suddenly realizing the fatal flaw in her plan. She had all the intention and desire in the world to activate it, but none of the knowledge.

The mystic rune activated of its own accord, needing only the desire of its wielder. It crumbled to dust, as did the eggshell-like layer that encased the child.

"Gita? Gita!" Shara leapt into her sister's arms. She was perhaps four years old and did not understand the destruction happening all around her. Everywhere, buildings collapsed and burned.

"Come on. We've got to go!" Jenner scooped up the little girl. They and the others sprinted towards the castle's fallen gates.

The dead littered the fields all around the razed villages. Far in the distance, they could see the mustering groups of humans and vyrm. Telltale flashes of light blinked as every capable person used the portal to escape the dying Prime dimension.

Directly in their path, a massive crack split the ground and opened a fiery fissure. The ground shifted and began to kilter upwards, separating them from the other side where the portal was.

"We've got to jump!" Zabe howled.

Shara clung to Jenner and Jackie and Claire both skidded to a stop. In a second they would lose the option, but even if they cleared the flames, the fall didn't look survivable to any except maybe the lycans.

"Come on, Cerci... where are you?" Zurrah screamed at the sky.

A skiff zipped out of a nearby gulch and screeched to a halt alongside them. "Do you guys need a lift?" Chira asked, activating the loading plank for them to climb. He bobbed his head to his vyrm copilot, who rode shotgun with a pair of binocs as he helped search for survivors. "This here is Chartarra. You might or might not not know him... but we've all probably tried to kill each other in years past."

"A pleasure," greeted the scarred vyrm who helped them aboard.

They clambered into their seats, and Chira punched the accelerator.

He whipped around to give them some room to run and then threw the speed to max. They sailed over the flaming gorge before gravity grabbed them and yanked the vehicle's weight back towards the ground. The skiff bounced along the dirt and stones kissed the vehicle's bulk; the impact of the crash overruled the hover thrusters momentarily as the skiff bottomed out for a few moments and then hopped back into the air.

Claire clutched the railing and gasped for breath, not realizing she'd been holding it in. "Thank you, Chira—we did not think we would make it."

The loyal general nodded. "I was making the final rounds, trying to locate any other survivors and whisk them to safety." He ruffled his own hair. "Honestly, I didn't even know you guys were out here—none of us did except Basilisk. He and Caivev said you were here, somewhere, trying to take down that snake." Chira looked at her hopefully. "Did you do it? Did you kill Nitthogr?"

She nodded resolutely. "Not just Nitthogr; Sh'logath has been defeated once and for all."

Behind Chira and his skiff, his passengers watched as the mountains collapsed in the distance, like melting wax. One at a time, the towers of the Prime's royal castle fell.

The battered transport craft slewed to the side and came in for a landing adjacent to the portal. Jarfig looked down and at the box he still held onto without thinking about it. He knew only enough about the inter-planar gates to understand that they normally required blood to operate them—a planetary evacuation of this scale would have required so much of it... but the gate-box had kept it open with no sacrifice required.

Basilisk and Caivev waited for them on the platform. Trenzlr stood by and nodded to the princess when their eyes met. Crowds of people still remained, but at the rate which they poured through the portals, the population would all be able to escape before the tectonic disruption and lava sprays had gotten to them.

A single-file line of vyrm prisoners walked towards them from the battlefield. They walked with hands clutched behind their heads and picked their way through a maze of busted planetary crust. Only a safe path remained for those on foot.

The prisoners wore the colors of the Black. With Sh'logath's hold on them broken, the enemy combatants had come to beg for leniency. A distinct figure led them through the trail to safety; his kingly robes fluttered on the hot winds and eddies of steam. J'v-Ellah walked up the steps to the platform with his captive army of vyrm in tow.

Basilisk and Caivev both knelt before the Architect King. The vyrm emperor grinned and shook his head in borderline disbelief. "You told me once that this would happen: that I would bend my knee again... after I came to grips with my unanswerable question... but I did not imagine the rest of this."

"And did you answer it?"

The Emperor inclined his head forward.

J'v-Ellah returned his nod with equally measured grace. "Please accept these soldiers into your service," he said of the Black.

"But they are enemies," Caivev said, "Traitors. They deserve to stay here and perish in the flames."

The Architect King looked down at them. It was clear that they could hear the exchange. "I agree. That would be fair... but we do not always get what we deserve. *Sometimes we receive mercy instead*, whether we understand that or not. If we all gave and accepted only what was deserved, life would have ceased long ago."

He looked into Caivev's eyes. "I desire mercy for them. Like *you*, they are *also* my children—even if by adoption." His eyes sparkled.

Caivev bowed and stepped aside so the remaining vyrm could access the gate.

Claire, Zabe, and all the others watched as J'v-Ellah turned to Basilisk. "I am true to my word. You answered my question and have knelt to my authority. Now that you know what it is, I will grant you the desire of your heart, as promised."

The Architect King looked over the collected crowds of humanity and vyrm. "Basilisk, keep my children safe and remember that the Prime is eternal. It is not a mere place—it is a people and a connection to my spirit which will never end. It may dim and it may brighten, but my flame will never go out."

In the blink of an eye, the Architect King disappeared.

Basilisk stood in awe of the responsibility that the King had bestowed upon him. The full retreat was already well underway, but he gave the official declaration, anyway. "Hurry, everyone. Back to the Deso... Back to *Edenya*," he corrected.

With the world dying all around him, Gerjha blinked. His head swam, and he fell in and out of consciousness as if in a fever dream. He could feel the heat of the lava flows burning all around him and he heard the crunching sounds of collapsing structures. The Prime rumbled in its death throes. He gritted his teeth against the agony he felt in his torso where he'd been split open by the blade of his countryman, a fellow Maethan.

He groaned as he felt a pair of strong arms lift him up. Gerjha's eyes came into focus, but barely. The prophet felt cold, despite the abundance of lava. He knew he was bleeding to death and that he had probably slipped beyond the ability of medical professionals to heal.

"Wh-who are you?" Gerjha croaked through his growing partial blindness. Acrid smoke bit his eyes, though he guessed the lack of blood had more to do with their malfunction than anything else.

"You do not recognize me?"

Gerjha's eyes widened. "You are the Architect King... the god and master of the Tesseract?"

The man nodded as he carried the wounded vyrm. "I am known by other names as well, for those who know them."

Gerjha put a hand on the man's cheek. He whispered reverently, "You are Maetha?"

The Architect King's skin turned scaly. "I have also been called J'v-Ellah, amongst other things."

Gerjha sighed. He remembered that J'v-Ellah was the earliest name of the creator of Edenya. Children's stories insisted that the vyrm had worshiped him prior to drifting off and into their own devices; that slow fade had led to the Thousand Elders and the summoning of Sh'logath. Most vyrm rejected that story with knee-jerk vitriol—its truth indicated their species had fallen from grace and were without excuse. *The strong always hated weakness exposed,* Gerjha thought.

He asked, "Am I dead?"

J'v-Ellah shook his head and spoke with a calm and comforting demeanor. "No. But you will be soon."

Gerjha touched the wound on his torso as the Architect King carried him across the burning plains. There was no more blood to lose, it seemed, and the pain had lessened. Sadness did not over-whelm him—he felt an overwhelming sense of resignation. Gerjha understood that it had to be this way—there was purpose in even the end of life.

"I made you promises while you were yet in your mountain-top circle, Gerjha. Do you remember them?"

"I... they were mere whispers... I remember them," he gasped groggily, "but also I do not."

J'v-Ellah smiled at him, carrying him as if he were no heavier than a child. "That is okay. I remember them for you, and I do not go back on my word. I promised you that you would see the fulfillment of many divine promises... and I have one I pledged to show you."

They winked through the dimensions and left the Prime. J'v-El-lah stood where the trouble all started: the sanctum of the Thousand Elders.

"Are we... are we in Straruck?" Gerjha asked, recognizing the massive, crumbling tomb and the monument to Sh'logath's followers.

"We are. This is where evil was unleashed and this is where all will be made new." J'v-Ellah carried his friend outside and leaned him up against the exterior of the building.

Gerjha sat with his back to the main building in Straruck. The massive, domed structure groaned; it was here that the ancient vyrm had built an altar to themselves and honored their own unique kinds of brilliance. Gerjha watched as grass sprang up from the cracked and desolate landscape; the plains began to turn green with seed and stem.

The wounded prophet whispered, "Edenya has returned," and then his chin dipped gently to his chest, never to rise again. With Gerjha's last breath, the building at his back began to crumble. It collapsed in on itself, ending the reign of the Thousand Elders once and for all.

J'v-Ellah put one hand against the vacant eyes of his servant, closed them. He walked out and into the vast, lush Plains of Neggath and evaporated like a cloud of ash, promising aloud, "I will always dwell unseen with my children, *all of my children.*"

Chapter Twenty-Seven

*E**denya*

Basilisk sat amongst his new council of political advisers. It included a number of humans and vyrm in mixed company. Several days had passed since their return to Edenya. There had been many tense moments and exchanges, but luckily they had weathered them all thus far.

Temporary housing had been in supply after Jeerzha's rebellion, but there were many other issues that required boundaries or rules established to keep the peace. This new paradigm was something that none of them had ever lived with and new changes came along with a vibrant, living Edenya where both humans and vyrm coexisted. None of had ever seen that before; none had even entertained such a notion prior to the Prime's breaking.

Cries had gone up initially from the humans demanding that Claire be propped up as a co-leader or have some influential position of power established for her. In a very public gathering, Claire declined a position when offered.

"Before departing, the Architect King established that Basilisk had been the ruler he had groomed for this role. Much about his being dunnischkte had prepared him for this. He is made of two natures—one that can relate to both cultures, as can his wife, Caivev. I will not reject what the Creator King has made law."

Behind her, Shandra nodded her approval and agreement. Their people had come to look to the last remaining cleric of the Veritas as their de facto religious guide. She'd even proved popular amongst the vyrm who had lost both Gerjha and the volatile Charsk. She and Trenzlr had begun working in close proximity, overlapping in shared knowledge and filling in the blanks for each other where there existed gaps.

Together, they began recruiting for a new hybrid order of Maethan and Veritas clerics. Given access to the ancient writings preserved in Basilisk's library, they poured over texts containing both wisdom and arcane lore.

Trenzlr whistled. "I wonder what Vikrum Wiltshire would think of all this?"

Shandra cocked her head. "You know Wiltshire? But, how?"

"I was close with Tay-lore," he reminded them. "Tay-lore often talked *about* him and *with* him. They shared much knowledge and did each other favors all the time. This seems like the kind of library he would appreciate. It seemed he was always chasing after some kind of mystic book or ancient, powerful artifact." Trenzlr turned the book he was reading over to Shandra. "He and Tay-lore often traded texts for research and personal projects."

The book he passed listed other creatures at least as foul as Sh'logath and many wicked spirits just as malicious as tricksters like Akko Soggathoth. She turned a leaf and scanned a story of another monster who tried to use his power to create reality-crafting crystals: artifacts that could rule minor facets of reality as they interlinked with the Feylands, a separate reality altogether.

Shandra closed the book. "We are doing the right thing here, rebuilding a corps of magic users. We must have those equipped and educated to defend."

Trenzlr bobbed his head. Magic had weakened somewhat with the loss of the Prime, but it still existed. "With creatures like these still out in the wild, we must be ever vigilant."

Shandra agreed, and picked up the next book, *The Tales of Myrddin the Cambion*; and a pile of loose leafs fell from the binding. A page she picked up was labeled *1-The Tragic Lovers of Suranvyn*. Shandra shuffled them back together, glanced at a clock, and set aside her studies. She had some place else to be.

Jenner and Gita walked up the slopes of the Emperor's garden, hand in hand.

Waiting for them at the end of the walk stood Shandra. Jarfig stood by her side, holding the hand of the child, Shara. Behind them towered a statue of the Architect King. This one had been commissioned for crafting as a memorial by the Imperial family. The inscription plate asked a question; *What do you value and to whom do you bend a knee? Answer truly and there I shall be.*

Gita blushed as Shara waved happily. "My sister's getting married," the child happily told Jarfig.

"Oh, is she?" Jarfig asked, as if he was unaware. "You know she is marrying my son? They are going to live here in Limbus forever so that I can be a proper grandpa, and so you can be an aunt."

Jenner grinned. His father had spoken loud enough for them to hear, and he was sure it had been on purpose. Jenner had no intentions to do anything other than what Jarfig had described. He'd lost enough years with his father and he and Gita had both lost enough family already. They'd both lost their taste for battle.

The two held hands as Shandra officiated. Her voice and demeanor sounded sad, but she performed her role dutifully. Duty had wrapped up every free minute since the Breaking and she was bound by it. Shandra did not have the same freedoms the others now enjoyed—the oath of the Veritas still endured, as long as she lived.

Her thoughts spun off into the weeds, distracted by a stroke of envy for these young lovers. She paused, mid-sentence, quite unsure what she had been saying.

"Mirror?" Jenner asked.

"I'm sorry, what?"

He cocked his head. "You said 'mirror.'"

Shandra shook off the fugue and concentrated. Her thoughts slipped back to Sam Jones with frequency, though she'd tried to keep busy enough to avoid errant daydreams.

What would it have been like if he and I were on the other side of this altar? Would that have even been possible had I not activated the mirror?

She knew that question would haunt her forever, but she *had* made the difficult choice. What remained now was duty. Shandra started her sentence again. "I now pronounce you *husband* and wife."

The young lovers kissed and Jackie clapped enthusiastically. She sat next to Claire, who also applauded. Their husbands sat on their respective sides. Zurrah sat adjacent to his brother, though he'd not yet broken out of the funk of being trapped within the Edenya realm, and not knowing what had happened to Cerci.

Jarfig had carried the key that controlled the gates into Edenya, but it did not seem to work within realms other than the Prime—not without being calibrated first. Gita explained how it had been done by Shjikara and the loss of the Prime had somehow altered that calibration. None knew how to reset it without the sacristy codex. Basilisk had secreted away the gate-box, claiming, "There is an inherent danger to dabbling too deep in things we do not understand."

Under Shardai the First, who protected the royal family during the earliest days of Vanganrda, and lasting until Zahaben's tenure, all planeswalking was restricted because of those potential dangers it opened. That rule had grown somewhat lax under Zabe's supervision. None spoke of it, but all knew that it may have factored into the loss of the Prime.

The back of Zurrah's legs tingled with an odd heat as a familiar voice sounded behind him. "Hey... what did I miss?"

He whirled around to find a glowing, geometric portal burning in the air behind him. Cerci winked. The portal expanded, and she leaped through and into his arms, covering him in kisses. "I was so worried when I couldn't open a portal to the Prime... like it just *wasn't there anymore.* I assumed my new machine simply didn't work. You have no idea how worried I was! And then I thought to try here."

"Oh, I can imagine," Zurrah said, and he held her tight.

"I think this garden is someplace special," Zabe told Basilisk. He and the dunnischktets shook hands beneath the shadow of the Architect King. "This is where it all began between us, though the statues are no longer quite so insidious."

Claire also shook his hand, but instead of shaking Caivev's, she leaned in for a tight hug.

"Oh yeah," Caivev had to peel Claire off of her. "I forgot that you were a hugger."

Behind Claire and Zabe stood Wulftone and Jackie. They were all returning to Earth together. Jackie had parents there and life already established. For Claire and Zabe, the release from royal duty opened up a host of new possibilities.

"You know, any of you are welcome here at any time," Basilisk said.

Wulftone bowed. "We will probably drop by on occasion to catch up... make sure everything is going well here, but we're eager to restart simpler lives on Earth."

Zabe agreed. "And besides, someone's got to keep an eye on Cerci and Zurrah. Those two can certainly get up to trouble without supervision... but at least we'll never lack resources," he shrugged. "Deep down, though, I'm rather looking forward to settling down like a couple of normal people, just Claire and I. Perhaps we'll start our own family. I don't know *what* we'll do just yet. But I think that we'll be fine."

"I'm sure you will be, son of Zahaben and of J'v-Ellah." Basilisk said.

Zabe bowed again and watched the portal open behind him as he unslung his baldric where the Stone Glaive hung. He climbed the base of the statue and slung the weapon over the shoulder of the Architect King's statue to complete the memorial. "I think, I hope, that I am done needing this."

Basilisk winked at him in return. "For your sake, I hope so. I desire those good things for you: family and peace. I think only trouble and duty will follow whoever wields that blade."

"Surely we will all see each other again," Claire said, and then she and her husband stepped through the portal to earth. Wulftone and Jackie followed.

Zabe handed a scroll to Cerci.

"What is this?"

He shrugged. "I don't know. It's from Shandra, something she found in Basilisk's library. She said that you might be able to understand it."

The unfurled parchment had a familiar looking rune drawn upon it, followed by a series of mathematic equations. She suddenly recognized it from Walther's lab and grew very excited. Cerci scanned the math, which resembled hieroglyphics more than anything else. This version was more complete than the previous version that she'd seen in the lab as they'd extracted Jarfig.

As Cerci stared at it, something in her mind clicked. *This looks awfully similar to the amulet that teleported Wiltshire.* The math crashed into her and all at once.

"Hold on to your butts, everybody!" She started working out the numbers on her white board and then opened the laptop connected to the rift maker. "We've got one more mission."

The Feylands: Arcadeax
...The Unseelie

Wiltshire's feet stamped rapidly as he crashed through the dark trees of the cursed forest. Thorns and bracken tore at his clothes. It didn't matter; they'd been mostly ripped to shreds during an altercation with orcs. That was a couple of days earlier, and he'd been running ever since.

He'd quickly realized that he was trapped in the Feylands, some dimension where the spider queen ruled. This place was not friendly to humans. A few elven traders and a gnome had been kind enough to fill in a few blanks, but none had been willing to anger the Spider Queen by offering him significant assistance.

His feet pounded the mossy forest path as rapidly as his pulse echoed in his ears. Wiltshire spotted it in the distance: a serene world beyond the edge of the dark forest. The gnomish informant told him of pockets of light that still held out against the Spider Queen's dominion. If he could just get to one of them, he could seek refuge, find a hot meal, and begin searching for a way home.

Wiltshire put on the brakes just in time. He skidded to a stop just before falling over the edge of a sheer cliff. Telltale insectoid sounds loomed larger behind him. Giant spiders and swarms of other vermin had found him; they'd surely be all over him within a few minutes and he had run out of road to flee by.

The cliff dropped vertically for hundreds of feet and he had no idea how he could climb down before the queen's minions fell upon him. A river ran through the bottom of the trench he stood above, but at this height, even a water landing would likely kill him—if he could even reach the river. *If* it was not filled with jagged rocks and ravenous creatures.

He pulled out his final magazine from the backup nine millimeter handgun he still had on him. The shorter model was lighter and less accurate. Wiltshire scowled. He knew he didn't have enough ammunition to deal with them all. The last patrol that she'd sent after him was enormous. He'd been sly enough to lose them in the woods, but wits and luck were in shorter supply than his bullets.

Wiltshire racked the slide of his handgun. It sounded dirty and in need of a good oiling. He only hoped that it wouldn't jam before he fired all six remaining rounds. He wanted to take as many of those monsters down with him as possible.

Suddenly, a familiar triangle shape ripped open in the sky. Wiltshire spotted the familiar faces of his friends from Earth.

Cerci spoke with a jokey nonchalance. "Hey buddy, need a lift? We're glad we finally found you—it was no easy task, you know."

"You have no idea how glad I am to see you." Wiltshire jumped through and just in time. The rift closed behind him. Moments later, a horde of giant spiders led by a cluster of driders burst out from the woods in search of him.

The driders, dark elves from the waist up that attached to giant spider bodies, growled as the trail ran cold. One of them looked over the lip and searched in vain for a body. "The Queen will not be happy with his escape."

Chapter Twenty-Eight

EPILOGUE

*O*ne Year Later...

Claire, Caivev, Jackie, and Gita sat together in Limbus. Both vyrm and humans strolled through the familiar place where so many new statues and sculptures now stood, telling the story of the Tesseract.

Caivev had named the place The Garden of the King and made it publicly available. The girls laughed as they caught up together.

Their guys clustered off to one side, heavily involved with some kind of board game they'd brought from earth. Basilisk was handily destroying them all at it and with barely a glance at the rule book.

"I have enjoyed our visits, Zabe," Basilisk said as he scooped up and removed a number of Zabe's pieces. "We have become more than just a disjointed people... folk connected by threads that span across the multi-verse."

Wulftone reached for the dice. "Are you saying that you think of us like friends?"

Basilisk grinned. "Friends are the family that one chooses," he said. "But I'm still going to wipe you off the table in two more moves."

Wulftone looked down, confused as to how he might pull off such a move, but was convinced that it was probably true, somehow.

Zurrah asked, "I also enjoy these visits, but do you think that our having the machine is too dangerous? Should we dismantle the gate machine after returning?"

Cerci looked forlorn at the notion. She leaned against Zurrah, more comfortable in the circle of men than with the other women; she'd always felt that way. The rift remained open and burned nearby, just past the statue of the King where the Stone Glaive hung. It remained open to allow for their easy return.

"Do you think this will be our last game together?" Zurrah asked.

Cerci patted his shoulder playfully, ignoring what was probably a serious question that they might have to answer someday. "I don't think you're losing quite *that badly* that you should flee an entire dimension and never return." She grinned and drew some smiles from the others.

Claire looked over and smiled at Zabe. He smiled back.

Looking beyond her husband, Claire felt a pang, like a kick inside her belly, when she spotted him.

Sam Jones had returned. He walked up the approach.

She stood and saw that it only looked like Sam. When Claire met his eyes, she could tell that it was J'v-Ellah. Still, she was happy to see him, even if it reminded her of the sacrifice her father had made.

He embraced his daughter.

"Are you back?" Claire asked. "I mean for good... are you staying?"

J'v-Ellah shook his head and walked towards the rest. The others watched, still amazed and mystified by the man's appearance. "I am not back to stay... at least, not like this. I'm sorry, daughter. I know you had hopes, but I knew it was important that you had one final chance to say goodbye."

Claire cried and leaned in to hug him. She had to lean and bend, discovering that her belly was in the way. The child inside her stretched and kicked, making J'v-Ellah smile as he felt it.

He said, "Life goes on. It is for life that I sacrificed what I did... chaotic, messy, painful life."

Claire hugged his neck and buried her nose in it. He'd sounded every bit of Sam Jones in that moment, and she knew why it had to be Sam all along to make the sacrifice. "We're naming the child Sam, either way. Samuel, if it's a boy; Samantha if it's a girl."

J'v-Ellah smiled with twinkling eyes. "I think the name will fit perfectly."

He turned and addressed them all. "While it seems like the most intense parts of our adventure together have wound down... I still have plenty more adventure left ahead of me."

Claire winked at him and rubbed her belly. She pointed to it. "You and me both."

The Architect King turned and smiled at them all, noticing the melancholy faces on each of them. "I will always be with you. All of you. Even though you cannot see me." He met Claire's eyes specifically. "I love you, my children."

A lone tear streamed down Claire's cheek, and she squeezed him again.

"Goodbye, daughter. Peace will finally follow you, but I must depart in order to ensure that future." He kissed her forehead and then whispered something secret into her ear, and then he disintegrated once again, much like Shandra had described to them before.

Zabe went to her side. "What did he say?"

She tearfully hugged her husband and kissed him. "He said that we are safe. Everything will finally be okay."

The End.

Vikrum Wiltshire will return in his own series, and you can find out more about the formation and purposes of his mysterious Red Order in the *Hidden Rings of Myrddin the Cambion* series, starting with book 1: *Hoods of the Red Order* (and including a fuller arch of the odd boggart, Bwbych.) The Feylands, only briefly seen, is the land of Arcadeax, and Wiltshire is not the only human to have been trapped within. There is much to see in a fey land of magic, legend, and duels. You can read about it in *Curse of the Fey Duelist*, starting with *A Kiss of Daggers*.

https://books2read.com/kissofdaggers

WHAT'S NEXT?

The interconnected worlds of the multiverse intersect a few different literary universes. There are the Casefiles of Vikrum which quite obviously intersect the books featuring Claire and Zabe, but there is also the time mystic adventure series with an overlap from the Red Order (*The Hidden Rings of Myrddin the Cambion*) and also a fey world briefly seen in book 3, *The Architect King*, where *Curse of the Fey Duelist* occurs.

Keep up to date and stay in touch with the author at this link: https://www.subscribepage.com/wolvesofthetesseract and add your email to be added to the newsletter list!

Glossary

Abyssal Auraphage – a kind of monstrous, supernatural bloodhound from the Darque.

Apex – the kind of tarkhūn mutation that resulted in massive, hulking warriors. The smallest apexes are slightly larger than the largest of the Black.

The Architect King – the Creator God. He is currently in stone form, trapped within Basilisk's stronghold at Limbus until some prophesied day.

The Awakening – A ritual dedicated to calling Sh'logath into existence.

The Black – common, lowest Caste of the species. Also called Blackborne.

Carrion Worm - a type of insectoid creature that resembles a giant millipede; it carries its young in its mouth and has caustic enzymes that act as a sort of acid as well as chemical electricity.

Chamber of Mysteries – an impenetrable vault where the arcane artifacts collected by the Royal Family are kept; also home to the Tesseract.

Churdachk – a kind of vermin pack animal in the Desolation; it resembles a large rat and is slightly smaller than a mule.

Darquematter – lead-like metallic substance with magical properties originating from the Darque dimension.

Desolation – a realm of the multiverse; formerly known as Edenya before the Syzygyc War ravaged the landscape.

Dimensional Inversion Pendant – a mysterious artifact made from darquematter; it alters the link between a Prime and his or her variants.

Drakoise - a kind of shelled reptile native to the Prime.

Dunnischkte - a religious ritual to gain a hybrid status between vyrm and human.

Dunnischktet – someone who has completed the Dunnischkte; he or she gains nigh-immortality and the ability to shift between hybrid, vyrm, and human forms.

Edenya – the name of the vyrm realm before it was called Desolation.

Eternal Sky – one of the thirty three dimensions of the multi-verse.

Frostmancer – tarkhūn with special abilities including ice/cold control.

Grimmorium Nitthogr – a journal kept by the fallen Veritas cleric Nitthogr; it is an arcane work that is the culmination of all the sorcery he learned in his earlier years before Sh'logath taught him even deeper and viler magics.

Guardian Corps – royal guards tasked with protecting the royal line and also the chamber of mysteries; some corpsmen decide to join the Veritas, a secretive monastic order drawn from their numbers.

Hierophanticus – a darquematter object imbued with arcane power to do a specific task.

Heptobscurantum – human branch of the vyrm's cult of Sh'logath.

Homo diurnus – android species created by the Technite people; Tay-lore is their last remaining, known member.

Kortath – The mountain range where rovers made their ancestral home. Their chosen prophet resides in the mountains to await instruction from Maetha.

Lich – tarkhūn with psychic abilities; they are always identified at a young age and pressed into service of the Sh'logath cult.

Limbus – the home to Basilisk, the recognized leader of the Tarkhūn, and the capital of Desolation.

Lycan – a werewolf hybrid form which can be assumed by certain members of Zabe's lineage.

Mae'le-ggath – the original form of dualistic religion practiced by the vyrm in which Sh'logath was one of two philosophical forces.

Maetha – a kind of vyrm savior of prophecy that predates Mae'le-ggath.

Multiverse – thirty-three connected dimensions of the Tesseract which can be traveled via pathways that open up based on the astral alignment/calendar.

Plains of Neggath - region in Desolation where the Sh'logath cult birthed the great Agod; the area is a veritable wasteland and often the home of Rovers.

Planeswalk – traveling to different dimensions of the multiverse via the power of the Tesseract.

The Prime – the main realm of the multiverse: the ultimate reality. It also refers to a person who lives within this realm; each Prime has dimensional copies living on the different realms of the multiverse.

Pyromancer – tarkhūn with special abilities including fire generation and manipulation.

Rovers – unaligned vyrm tribes. They are typically either Seekers of Maetha or Followers of Krakkath, two different theologies that some vyrm adhere to.

The Seven – Illuminati-like ruling council of the Heptobscurantum.

Shade – tarkhūn with extreme camouflaging ability; some have even gained the ability to completely shapeshift their forms.

Sh'logath – the Devourer, Nega-God, Agod of Destruction, the Reality Eater... all are names to describe the terror that lurks on the verge of reality.

Straruck – the Holy city in the Neggath region; it has holy significance to the vyrm (their religion's kind of Mecca).

The Syzygyc War – the war that waged many years between the Prime and Desolation as they sought to awaken Sh'logath; it was prevented by the Architect King.

Tarkhūn – high caste of vyrm that once ruled their race before a schism led by Nitthogr long ago. They are a rarer, but stronger breed. Some, who resemble members of The Black, have developed additional powers.

Tesseract – a gem created by the Architect King; it is the key to all power in reality and the embodiment of the multiverse.

Thousand Elder's Sacrifice – the sacrificial torpor they entered into in order to make Sh'logath real in a ceremony they called the Birthing.

TRX718 – a high powered blaster pistol Zabe is fond of.

Tyradon – fast, heavily armored battle lizards used by the Tarkhūn military; they are much larger than churdachk, tire less often, and will prey on creatures up to one and a half times their size in the wild.

Veritas – the religious order that seamlessly integrates into the Prime culture and is dedicated to the Architect King.

Voice of the Thousand Elders – the chief Cleric of the Vyrm's Thousand Elders. He stayed alive and died of old age, although his spirit remains disembodied and tied to the Thousand Elders will.

Vyrm – reptilian humanoid race whose home realm is known as the Desolation.

Dramatis Personae

Akko Soggathoth – An ancient and mischievous demigod released from his prison within the Darque by the Texas Black Goat Cult.

Andrew Thornton – A member of The Seven who rule the heptobscurantum

Atticus Sexton – A paranormal investigator and Red Order brother; Vikrum Wiltshire is his partner

Basilisk – The leader of the tarkhūn. He is the brother of Nitthogr who died at the Nebraska Worldgate incident. He is a Dunnischktet.

Bithia – The Prime version of Claire Jones.

Bruce Cannon – A member of The Seven who rule the heptobscurantum. Hired Vikrum Wiltshire to save his life

Caivev – A traitor to the Prime who was seduced by Nitthogr. She was once a skilled intelligence officer under Zahaben.

Cerci Heiderscheidt – Walther's head assistant, she is a scientist in her own right and commands three assistants underneath her.

Charobv – One of Caivev's generals. He was a skilled sniper and has a warrior son named Chartarra.

Charles Summers – A member of The Seven who rule the heptobscurantum

Charsk – The vyrm high priest of the Sh'logath cult.

Chartarra – One of Caivev's assassin-warriors.

Chira – One of Zabe's Corpsmen; he took over the Royal Army after Harken.

Claire Jones – Just a simple girl from Earth who wound up with the mind and soul of the Prime's ruler, the daughter of the Architect King, fused to her.

Druen – Leader of the Merciful Hammer in the Veritas and Shandra's immediate superior.

Gerjha – A prophet of the rovers/Seekers of Maetha, and a cousin of Trenzlr.

Gita – A young recruit for the Guardian Corps and friend of Jackie.

Harken – A local hero who arose during the Black's occupation; post-Nebraska he rose to lead the Prime's Royal Army.

Idrakka – A tarkhūn frostmancer secretly sent to infiltrate Caivev's team over a period of years. Secretly he is the brother of the shade, Jarkara.

Jackie – Claire's best friend who followed her to the Prime. The two are as close as sisters.

Jacob Sisyphus – A former pro wrestler and magic wielder of Earth. He is a member of the Heptobscurantum.

James Shianan – A former pro soccer player with worldwide fame. His is a form taken by Nitthogr

Jarfig – Prime version of Jacob Sisyphus. Captured years ago he is used as a blood bank to boost Sisyphus's magic abilities.

Jarkara - A shade spy sent by Basilisk. He is one of the more talented shapeshifters and Vivian suspects he was sent as a mole to infiltrate her team. Brother to Idrakka.

Jenner – Professor Jarfig's son. He was fifteen when he lost his father and is possessed with the singular purpose: to find and rescue his father or punish those who took him.

Jonathan Trask – A member of The Seven who rule the heptobscurantum. Turned out to be a Tarkhūn traitor and spy

Kreephast – One of Caivev's generals. He is a member of the Black, but his disguise skills rival those of a shade (he is also General Nyagittari). He is very religious and well versed in history.

Krenyr the Hunter – One of Nitthogr's shades. He is at the pinnacle of ability for disguise and can even change his genetic code to match that of his target, when necessary.

Minas – The leader of the Order of the Flame within the Veritas.

Ma Kechewaishke – A Native American woman who helped Claire access the astral plane

Miles Jecima – A linguist with specialty in dead, ancient, and unknown languages. He is good friends and peers with Sam Jones

Nitthogr – Sorcerer and leader of both The Black and the heptobscurantum. He and his brother were, long ago, members of the Veritas—a monastic order in the Prime

Percival Wainsmith – Independently wealthy man with many influences abroad; he has joined the Heptobscurantum's Seven.

Perribelle – Leads the Wax Order of the Veritas.

Peter Greyson – A member of The Seven who rule the heptobscurantum

Pietro Walther – A pseudoscience doctor who was originally recruited and equipped by Bruce Cannon.

Pollando – The mute leader of the Order of Mystics within the Veritas. He is a highly trained psychic.

Praetor Russo – In charge of a large region of Red Order members

Quintin Hall – Formerly with the Red Order. He is still a paranormal investigator but has gone private. Hall remains in touch with Vikrum Wiltshire

Regorik – Nitthogr's second in command during the first invasion. He was a tarkhūn apex who shifted allegiances because of his ideology and faith in Sh'logath

Respan – A scientist and R&D expert who works for the Guardian Corps.

Robert Schaeffer – The Earth version of Zabe. He looks like Zabe... but they are not the same person

Percival Wainsmith – Independently wealthy man with many influences abroad; he has joined the Heptobscurantum's Seven.

Pietro Walther – A pseudoscience doctor who was originally recruited and equipped by Bruce Cannon.

Sam Jones – Father of Claire Jones. Archaeologist. Widower. Occasional kidnapping victim.

Shandra – A Cleric of Veritas and member of the Merciful Hammer. She is responsible for tracking down ancient artifacts with arcane power.

Shardai – Zabe and Zurrah's grandfather and the father of Zahaben. He was named after Shardai the First who was a child soldier during the Syzygyc War. Shardai originally commanded the Guardian Corps before his son and grandson; he died shortly before the Battle of Nebraska.

Shjikara – High Cleric and leader of the Veritas.

Skrom – Caivev's behemoth tarkhūn general; he is perhaps even more devoted to her than Regorik was to Nitthogr.

Tahnak – A member of the Guardian Corps whose life was upended while trapped in the Darque dimension. He gained some expertise on darquematter while trapped there, but with a cost.

Tay-lore – A quirky android member of Guardian Corps and last member of the technological homo diurnus race. He is fully devoted to Claire/Bithia. He finds killing highly distasteful—but he would make any sacrifice at his queen's request.

Theera the Undying – An unkillable servant and personal henchman enthralled and empowered by Akko Soggathoth.

Thomas Chelish – A member of The Seven who rule the heptobscurantum

Trenzlr – A Blackborne vyrm and Seeker of Maetha who fell through a portal and into the Prime.

Victor Adams – A member of The Seven who rule the heptobscurantum

Vikrum Whiltshire – An occult detective from Earth, Tay-lore is often in contact and once hired him to digitize the arcane library found at the Texas Black Goat Cult.

Vivian Shianan – Works for the Special Research Division of the government which looks into paranormal phenomenon and dispels questions. Half sibling to James Shianan. See Caivev.

Wulftone – Cousin to Zabe and second in command of the Guardian Corps; he was raised in the same home as Zabe's brother when his parents died.

Zabe – The son of the great General Zahaben and protector of the Royal Family; he leads the Guardian Corps.

Zahaben – Captain of Princess Bithia's personal guard and leader of the Guardian Corps

Zurrah – Zabe's brother who was captured and presumed dead at a young age.

About the Author

Christopher D. Schmitz is an indie author from the fly-over states who dabbles in game design. He has published award winning science fiction, fantasy, and humor. He's written and freelanced for a variety of outlets, including a blog that has helped countless writers on their publishing journey. On any given weekend, he can be found at pop culture and comic conventions across the USA or playing his bagpipes for people. You can look him up at www.authorchristopherdschmitz.com.

ALSO BY CHRISTOPHER D. SCHMITZ

www.ingramcontent.com/pod-product-compliance
Lightning Source LLC
Chambersburg PA
CBHW061042190726
48286CB00006B/1570